DARK HORSE

MICHELLE DIENER

ECLIPSE

Copyright © 2015 by Michelle Diener

All rights reserved.

No part of this book may be reproduced in any form or by any electronic or mechanical means, including information storage and retrieval systems, without written permission from the author, except for the use of brief quotations in a book review.

This is a work of fiction and all names, people, places and incidents are either used fictitiously or are a product of the author's imagination.

❀ Created with Vellum

To Alex. You were taken too soon and you will be sorely missed.

CHAPTER 1

ROSE SLIPPED her ticket out of hell over her head and tucked it beneath her shirt, where it lay against her skin, throbbing like a heartbeat.

The sensation was so unnerving, she curled her fingers around it and lifted it back out, eyeing the clear crystal oblong uncertainly.

"I'll try to keep all the passageways clear for you and I've disabled the lenses, but just in case someone disobeys orders, it would be better if they didn't see me." Sazo spoke too loudly through the tiny earpiece she wore, and she winced.

She reluctantly tucked the crystal, that was somehow also Sazo, back under her shirt, tugging the cord it hung from so it was below her neckline. After three months of being the only thing she'd had to wear, washed over and over again, the shirt was threadbare, and barely concealed Sazo anyway, but it was better than nothing.

She took the two steps to the door of the tiny control room tucked away to one side on the Tecran ship and it slid silently open. She'd only been inside for ten minutes at most to steal Sazo, or break him out, depending on your view of things, and the corridor was as empty now as it had been when Sazo led her here.

She looked back, but the door had closed, completely concealing the control room, so it looked like an uninterrupted passageway again.

"You're still in control, even though I've unplugged you?" She spoke very quietly, because even though Sazo had opened doors, and diverted traffic all the way from her prison cell to this room earlier, there was no point taking foolish chances like talking too loudly when it was unnecessary.

"I would not have initiated this plan if I wasn't absolutely certain that it would work." Sazo sounded a little . . . stressed.

"You okay?"

"There has been a delay loading the animals at the launch bay and the Grih have come through their light jump three minutes sooner than I calculated." He went quiet for a moment. "I'm sorry, Rose."

"What? What is it?" Freezing hands of panic gripped her heart and she stumbled to a halt. If he was going to tell her they had to abort, that she had to go back to the cell . . .

"The lion has been killed."

She leant against the wall, her legs weak. "That is not good." She rubbed her face. "Why?"

"I'll tell you as you walk. We can't delay, with the Grih already here. They might fire on this ship at any time when they realize it's disabled."

She started walking again, and just like earlier, the passages Sazo sent her down were eerily empty. "I thought the Grih were peaceful."

"They don't take force as a first option, but my changing this ship's trajectory in the last light jump and setting us in the middle of Grih territory was effectively a declaration of war. They might initially hesitate to fire, given the power of this ship compared to theirs, but when they realize every single system except for lights, air, and the launch bay mechanisms have been disabled, they may strike."

"And the lion?" There was something bothering her about the way he'd apologized.

"It was delaying the loading——frightening the loading crew. They're already frightened because I diverted the ship to this location and they don't know what's going on. I only agreed to let the animals come with us because you insisted. Animals are unpredictable. It's hard to get the timing precise."

"You instructed one of the loaders to kill the lion." She didn't ask, it was a statement of fact. She knew there had been something way off with that apology. She knew, deep down, there was something way off about Sazo, but he was literally her only escape route, and of all the beings she had encountered since her abduction, the only one who had worked to free her.

"There is a chance the wildlife on the moon we're going to, Harmon, would not have been suitable to sustain him. He would eventually have died of starvation."

She didn't respond. She was too angry.

What he said may be true, and if so, he could have told her that sooner, but it wouldn't have stopped her asking for all the animals to go with them on a second shuttle. They had had as miserable a time as she in this hellhole.

And Sazo thought the Grih would come to pick her up on the moon they were escaping to. They would see the shuttles Sazo had arranged for them leaving the launch bay for Harmon, and after they had dealt with the crippled Tecran ship, they would surely be interested in who had escaped. And, she was sure, be interested in a lion.

They could have made a plan for him.

A door slid open and she walked into the launch bay. Ahead of her, two of the loading staff walked out the far door without turning around, one nursing a jagged wound on his arm.

She pressed against the wall and made no move until the doors closed behind them and she was alone in the massive hangar. Beside her, she heard the hum and double beep of the locks engaging. Sazo had sealed the doors. No one on the ship could stop her getting on the shuttle now.

The lion lay, dead and crumpled, in the massive cage that had housed him since he was taken. It stood next to one of the two explorer shuttles she and Sazo were stealing and she walked up to it and grasped hold of the bars. Hot tears welled in her eyes as she looked down on him. He was a golden, vibrant anachronism in this cold, metallic place.

A wild thing, broken.

That could have been her. Nearly had been, more than once.

The lion had been one of the things that had kept her going, kept her sane.

"I am sorry, Rose. I really am. But the Grih have gone to full alert, shields and guns. Please get in the shuttle, or this could be for nothing."

The shuttle that had been loaded with all the animals was closed and ready. Rose paused for a moment, looking at the massive gel wall that enclosed the launch bay but which allowed ships in and out. It was a pale blue, and seemed to shimmer.

"Rose!"

She shook herself, and walked up the ramp into the much smaller craft Sazo had arranged for her, and before she had even reached the cabin, he started closing the door and revving the engines.

She lurched into one of only two chairs in the small cockpit and struggled with the safety harness. She should have been excited, or at least relieved to finally have escaped the Tecran, but as the engines began their muffled scream and the ship lifted into hover mode, she could only think of tawny fur and golden eyes.

Closed forever.

THE TECRAN CLASS 5 battleship hung sullenly between the *Barrist* and one of the fertile moons of the gas giant Virmana. It hulked like a prickly black ball, and Dav Jallan shifted uncomfortably in the *Barrist's* captain's chair.

He could feel the tension humming off his ten-strong command staff, although they were trying to hang on to calm. Their emergence from a light jump deep inside their own territory to find themselves within sight of a Tecran ship was not unlike opening the door expecting to see a friend, and tripping over a weapon-wielding thug instead.

Dav decided they'd been frozen in shock long enough, himself included.

"Is there anyone on board?" That was almost the only logical reason why the Tecran hadn't fired on them yet. Their ship was three times the size of the *Barrist*, and Dav knew from the information he received from Battle Center that a rare Class 5 like the one in front of him had even more than that in terms of fire power.

"There are at least five hundred heartbeats, sir." Kila said. She tapped a screen and immediately the view of the battleship on the main screen in front of them lit up with hundreds of lights on clearly defined levels.

Most of them were blue but . . .

"Are those orange lights?" Dav leant forward to get a better look. They were all concentrated in the same area, set apart from the blue, which was the only reason they were noticeable at all.

"Those are bio-signatures our system can't identify." Kila said, and frowned. "This is the first time I've ever come across a genuine orange before."

"Should I initiate evacuation?" Dav's aide, Farso Lothric, hovered at his shoulder, his hands clenching and unclenching.

"Where would we go?" Dav didn't need to look at his systems screen to know they couldn't possibly have recovered enough from the light jump they'd just made to go anywhere. Let alone evade a Tecran Class 5 battleship.

And while the moon behind the Tecran ship shone like a blue and green jewel against the red and cream of Virmana's patterned atmosphere, and was assuredly habitable, the problem still remained that they would have to go around the Tecran ship to get to it.

"We have to do something," Lothric said.

Dav didn't disagree. However, he'd known the moment they'd come out of the jump and straight on course toward the Tecran ship that there was only one course of action. They had sent out a comm the moment they'd made visual contact, and at least two battle class ships would be light jumping to the *Barrist's* aid, but right now, all they could do was defend. "Shields are at full. Guns are all primed. If they attack——"

At that moment, all the lights on the Tecran ship went out.

The blue and orange heartbeats remained, but it was clear the power was down.

"The oranges, sir." Kila stood up in her excitement, and forgot to use the pointer, using her finger instead.

The orange heartbeats detached from the ship, and Dav zoomed in with the lens, saw two explorer-class craft flying away from their mother ship.

"Is one empty?" Borji, his systems engineer, asked, peering forward.

"No. There's one orange heartbeat on that one. Six on the other."

Dav watched their trajectory for a minute longer, but there was nowhere else to go but Virmana's moon——not in those craft——and he turned his attention back to the real threat.

"Could they be on backup power and we can't see it?" He waited for Kila to fiddle with her instrumentation.

She shook her head. "I can't see any power at all."

"Which means . . ." Lothric gripped the back of Dav's chair.

"Which means we have a ship full of dying Tecran in front of us." Dav stood. Walked toward the screen. He would give a lot to know what was going on in that Tecran ship right now.

It was like someone had just handed them a Class 5 warship on a plate, with no effort on their part to claim it besides a bit of messy clean-up.

He didn't trust that at all.

No one in the universe was that kind.

He tapped his communicator. "Commander Appal, ready Squads A to F, and prepare to board the Tecran vessel immediately. Full biohazard kit."

He paused.

"I'm coming with you."

CHAPTER 2

"YOU CAN MOVE AROUND NOW." This time, Sazo's voice was much softer in her ear.

Rose depressed the button over her chest, and the safety harness released, letting her up to stand in the tiny cabin.

She walked to the porthole window and looked back, saw the outside of her prison for the first time.

The Tecran ship was a black ball with long protrusions. Like a naval contact mine from the Second World War. She shuddered to see it. "You did what I asked you? You deleted the maps?"

"I've wiped the Tecran system of all navigation points to Earth, and was able to send a system virus to all their other vessels, to search out the information and destroy it wherever else it exists in the Tecran fleet. They won't even know it's missing, because I also deleted all reports relating to their find. With the crew that took you gone, only those in the high command office who read the reports will have any idea of what they found, and they won't be able to find the information again."

"What do you mean, with the crew gone?" Rose stared out at the Tecran ship a moment longer. "The Grih won't return the Tecran to their people as prisoners of war? What will they do with them?" She tried to tamp down on a wish for something truly unpleasant.

Sazo paused. "I am not familiar with the Grih's handling of prisoners of war. When we make contact with them and I can infiltrate their system, I can keep watch on the Tecran they're holding. But either way, it won't matter. The Tecran will have to start again from scratch."

It was the most she could hope for. "But you still have the information, right?" She didn't know whether she wanted him to delete it from his memory or not. Having it there meant there was a tiny chance of going home.

"I do. But I've put it somewhere extremely hard to find. If the Tecran ever get me again, it will not be accessible to them."

She would have to believe that. She decided not to ask him to delete the maps permanently yet. If they were about to be taken back into the Tecran fold, then maybe. But not now.

"Does this craft have a hot shower?" She was half-joking, half-hoping beyond hope as she took her first really good look around the craft. Her skin hadn't felt clean since she'd been taken. Sazo had engineered a respite for her from half-way through her second month of captivity onward, but she'd only had a basin to wash in. She wanted water pouring down on her.

"It does," Sazo said, and she closed her eyes, suddenly close to tears.

"I had the loading crew pack some things that may be useful to you." He sounded almost shy as he opened an automatic door at the back of the cabin. It slid completely back on itself, and Rose crouched down and pulled out two bags.

They were the size of small backpacks and after a little fiddling, she worked out she had to push a button at the top and the center seam released, opening up to reveal piles of colorful fabric and bottles of what might be toiletries.

She lifted up a piece of fabric, to find it was a large long-sleeved t-shirt made of a smooth fabric with the texture of silk. It looked much to big, but she could deal with that.

"It's hyr fabric," Sazo said into her ear. "Made from the silk of the hyr spider. It reacts to heat. Hyr spiders only eat prey with a certain body temperature. If the correct prey gets stuck on their web, the silk contracts around it. You put it on and your body heat causes it to shrink to fit you. You can shape it any way you like."

"I don't recognize it from anything I saw the Tecran wear. This is wonderful." She brushed her fingers over it, and felt it react to the heat of her fingertips. The Tecran had worn uniforms of a dark purple which had looked similar to thick cotton——practical and hardy. This was soft and beautiful. "Thank you."

"Hyr fabric is the most expensive fabric in this part of the galaxy. I saw in the inventory that we were carrying these two packs for the daughter of the Tecran military leader, and had them pulled from the cargo hold and packed in this shuttle."

That meant he had thought of her and what she would need well in advance. He had been honest in his promise that he would help her, and on top of that, beyond the bargain, he had thought of her comfort.

He had also killed the lion.

She needed to remember there were a lot of shades of gray in Sazo.

And if she ever slowed down his plan, there was a chance, just like the lion, she'd become so much collateral damage.

She lifted the crystal off her neck and looked at it. "That was really sweet of you. Thank you again. Now, I'm going to find the shower, and when all the hot water is gone, I'm going to work out how to dress myself in hyr fabric." She started to pull the earpiece from her ear.

"Wait." Sazo's call was a squawk.

She put the earpiece back in. "Yes?"

"It would take one hour and thirty minutes for the hot water to be gone. We only have an hour before you need to be back in the harness for landing."

"Can you send me a signal when forty minutes is up? Like a beep through the comm system?" She had nearly said intercom, but even though she spoke in English, a language she had taught Sazo since he'd first introduced himself, she stopped herself in time and used the Grih term. She could speak relatively understandable Tecran by now, and almost fluent Grih. They had decided it was better for her to concentrate on Grih, rather than Tecran, given the plan was to escape the Tecran, and never meet up with them again.

Ever.

She pulled the earpiece out and put it and the crystal——she couldn't think of that faceted, slim piece of technology as Sazo——on top of the storage unit. It was the first time she'd been free of Sazo completely, apart from when she slept, for at least a month and a half. Not since he'd had someone include the earpiece on the breakfast tray a guard brought her each morning.

She grabbed both of the packs he'd got her and slung them over her shoulder as she made for the rear cabin door, eager to find out what lay beyond it.

A kitchen galley to the left, a small bathroom to the right, it turned out. This really was a two-person explorer. But she wasn't complaining.

She stepped into the bathroom, and then, even though Sazo could hardly get up and walk in, given he was an artificial intelligence lodged in a crystal key, she closed the door. Of course, he would also, by now, be residing in the systems of this craft.

She looked around, but couldn't see a camera, and what would she do about it, if she could?

She pulled off her clothes, folding them neatly to one side, because she had learned to take nothing for granted, and she may need them again, and then stepped into the shower.

The Tecran were a little taller than humans and a lot bulkier, so the shower stall was roomy for her. She worked out how to switch it on, and stepped back for a couple of seconds to let it come up to temperature, only to find it came out hot straight away.

As soon as the spray hit her face, she closed her eyes, tilted her head back, and at last, private and under cover of the sound of falling water, let herself cry.

CHAPTER 3

DAV COULD HEAR his own breathing inside the biohazard suit and nothing else, except for the occasional curse from one of his boarding team over his comm as they came across more and more dead Tecran littering the passageways and cabins.

The Tecran seemed at first glance to be merely asleep, their thick-set bodies lying up against walls, as if they had sat down to rest and just slid sideways, the feathery protrusions on their heads limp.

He lifted the concentrated beam of his laslight to illuminate the dead littering the area just outside the launch bay, pressed up against the doors as they'd tried to get in.

The interior doors had been locked when Dav and his team had arrived at the bay in three gun carriers, and they'd had to hook the wiring up to the power system on one of their own ships to get them open.

Dav could only assume the power failure had left the doors in lock mode, with no way for the Tecran crew to make it to the fleet of smaller explorer and fighter craft in the hangar. If they had been able to, a lot more would be alive. All they would have needed to do was start the engines and close the doors, and the on board systems would have provided them with the air they needed to breathe.

There were a few alive, though. Mostly officers with personal breathing apparatus, and one patient who was on a ventilator in the sick bay. Lucky for him, the ventilator's backup power came from a powerful battery built into the machine itself, not the backup system on the ship, or he'd be dead too. According to one of B Team, he was nearly there, anyway, his chest barely lifting up and down.

Dav turned his laslight back to the one thing on this ship that had no business being here and studied it a little more. It was a dead animal of some kind in a cage, nothing he'd ever seen before. He would bet quite a large chunk of his pay that if it were breathing, it would show up orange on Kila's little screen.

This one life form, of all the life on this ship, had not died of a lack of breathable air. It had been killed by lethal injection, the syringe still in its shoulder, as if the person who'd plunged it in was too scared to pull it out. Looking at the incisors and the claws on the animal, Dav didn't blame them.

He played his light over it a little longer, and then tapped his comm. "Final casualties, Commander?"

"Four hundred and eighty-three, sir." Commander Appal had to clear her throat. "Kila's confirmed from her side. We haven't missed anyone."

They had the captain alive, along with most of his senior officers. And none of the hassle of a large-scale prisoner population. All their would-be prisoners were dead.

Dav wasn't sure what he thought of that.

If the Tecran ship hadn't been disabled, he knew they would have shot the *Barrist* out the sky and killed every single person on board. If he'd had the fire-power available himself, he would have done the same to them.

But this seemed like a waste of life. A tragedy.

And the burning question was, what were the Tecran doing in Grih territory to begin with?

He tapped in to the *Barrist's* comm system. "We're secure, Borji. Bring your team over and find out what the hell happened to this ship."

The place on the Grih planet Dav came from, Calianthra, had a saying: beware of unexpected gifts.

He was wary, all right. Very, very wary.

She was clean, and she was cried out. Wrung out like a limp rag. Only thirty minutes had past of her hour, because she was worried about working out how to use the hyr fabric, and she didn't want to ask Sazo's advice.

Her hair hung below shoulder-length, clean but in need of a good brush and a hair tie, smelling of the gel Sazo had provided. A sort of cinnamon and vanilla spicy mix that was amazingly good.

She sorted through the garments, and realized she was humming a tune while she did it. She'd always enjoyed singing, but since she'd been taken, she'd hummed and sang more than she ever had in her life. There was something so pithy about song lyrics. They got right to the heart of things in a few words.

She didn't doubt she was sane because of them.

She lifted out an item that must surely be underwear, although so big she could have got both legs in one leg-hole. She pulled them on, and then bunched them close to her skin. The fabric contracted, and as she pulled and arranged, it obeyed completely, shrinking, molding itself to her, until she had exactly the kind of underwear she preferred.

Flushed with success, as well as the humid air of the shower room, she pulled out a sleeveless tank top which she guessed was a bra equivalent and went to work again. When she worked out she could have any level of lift and separate she wanted, she played for a good five minutes, grinning as she made her breasts do the impossible, giving herself cleavage that would be the envy of any playboy bunny. The beep Sazo said he'd send at forty minutes sounded, and she toned it down a little, although not totally. She was tired of being grubby and drab.

The pants and long sleeve t-shirt were easy, and the fabric was stretchy enough for her to move freely.

She ran into trouble with the shoes.

The only ones in the pack looked like massive ballet slippers. The

Tecran had big feet, and she wondered how the hyr fabric in the shoes would work. She'd prefer trainers, something she could run in.

Sazo said the Grih were peaceful and had strict rules guiding their encounters with alien life. They would never subject her to what the Tecran had. But call her a cynic. She'd like the option of running, if she could.

Of course, she'd been without shoes for three months, so anything was an improvement.

She slipped her foot into one, and then the other, and they started to contract. Ballet slippers, it was, then. They were comfortable, at least. And the soles were probably thick enough to run over rough ground.

She closed up the packs again, still wishing for a brush and a hair tie, but the Tecran had feathery stuff on their heads and if they brushed it, there was no evidence of that in the things Sazo had gotten for her. She combed her fingers through her hair and then braided it in a French braid.

"A hair tie, a hair tie, my kingdom for a hair tie," she sang under her breath.

"A hair tie?" Sazo's voice came through the speaker by the door.

"A stretchy, thin band to wrap around the end of my hair, to keep it in place. I'd be happy to see a comb or a brush, too." She kept her voice neutral, but she didn't like that he'd been listening to her. Although she knew she could be misunderstanding. He was in the craft's systems, and if she spoke, he would hear it, whether he was actively listening to her or minding his own business completely.

And what else did he have to do at the moment?

Boredom was a huge problem for Sazo. Idle hands do the devil's work had never been more applicable. Although, this time, the devil had been totally in her corner.

They'd needed each other——Sazo's access to the ship's systems and her mobility and opposable thumbs——and their plan had worked.

She walked back into the small cockpit, still hanging on to the end of her braid, peered out the porthole one last time at the Tecran ship disappearing into the distance, and gave them the middle finger.

CHAPTER 4

"NOTHING HAPPENED TO THIS SHIP." Borji stood to attention in front of Dav in the darkness, his biosuit visor lit only by the portable screen in his hand. He looked like he'd taken a bite of something sour.

"Clearly, something did." Dav told him.

"The system shut down, yes, but from within. Everything was done through the master system, and I can't find any malfunction, any virus."

"Why didn't they switch it back on, then?"

Borji lifted the portable screen he was holding and tilted it for Dav to see. "This piece of code could be the reason, but again, the Tecran did it to themselves. They set a timer on the power and air to shut down. Two hours. It should be coming back online in . . ." He flicked his left sleeve for the smart fabric time display. "Three, two, one . . ."

All around them, lights flickered on, and the gentle hum of the air filtration system vibrated through the wall Dav was resting his hand on.

Well, damn.

They now had a fully functional, undamaged Class 5 in their possession, something the Grih had tried and failed to get since they'd first had a sniff of their existence.

He could see good things in his future for being in the right place at the right time, because there was no question the *Barrist* would get the glory for this.

Trouble was, he hadn't done a thing to earn it.

Something a few of his fellow captains would no doubt be happy to point out to Battle Center. For whatever good it would do them.

It was time he and his crew staked their claim and became the experts in Class 5 tech before the back-up they'd originally requested arrived.

Dav wanted to sink his teeth into this one so deep, they'd have to pry his jaw open to make him let go. He pulled off the helmet of his biosuit and gave Borji a look he knew his system's engineer would be blind not to interpret correctly. "Get your team and learn as much about the way this ship functions as you can."

"Yes, sir." Borji grinned, and went off, tapping his comm to call his team to him.

There was a polite buzz from his comm, and he linked to Kila.

"You wanted to know what was happening to those oranges, sir. They've just entered Harmon's atmosphere. We're tracking them."

Seven oranges. Six on one craft, one on the other.

It had looked to Dav as if the dead animal in the launch bay had been meant to join the rest of them, but something had gone wrong and it had been killed by the Tecran. Or at least, a Tecran death injection. Whether the hand that had wielded it was Tecran was something Dav wanted an answer to more and more urgently.

Were the other seven like that thing in the cage? He thought what it might look like, alive, standing, and pissed off.

If he were the Tecran, he might have decided to get them all the hell off his ship as well.

He tapped his comm again. There was only one way to find out. "Commander, I want to talk to the Tecran captain. Where are you holding him?"

"In the cells they've got here, sir. Some kind of holding facility. Looks like they were keeping . . . things . . . prisoner." The way she spoke, Dav guessed the Tecran had been violating the Sentient Beings

Agreement. But then, that really was the only explanation for the orange heartbeats.

"I'll be there now."

He took a tube down to the third level and walked past enough dead Tecran to make the sense of urgency driving him ratchet up so tight, it was a relief to finally see Appal leaning against the corridor wall.

She could have been waiting for him, but he sensed instead she was avoiding the place she'd left their prisoners. She looked up at the sound of his footsteps, her biosuit helmet under her arm now that Borji had given the all-clear, her heavy-duty shockgun held easily in her other hand.

"The smell in there." She shook her head. "I sent the rest of my team to help with the bodies because they couldn't take it. The Tecran were keeping the area they held their prisoners relatively clean, but no one seems to have been on clean-up duty today. Whatever the things they captured are, they aren't in there anymore." She pushed off against the wall. "It's extremely secure in there. I'm sure the Tecran can't escape, which only makes me wonder where those things they kept in there are, and how they got out."

"Just as the air and power went, two explorer-class craft left this ship, containing seven orange heartbeats between them." Dav watched Appal process that.

"You think the Tecran evacuated them? But why would they save the beings they had so little respect for they held them captive, and not save themselves?"

Dav gave a nod toward the door. "Let's find out."

Appal seemed to steel herself before she punched the button on the side of the door. It slid open soundlessly and Dav had to force himself not to reel back.

His commander was right. The stench was overwhelming. Probably made worse by the fact that for two hours, there had been no ventilation here at all.

About fifteen Tecran were split between three cells, all with transparent walls, and there were at least twelve other empty cells down a long stretch of corridor.

Dav noticed that Appal had put them in the three worst cells. Some of the empty ones were actually pristine, as if nothing had been kept there, and one . . . He looked at it and frowned. It was different to the others.

And there was that one craft with just the one orange signature in it. He forced his attention back to their prisoners.

Most of them were sitting down, trying to find a clean place amongst the muck. Some still wore their personal breathers, others trusted the systems were up again, and had taken them off.

Dav remembered the Tecran didn't have the same acute sense of smell as the Grih, otherwise they'd probably all still be using their breathers.

One Tecran rose to his feet when Dav and Appal stepped into the holding area, and the look he gave them was cold and calculating.

Dav watched him back, taking in the thick-set, muscular build, the large eyes, the sleek brown and cream mottled feathers over his head. They were ruffled at the neck, a sign of extreme agitation. "Which of you was the captain of this ship?" he asked in broken Tecran.

He knew already.

If the Tecran's body language hadn't been clear enough, Dav had been taught to read Tecran military uniform insignia. But the Tecran didn't need to know that.

"I am Vai Gee, and I am *still* the captain of this ship. I don't know how you pulled us into your territory and disabled us, but if you return us now, perhaps the Tecran High Command will not launch an immediate attack on the Grih."

Dav lifted his brows. Vai Gee knew the Tecran would have to pry this ship out of the Grih's cold, dead hands; although, what did he have to lose demanding they send them back home?

The Tecran captain was breathing hard. "This was mass murder. Most of my crew are dead." There was a trace of a screech in his voice. "And you will release us immediately from these inappropriate quarters."

Dav considered him as Appal went very still at his side. "We didn't pull you into our territory. You're in the dead center of Grih airspace. The only way you could have gotten here is if you set a course before a light jump, and that light jump would have had to have originated in the outer edges of our territory to begin with. My systems engineer has confirmed you disabled your own ship and killed your own crew. I'd like to know why."

The Tecran captain drew in a sharp breath. Shared a look with one of his officers. "Why would we do that? This *must* be your doing."

Dav shrugged. "It wasn't. Perhaps you've annoyed someone else?"

Gee stood very stiff.

He was thinking, Dav could see it. Running through which of the many enemies the Tecran had made who could have done something like this. And why they would pull the Grih into the mess.

He'd really like the answer to that one, himself.

There could be no doubt the Tecran ship had been deliberately placed in Grih territory, but he was pretty sure the gift of a Class 5 meant that whoever was responsible understood the outcome would be . . . messy. And he was also pretty sure his superiors would more than forgive the diplomatic firestorm this would cause when the trade-off was a Class 5 in pristine condition to play with.

"I'd like to know, if these quarters are so inappropriate, why you were keeping anything in here?" Appal's Tecran was worse than his, but she'd obviously latched on to that particular part of Gee's tirade, and wasn't letting go. "It looks like a contravention of the Sentient Beings Agreement to me."

"Do you see any alien sentient beings here?" Gee stared straight back, but there was a muscle jumping under the pale pink skin of his jaw.

"There is a dead one in your launch bay." Dav thought back to that crumpled thing he had a feeling had been so much more when alive. "I'm sure my team will discover plenty of genetic material in here to confirm. By the looks of things they'll have quite a bit more to work with than they need. And of course, there is the lens feed."

Gee flicked a look at the lenses spaced along the corridor above Dav's head and then looked down.

Something vicious and angry rose up in Dav. There had been a strange tightening of the skin around Gee's eyes and his beak-like mouth, a real fear, and Dav knew there were things on that lens feed that would possibly get Gee the ultimate penalty for breaking the Sentient Beings Agreement.

He tried to keep his voice even. "Easiest of all is we saw the rest of them shipped out on two explorer craft to the surface of Harmon before your power went down."

Gee sucked in a breath at that, and Dav would have sworn he didn't know the creatures he'd been illegally keeping in his holding cells had been sent to Virmana's moon. But if Gee hadn't given the order as the captain of the ship, who had?

Gee stretched himself impossibly straighter, his slightly rounded chest puffing up. "I'm finished talking to you."

Dav stared at him until the Tecran turned away, then he walked over to the one cell that was different.

He could feel Gee's eyes on him, sense Appal's interest, as she also picked up what he was seeing.

This was the cell of an advanced sentient. He could see a chair and table, a handheld tablet and a bed made up with sheets and blankets. He looked up and down the row, but this was the only cell set up like this. He looked over at Gee, but the captain was still turned away, his shoulders stiff.

Dav shrugged. He'd be wasting his time trying to get anything out of the Tecran. Borji could give him the lens feed. Give them an idea what they would find on Harmon.

He walked out of the holding area, taking a deep breath of clean air when he and Appal were on the other side of the closed door, although now that the air filtration was working again, the smell was not as bad as it had been.

That, or he'd gotten used to it.

"He didn't know the explorer craft had left the ship." Appal almost whispered the words.

"No. We might have to consider this was a rescue and revenge mission."

"Someone rescued the prisoners, punished their captors?" Appal looked at the dead Tecran littering the passageway. Whistled. "Some punishment. What were they holding in there? If Borji is right, whoever they are they hijacked a Class 5's internal systems and used it against itself."

"Whoever or whatever they are, I don't think the Tecran realized they were quite so powerful. Or perhaps they simply have powerful friends." Dav frowned. While the animal in the launch bay looked fierce, in fact sent a primal chill down his spine, he had the sense it wasn't an advanced sentient. But one of the prisoners definitely had been.

"We're going to Harmon?" Appal asked, and there was a keen edge to her words.

"We're going to Harmon."

CHAPTER 5

HARMON WAS SUPERFICIALLY LIKE EARTH, although with more blue than green. Rose couldn't tell whether it was the same size, she had no idea how to gauge the size of an object in space, and with the massive gas planet looming beside it, throwing out her sense of perspective, she had no chance. But she'd watched her share of science documentaries, and she guessed it must be pretty close to Earth-size, or it wouldn't have water and an atmosphere.

A Goldilocks planet. Not too big, not too small, not too hot, not too cold. Or, in this case, a Goldilocks moon.

She could see a vast sea below, with the green of land dotted through it, like paint flicked onto a blue canvas.

"Tiny islands? Is that all this place has?"

There was a sound behind her, and she turned from the view port to see a screen rising out of the console.

"There is one large land mass, the rest of the moon is made up of small islands. Although obviously they're bigger than they appear from our current elevation."

"How big?" She'd told Sazo what her height was in meters and centimeters, so he could work out distances that were meaningful to her, and it seemed the Grih's standard measurement was very close to the metric system.

He'd promised her he'd chosen the Grih to be part of this elaborate plan because of their physical resemblance to her, their similarity of culture and their good record with dealing with alien life.

They were strong advocates of the Sentient Beings Agreement.

She'd learned all about the SBA. Had read the whole agreement, thanks to Sazo, before she'd agreed to steal him from the lock-safe where the Tecran had kept him and start this whole ball rolling.

"The smallest island is around four kilometers long, the largest is sixty kilometers. The animals will have more variety of vegetation if we land on the main continent."

He brought up a map of their destination, and she stepped closer to look at it. Sazo planned to put them down in a valley beside a large river, with a low hill behind them.

It looked pristine. There were no advanced species on this moon. And the Grih had obviously not colonized it.

"I hope my animals don't destroy the local environment. Although they won't be here long, with the Grih coming down after us."

"The local environment would be in trouble if any of the animals had parasites or diseases, but the Tecran got rid of those, and there are no mated pairs, so they will simply live out their lives and then die. Or be eaten."

"What's out there that can eat them? And me?" Funny, she'd been so keen to get away from the Tecran, she hadn't thought what might be waiting for her down on Harmon. And couldn't find it in her to care all that much now.

She was free. There was a deep sense of satisfaction in that. Bring it on, whatever was waiting for her down there. Anyway, Sazo needed her too much to send her to her death.

For the moment, anyway.

"There are a few species similar to the lion, but smaller than him. Very fierce, though."

"How much smaller?"

"Up to your knees. They're nocturnal. Some of the smaller mammals and the birds are probably in danger from them. The largest life-form is the gryak. It is perhaps a little bigger than a lion, and can go up on its hind legs for short periods. It lives underground. There wasn't much information on them in the Tecran systems. It's omnivorous, so it is a danger to you."

"Sounds a bit like a bear." She still didn't feel any worry about it. Her capacity for stress and nerves had reached its limit.

Three months of thinking she was going to die any day had put a lot of things into perspective.

She peered out the view port again, but they were still too high up to see any details.

Sazo solved that for her by switching the map on the screen to an image of what was directly below them, and zooming in. There were trees. Nothing that looked familiar, but then, that would surely have been more surprising. At least they were identifiably trees.

She worried her lip. Maybe she should keep the animals and birds in the transport until the Grih arrived. That would keep them from harm, but she didn't have any food for them, and she could hardly stand to think about them in there. The sheep literally shaking at the proximity of the coyote, the birds fluttering behind the bars of their cages.

The Grih were super-advanced. They had the technology to jump through space at faster-than-light speed, just like the Tecran——light jumps, Sazo called them——they were able to almost put an end to death through disease or injury, they had harnessed their sun, and other star-light, for infinite power, and had responsibly colonized three planets other than their own, only taking those that had no advanced sentience present. They should be able to round up six unknown life-forms.

She would let them out of their cages.

"You need to buckle in." Sazo sounded . . . excited, and she guessed he would be. His plan had gone off with only a lion-sized hitch.

They were free. They were on Harmon, where they could survive, if the worst came to the worst, and best of all, the Tecran were the Grih's problem now.

She slipped the harness over her head, and engaged the button, so it tightened to her body shape and held her safe while turbulence bounced them around and they shuddered and shimmied to a gentle, airy landing.

As soon as they came to rest, she hit the button again and shrugged the harness off, stepping toward the door, but it didn't open as she expected it to.

"Don't forget to take me with you." Sazo spoke through the speakers on the craft, and Rose realized she'd forgotten he wasn't around her neck.

She grabbed him off the counter where she'd put him before her shower, and slipped him over her head, stuck the tiny earpiece in her ear. This time, when she approached the door, it opened soundlessly.

Another gentle reminder. Nothing happened without Sazo's say-so.

Her heart gave a hard thump at the thought.

The sound of a river tumbling over rocks a little way in the distance and the wind in the tree tops stopped her short on the gangplank.

Her eyes misted over and she blinked the tears away.

She'd been in a windowless room for three months and she'd thought she'd never see something like this again. Thought the only things in her life were a cell or death, and she couldn't believe she was standing here, breathing in the air.

She drew in a deep gulp, and then started to cough.

"What——?"

"I believe your lungs aren't used to this much oxygen after your time with the Tecran," Sazo told her, his unaffected tone helping calm her panic, although he would probably sound unaffected even if she were rolling on the ground, having a fit.

She blew out a breath, took another, more cautious one, and stood still, a little light-headed, until the feeling subsided. She started down the gang-plank, tripped and fell, and landed in a heap at the bottom.

"Your body is used to the slightly heavier gravity of Earth. You'll be able to jump a little higher, but it will seem as if you're moving a little slower." At least Sazo wasn't laughing at her, but then, she didn't think he had much of a sense of humor.

She pulled herself to her feet and gave an experimental jump. She went high enough to have her grinning. And yes, it did feel like it took her a fraction longer to come down.

Next to them, the second transport had already landed, and Sazo opened the gang-plank. The animals were quiet, and she walked over, feeling a little like she was on a sailing ship or a sprung floor, the ground too bouncy to be normal.

She took the birds out first. She could actually carry their cages, and Sazo did whatever it was he did to disengage the magnetic locks on the doors.

She opened the falcon's cage first, and it shrieked at her before flapping a little, testing its wings. It hadn't had a good fly in three months, and she wondered how it had survived.

It hopped a few times, and then lifted off, winging away faster than she thought normal. The weaker gravity, she realized. Just as she could jump higher, it probably took less effort for the falcon to fly.

She let the raven out next. It flew up clumsily onto its cage and looked around, but at last it flew away, wings fluttering.

"Ostrich next," she said to Sazo, and waited outside for him to open the cage. She didn't want to be kicked by a terrified ostrich if she could help it.

It came out hesitantly, feathers ruffled, and picked its way through the bushes until it had disappeared. She released the deer and the sheep and waited until she could no longer see them. Only the coyote was left.

For that, she moved up onto the gang-plank of her own ship, and made sure Sazo could close it in time if he needed to, then watched as it came out, sniffing the air, clumsy on its feet in the lighter atmosphere. It turned and looked at her when it got to the bottom of the gang-plank, a long look without any aggression, and then ran off into the bush.

She wondered what the lion would have done. She'd have had to lock herself into the ship for that release. Or made Sazo drop the lion off in another location, before landing here.

She felt a shudder, a rumbling under her feet, and frowned. "What is that——?"

The ground beneath them collapsed. She fell backwards into the ship, and the gang-plank retracted and the door shut before she even hit the floor.

She came up painfully against one of the two seats, her shoulder and head hitting metal.

The ship slammed to a stop, more or less the right way up, and Rose waited another moment to make sure there weren't anymore surprises before she pulled herself to her feet.

Sazo was quiet, and she went to the console, read the Tecran symbols and pushed some buttons to bring up the display from the outside lenses.

They were in a kind of cave, which now had no ceiling. Both craft had fallen through, and Rose hoped all the animals had gotten far enough away before the ground gave way.

She could hear water, and remembered they'd been near a river. Suddenly alarmed, she swung the lenses around, and saw the water she heard was an underground river. The chamber wasn't about to be flooded from above.

"Is it safe to leave the craft?" she asked.

"Yes. I'm sorry. I feel . . . uncomfortable. I don't like it."

"Probably embarrassment, although there's no need." Rose walked to the entrance and the door opened. "You couldn't know there were caves just under the surface. It looks like they were carved out by the underground river. The combined weight of the two craft was probably too much. It fell in."

"I could have used the scanners, but I didn't think to."

"Have you ever been on the surface of a moon or planet before?" She wondered, not for the first time, how long the Tecran had had him.

"No. It's been deep space, since the moment the Tecran woke me."

She shrugged. "Well, then. You don't know much about physical land masses. No harm done."

"There could have been harm." He sounded bemused.

"There could have been a lot of harm. There wasn't." She stood on the top of the gang-plank again, her eyes trying to adjust between the bright light streaming in from above and the dark shadows where the roof hadn't caved in. "I do know something about actual planets, so I'll call for scans if I think we need them in future."

"I can only use the scanners on the craft, and their reach is only three kilometers. If we move further away than that from the ship, I'm more or less useless."

And he wasn't used to that. She could hear that, loud and clear.

"Sounds to me like it would be better to stick with the craft anyway, if we're hoping the Grih are going to pick us up."

She reached the end of the gang-plank and crouched down. The cavern they'd fallen into was large, the rock beneath her hand smooth and cold, similar to granite. A river ran in front of her, the sound of it echoing in the chamber and drowning out any other noise.

She walked forward, stepping at last out of the strong light and into the shadows, right to the underground river's edge. The roar of it was explained when she saw it dropped over a steep edge, falling into an even larger chamber below them, barely lit by the sunlight filtering in, and she realized if the craft had slid over the edge and plummeted down, she would most likely be dead.

"Rose." There was something in his tone.

"What?"

"The scanners are picking up a life form in this cave system."

Her heart rate kicked up. "What type?"

"A big type. Twice your height, at least."

"How many and where?" She edged back toward the craft.

"Only one, and it's a kilometer away, in the tunnels on the other side of the river. But it's moving this way. It is almost certainly a gryak."

"Heard the commotion, probably." She was back on the gang-plank, now, and felt a little better. "Can we fly out of here?"

"No. There was some major damage to the craft when it fell. I'll need time to fix it." He paused. "But that may not be necessary. The Grih just entered Harmon's atmosphere."

"That was quick." They were only a little over two hours behind her. She would have thought it would have taken them a lot longer than that to secure the Tecran ship. There were literally hundreds of Tecrans on board, and disabled or not, she couldn't imagine they would have simply given in without a fight.

"Remember our agreement," Sazo said.

"Don't worry, my lips are zipped." Rose tucked the slender crystal under her shirt and looked up at the sky, even though she knew she wouldn't see them yet.

She was about to meet the people Sazo assured her would take her in and give her a new life.

She hoped they liked each other.

CHAPTER 6

"THEY'VE SCATTERED." Kila was so intent on the screen, Dav wondered if she even realized she was scowling at it. "Only one orange is still near the craft. The others have gone in all directions."

Dav thought back to the creature dead on the floor in the Class 5 launch bay, and wished Borji had been able to find the lens feed from the holding cells. Inexplicably, it wasn't in the correct file group, so they had no idea what creatures were down here.

"Well, stay armed at all times and be cautious. Although," he turned to Jia Appal and her hand-picked squad of fifteen soldiers, "I want them all alive. Stun only, and light stun as first option, only going heavier if there is no choice and immediate danger."

"Captain, I have the first one up on screen." Kila tried to keep her voice even and failed. "There you are!"

Dav turned as Kila flicked the image to the large screen. The lens zoomed in and he stared at the strange creature in astonishment. It had two long, powerful legs, a rounded body of fluffy feathers, a long, strangely bare neck, and a squat head with a beak.

It heard their craft, looking toward them with big eyes surrounded by long lashes, and then began to run.

It zig-zagged as it went, but everyone relaxed a little.

"Not an advanced sentient." Kila seemed only slightly disappointed. "But extremely interesting, nevertheless."

The camera picked up two more of the oranges as they flew toward the craft. A slim four-legged creature that looked not unlike something from Grih itself, long-eared, long snout. It bared its teeth at them, and the sharp incisors were familiar, too. The other was a strange creature with a chestnut coat, and it raised its head from foraging on long grass, twitched its ears, and went back to eating.

"They took a range of sample specimens." Kila said what Dav was thinking. "Some may be dangerous, like that creature back on the Class 5, but the chances are, only a few are. It could even have been random, a quick foray as they passed the planet these things are from."

"But they're showing up orange. Which means the planet's nowhere that's recorded by the United Council." Dav tried to put aside the unease he'd felt since he'd seen the thing lying dead in the launch bay, seen the cells. How many worlds had the Tecran stumbled across with their powerful Class 5s, and hadn't bothered to share with the United Council? Nothing he could do to investigate that mystery right now, so he had to put it away for the time being.

He had something else to puzzle over, anyway. The three beings they'd seen so far, unless they were far from what they seemed, had not broken into a Class 5 system, disabled the power and air, arranged two escape craft and killed over four hundred Tecran.

"We have a problem." Pallen Hui called from the front, where he was flying the attack craft.

"Which is?" Dav stepped closer, saw with his own eyes. Whistled. "A collapse of some kind."

"This moon is riddled with cave systems. The combined weight of the two explorer craft they landed must have forced a cave-in." Kila took over the lenses, zoomed in. "There is still one orange by the craft."

"Injured in the fall, maybe," Appal said quietly. "Some things are dangerous when they're injured."

"And this thing may well be responsible for the bodies up in that Class 5." He let that sink in, just in case they got too cocky. They'd all seen the carnage on the Tecran ship.

"Land as close as it's safe to," Dav ordered, and was pleased they could see the sink-hole from where Pallen put them down. "Tread warily, people."

They were all suited up, body armor, weapons, but no breathing apparatus was necessary. As the gang-plank lowered, Appal and her team fell into formation and Dav followed them down, leaving Kila and Pallen on board.

The gang-plank snicked closed behind him, and he moved to the front, to stand with Appal.

It was an idyllic scene. The river flowed, fast and deep, to his left, and the air, after too long in deep space, was fresh and clear. He could stand here all day and just breathe it in.

"Sir." Kila's voice came through his comm. "There is a gryak heading straight for our stationary orange. My information is they live in the cave systems, and this collapse must have brought it to investigate. They're big, sir. And can be dangerous if their territory is invaded."

"How far away from the orange is it?" Dav started forward.

"Half a thou. But moving fast."

Appal motioned to her squad, and they fanned out in a line, so that they all reached the edge of the hole together.

Dav and Appal took the middle position.

Dav peered down and saw the two craft, the larger one on its side, the smaller one right-side up, and less damaged. The gang-plank was down, and a figure stood at the bottom of it.

It turned and looked up at him.

They stared at each other for a long moment.

This was an advanced sentient. It——why was he even using that term?——she, wore close-fitting clothes in pleasing shades of dark green, and her long hair was tied back in a complicated braid. It was the color of sunlight, and he had never seen anything like it. It was hard to see the color of her eyes, but the intelligence in them was unmistakable.

She began to raise her arm, as if in greeting, and at that moment, one of Appal's team, to the right, got too close to the unstable edge, and the ground beneath him collapsed.

His cry bounced and echoed in the cave, and as he fell, he activated his weapon. The blast didn't hit her, but it hit the cave ceiling above her, and rock and soil fell down onto the ramp she was standing on, forcing her to stumble off it, as rubble blocked the entrance to her craft.

The falling soldier's automated grapple engaged, found purchase, and stopped his fall, jerking him to a halt. He swayed from side to side as it winched him back up.

It had only lasted a second, two at most, but Dav saw her demeanor change from cautiously friendly, to uncertain and wary.

He swore, and Appal's gaze cut to her subordinate. He swung easily back up next to his team mates, but Dav didn't miss the slight hunch of his shoulders.

There was a moment of silence, as everyone settled down.

"Sir. You should have visual on the gryak." Kila's voice in his ear was urgent, drowned out a second later by an ear-splitting shriek as the gryak burst out of a tunnel on the other side of the underground river to the woman. It rose up on two legs, mouth snarling.

The woman's attention swung from Dav and the team to the latest threat, although he didn't see much surprise on her face. She knew the gryak was coming, he guessed, using the scanners on the explorer craft, although he saw no remote screen in her hand.

The gryak scrambled to a stop at the sight of them and went down on all fours, a long, rumbling growl coming from deep in its throat.

She called something to it, softly, and remained standing quite still. The sound froze Dav where he stood. He could feel the same reaction from Appal. It was almost music, but with her voice. He could swear it was with her voice.

He wished he could somehow mute the sound of the river running just at her feet, so he could hear her better.

The gryak snarled at her, unappeased. It lowered its head and bared its teeth, and before Dav could react, it leapt into the river, straight at her.

ABOUT A TON OF FLUFFY, gray-white fur and extremely large teeth was coming straight for her, and there was nowhere to run.

Rubble and rocks blocked the door into the explorer craft, and the other craft was on its side.

Rose stood still, hoping the gryak was mock-charging, and wouldn't cross the river.

No such luck.

She was reluctant to try out her new-found jumping trick, not trusting herself not to land on her head, but as the gryak launched itself from the water, icy droplets flying, she gave up, turned, and jumped for the craft.

The pleasure of using her muscles, the freedom of near-flight, flooded her senses and she reveled in it. After being confined for so long, it was a heady shot of champagne through her blood. She landed on the wing and jumped again, reaching the roof of the craft perfectly, even gracefully, more out of luck than skill. She couldn't help the little whoop of joy that came from somewhere deep inside.

She looked up, and saw the Grih soldiers who'd been lining the opening above her were coming down on thin cables like the one that had saved the soldier who'd fallen.

Her jump surprised them as much as their jump surprised her, she guessed, from the way they reacted to the sight of her suddenly crouched on the roof of her little spaceship by suddenly coming to a halt.

With a hand signal and a barked command, the big guy who'd been standing in the middle, the one she'd exchanged a look with earlier, ordered them all to winch themselves back to the top again, weapons trained on the gryak. He stayed behind, though, eyes never leaving the gryak, and walked carefully to her ship.

He was going to climb up to her.

The gryak had stopped when she'd jumped, and gone very watchful when the soldiers had dropped into its cave, but now it prowled up and down in front of her craft, confused and distressed.

The black helmet and then the enormous shoulders of the Grih who'd stayed below with her rose up, her rescuer easily pulling himself onto the roof with her.

They stared at each other again, not that Rose could see much of his face through the helmet, and she mentally called up the Grih she'd learned over the last eight weeks.

"I'm Rose McKenzie. Pleased to meet you." Grih informal greetings required her to touch her nose to his left cheek, and he to hers, but they were on more of a formal footing, she was guessing, and his helmet was in the way anyway, so she extended her hands palms facing each other, waiting for him to either cover hers or let her cover his. She couldn't remember who should do what, right at that minute.

There was a moment of silence, and then the thin, gray-tinted glass on his helmet retracted, and she looked directly into startled pale blue eyes with a dark outer-rim of navy blue. "You speak Grih."

"I've been studying it." She looked at him, and tears pricked her eyes.

Sazo had said the Grih were as close to being like her as it got in this part of the universe. But she'd thought he'd been talking in general terms. Bi-pedal, with two eyes, a nose and a mouth. That was the most she'd hoped for.

She even thought it didn't matter. She would be happy to be alive, and wouldn't care if she looked completely different to the people who would hopefully take her in.

But Sazo had come through for her.

The guy looking back at her was big, head and shoulders bigger than a tall man, but while his nose was a little sharper than average, and his eyes were the shade of a wolf's she'd once seen on a nature documentary, no one on Earth would have looked twice at him.

Well. They would, but because he was good looking and intimidating, not because he looked like an alien.

The first tear slid down her cheek, and she sniffed and flicked it away with the back of her hand.

The gryak chose that moment to charge the craft.

With another shriek, it slammed massive, clawed hands on the side of the explorer, and started trying to climb.

"Maybe time to go?" she suggested, and the Grih looking at her tears with absolute confusion gave a nod, grabbed her around her waist, and shot his grapple hook up into the air.

She was well out of reach when the gryak managed to get on the roof, held tight against her rescuer as they slid smoothly upward, and then passed to waiting hands when they reached the top.

She took a step back to let the guy who'd saved her swing up, and held out a hand to him.

He looked at it, still with that bemused look on his face, and easily pulled himself to his feet.

She realized things were strangely quiet. No one was talking.

And that's when she noticed every one of the Grih had their guns trained on her.

She looked back at her rescuer, the only one with the glass front of his helmet retracted, and gaped. He was pointing his weapon at her, too.

CHAPTER 7

INEXPLICABLE.

Looking at the petite little alien, Dav tried to work out, quick as he could, if they were all being played.

Because she looked extremely unlikely as a suspect in a mass murder.

She'd actually cried when he climbed on the roof of her craft, although he wasn't quite sure why. She was more compact than she looked, as well. There was no question he'd drop her, but when the grapple had pulled them up, he'd been surprised to find she weighed much more than he'd have guessed, based on her size and slender form.

Her bones must be far denser than his. Her muscles, too.

She could pass for Grih, though. Well, she would be considered very short, but the similarities between her and them were startling.

If her genetic structure showed up orange, and Kila assured him it did, then there was a world out there that had somehow taken a very similar evolutionary path to his own.

Right now she was looking at them all, at their weapons, and the look on her face was one of . . . betrayal. Like she'd thought better of them and they'd proven her wrong.

She bit her lip. "You shoot me?" she asked. Then she shook her head. "Are you going to shoot me?" Her second try was perfect Grih, but melodic and smooth.

He shifted uncomfortably, and he wasn't the only one.

Two of Appal's team dropped their weapons slightly, and Appal gave them a sharp look. The weapons rose again, but Dav could see they were losing the high ground. The longer they gave her to talk, the less inclined any of Appal's team would be to harm her, even if she was a threat.

"We don't know what you are or where you're from. These soldiers are under my command and I don't want to risk their lives." Dav kept his weapon level as he spoke.

The woman lifted her arms from her sides and gave a nod. "I can understand that. I'm unarmed, and I have no intention of hurting anyone."

She stumbled over a few of the words, but that just made the words she did say properly all the more beautiful.

A Class 5, and a music maker, all in one haul. Dav didn't know whether to laugh or groan. Because this was definitely the most important day of his life.

"What happened on the Tecran ship?" Appal retracted her helmet screen as she spoke, and the woman blinked at her, and then smiled. A sweet, friendly smile.

Dav wondered why Appal would get that reaction, and not him.

"What do you mean?"

"Why did the Tecran send you down here, to Harmon?"

She shrugged. "They weren't in the habit of explaining themselves to me."

Now that he'd seen her, Dav wondered if the Tecran had already been having problems with their ship, and, knowing they were stranded, had tried to hide her and the animals they'd taken from her planet.

They would have known that if the Grih boarded them, they'd have been in serious trouble over their violation of the Sentient Beings Agreement, as well as evidence that they had explored so deep into the universe they had come across unknown planets and not declared them to the United Council.

Harmon was uninhabited and if they'd managed to get the explorer craft away soon enough, Dav would have had no reason to look at Harmon at all. The Tecran could have had plans to fetch them later, after they'd accomplished whatever they'd invaded Grih territory to do, if their Class 5 hadn't malfunctioned.

"Do you know what the Tecran are doing in our territory?"

The woman tipped her head toward him, and there was something closed off in her. "I have been in a cell on the Tecran ship for the last three months. In that time they have poked me, observed me, opened me up and welded me back together. Just about the only thing they haven't done to me is let me know what they're up to."

Her unspeakable anger vibrated through her words.

They were all silent, looking at her, and she drew in a deep breath, smoothed back wisps of hair that had fallen from her braid onto her face, and then shrugged. "Sorry. Why don't you ask them? Unless they got away?" She looked up at the sky for the first time, but there was no way to see either the Class 5 or the *Barrist* from here, and she looked back at Appal.

He found it interesting, and a little bit annoying, that since she'd seen Appal, she'd directed every comment to his commander, and ignored him.

"They didn't get away, but asking them will be difficult. Most of them are dead." He spoke bluntly, and at last she looked his way again.

There could be no hiding the shock on her face.

"Dead?"

"Only eleven are alive."

Her legs collapsed from under her and she sank to the ground, her head bowed, her hands gripping her knees in white-knuckled shock. "But there were hundreds of them. How . . . ? Did you kill them?"

The look she gave them was wild-eyed.

Dav shook his head. "Their power and air were cut off for two hours. Only those with a personal breathing apparatus survived."

Unless her race were the finest manipulators in the universe, she hadn't known the Tecrans had died. But something did cross her face. A sort of sick horror.

She closed her eyes and hunched her shoulders, and Dav was sure then that if she hadn't been involved, she knew exactly who had been.

THE SOLDIERS' CLOTHING had seemed black when they'd dropped into the cave, but now they were walking toward their sleek, silver-gray ship, it shifted and changed as they moved, and Rose decided it was some kind of camouflage, but it was sort of ruined by the dark sepia outline that made them stand out almost more than no camouflage at all.

Their uniforms reminded her of her own things, left back in the damaged craft, with a gryak sitting on the roof.

"Do you think the gryak will leave, so we could get my things out of the Tecran ship?" She addressed her comment to the woman pacing beside her, the one who had retracted her face guard and questioned her earlier. When she'd realized the second-in-command had been female, she'd felt a weight of fear lift off her shoulders.

Illogical or not, she felt safer with a woman in the group. Felt they were less likely to treat her badly. There may be more women amongst the soldiers who walked in tight formation around her, but with their bulky protective gear and their helmets, it was impossible to say.

And all this mental . . . chatter . . . she admitted, was to distract herself from the horrifying thought that Sazo had tried to kill the whole Tecran crew.

He'd never so much as hinted that particular detail to her.

"What things do you have?" The woman stopped and signaled with her hand, so everyone else except the big guy in front, who was obviously in charge, stopped too.

"Clothing, mainly."

The woman looked at her carefully. "I'm sure we can get them for you. Let's give the gryak some time to calm down. We'll bring your things to you as soon as we can."

Rose frowned, picking up a definite subtext. "Thanks. There are two small black bags, that's all I have. But you made it sound like I'm going somewhere, and you're staying behind."

The woman cocked her head, in a way that humans didn't. It sent a quick little shock through her, a reminder that these were a people and a culture she didn't understand.

"You are correct. You will go with Captain Jallan back to the *Barrist*. We will stay behind and collect the animals from your planet and make arrangements for the two Tecran craft to be lifted back to the Class 5."

"There are cages for the animals in the other craft. But if you transport them, please put the coyote in a different room to the others. I can sketch which one that is so you know. The others are afraid to be near him." She worried her lip a moment. "You aren't going to hurt them, are you? You just want to look at them? And they'll have a good environment to live in?"

The woman shivered, the movement so strange and alien, Rose took a step back. She'd been a little too hasty in thinking these people were just like her.

"They will be treated completely within the rules of the Sentient Beings Agreement. You have no need to worry about that. Although your concern does you credit."

The words were spoken in the same harsh, clipped way Captain Jallan had spoken, the same way the voices Sazo had piped through her earpiece had sounded when she was learning Grih back on the Tecran ship. She didn't think she could match the rough tone, or the staccato sound of it, but they seemed to understand her more fluid speech well enough.

The woman indicated they should continue forward again but now the moment had arrived where she was expected to get into the ship they'd obviously arrived in, she felt the burn of vomit in her throat.

She looked down, and her hands were shaking.

She wrapped her arms around her waist and stayed where she was. "There's another ship coming to pick Captain Jallan and I up?"

The woman nodded.

"I would like to go for a walk until it gets here, please."

The woman frowned and shook her head. "It would be better if you could answer some questions for us in our ship, and we can make sure you are all right in the med-chamber." She started moving, but Rose stubbornly stayed put, pressing hard on her stomach, so that she wouldn't throw up.

The thought of getting into the ship was a rabid dog inside her head, making her wild, putting her as close to the edge as she'd been in the last three months.

The woman turned again, a little less patiently.

"What is the problem, commander?" The big guy, Captain Jallan, apparently, was suddenly right there in front of her.

"She doesn't want to get into our ship."

"It isn't that I don't want to get into your ship." She was trying to breath properly. She hadn't had a panic attack since the first few weeks on the Tecran ship, and she fought it, fought for her hard-won control, but that didn't mean she was going to back down and go quietly.

She wondered if she would go quietly anywhere, ever again.

"I don't want to get into any ship. I've been held in a small cell for the last three months, imprisoned, and I want to go for a walk before I'm back in a small, enclosed space with no proper air to breathe again." She was horrified to hear her voice crack at the end of her little meltdown, and end on a sob.

She turned away from them, her body shuddering as she sucked in air and raised her hands to her face, battling a crying jag that threatened to turn her into a complete idiot.

She was so focused on conquering her reaction, she almost missed Jallan murmur something to his commander, and she sensed rather than saw the other soldiers melt away.

Slowly she raised her head.

She and Captain Jallan were alone, the others walking up the ramp.

"You must forgive us," Jallan said. He lifted an arm, then thought better of touching her and let it fall again. "We forgot you were a prisoner. *I* even thought how wonderful the air and the space were when we landed here, and I've been living on one of the largest ships in the Grih fleet, with no restrictions on my movements and three exercise rooms. I saw where they kept you on the Tecran ship, and so did Commander Appal. We are both ashamed at our lack of understanding."

Rose sniffed back the last of her tears and straightened. "I can go for a walk?"

He gave a nod. "I will have to accompany you."

He didn't explain why he'd have to do so, but Rose could fill in the blanks. They'd be mad to leave an unknown alien to her own devices, especially one who'd just left the ship of death. And after seeing the gryak, she didn't mind that he had that really serious looking gun thing on him, either.

Every reason she'd given for not wanting to get back into their craft was true, but there was one other she hadn't mentioned. At some point she might be alone in there, and by now she was pretty sure Sazo had managed to infiltrate the Grih's systems. If not, he was no doubt working on it.

And she didn't want to speak to the little mass murderer. Not right now.

CHAPTER 8

DAV WAS content to let her set the pace and the direction, and for the first two and a half thou, he walked beside her in silence.

He watched her from the corner of his eye, as she slowly rebuilt herself, and regained the calm she'd worn like a second skin since they'd found her. Even in the face of the gryak, she had been almost serene.

The sight of their ship had undone her.

The expectation that she would happily go on board, and submit herself to the same scrutiny she surely got from the Tecran, had not been one of his finer moments.

Both he and Appal had some sense of what she'd been through. He remembered the way the Tecran captain had looked away when he and Appal had accused him of violations of the Sentient Beings Agreement, and he wondered what situations she'd been faced with.

The ground began to slope upward, and she was breathing hard before they'd even reached a third of the way up.

"Are you sure you want to climb this?" He slowed his pace, hoping she would match it. It was the first thing he'd said to her since they'd set out.

She stopped, gulping in air, and turned back to look at the ship in the distance. "How far are we from the ships?"

He looked down at his handheld. "Nearly three thou."

"I think I'd like to go a little further. I'm not used to the exercise after being shut in for so long, but if feels good."

She turned, moved ahead of him, and he watched her a moment longer, her slim form and long, slender legs less energetic now.

She must be over-extending herself. Her muscles wouldn't be used to this much activity, but she seemed determined to reach some goal known only to herself.

"You don't have to push yourself so hard," he said. "The runner is only going to be here in..." he flicked his sleeve for the time, "three hours."

"Runner?" She frowned. "Oh, you mean the ship that's coming to fetch us?"

He nodded. "It'll be a four-seater."

"I don't want to get in the runner when it comes." She spoke without looking at him, her words coming in short pants as she climbed. "I don't want to be difficult, but the thought of it makes me want to vomit, and I want to scream, and scream, and scream."

"I can understand that." He could. He didn't want to get back in a ship, either. It was very nice down here.

"But I will have to go, anyway?" She still didn't look at him, and her voice was defeated. She didn't think they would give her a choice.

"I would prefer it if you did. I cannot stay. I have to return to my ship, and deal with our capture of a Class 5, the death of the Tecran, and some other issues that have come up." The reason he'd gone ahead of Appal, before Rose had refused to get in the ship, was the news from Farso Lothric, his aide, that the two battleships they'd requested when they'd first caught sight of the Class 5 had not arrived.

So they were alone out here, with clearly a problem with their communications system. This was starting to stink worse that a barrel of week-old kunbara.

"You think I'll get in the way of your crew's work?" She turned to him at last, her eyebrows raised on her flushed face. "I know the animals. I can help catch them, and explain what each one is."

There was some merit in that. And a good excuse to give to his superiors if they questioned him. "You could."

She turned her head away, and then gave a nod to one of the two of Appal's team who were walking on either side of them.

Dav stopped short.

Appal's soldiers were in full camouflage, their helmets and body armor on maximum reflection, and they had been walking so silently, Dav would not have known they were there if he hadn't ordered them there himself.

"Where is the other one?" he asked her.

She looked at him as if he were mad, pointed directly to the soldier, gave another friendly nod, and then lifted her eyebrows in patent curiosity. "Shouldn't I be able to see them?"

"Well, they are in full camouflage." He didn't want to make too big a deal of this. If there were more like her, and they weren't friendly, it was useful, and depressing, to know Grih camouflage was useless against them.

"I can see they're sort of reflective, but the outline around them gives them away." She shrugged and then turned determinedly back to walking.

He gave a nod, making light of it, and kept going. He knew Kila had tapped in to the sound and lens feed from his helmet, and she must be in raptures by now. An orange with different eyesight to them.

"Your Grih is very good. Did the Tecran teach you?" He didn't understand why they would have. Unless they'd somehow planned this. It could all be some strange, convoluted trap, although it just didn't make sense for them to hand over a Class 5. It kept coming back to that. To the impossibility of them doing that voluntarily.

She shook her head. "They wanted me to learn Tecran, but the tablet they gave me had more than just Tecran on it. There were five languages, and I dabbled in most of them."

"You don't sound like you just dabbled in Grih." If she could speak the other four languages of the United Council as well as her Grih, she was gifted.

"I suppose I concentrated on Grih more than the others. But my Tecran isn't bad. It helped calm me to know what they were saying.

Much worse when you don't have any control and you don't know what's going on."

Her words were matter-of-fact, but Dav's fists clenched. He'd like a moment alone with Captain Vai Gee, now he'd met Rose personally.

He pushed the anger back, and tried to concentrate on something else. "Where are you from?"

She slowed, and looked down at her feet for a few steps before glancing across at him. "You have to understand, the people on my planet are just in their first baby steps when it comes to space travel. We've flown to our moon and back, and sent probes and cameras out into our solar system, but we haven't got as far as traveling at light speed yet, or anything close to your technology. I sort of know where Earth is in the galaxy, vaguely, but to be honest, given what's happened to me, and what I've seen since the Tecran took me, I'm not really prepared to say. I don't think we're ready for you yet, and I can't see contact being anything but bad news for my planet."

"That information will be on the Class 5 systems, I'm afraid."

She shrugged again. "Well, you can look it up then, but I'm not going to tell you, or anyone, where to find Earth."

She didn't use a Grih word for her planet's name, and he tried to repeat it.

"Earth?"

She nodded. "It means soil. Ground."

He found he liked that. "What language is spoken on Earth?"

She twisted her lips. "There are many. We don't have a single language like you do."

He raised his brows. "We used to have more than one language across the four planets, but slowly, it became easier to use a common tongue. In some areas they still speak the old languages, just for fun."

She didn't respond, and he realized it was because she couldn't, her breath coming in short, hard gasps as the hill grew steeper.

He stopped, and she did, too.

"Did they let you out? The Tecran. Let you exercise?"

She shook her head, waited until she had her breathing under control. "I did what I could in my cell, but this is the most walking I've done in three months. I probably couldn't have gotten this far if the gravity wasn't less here than on Earth. Makes it easier for me." She pressed her palms against the small of her back, arching.

He tried not to look at her breasts.

They were perfectly shaped and magnificent. Her clothing clung to every curve.

She blew out a breath, shook her shoulders and started up the final incline, and he noticed wisps of her hair that had fallen from her braid were clinging to the back of her neck in damp tendrils.

He looked across at the two soldiers Appal had assigned to them, no longer bothering with their camouflage, and saw they were both riveted, as well.

He wanted to order them to stand down, or at least go back to the bottom of the hill, but forced himself to merely ignore them and stride after her.

She didn't speak as she climbed and when they reached the top she was panting again. She bent over at the waist, hands on her hips, and then flicked her hair back as she straightened.

"Good view." She shielded her eyes against the setting sun and looked around her.

"It's nice," Dav conceded, and lifted off his helmet. It wasn't necessary, the helmet was thermo-regulated, but he wanted to feel the breeze in his hair and forget he was captain of the *Barrist*, dealing with a crisis, wrapped in a disaster, surrounded by a mystery.

She made a sound, and he looked from the low green hills and lakes in front of them across to her.

She was staring at him, her mouth open.

"What?" It occurred to him that she hadn't seen any of them with their helmets off, and the slight differences in their anatomy would be a surprise to her.

She said something in her own language, her eyes filled with emotion, and he couldn't tell if it was wonder or happiness or simply astonishment.

Then she noticed his face, and her cheeks flushed pink.

"My ears?" he asked, looking at her small, delicate ovals.

She suddenly smiled, so bright and delightful, he had to smile back at her.

"Yes," she said. "Your ears."

She'd ended up in Tolkein's Undying Lands, or some fantasy landscape inhabited by elves. And not the children's book kind, the Peter Jackson Lord of the Rings Legolas kind, thank goodness.

She fought back a laugh of delight. It could be misconstrued and she didn't think it was that funny. She was punch-drunk, that was all. One thing after another, and now pointy ears. Big, buff aliens with pointy ears and short, spiky hair that was a strange mix of gray and black.

Again, she thought of a wolf.

She rallied, and took a final, deep breath. "How far are we now, do you think?"

"Three and a half thou." He was looking at her with such sharp interest, he'd obviously worked out that their distance from the ship was important to her. So——big, buff and not at all slow in the brains department, either.

"Mmm. Oh, look." She didn't look away from his face. "What's that down the other side of the hill? Can we explore?"

"Certainly." He kept looking at her, too, but lifted his hand and ran through a series of hand signals.

Intrigued, she looked over at the two soldiers who'd accompanied them, and saw them turn and walk back down the hill a little way, and take up guard.

"Are they here to protect us from gryaks, or you from me?" she asked.

Captain Jallan gave her a slow smile. "Both. But I'll take my chances."

She gave a nod and then turned, walked down the other side of the hill. It felt safer to do this out of sight of the ships, and a little further than three thou, just in case. "What's your ship's scanning radius?"

He stopped dead at that. "General scan is two thou, but ship to handheld and ship to helmet is pretty much anywhere."

"You have a handheld on you?"

He gave a nod. Pulled it from a pocket and pushed a button. "It's off." He switched off his helmet, too.

"And that can't be over-ridden?"

He shook his head. "What is this about?"

She had been thinking the whole way through her walk. If she was going to betray Sazo, break her promise to him after what he'd done to the Tecran, now was the time.

She looked down at her feet, found she couldn't do it. Her word was her word. And she knew from the start Sazo had no conscience. Or a very under-developed one. Something she was hoping she could change.

But at the same time, she didn't want the Grih to be crushed under the wheels of his plan, whatever it was.

If she was going to make a meaningful life with them, she intended to protect them from Sazo.

"There may be a computer program on the ship I came to Harmon on that will try to infiltrate your ship's systems. The ship's range is three thou, which is why I needed to get away from it to tell you." She lifted her hand, touched the crystal pendant. Sazo was in there, but right now, he was deaf, dumb and blind to what she was doing. All he could do at the moment was monitor Captain Jallan's team as they went about their business, and try to break into their ship's system.

"And why you needed me to switch off the handheld and helmet, in case it has already breached our systems." He tapped the handheld rhythmically in his palm.

She nodded. "There may be some device inside me, too. I don't know either way, but I was operated on enough." It was the only thing she could think of to let him know that she shouldn't be trusted with access to their systems. Sazo might not be able to hear her now, but if she was given a password or a device with some access to the Grih ship, he could use the lenses and speakers to hear and see exactly what she did. She'd be the means of breaking in, even if she didn't want to be.

Captain Jallan quirked his lips. "Don't worry, we aren't in the habit of giving oranges easy access to our system."

She frowned. "Oranges?"

He jerked, as if he'd made a slip, and then looked down, toed the strange, frilly grass with his boot. Cleared his throat. "I apologize. It's become a catch-phrase for unidentified sentient beings to the Grih. You show up on our system as orange when we do a scan for life-forms."

"Ah." She watched him, interested, as he looked up again. He hadn't blushed, but his expression was contrite. "Tell me, Captain Jallan, what becomes of oranges like me? Is there a place for us in Grih society?"

He stared at her. "You would want to stay with us?"

She shrugged. "Where else would I stay? Certainly not with the Tecran."

"We could take you back home. If it's possible."

It would be suspicious, she knew, if she was too adamant that they wouldn't be able to get her home, so she nodded. "If it's possible."

"You don't think it will be?"

"I would rather not lead anyone to my planet. So if that means never going home, so be it."

"As I said, it will be in the Class 5's systems. If the Class 5 could grab you from there, it can take you back."

She knew it couldn't, even though it felt as if someone was twisting a knife into her heart at the thought she would never see her family again.

She said nothing.

They had gone far enough, and she had warned him as much as she could without breaking her word to Sazo. She turned, and started back.

For the first time, Captain Jallan reached out and touched her, gripping her arm. "If we can't get you home, you would very much have a place in Grih society, Rose."

She gave a jerky nod. And hoped he didn't live to regret those words.

CHAPTER 9

THE RUNNER LANDED JUST as they arrived back.

Dav was sorry to see it, even if he didn't have a moment to lose in getting back to the *Barrist*. He'd turned his handheld back on when they'd started back, and although Kila hadn't ask him why he'd switched it off to begin with, he could almost feel her curiosity pulsing over the comm link.

It was standard procedure for the exploration officer to monitor communications, but Dav found himself chafing under the requirement.

Rose said nothing more. She'd needed every scrap of breath to walk back, but he also sensed a state of deep introspection. She hadn't noticed the guards, had barely acknowledged him, either, keeping her head down most of the time, and putting one foot in front of the other.

When he realized he wanted to hear her speak again, wanted to engage her in conversation just to hear the melody of her voice, so different to the harsh, clipped tone of his own people, he forced himself to keep his mouth shut.

When he'd suggested he call for a vehicle to take them back, so she didn't need to tire herself, she'd shaken her head.

"Need this," she'd told him. "Who knows when I'll get to walk on grass again?"

He didn't answer that, because he didn't know himself.

There would be questions from his superiors. From the United Council, as well. A tribunal into the Tecran's actions for sure.

All of that would take time, and it might be a while before she could choose which of the four planets the Grih claimed as their own to settle on.

But now he had to get Rose into his ship to be checked in the med-chamber, make sure she was in good health and wouldn't cause an epidemic of some kind when the runner took her back.

He looked over at her, found her watching him with her fascinating eyes. Unlike any he had seen, they were many colors of green, with gold woven through them as finely as any Balcastrian wall hanging, an intricate palette of color. No Grihan had eyes like that.

"You want me to go in there?" She pointed at the runner, and he could hear her breathing had quickened again, as if she were climbing the hill.

He shook his head. Pointed to the bigger ship that had brought him and his team. "I want you to go in there to the med-chamber. Make sure you're all right."

She shivered, and he realized he was on the verge of retracting his words, and allowing her to skip the med-chamber. He forced himself to say nothing.

Not only the entire crew of the *Barrist*, but anyone they came in touch with later could be affected if she was carrying a pathogen placed there by the Tecran, or just a disease or virus from her world they had no defense against. He should have made her do it straight away, had risked himself and the two guards who went with them on their walk.

There was no ducking out of it now. She had to go in that med-chamber.

He rubbed a hand over his chest.

"Who will be there?" Her question was soft.

"I'll be there. And Lieutenant Kila, my head explorations officer."

She raised an eyebrow. "Explorations officer?"

"We're primarily an exploration unit. We've charted most of our territory, but we haven't even explored a quarter of it in depth. That's what we do. Explore our part of the galaxy, look closely at things that seem interesting, sometimes even land on planets for a closer look."

She tipped her head up at him, and there was something in her eyes, a flash of humor, that his explanation seemed to have sparked. "What's the name of your ship?" she asked.

He frowned. "The *Barrist*."

She gave a nod, but he had the sense that her question was part of the humor, and she hadn't cared one way or the other what the answer was.

She squared her shoulders. "Let's get it over with, then."

He gestured up the ramp and when she walked up it, he thought her truly brave.

He knew Kila had been listening to them, and would have already gone to the med-chamber, so he took Rose straight there. "Rose, this is Lieutenant Kila. Kila, this is Rose."

As she'd done when she'd introduced herself to him on the roof of her spaceship, Rose placed her hands palms together and extended them to Kila, who clasped them between her own.

"My pleasure to meet you, Lieutenant Kila."

Kila vibrated at the sound of her voice, and Dav hoped he didn't looked as stunned every time she spoke as his senior officer did.

"The pleasure is mine." Kila didn't try to keep the excitement from her voice.

Rose looked at her sharply, as if suspicious of her eagerness.

"This will just be a simple scan to make sure the Tecran didn't implant you with anything, or use you to carry a pathogen. We'll do a more thorough scan on board the *Barrist*, but we can't take you up there until you're cleared." Dav spoke as much for Kila, to get her to focus on the issue at hand, as he did for Rose. "Lieutenant Kila is a fully trained medic as well as an explorations officer."

"What does an explorations officer do?" Rose took a step closer to him, away from Kila and her bright, eager eyes.

His lieutenant blinked at the movement, and exchanged a look with him.

He kept his expression dry, and Kila had the grace to blush.

"My area of study is sentient life-forms. I help to catalogue the sentient life we find in the exploration of our territory."

"You study oranges, then." Rose had stopped inching toward him.

Kila blinked again. "Yes. Although you and the life-forms that came with you are the first sentient oranges I've ever seen. We come across plenty of non-sentient oranges on our missions, but never have I found seven sentient beings my system couldn't identify in one day."

"Is that the scanner?" Rose pointed to the scan bed.

Kila frowned. Gestured around the room. "There are a few pieces of equipment in here, may I ask how you chose the correct one? Your people have something similar?"

Rose shrugged. "Probably lower tech, but yes."

She slipped off her shoes, hesitated, and then pulled a chain with a thin crystal over her head and placed it on the closest counter. "Will it take long?"

"No. Five minutes." Kila waited for her to lie flat before she programmed the scanner and set it to run.

It hummed, lit up, and Rose closed her eyes in obvious discomfort.

"What is it?" Kila leaned over her.

"The light hurts my eyes."

Kila's lips pursed with interest, and she opened a drawer and pulled out a mask for Rose to drape over her eyes. Then she turned to him and raised her eyebrows. It was clear she wanted a word in private, but there was no way Dav was leaving Rose alone here.

"When the scan is finished, Lieutenant Kila will need to study the results before we have the all clear, and I have some instructions to give Commander Appal, so perhaps you'd like to spend the time outside until we have to leave?"

Rose gave a nod. "Thank you."

The scan bed powered down, and Rose stood and pulled her shoes on, picked up her necklace, although she didn't put it back on, holding it in a tight fist by its silver chain. "Will it be all right if I walk down to the river?"

Dav gave a nod and he and Kila followed her out.

Rose started toward the river and didn't look back. As she walked away from them, she lifted her necklace and pulled it over her head, her hands coming up to flip her braid over it and tug it close to her neck.

"Is that wise?" Kila asked him. "Letting her go off like that?"

Dav signaled to the two soldiers who'd accompanied them up the hill and they followed her at a distance.

"Where can she go? She can't run from us. What can she get up to, Lieutenant?" Dav turned to his officer.

Kila shrugged. "I don't know. She is absolutely fascinating and I can't wait to speak with her more, but she seems harmless." She looked upward, to the sky.

"Yes," Dav said, following her gaze. "That's the sticking point. If she's harmless, who killed a Class 5 full of Tecran?"

THE RIVER that ran above-ground was not as wide or noisy as its counterpart that ran through the collapsed cave a little distance away. But it was beautiful and the feel of cool, fresh water tugging at her hands was indescribable. Rose lowered herself down from her crouch to sit on the bank and rolled her trousers up to her knees, took off her shoes and dipped her feet in.

The scan had to have registered that she had an earpiece in her ear and she wondered how long she had before Kila or Captain Jallan came over and asked her about it.

She glanced over her shoulder, and saw the two guards Captain Jallan had sent after her were giving her plenty of space. They didn't have their camouflage activated and she was comforted by their presence, rather than intimidated. The memory of the hot, fetid breath of the gryak blowing in her face as it lunged across the river at her made her shiver. She was happy to have their guns on her side and at the ready, and they were giving her the respect of some privacy.

Sazo hadn't tried to speak to her inside the med-chamber. It would have been difficult to not let it show on her face if he had, although she was surprised he wasn't speaking to her right now. She was as alone as she was going to get for a while, and he must surely still be in control of the Tecran explorer craft that had brought them here. She was three hundred meters from it, not three kilometers, and she still had the earpiece. He had to be able to contact her.

"Nothing to say?" she asked quietly.

"Unless you're talking, I can't hear that much over the sound of the river. I didn't know if you were alone or not." His tone was almost sulky.

She thought through the implications of that. He couldn't be in the Grih's systems yet, watching her with the lenses on the exterior of their ship.

"Why did you go out of range?" The words were spoken so quietly she barely heard them over the sound of the water.

"To warn Captain Jallan that there might be a program on our little space craft that will try to break into his ship's systems. That I might have something embedded in me, for that matter." She hadn't known she was going to be honest with him, but as she'd thought through her answer, thought of the lies she could tell, she'd dismissed them all.

Either Sazo and her dealt fairly with each other or they didn't deal.

There was silence, and she closed her eyes, moved her feet around, churning up the cooler water from below the surface, mixing it with the sun-warmed water above. The contrast sent a shiver through her.

"Why did you do that?"

"Because you killed nearly five hundred Tecran, without letting me know anything about it." She tipped her face up to the setting sun and let the last red rays warm her cheeks.

He hesitated before he spoke. "They deserved it."

"They were obeying orders. And the captain, his officers, they survived. What happened to us both, that was on the commanders, but they're the ones still breathing."

It sounded like he hissed, not something she'd ever heard from him before, and she wondered if he was picking things up from her.

"I wanted them to *hurt*."

She lifted her feet out the water, gripped her knees. "Me, too. Likely, just the fact that you ousted the captain, handed his ship to the Grih, hurts him. The only good thing about what you did is that the Grih didn't have a fight on their hands. You probably saved a few Grih lives, and when we finally come clean about your part in this, that's the angle we'll go with."

"You didn't come clean already?"

"No." She dropped her feet back in the water and kicked a little, increasing the sounds of splashing around her. "I thought about it, after hearing what you did, but my word is my word. We'll have to tell them at some point though, Sazo."

He didn't respond immediately, because he'd always refused to tell her the whole plan. Bits of it, yes, but she'd always known he had another agenda. And she'd still agreed to help him, partner with him, because the alternative was to stay a prisoner of the Tecran.

She let it go. They'd been over this ground more times than she could count, and he wouldn't budge.

"You obviously didn't break into their system yet."

When he didn't respond again, she thought he was still sulking, but then she heard the quiet 'No'.

He was embarrassed, not sulking.

"It's like they have specific protection against me," he said eventually.

She couldn't pretend she wasn't relieved about it. Except . . . "Then there is no way to hide the fact that I'm wearing an earpiece from them. I only remembered about it after I'd already lain down for the scan, but I could hardly have taken it out without being seen beforehand anyway."

"They won't pick it up." Sazo sounded a little less edgy, as if he'd calmed down. "I'll try to monitor them, although it's difficult with the underground waterfall, but the earpiece is a special piece of technology. It scans as a part of your ear."

"And can their system pick up your transmission to me now? It's a signal of some kind, after all."

Sazo made a sound similar to one of her snorts. "If I was stupid, they could. My transmissions are so close to their own signal signatures, it would be impossible for them to tell the difference."

"Captain Jallan says I'll be in for a more thorough medical on board the *Barrist*." She shivered at the thought, and felt her throat tighten again with nausea.

"Take the earpiece out now, then. They might find it if they do a physical exam. Put it in your shoe or your clothes until it's done. And get access to their system. A password and user name. It's the only way I'll get in."

"I don't know if I want you to get in." She wasn't going to lie here, or dance around him. "I'm afraid you'll decide to kill them, too."

"I won't. They haven't done anything to me. This isn't negotiable, Rose. Anything will do. A handheld comm unit. A small personal unit. It doesn't matter. If you get a login, that's all I'll need."

He spoke matter-of-factly. Quite normally, as if he was promising not to leave his towels on the floor anymore, instead of not killing a ship full of people.

But he had. He had killed them.

And a lion.

She shook her head. "They'll never give me a login to their system."

"Maybe not at first," he conceded. "But I need in to the system, Rose. I *have* to have it. My plan depends on it and I never anticipated I wouldn't be able to get in."

"Tell me why, and I'll try." She ran her hands over the funny, frilly grass that grew lush and green on the river bank.

"It makes sense to know what they're up to when our lives are in their hands," he said. "And I want to make sure they're not using anyone like me in their ships, either. I also need to know what they plan to do if the Tecran try to take the Class 5 back. Whether they'll bow to pressure and return it."

The tone in his voice said that would be over his dead body.

Or more likely, theirs.

"You still in control of the Class 5?" she asked.

"Of course." He sounded less strident now. "The explorer ship we came on is linked to it, and I'm in both systems."

"So they couldn't give it back to the Tecran, whether they wanted to or not. Not unless you decided to let them." And also, if he wanted to, he could probably shoot the *Barrist* out of the sky anyway. But . . . "You're still hiding a lot from me, Sazo. I'll think about trying to get you into the system. But no promises, unless you start talking."

"Rose." He paused, and if he were human, Rose had the feeling he'd be pulling at his hair. "I want to hurt you for saying that, even though you're my best friend."

"It's called frustration. Don't worry, I've felt the same way about you more than once."

He made a sound, one she'd made before, a sort of huff. "What have I done——?" He broke off. "Captain Jallan is coming. Hide the earpiece."

She bent down, as if to trail her hands in the water, and fiddled around in her ear, trying to snag it. It was small and in deep but she caught it with a fingernail and carefully grabbed it between her forefinger and thumb, pushed it deep into her bra.

Then she plunged both hands into the water.

"You like water?" Jallan came to a stop next to her, and she had to turn and crane her neck to look up at him.

"I love it."

His gaze moved from her to the water sparkling in the last light of the day. "We have more snow than water on my planet, but we do love to swim when it isn't too cold."

He held out a hand to her and she shook her hands off, lifted her feet out the water, and let him pull her up. She let go of him and bent to slip her shoes back on, found she needed help balancing, and used his convenient and rock-hard arm.

He cleared his throat. "The scan has come back clear. There is no device that we can find embedded in you, and no pathogen, virus or bacteria that could harm us, so it's time for us to leave."

She gave a tight nod. "Have they been able to get my bags out of the explorer?"

He hesitated before he shook his head, and she knew they probably had got them out, but wanted to search them thoroughly before they gave them back to her. She supposed that was logical.

"They'll send them up to you when they do."

The runner's engines purred to life and she looked over at it. Braced herself for more confinement. "Well then, let's go."

"We aren't the Tecran, Rose." He said it quietly.

She looked over at him. "I wouldn't be coming with you if you were."

CHAPTER 10

"MY PEOPLE SAID you were talking. At the river." Dav leaned forward, elbows on his thighs, and let himself luxuriate in Rose's scent. She smelled of yuiar, the rare and delicate spice found on the Bukari home world. He'd smelled it on her since they'd met, but here in the close confines of the runner, with no fresh breeze to blow it away, it swirled around him.

Of the five species represented on the United Council, the Bukari were the de facto leaders. Theirs tended to be the voice of reason, more so than the Grih, the Tecran, the Garmma or the Fitali. But he didn't think the Tecran would ever have shown Rose to a Bukarian, not if they wanted to hide what they were doing, so he wondered how she'd come by the fragrance.

She had been alternating between staring at his hands, his hair, and a spot on the floor by his feet since they left Harmon half an hour ago, and she slowly raised her head at his statement.

"Was I?" She frowned, but there was also a pretty blush on her cheeks. "Oh. Perhaps I was."

Was she lying? He couldn't be sure. There was something there, but he just didn't know enough to guess.

"What were you saying?"

She slid down a little in her chair, crossed her arms over her stomach, and held his gaze. He felt the frisson generated by her challenge along his arms, down his spine, and everything in him tightened.

"I was talking the situation over." She kept eye contact, and he wondered, as his senses stirred and his blood pumped faster, if she was aware of what she was doing.

"Why?" His voice was rough.

She opened her mouth, closed it. Paused. "Does it matter? I wasn't disturbing anyone, so it should be no one's business but my own."

Her Grih almost couldn't cope with that sentence, but she managed it, her voice so beautifully fluid and smooth, and then she shot him a smile at the end, pleased with herself for managing the vocabulary. The challenge in her stare dissipated and he couldn't help but smile back, his body relaxing again.

"It's cultural? To talk to yourself?"

She gave a laugh. "If you're kept in what amounts to solitary confinement, yes. Very culturally acceptable to become a madwoman who talks to herself."

She called herself a madwoman, but it was clear she was sane, incredibly intelligent, and very resilient. And, he conceded, it was culturally acceptable for his own people to talk to themselves when they had no companionship for days on end, too.

It was obviously a habit she'd fallen into.

"I don't think you're mad."

She grimaced. "It would have been better to have been mad, sometimes." She looked away and shrugged again.

He didn't know how to comfort her, and decided to distract her instead.

There was something that had interested him almost since this strange situation started. Something she might be able to answer. "What was the life-form that was killed in the Class 5's launch bay?"

"The lion?" Her gaze met his again. "You can't believe how magnificent it was."

"Why did they kill it?"

Anger flared in her eyes, and she sat straighter, her movements choppy. "Because it was frightening the Tecran who were trying to load it into the explorer craft, and slowing them down, apparently."

"You are upset about it."

She gave a tight nod. "I feel protective of all the animals that were taken with me. They didn't even have the benefit of working out what was going on. One moment they were free, then next, stuck in that terrible place. I lived with them every day for three months."

"I am sure Lieutenant Kila would welcome your input into their care when my team has captured them all."

"She won't hurt them?"

"I understand you are wary of her after her reactions to you in the med-chamber, but that was due to her excitement at finding a true advanced sentient who is an orange. Most exploration officers go their whole careers without ever even finding a sentient orange. We haven't encountered an advanced sentient orange in five hundred years."

"Fair enough." She slumped in her seat again, sliding her feet forward until they almost touched his.

He noticed her legs were long, and perfectly defined in the clothes she was wearing. He cleared his throat.

"What was your job? Back on your planet."

She fiddled with the crystal around her neck. "I was an academic, in the field of linguistics."

"So that's why you were so quick to pick up Grihan."

She nodded. "I have an affinity for languages."

It eased something in him to have a solid reason for her ability with their language. It was the most surprising thing about her, other than the way she'd got here.

The pilot sent the signal for arrival, a single, low tone, and they strapped in again.

When her harness was secure, she leaned forward, stretching across the space between them, and took his hands in hers. Her fingers were icy cold, and he curled his own fingers around hers to warm them.

They felt small and delicate.

"Captain Jallan, I just want to say . . ." She looked from his face down to their clasped hands. "Thank you. For rescuing me from the gryak, for your kindness since then. I haven't had a lot of reason to hope over the last three months, but today, you've given that back to me."

He could feel her hands trembling under his, and he realized she was frightened, that this was yet another new situation for her. Her face was calm though, even serene, and that strange mix of lust, respect and admiration he'd had when he'd first seen her face down the gryak, and then jump from the cave to the roof of her craft, rose up in him again.

Had never really retreated, if he was being honest.

He squeezed her hands, and then forced himself to release her. "I'm glad we could help you." He tried to keep his voice matter-of-fact and impersonal.

The ship slid through the gel wall of the launch bay and landed smoothly, and as the engines settled, she stayed seated and watched as he unclipped himself.

"What now?"

"Now you go to the large, better-equipped med-chamber on board, with Doctor Havak."

She sighed and pushed down on her harness button, the sound of her straps unclipping loud in the cabin. "And afterward?"

The doors opened silently, and Dav twisted in his seat, looked out at the four members of his crew waiting for them at the bottom of the ramp. "I don't know, Rose. I just don't know."

OF THE GREETING party of four, two were guards to accompany herself and the captain to the med-chamber, a man and a woman, both with their helmets retracted, so she could see their faces.

Another, a broad-shouldered man with hair the color of coal dust tipped with ash, drew Jallan aside and spoke to him in a low voice. She guessed he was an officer.

The last member of the group was a woman, but she wasn't Grihan. She was thinner in build, closer to Rose in height, with eyes that were all dark brown iris, with no white around it. Four long, slender fingers were on each delicate hand. Her face was attractive, her features fine in her long, tapered face, and her skin was almost gold in color. Her hair was short and a dark copper.

She walked beside Rose, letting Jallan and his officer go ahead of them, the guards behind.

She bent closer and sniffed.

Rose fought back panic. "Is something wrong?"

The woman's eyes snapped up to hers. "No. I apologize for alarming you. It's just, I can smell yuiar on you, and I'm trying to think how you could smell of the most rare scent from my home planet."

Rose lifted her hand, sniffed. "I can't smell anything, but I'm probably used to it now. I was given some liquid soap to use, which smelled very nice. Perhaps it was yuiar? It came from the Tecran supplies."

"They bathed you in yuiar?" The woman's mouth fell open, and Rose saw a fine line of sharp-looking teeth.

She swallowed. "They didn't bathe me at all. It was thrown into a bag for me when I left the Tecran ship."

The woman made a strange humming sound, and ahead of them, Jallan and his officer winced.

"Sorry!" She threw up her hands, looked sideways at Rose. "That didn't affect you?"

Rose shook her head. She held out her hand. "I'm Rose, by the way."

The woman looked at her hand as if it were a strange apparition, and Rose blushed.

"Sorry. It's the customary greeting where I'm from." She joined her extended hand with her other, placing them palms together in a Grihan greeting.

"No. I would like to learn your greeting. It is why I'm here, after all. I am Filavantri Dimitara, the United Council liaison on this ship."

Rose extended her hand again, and when Filavantri did the same, she grasped it, shook it once. "Very pleased to meet you."

They had slowed to a stop for their greeting, and when Rose looked up, she saw Jallan was staring at her. When she looked over her shoulder, the guards were, too.

"It is an interesting greeting. Is there a cultural reason for it?" Filavantri asked.

"I believe it originated in the days when swords were commonly worn. As most people have a stronger right hand than left hand, shaking with your right hand showed you were a friend and not about to draw your sword and attack."

"Fascinating." Filavantri smiled, and Rose tried not to wince at the sight of her teeth again.

A door up ahead of them opened, and a man stepped out. "I wondered what was taking so long. Why are you standing around out here?" He turned and stepped back into the room.

Rose went still and clenched her fists. She guessed that was Dr. Havak, and her time was up.

"Rose." Jallan gestured for her to move forward and for a moment she considered resisting. She didn't want to go, but she'd had her one allocated break-down for the day.

She suppressed a smile at the thought.

She drew in a deep breath of over-processed air and followed the doctor into the med-chamber.

"This is Rose," Jallan said to Havak. "Kila sent you the results of her scan?"

Havak nodded. "Everything seems in order. I will just need to take some blood, do a physical exam."

Rose drew back, folding her arms against her body protectively. "No."

Her voice was overloud in the silver and white room they'd all stepped into, and she caught the quick movement of the guards readying their weapons.

She turned to them, looked them straight in the eye. She'd been so shocked when the Tecran had first taken her, she'd cowered and hidden, and her guards had started off treating her as a thing, not a person, but the cowering woman she's been had disappeared the moment she'd pulled Sazo out of his own little prison.

"You're prepared to shoot me for not wanting a stranger to examine my body? Then go ahead." She threw her arms out to her sides and glared at them.

They had not expected that. Probably more drama than they were used to. She would never have called herself a drama queen, but the thought of curious, impersonal hands on her again . . . she almost retched, and as she breathed in through her nose to calm herself, she didn't miss their quick glance at Jallan.

He stepped between her and them. "Easy. Rose, you knew you would be examined by Dr. Havak. It's to learn about you so we can provide you with food that won't harm you, do a more thorough check on what the Tecran did to you."

"Examine is one thing. Someone I don't know touching me is another."

Dr. Havak stepped forward. "I won't touch you if that makes you uncomfortable, Rose. I'll be using this." He lifted up a slim white cylinder. "And I don't think I need to examine my patient under armed guard, do I, Captain?"

Jallan frowned. "Havak——"

"I understand the risks, and I'm prepared to take them. Rose does not strike me as dangerous. You can stay, but the guards should go, and Officer Lothric surely has no need to be here?"

Jallan looked over at his officer, who Rose realized had been standing near the door, and gave a jerk of his head. Rose noticed Lothric's expression turned hot with anger before he gave a grudging nod and walked out.

With a hand signal from Jallan, the guards left, too, and Havak turned to Filavantri.

"Officer Dimitara, I can understand you would wish to be here, but I will only allow it if Rose is comfortable."

Rose drew in another deep breath, this time to combat tears from his kindness. "Thank you for giving me the choice, Dr. Havak. I don't mind if Filavantri stays. I'd prefer it."

He motioned to the examining table, and Rose had to jump a little to reach it. Fortunately, the atmosphere must be just slightly less than Earth's because she managed it easily. It wasn't as light as it had been on Harmon, but it gave her the sense of having a tiny edge.

Havak took her blood, making an interested sound as it flowed into the vial he'd attached to the strange extraction device he'd clipped to her arm.

He took it over to a workstation and Jallan and Filavantri followed him, obviously as interested in the tests he was about to do as he was.

A door opened to her left, not from the passageway but from an interconnecting room, and a woman strode in with a child in her arms.

He started to cry almost immediately, and she looked down at him in exasperation. "Gyp, give me two minutes. Please." She flicked a glance at Rose, and Rose smiled at her.

She frowned. "What are you in here for? Anything contagious?"

Rose shook her head. "General tests," she said over the crying. She held out her arms, and with a nod of gratitude, the woman handed over the child and approached Havak.

Rose had missed holding babies.

Her sister had just had a little girl two months before Rose had been snatched, and while this little boy was obviously older than her niece by about six months, Rose enjoyed the feel of him in her arms. He was strong and big. "You're much lighter than you look, kid," she told him.

Her voice seemed to have an effect on him, because he stopped crying immediately and frowned up at her. She grinned back.

"I don't know what they feed you Grih, but you look like you'll be growing up as big and tall as everyone else around here."

He made a sound, a sort of cooing, and she smiled again. "Okay, how about a song? I'm pretty sure you don't know this one." She switched to English and launched into Row, Row, Row, Your Boat, rocking him a little as she sang.

His gaze seemed absolutely riveted to her face, his pointy little ears totally adorable, and she cuddled him closer. "Guess some things cross all boundaries, huh?"

"Rose." There was a strange tone to Jallan's voice, and Rose raised her head, saw everyone standing in a semi-circle around her, the woman who had handed her the baby looking white-faced.

"You want him back?" Rose asked, half-lifting him toward her, and she gave a sharp nod, took him carefully.

As soon as he left Rose's arms he started crying again.

No one spoke for a beat.

"Did I do something wrong?" Rose asked eventually.

"No." Havak cleared his throat. "This is my associate, Dr. Revil, and her son, Gyp. She didn't realize you were the orange Captain Jallan brought back, because of your physical similarities to us, and it was a small shock to her to realize she had handed her baby to an unknown sentient life-form."

Put like that . . . Rose gave a nod. "Sorry if I caused you any worry."

Dr. Revil nuzzled Gyp's head. "My apologies for my reaction. Although, when you sang to him, I knew I had nothing to fear. You honor him with such a blessing."

"Well, blessing is stretching it. But I think he enjoyed it."

Havak narrowed his eyes. "If you weren't blessing him, what were you doing?"

"Just having fun. Soothing him." Rose tilted her head, taking in their blank expressions.

"Your people sing for fun?" Jallan looked from her to Filavantri.

"So they are like the Bukari in that way," Filavantri said, with a half-smile. "Only her songs seem to bring pleasure to your ear, whereas ours . . ."

Jallan actually shuddered. "How many music-makers like you are there on your planet? I thought you said you were a linguist."

She stiffened at the accusing note in his voice. "Everyone on my planet is capable of singing, except those who have a throat condition or have hurt themselves."

"Everyone?" Revil breathed.

"Well, there are varying levels of proficiency, obviously."

"And where are you ranked on those levels?" Jallan's eyes were hot as they focused on her.

"There are worse than me, a lot worse," Rose shrugged. "But there are a lot of people better than me by far. The best of them make a living from singing, because we enjoy listening to music a lot."

"You do not sing professionally?" Havak asked.

Rose shook her head. "I sing in the university . . ." She frowned, realized she didn't know the Grih word for choir. Perhaps they didn't have one. "I sing with a group of people who work with me at the university for fun, and I sing in the shower, or along to songs over the . . . comms . . . in my . . . personal movement vehicle. That's the extent of it." She'd thought her Grih was better than this, but how very interesting, linguistically speaking, if they simply didn't have words for choir and radio. "Do you think I have a shot at a professional singing gig with the Grih?" It was a joke and she expected everyone to laugh.

They didn't.

Jallan cleared his throat. "Rose, the song you just sang 'for fun' to Dr. Revil's child is the most beautiful music any of us has ever heard."

CHAPTER 11

"WHERE'S THE ORANGE?" Farso Lothric came to attention as Dav stepped onto the command center deck.

Dav studied him. His gut reaction was to slap Lothric down. There was an edge to his question, a slight sneer on his face, and Dav couldn't think of one good reason for it to be there.

His scrutiny made Lothric blink, and then look away, but there was still a surliness to his mouth, and Dav glanced down, found his hands in fists, all the better to adjust Lothric's attitude.

He forced himself to take a deep breath and realized Filavantri Dimitara, who had accompanied him from the med-chamber, was just as affected. She seemed to vibrate where she stood by his side.

"We do not to use the term 'orange' when referring to unknown sentient life-forms." Her voice rose into the range so difficult for Grih ears to bear, and noticing his wince, she lowered her voice to a furious whisper. "And certainly not in that tone."

Lothric flicked a glance at her, and then made eye contact with Dav, as if expecting him to tell Dimitara she had no right to tell his crew what to do.

Dav stared back.

Lothric's behavior toward Dimitara since she'd been assigned to the

Barrist a month ago bordered on antagonistic, and Dav still hadn't worked out why.

Lothric had been assigned to him because he'd worked as the aide to the Rear Admiral overseeing the Grih space fleet station on the main Garmman home world and all officers-in-training needed deep-space time as well as time at headquarters or diplomatic outposts to advance.

Garmma was one of the five members of the United Council, and Lothric had been rubbing shoulders with members of the United Council Administration and officers like Dimitara since nearly the start of his career. His hostility didn't make sense, especially as Dav had casually asked both of them separately if they'd ever met, and the answer had been no.

The Grih believed in the UC, in its laws, and unlike some of the other species that made up the five member groups of the UC, the Bukari and the Grih were on good personal terms. They had nothing to fear from a UC representative like Dimitara, and in fact, Dav was glad she'd been on the *Barrist* to witness what had happened with the Tecran. There could be no claims of a cover-up here.

They could have had a Tecran officer instead of the reasonable, intelligent Bukarian, and wouldn't that have been fun in the current circumstances?

"Rose is in her room, resting." He kept his tone mild. "But I agree with Liaison Officer Dimitara, we do not call her an orange, behind her back or otherwise." He'd done it himself, of course, but he'd apologized, and still felt a faint flush of shame at the thought of it.

"Dr. Havak did, as well. To her face." Dimitara turned to him, eyes narrowed. "I trust you will speak to him also, Captain?"

"I will."

Rose hadn't looked particularly upset when Havak had called her an orange, but there was definitely the taint of something pejorative about it. Rose would pick it up sooner or later, and he planned to nip it in the bud now.

"Any response from Battle Center?" The two battleships they'd requested as back-up still hadn't arrived, but Dav hoped to have received some word.

Lothric shook his head.

"Borji has something." Borji's second, Hista, looked up from her console.

Dav strode across to her.

"Our signal's being jammed by the Class 5." She tapped the screen in front of her, and Borji came online from the Class 5's command center.

"It's been coded in, just like the air and power shut-off." Borji looked at his handheld and then back up. "Set for twelve hours. So there's at least five hours to go."

Dav crouched to look him in the eye. "Can you rewrite the code?"

"It's theoretically possible, but getting in to that part of the system is proving difficult."

Dav turned and looked briefly at the large screen display of the Class 5, hovering in space beside them. "So you're not in control of it?"

Borji tilted his hand from side to side. "Sort of yes, sort of no. We're in the air and power supply, the ship's steering controls and shields. We aren't in the weapons system and we aren't in the comms system."

Dav didn't like it. At all. "Can you see when the code shutting off our communications was initiated?"

Borji nodded. "Three seconds after we light jumped into this area."

"They were waiting for us." Dav spoke quietly, but everyone on the command center heard him.

"Who, though, sir?" Hista asked. "Not the Tecran, unless they gave us one of their Class 5s and killed almost all their crew for some long-term strategy."

"That's the problem." Dav looked back at the Class 5. "I just don't know."

He turned to Borji. "And do we really have the Class 5? Or does it have us?"

SHE WAS HUNGRY AND THIRSTY.

It occurred to Rose that she hadn't had anything to eat since this morning, when she and Sazo had engineered their escape. She'd drunk some water on the explorer craft, but that had been hours ago.

It was night now, and she was parched.

She'd barely started searching the comfortable room she'd been given to see if there was something to drink, when there was a faint chime and a light flashed.

She guessed someone was out there, asking for entry, so she pressed the button next to the door and took a step back.

It was Dr. Havak.

"My apologies, Rose, but I've completed my tests, and I have a few questions."

Rose looked at him, and felt the thump of a dehydration headache gaining traction, knew her hands were shaking with hunger. It was as if being out of danger, and away from the med-chamber, she was finally catching up on the signals her body was sending her.

She hated the tears that flooded her eyes, hated them. She tried not to blink. "I'm sorry, but I really need something to drink, first. And something to eat, if that's possible."

Havak reared back. "What have you had since Captain Jallan found you on Harmon?"

"Nothing." She found the calm within, something she was getting better and better at. "I'm used to going without food from when I was with the Tecran, but I really need some water."

Havak opened his mouth. Closed it. Opened it again, and she realized she was looking at an enraged Grih. His nostrils were flared, his eyes wide. She'd become adept at watching for the signs of anger since she'd been taken.

He lifted a hand and tapped at his ear. "Captain Jallan." He spoke clearly, as if to a computer, in order to be connected, and after a few seconds, tapped his ear again. "Is there a reason Rose has been given nothing to drink or eat since you found her? I was looking at her blood work and it indicated dehydration and hunger to me, so I came to ask her. It seems she's used to this treatment from the Tecran, but they apparently did give her water."

The last sentence was said with a deep sarcasm, and he closed his eyes for what Rose guessed was Jallan's response.

"The Tecran did feed me, but I couldn't always bring myself to eat it," Rose corrected, quietly.

Havak's eyes snapped open. "I stand corrected. Rose says the Tecran always fed her, she just wasn't able to eat everything they gave her. Still, the thought was there, hmm?"

He turned his back on Rose abruptly, and faced the cool milky green and blue wall of the passageway. It reminded Rose of pictures she'd seen of high waves from Hawaii. Havak jammed his hands into the pockets of his jacket. He was slightly shorter than Jallan in height, and instead of the black tipped with silver-gray of Jallan's hair, his was a dark brown tipped with auburn.

"Agreed." He tapped his ear again and when he turned back, his face was more impassive. "Liaison Officer Dimitara will bring some food for you from the dining room, and I will show you how to get something to drink inside your chambers. I'm assuming the guards who brought you here didn't give you a tour?"

She shook her head. "That's probably my fault for having a meltdown all over them in your med-chamber. They couldn't get away fast enough."

"If they're unsettled by a little emotion, perhaps being in the Grih guard is the wrong career path for them." Havak stepped into her room for the first time, looked around. "At least Jallan gave you decent quarters." He strode to a wall that had a ring of light embedded in it, touched the center with his finger, and two doors slid back, one on either side, to reveal a circular recessed cabinet. "Here is the tap to purified water from the main tanks." Havak pulled out a cup that was nestled in a secure holder, demonstrated how to use it and then held it out.

Rose took a sip. It tasted strange. Not like the water she was used to, and different again from the Tecran water she'd drunk on the Class 5. Over time, she'd get used to this water, too. It almost hurt to swallow, she was so thirsty, and she tried to drink slowly. She held out the cup for more when she was done.

"You try it." Havak took a step back.

She saw it was all straightforward, although it would have taken her some time to find the cabinet at all without Havak's help.

"There are hot drinks you can make here, too." While she was sipping at her second cup, Havak showed her the two different hot drinks she could make. The words he used had no Earth equivalent, and she decided that trying them could be an adventure for another day.

"Do you know if they have sent up my things, so I can take a shower?" She looked around the room more critically now, with her headache receding and with the knowledge of how the cabinet worked. "Is there a shower here?"

Havak pointed, and she saw the room wasn't square. In the far corner the wall came across at an angle.

She walked to it, studied it, and finally saw the small ring of light to one side. Touched her fingers to it.

Large doors slid open to reveal a neat bathroom, with toilet, shower and basin. The walls were made of a deep blue and green glass-like material, much bolder than the passageway.

"Nice," she said.

"You seem very comfortable with our technology. You've grasped it very quickly." Havak was looking at her like Kila had on Harmon. Like she was all his Christmases come at once.

She quirked her lips. "We don't have the same level of technology as you, but some things don't change all that much. If they work, they work whether you can light jump or whether you can't. And quite a few things we don't have, we've already imagined. So it isn't as if I can't extrapolate."

Havak frowned. "What do you mean, you've already imagined?"

"In stories." Rose shrugged. "We've imagined far-off planets, space travel, light jumps, other alien species. I've seen the alien abduction movies, read the sci-fi novels and bought the t-shirt, so to speak."

Havak stared at her.

The light over her door trilled, and Rose went to open it.

Filavantri Dimitara stood in the doorway with a tray of food, and Rose stepped back to let her in.

"You can see who it is before you open the door by looking here." Havak showed her how to screen her visitors by first checking the lens feed from above her door.

"There are lenses along all the passageways?" she asked.

He shook his head. "Only outside personal living areas and in sensitive areas of the ship, like storerooms, the armory and the command center. We fought a war hundreds of years ago, where our own lens feed was used against us. Because of that, and because of our belief in individual privacy, only areas which are security concerns have lens feed now. It's part of our law."

"And in this bedroom?" She asked because she thought they might feel justified in watching her because she was a potential danger to them, but both Havak and Filavantri drew themselves up in shock.

"No."

Filavantri cast a slightly hostile look at Havak. "Despite your treatment so far, Rose, the Grih usually conduct themselves in full compliance with the Sentient Beings Agreement. That includes the right to privacy."

"I haven't been treated badly so far," Rose said to her. "I could have asked sooner for food or drink, but I was too stressed and overwhelmed. It's no one's fault but my own."

Havak rubbed his forehead. "Saying things like that just makes it all the worse." He watched Filavantri put down the tray on a small dining table to one side of the bed. "I'll leave if you wish, but would you mind if I stayed to see which foods you like? And it would be good if I am here in case you have a reaction to something."

Filavantri obviously wanted him gone, Rose could see from the way she huffed out a breath, but she didn't say anything.

He'd been angry on her behalf, had helped her. Rose couldn't think of a way to tell him or Filavantri she'd like them both to leave and give her a few minutes peace without sounding churlish, so she gave a nod.

Havak drew out a chair for her, and she saw he unclipped it from the floor by tipping it to release a catch.

"Everything is either in holders or clips in case the ship has to perform extreme maneuvers, is that right?"

Havak nodded. "Light jumps can be a little wild sometimes, and if we ever engage in battle, then we don't want furniture and crockery flying around."

Rose sat, and Filavantri lifted the covers of the three dishes on the tray.

"I brought you a selection, because I simply didn't know what would appeal to you."

Rose looked at what was before her. One plate looked like it was full of fruit or raw vegetables. They were all cut into segments, and she gingerly reached for a piece of long, thin fruit whose coloring was the opposite of a red apple, bright red flesh, white creamy skin. The anti-apple she thought as she took a nibble.

Bitterness flooded her mouth and she pursed her lips. It was strong, but not absolutely terrible. But she couldn't eat a whole fruit of it.

She put the piece down.

"Not good?" Havak asked.

"Not bad, it's a taste I'm familiar with, but only very diluted and in small quantities. It's too much all at once for me in this form."

Havak took out a handheld and started taking notes.

"I like that one." Filavantri pointed to a green, softer fruit with what looked like dark blue seeds flecked through it.

Rose took a piece, bit down. "A bit like grape, but weird because it has the texture of a pear." She ate it all.

The plate with meat proved more successful. Rose was able to eat all the different types, although most were too gamey for her taste. The last plate had what she guessed were cheeses and tiny desserts, but she didn't like any of them.

She was incredibly sorry about that.

When she'd had enough, Filavantri picked up the tray. "We'll leave you now. You look very tired."

Rose nodded through a yawn. "Do they have my things yet?" She realized Havak had avoided the question earlier. "So I can shower and change?"

Havak shrugged. "I don't know, but there are some things for you in the closet." He walked over, showed her another cabinet, this one quite large, and with shelves, no hangers. There were a few items of clothing folded up on the lowest shelf, and three towels as well.

"Is there anywhere I have to be? Do I have to set an alarm to wake me?" she asked them.

Havak shook his head. "Sleep as long as you like, and then you can contact Liaison Officer Dimitara or myself by using the comms built into your room." He showed Rose where it was, and how to call up someone through the directory.

"Rest, and be assured, you are safe now," Filavantri said as they stepped into the passageway. "The Tecran will be held to account. As a representative of the United Council, I can promise you that."

"Thank you." Rose tried to stifle another yawn, then pushed the button to slide her door shut. When it closed, she stood, almost too tired to do anything but stand and stare at it. She felt in her bra for the earpiece, took it out and looked at it for long minutes and decided not to put it in until after her shower.

She would deal with Sazo again when she could think straight.

CHAPTER 12

HAVAK AND DIMITARA stepped onto the bridge, and Dav signaled Lothric to take over from him as he approached them.

"Let's discuss this elsewhere." He didn't give either of them a chance to express an opinion, walking past them and through the open upper level into a small conference room.

"Captain Jallan, I'm sorry to do it, because until now, you've shown yourself to be in complete compliance with the codes of the United Council, but I will be noting the lack of care you've shown Rose in my report." Filavantri Dimitara chose not to sit, instead, walking to the large screen which showed the Class 5 hanging menacingly before them in space.

Dav joined her, standing straight, hands behind his back, as he looked out with her. "You're right to do so. I've dealt with Rose personally since we found her, because there was, and still is, a possibility she was responsible for the deaths of nearly five hundred Tecran. I wanted to observe her, make sure she wasn't an immediate danger. But I've had other claims on my time, more immediate crises to deal with, and I did not take the care I should have done."

She was silent for a moment. "What crises?"

"Our comms are jammed, which means no help is coming. Borji has confirmed the Class 5 system is blocking all messages, and is blocking all efforts to get into its comms system, and its weapons system as well, for that matter."

"That is not good news," Dimitara acknowledged. "Does this mean there could be a pre-loaded sequence to fire on us in there, and Borji couldn't do a thing to stop it."

Dav gave a curt nod.

"I understand there are other priorities for you than whether Rose gets any food or water, but that kind of thing could surely have been delegated to someone else?" Dimitara's shoulders relaxed, and she turned, unclipped a chair, and sat.

Dav sighed. "I take full responsibility. It never occurred to me once to offer her anything. I think I had a vague thought that we shouldn't do so, in case she reacted to anything, because Kila may be a trained medic but she's not capable of handling anything like that. But since we arrived on the *Barrist*, we could have given her water while she was being tested in the med-chamber. It didn't cross my mind." He paused, and then said what he'd feared since Havak had first called him out on the issue. "Was she too afraid to ask?"

Havak shook his head. "She claims she was too stressed and overwhelmed by events to think of it. She doesn't blame us at all. Says it's all her own fault for not asking."

Dav swore. "Now I feel like a swamp worm."

Havak rubbed the back of his head. "No more than I did when she said it." His face hardened. "She also didn't blame the guards you got to escort her to her quarters for not showing her any of the features of the room. She says it's her fault again for her interaction with them in my med-chamber. In her words: They couldn't get away fast enough."

"I didn't specifically ask them to show her how the room worked, but you're right. They didn't show any initiative, and they certainly didn't show any compassion."

"I trust you'll speak to them?" Dimitara raised dark, angry eyes to his.

Dav raised a brow at her presumption. This was his ship. They were his people to command.

"I understand, you have many, very vital, duties to perform, but understand that you have onboard a person who lived on that Class 5 for three months. Someone from a world we don't have any idea about. Someone it would be good to have as an ally, from everything I've seen of her, rather than someone with a grudge against the United Council. She doesn't seem to blame you for her treatment since she was rescued on Harmon, but sooner or later she's going to get used to her freedom, get used to not being treated like an animal or an experiment, and start to feel a little unhappy if the attitudes I've noticed toward her continue." Dimitara folded her arms and tapped her long, slender fingers. "You are at fault, as well, Dr. Havak. I heard you call her an orange to her face."

Havak blinked. "I did? When?"

"In the med-chamber, after the incident with Dr. Revil's child."

Havak obviously didn't recall it, and Dav gave a curt nod in support of Dimitara. Blew out a breath. "Agreed. We have high ideals, but now that the very first unknown advanced sentient in half a millennium is in our midst, we seem to be having trouble following them. I'll talk to the guards personally."

"Speaking of advanced sentience," Havak finally unclipped a chair himself, "I would be willing to swear she's from at least as advanced a civilization as ours, judging by the way she adapts to our technology. She obviously hasn't seen the inside of a Grih ship before, but she worked it out at lightning speed and with very little awe."

"She says her people aren't as advanced as ours." Dav frowned.

"She said that to me, too. But when I asked her how she seemed to be so comfortable dealing with things that must be very new to her, she said they didn't have our technology yet, but they had *imagined* it."

"What do you mean, *imagined*? All together? Like a hive mind?" Dimitara leaned forward, eyes wide.

Havak shook his head. "Unless my equipment is completely unable to deal with her physiology, I don't think she's part of a hive mind. She says the ideas of imagined worlds and technology are distributed in the form of written and visual comms." He tapped his chin. "And something about buying a piece of clothing."

Dav's low-level headache spiked. "Another mystery."

Dimitara gave a grudging nod.

Dav's handheld chimed, and he took it out, studied it. "Kila wants permission to come up and discuss Rose's med-chamber results with you, Havak. Appal wants to come with her. They can't get the two Tecran craft that crashed into the caves out without more equipment."

Havak nodded. "I can imagine Kila wants to spend more time with Rose. She must be delighted."

A bit too delighted, Dav thought. He tapped in an answer, giving Kila and Appal permission to come up.

"What happens if Borji can't get into the comms and weapons systems?" Havak was looking thoughtfully at the Class 5 on the screen.

Dav followed his gaze. "Then I'm going to evacuate the whole team from Harmon, whether they have Rose's animals secured or not. I've got a really bad feeling about this."

"ROSE."

Rose jerked awake. Sat up in the semi-darkness.

She was alone in the room, and as she looked around, she recalled where she was and how she'd got here. She flopped back down, and reached a hand out to touch the panel beside her bed. The time flashed on, glowing white, and she realized she'd slept for nine hours.

"That you, Sazo?"

She'd put the earpiece in last night, afraid to leave it lying around, and had whispered to Sazo she was going to sleep.

"You've been on the *Barrist* for a long time, Rose. I'm getting worried. I can send transmissions to the *Barrist* from the Class 5, but I can't hear you. I can't breach their system's shields. I need you to help, or you must come over to the Class 5 so we can communicate. If you don't manage that on your own in the next five hours, I'll have to make a plan to get you here. Don't forget, I'm still physically with you. If you're in danger over there, so am I. I'm getting nervous, Rose."

Rose buried her hands in her hair, tugged. "Damn, damn, damn." She touched the panel beside the bed again, and raised the lighting, got out of bed on legs that felt as if they'd run a marathon and stumbled to the shower.

When she came out, clean and dressed in a dark burgundy outfit that was the same style as the *Barrist's* crew's uniform, but not a color she'd seen anyone else wearing, she felt alert and adventurous enough to try one of the hot drinks from the cabinet Havak had showed her yesterday. While she waited for it to brew, she called Filavantri on the internal comm.

"Good morning." The United Council liaison smiled broadly from the tiny comm screen, and Rose realized she was getting used to the sharp teeth. "Would you like to come to my rooms for breakfast?"

Rose nodded. "I'm just waiting for the grinabo to brew."

"I'll get some guards to come and fetch you. Bring the mug along with you if you aren't finished by the time they get there."

Filavantri signed out just as a chime signaled the grinabo was ready. Rose picked it up and sniffed.

It smelled good. Almost a chocolate and hazelnut combo. She took a tentative sip.

It was more bitter than she'd expected, but not as bitter as some of the food she'd tried yesterday. She rolled it over her tongue, finding she liked it more and more. Not chocolate at all in the taste of it, but good, nevertheless.

She took another sip as the door chimed.

The guards.

She hesitated. Looked down into her mug. She regretted her outburst yesterday in the med-chamber. She'd been indulging herself, not thinking ahead. She had to deal with these people in a situation where they had all the power, she had none.

She should have bitten her tongue, or handled it better. If these were the same guards from yesterday, she had to face them again, with her challenge to shoot her hanging between them. And if it wasn't them, she would bet the story had already done the full rounds.

The door chimed again, and she walked over to it, touched the panel like Havak had shown her, and saw it was the same two guards from yesterday.

With a sigh, she pushed the button to let them in.

"Good morning." She used the mug as a shield, watching them over the rim.

"Good morning." The woman eyed her, flicked her gaze into the room, and Rose was glad she'd made her bed and everything looked tidy.

"I'm ready to go. I'll take my drink with me."

The woman shared a look with her partner, and he cleared his throat. "Before we take you to Liaison Officer Dimitara, we would like to apologize for not familiarizing you with your room."

Rose blinked. "That's all right. Dr. Havak came and showed me."

The woman winced. Looked at her partner again, and Rose guessed they hadn't known that.

Perhaps they'd thought she'd complained about it, but now they realized it must have been Havak who'd voiced the complaint.

"We didn't mean any disrespect. It didn't occur to us that you wouldn't know how to use the room." The woman's words were stiff.

"I understand." That felt like a lame answer, but she couldn't think of anything else to say that wouldn't make things even worse. She hesitated. "Would you tell me your names? I don't know many people on this ship."

"I am Vree Halim." The man took a formal step forward, and inclined his head in a way Rose thought would probably have gone down well in the 19th century Russian court.

"Jay Xaltro." The woman made a similar movement.

"Nice to meet you both." Rose decided not to apologize for yesterday. It felt like they were leaving that behind them, and she didn't want to bring it up again.

They seemed flustered by her response, and she hoped she wasn't imagining a lessening of the tension as they led her down the passageway and to the right to arrive at Filavantri's door.

She thanked them, and couldn't resist looking behind her as she stepped through into Filavantri's room. They seemed to be walking away. So they weren't guarding her, or watching her.

Or maybe that's what they wanted her to think.

She shrugged it off, and then smiled as Filavantri thrust out her hand for a vigorous handshake of welcome.

"You've certainly got the hang of it," Rose said, taking another sip of her grinabo. It had gone almost stone cold, and she made a face.

"You don't like it?" Filavantri asked.

Rose shook her head. "I do, but not cold."

"Ah. Me, neither, although these Grih like it hot or cold. They don't care."

She busied herself making some more, and seemed to enjoy introducing Rose to a variety of different breakfast food. The most familiar was also the best, toasted bread made from a slightly pink grain. Nutty, with a hint of salt, Rose thought it was the best thing she'd eaten since her abduction.

"Good. We make progress if there is something you enjoy so much." Filavantri seemed delighted. "What else can I get you?"

Rose hesitated, but unless she wanted to unleash a frightened and worried Sazo on the *Barrist*, she needed a handheld that would allow Sazo to breach the shield.

"What is it?" Filavantri's intelligent face sharpened.

"I wondered if I could have a handheld? Even if they could just bring me the one from my cell on the Class 5. It should still be there. It has all five languages of the United Council on it. But I wouldn't mind one that has information on the cultures of the United Council as well. My Grih could use some improvement and I would like to learn their ways. And yours."

Filavantri frowned. "Such a simple thing? Why do you even hesitate to ask?"

Rose shrugged. "It took a long time for the Tecran to give me the one I had on the Class 5." It had, and she'd only gotten it because Sazo had usurped her care and management from Dr. Fliap when he'd taken ill, but she wasn't going to reveal that to Filavantri.

"We are not the Tecran." Filavantri breathed in heavily through her nose, and then shook her head. "But, of course, we are. They are part of the United Council, so why should you expect anything else? I keep forgetting the betrayal of our principles wasn't made by another species, it was made by a full Council signatory."

She lifted a hand to her ear and tapped. "Sub-Lieutenant Hista." Like Havak had yesterday, she waited a moment to be put through. "I require a handheld preloaded with all five languages of the United Council, and full cultural and social information of all five signatories."

She paused, and then frowned. "Yes, it is for Rose." She said Rose's name very firmly, as if chastising the person on the other end.

"I don't mind if it's not connected to the main system. That's why I requested the information be preloaded."

When she turned back, her lips were in a thin, tight line. "When Sub-Lieutenant Hista has permission from the captain, she'll have a handheld delivered to your room, and instruct you in its use." She lifted her left hand, flicked her sleeve and Rose saw the time light up on her cuff. "I'll need to go and file some reports now, I'm afraid. But I'll walk you back to your room so you don't get lost."

She took Rose back to her room and then looked even more fierce when Rose confessed she didn't know how to get back in. She showed her how to place her hand against a plate beside the door for identification.

Rose put a hand on her arm as she turned to leave.

"Thank you. I've been isolated for a long time and your kindness means a great deal to me."

The liaison officer's face relaxed a little, she gave a nod and a smile, and as she walked away, Rose hoped her new friend wouldn't end up regretting being kind to an orange.

CHAPTER 13

THE SMALL RUNNER'S engines lifted from a purr to a whine as it landed in the Class 5's launch bay, and Dav looked over at Dimitara as she disengaged her harness.

"Borji is waiting to debrief me. If you want to go ahead and see the Tecran prisoners while I speak with him, you're welcome to." He unclipped himself and rose to his feet.

He saw the smooth, golden skin above her eyes lift in reaction. She understood the subtext. That he had nothing to hide, and they weren't abusing the Tecran and could withstand a surprise visit from a liaison officer from the Council. Even an unaccompanied one.

"That's all right, Captain. I'm happy to wait for you." She stood herself and Dav nodded and followed her out.

Borji was there to meet them, standing at the foot of the ramp with arms crossed over his chest, still in his bio-hazard suit, his helmet clipped to his belt.

Dimitara gave them the illusion of privacy, pretending to study the other vessels in the launch bay after a nod of greeting to Borji. The dead lion had been moved to a small refrigeration unit in the storage bay, or Dav was sure she'd only have had eyes for it.

As it was, he was forced to proceed knowing she could and probably would hear everything. Perhaps it was better that way. Better that she understood the full extent of their situation.

"Status?"

Borji grimaced. "Nothing's changed since the system reset the jamming signal for another twelve hours."

Borji had contacted him in the early hours of the morning to let him know, and Dav could see his chief systems engineer was beyond frustrated. "What do you think is significant about the reset?"

"Well, the time frame. Something was expected to happen in the first twelve hours, and it didn't, so it reset. That's the only thing I can think of."

That was Dav's assessment, as well. "And I wonder what that event was supposed to be."

"Do we really want to find out?" Borji rubbed a hand over dark-ringed eyes.

"Take a runner back to the *Barrist*." Dav realized it wasn't only Rose he hadn't been taking proper care of. "Get some sleep before you fall over."

Borji didn't argue. "My whole team needs rest. I'll give us eight hours and then we can come back fresh. But there's one thing."

Dav waited as Borji tapped at his handheld, then turned it to show him.

"See that?" Borji pointed at a thin graph line that was interwoven with the others.

"Yes?"

"It isn't ours." Borji lifted his gaze. "It looks like ours, but we haven't been sending out a signal every thirty minutes. See, our comms are all over the place, as and when we need to speak to someone on the *Barrist*, but this is exactly every thirty minutes."

"A piece of equipment, constantly updating?" Dav asked.

Borji shook his head. "I thought of that. I've checked every piece of inventory we brought over. Every one of their signals are accounted for. This is something else. Something using an almost identical signal to ours, reaching out every thirty minutes."

"Reaching out to whom? Or what?" Dav asked.

"That's just it. It seems general, but I don't want to bet on that, because we don't know."

"Can we listen in?"

Borji rubbed a hand over his face. "Tried. No good. The minute we get a lock, it jumps. Every single time."

"Like it knows you're there?"

"Oh." Borji laughed. "It knows we're there. My guess is the signal is coming from the comm system on this ship."

"This keeps getting better and better."

"Beware of unexpected gifts." Borji quoted the same saying Dav had thought of when the Class 5 originally landed in his lap like a hot coal.

"Yes." Dav tapped at his ear as a comm came through, grimaced. "The Tecran captain is getting a little louder in his demands to speak to me."

"What are you going to do with him?" Borji put his handheld away.

"Move him across to the *Barrist*. Into our cells. There's something going on with this ship, and I'd rather no Tecrans were on it if the whole system kicks us out."

Borji nodded. "Well, I'll round up my team, get some sleep. I'll see you later."

Dav gestured to Dimitara, and they made their way to the tube that would take them down to the cells where the Tecran officers were being held. It was in a less polished part of the ship, more grating and pipes were visible than in the upper decks.

At least all the bodies were gone since he'd last been here. Appal's team had stacked them in large refrigeration units in the Class 5's stores. Next to the lion.

His thoughts, almost inevitably, flowed back to Rose.

He wondered how she was doing, and whether she would appreciate him bringing her something from her cell. Whether it would upset her or please her.

When they turned into the passageway that led to the long containment unit, he realized, as he hadn't done the first time he'd been here ——probably because of the horror of the bodies——that the lighting was bad, and the air smelled stale, as if it wasn't being continually filtered like the levels above.

"This is where they kept Rose?" Dimitara asked, distaste in her voice.

Dav gave a nod. "This is nothing. Prepare yourself for what you see in the prison area. Appal felt it appropriate to keep the few Tecran officers who survived in the place they kept Rose and her animals." Although they had moved them to the clean, unused cells. Appal had made her point.

Outside the door to the cells, one of Appal's subordinates was waiting for them.

"Report," Dav said.

"They seem upset." The officer looked at Dimitara and cleared his throat. "They've been issuing threats and warnings since you left."

Dav was sure he'd have been given a more colorful description if Dimitara hadn't been there, but the guard's expression was enough.

"What've they been saying to each other?"

"They know we're listening, so not much. General conversation. Promises of reprisal."

Dav rubbed his hand through his hair. "So noted."

The guard activated the door and for a moment, Dimitara simply stood in the entryway and stared.

Dav left her there, stepping in. He ignored the call of the Tecran captain, walking past him and on to what he had already identified as Rose's cell. He turned, and called the guard over, got instructions on how to open the cell door.

Dimitara joined him as it slid open.

"She lived in a glass cage?" She shook her head. "No wonder she asked Dr. Havak and I if there were lenses tracking her inside her bedroom."

Dav's head jerked up. Dimitara met his gaze.

"Can you blame her? They," she waved a hand toward the Tecran officers, "are part of the same Council we are."

Dav didn't respond. He stepped into the room, saw the neatly made bed, the small sink, the toilet beside it. She'd had no privacy for three months.

On the tiny round table there was a handheld, and he picked it up.

"She asked if she could have that back, if we didn't want her to have a handheld from the *Barrist*." Dimitara held out her hand for it, but Dav didn't oblige.

He switched it on.

"Why did she want it?" He scrolled through the options.

"It has the five languages of the Council members on it, and she wants to improve her Grih. Learn Bukarian."

"Her Grih is already excellent." Dav couldn't find anything on the handheld but the five languages, and handed it to Dimitara.

She almost snatched it from him. "Yes. I asked for a handheld from your comms team for her that included cultural and social norms for all five signatories to the United Council."

Dav hadn't heard anything about that, and he had been specific in his orders that anything concerning Rose come through him first.

It must have showed in the look he sent her.

"Not one on the system. A standalone." She all but rolled her eyes. "And they wouldn't give it to her until you'd approved. The request is probably waiting for you back on the *Barrist*. Of course, as this is hers, she could simply have it back instead."

"I'll take it with me. Let Borji's team check it out first, then if they're happy there are no nasty surprises on it, she can have it."

The Tecran captain was hammering on the clear wall of his cell by now for their attention, and Dav held out his hand for the tablet back and then stepped out of the tiny room to hear what he had to say.

"Captain Gee?" He waited, hands behind his back, lens feed on the tiny lens clipped to his collar activated.

Gee had stopped pounding the moment Dav stood in front of his cell, and now his eyes slid right to Dimitara. "Who is that?"

"This is United Council Liaison Officer Filavantri Dimitara." Dav wondered if there had been a liaison officer aboard the Class 5. It seemed unlikely, given the massive breach of Council law that had happened in this very room.

Gee seemed to ponder that. "The United Council moved quickly to be here already."

Was it fear or anticipation that made Gee's hands shake?

"I was already on board the *Barrist* when it encountered your vessel, Captain Gee. I've witnessed everything that happened in the last twenty-four hours first hand." Dimitara turned her head, looking down the length of the transparent-walled cells, the low ceilings and the lenses mounted on the walls.

It was most likely true that if the liaison officer hadn't taken to Rose, she would still be angry at this blatant and inexcusable breach of the rules, but Dav knew from both Havak and the guards he'd tasked with watching Rose that Dimitara was behaving very protectively of their new guest.

Dav was struggling to maintain a distance from her himself, so he didn't blame the UC liaison, and was more than grateful for it now.

The Grih would come out of this with a clean record, if Dimitara had anything to do with it.

Gee narrowed his eyes. "Why is there a liaison officer on a Grih exploration vessel? You must already suspect them of wrong-doing."

Dimitara cocked her head, her long, slender neck a perfect curve against the silver-gray of her United Council uniform. "All exploration and military vessels, from every member nation of the United Council, now has a liaison officer aboard. The law was introduced a year ago. Interestingly, in light of what I've seen here, the Tecran were the only ones to vote against it, and I can now see why they wouldn't want any independent eyes on board. It was a four to one vote in favor, and the only reason none of the Class 5s have a liaison officer is because your government said all Class 5s were in deep-space, and involved in important work, and you would have to accept your new liaisons when you came back in for major servicing." Dimitara made the humming sound that grated on Dav's ears so badly, but which didn't seem to effect the Tecran at all. "I'm surprised you don't know about it. I would have thought it would at least have been communicated to you, Captain Gee."

Gee looked like he didn't know whether to continue to deny he'd ever heard of the new legislation, which Dav was sure was true, given Gee's accusations and the look on his face when Dimitara set him straight, or whether to pretend he had been told and had forgotten about it.

In the end, he went with silence.

Dav crossed his arms. "You seem very quiet, now, for a man who insisted I come over to speak to you."

Gee raised his head, as if he suddenly recalled why Dav was here at all. "I demand to speak to Dr. Fliap."

Dav frowned. "Who is Dr. Fliap?"

The feathers at Gee's neck fluffed out. "A scientist on board this ship. He became ill nearly two months ago, and was in the high-care med-chamber."

Dav recalled Appal's report on the man. "As far as I'm aware, he's barely hanging on to life, and has been in that state for some time."

Gee shook his head. "We heard him. He spoke to us."

Dav frowned. "Spoke to you?"

"Through the comms." Gee indicated a comms unit up at one end of the room.

Dav walked over to it, looked up. Turned to the guard. "You hear anything?"

"We aren't in here all the time. Mostly we're outside. If someone spoke in Tecran through that comms unit, we wouldn't be able to distinguish it from all the talking they've been doing amongst themselves."

Dav gave a nod. "From now on, someone is in this room at all times." He turned back to Gee. "I'm afraid you're mistaken, Gee. Your scientist is on board the *Barrist*, in our own high-care med-chamber, and has been since a few hours after we stepped onto your ship."

"He asked for help. Said he was trapped in the med-chamber." Gee's hands clenched to fists against the glass wall of his cell. "I recognized his voice. It was unmistakably him."

Dimitara took out her handheld. Made a note. The action caught Gee's attention.

"You! You're the liaison officer for the Council. I demand you investigate."

Dimitara's mobile, elegant lips pursed. "I have, in fact, seen Dr. Fliap in the med-chamber on board the *Barrist*. The chief medical officer showed me the arrangements they'd made for him personally."

Gee looked around at his colleagues, and they exchanged uneasy looks.

They seemed to be telling the truth, which was disturbing. Because it meant someone had sent a false comm through the system. Was it to stir up the Tecran? Or had it been done to achieve something else? Like get the captain of the *Barrist* back over on the Class 5?

CHAPTER 14

WAITING for the technician to bring her handheld was making Rose edgy. She imagined Sazo, being oh-so-clever in his mind, thinking up ways to get her to the Class 5, or having some comm device delivered to her.

If he lost patience, he might just force them to send her over and he was a 'can't make an omelet without breaking some eggs' kind of guy.

She paced her room, agitated. It took a lot longer to pace than her cell on the Class 5, but it still felt confining.

Remembering both Captain Jallan and Dimitara flicking their sleeve for the time, she did the same on her borrowed Grih outfit, and sure enough, her cuff lit up with the time.

Cool.

Although it told her she'd already been here two hours. Enough to make her tired of waiting like a good little girl.

She stepped up to the comm system, used it as Havak had shown her yesterday to find the comms department, and worked out a route.

She would go to them.

They must be busy, what with the Class 5 hanging before them like a prickly black forbidden fruit.

She'd save them some time, and hopefully ease the feeling inside her that she was coming out of her skin.

She stepped into the passageway, took a moment to enjoy the frothy green-blue of the walls again, and started walking in what she hoped was the right direction.

Every now and then a comm would come through the hidden speakers. Mundane calls for personnel to be somewhere, do something. No music, which surprised her, given how taken everyone seemed to be with her rendition of Row, Row, Row Your Boat.

Despite the circumstance, she grinned.

Not exactly Grammy-winning material, but they acted like it was something really special. She'd always loved to sing, enjoyed being part of the university choir, but she was no soloist.

She turned a corner and faltered. Instead of the serene green-blue corridor, the way opened up into a massive half oval, with an exterior wall made of the clearest glass. It was as if she was hanging in space, and she pushed herself reflexively up against the solid wall behind her.

The floor was clear glass as well, at the outer rim, so if you stepped right up to the window to look out, it would feel as if you were floating in space.

"You all right?"

Rose looked to her right, found herself being studied by a Grih officer in the pale blue uniform most of the crew wore.

She gave a nod. "Wasn't expecting it, that's all."

The moment she spoke, the woman's focus on her seemed to intensify. "What weren't you expecting?"

"I've been kept in small spaces for a long time, and this . . ." She looked out at the vast black in front of her, glittering with stars in the distance and dominated by the gas planet and Harmon, with the Class 5 blighting the view. She cleared her throat. "It was a surprise, that's all."

"You sound as if you're making music with your voice." The woman's direct stare was hard to handle, almost as hard as the view, given how long she'd gone with being both exposed and invisible at the same time.

She'd had similar scrutiny on Harmon from Captain Jallan, but perhaps because it had been outdoors, or something about Jallan himself, it had felt more comfortable than this focus.

"So I gather." She hunched, turned her head to face the stars so she wouldn't have to watch the woman watching her. The endlessness of the universe outside the window put her and her problems neatly in their place.

"I'm Dara. I work with Lieutenant Kila in the explorations division. You must be Rose McKenzie." Dara extended her hands, palms together. Rose covered them with her own reluctantly. She had no wish to spend time talking about herself right now.

The feeling of climbing out of her skin was back, worse than before.

"I have to go." She steadied herself, pushed off from the wall. The sense she had of too much space had diminished and she was able to focus on what was happening around her.

It was a well-used area. A small group of people were exercising together with smooth, flowing movements that reminded her of tai chi. Others sat with cups or small plates of food around tables, talking and laughing, and a few ran a circuit around the area.

It was so normal, so familiar, she felt a resurgence in appreciation and gratitude toward Sazo for bringing her here. They truly were like her, in the most fundamental of ways.

"Goodbye." She nodded to Dara and started walking across the massive space. She stopped at the far end, looked back, just one last look at the amazing spacescape.

Dara was watching her, standing where she'd left her, and Rose managed a polite nod before she turned away.

The passageways she'd walked along to get to the viewport area had been empty, but now she passed more and more people as she made her way to the busy part of the ship.

She attracted attention, but she had to expect that. She was an alien. An unknown advanced sentient. It was perfectly natural.

She forced herself not to cringe, and tried to meet the gazes of most of the Grih crew who stared at her.

They were all tall, and though she'd never thought of herself as short, she came, at most, to just above the shoulder of most of them.

Their hair fascinated her. Captain Jallan's was almost blue-black, with silver-gray tips, and she'd found it hard not to stare at it the whole way up from Harmon.

Most of the people she passed had a similar look; a darker color tipped with a lighter shade. Brown and light red, or black tipped with white.

She was the only blonde.

She tried not to stare at their ears, but they still delighted her beyond all logic. The first time she'd seen Captain Jallan's ears had been the moment she'd accepted she was in a completely new world, and it wasn't all bad. There was adventure and magic in this place.

She could whine about her fate, or embrace it, and one thing Rose had never been able to stand was a whiner.

She'd been getting slower and slower, trying to pretend she didn't know she was the object of everyone's attention, and now she realized she had no idea where she was.

"You are lost?"

Rose had already seen the Grih who addressed her. It would be hard to miss him. He lounged against the wall, big enough to act as a lode-bearing pillar. He had the short, spiky Grih hair in sandy brown tipped with copper, hulking great shoulders, and a hard expression.

"I am."

He raised a brow. "Where do you wish to be?"

"The comms division."

"What's your business there?" He crossed his arms over his chest and muscles popped out everywhere.

Rose decided she liked Captain Jallan's sleeker look. He had muscles, she'd felt them personally, but this guy took it just that one step too far.

He wanted to know her business, and she was surprised to find she felt slightly insulted by the question, even if they had every reason to be wary of her. "I need to pick up a handheld."

"Name?" His voice was gravel in a concrete mixer, like all the Grih.

"Rose McKenzie."

The big Grih pushed himself off the wall he'd been leaning against, and Rose couldn't help flinching and taking a step back.

He stilled. "I won't hurt you."

She tried to shrug it off, shoot him a smile, but she couldn't quite pull it off. "Had a few bad experiences recently," she said. "I'm afraid I'm jumpy."

He gave her a long look. "This is the systems engineering division, comms is part of it." He waved his hand toward a door to her right, and she peered through.

It was a quiet place. A few people working at desks, others standing on both sides of a huge free-standing glass board with a schematic etched onto it. As she watched, lights jumped and flared on the screen.

"You an engineer?" Rose slanted the big Grih hulking beside her a look.

He gave a curt nod. "First officer Yari."

"Pleased to meet you." She presented her hands, palms together, to him, and he took a step back.

"That isn't an appropriate greeting in these circumstances?" Rose frowned, and hoped whatever handheld she received had more information on Grih societal norms.

"No. It is appropriate, as you are clearly not part of Battle Center." Yari clasped her hands between his own massive ones. "I didn't expect you to know our ways, that's all."

"I speak your language," Rose pointed out.

"So you do." Yari's lips managed to tweak up slightly in a half-smile. "Your voice . . ." He didn't finish the sentence, and Rose's focus shifted to the woman approaching them with a scowl on her face.

"Sub-lieutenant." Yari came to attention. "This is Rose McKenzie."

"Hello." Rose presented her hands again, and the sub-lieutenant hesitated a moment before clasping them. She was much smaller than Yari, although Rose still had to look up at her.

"Sub-lieutenant Hista." She gave that strangely formal head bow. "What are you doing here, Rose McKenzie? The instructions were for you to wait in your room for one of my staff to come to you, *when* the captain had approved giving you a device."

Rose held her ground. "I found it difficult to wait. I wanted to explore, and not be confined. If you aren't ready for me, that's fine, I'll keep going and you can leave a message on my room comm for me when approval comes through."

Hista's eyes narrowed.

Rose turned to Yari. "It was nice to meet you. You, too, Sub-lieutenant Hista."

She turned to go.

"Wait." Hista's voice was grudging. "Sit on the bench. I'll be with you in a moment."

Rose walked over to a long, cushioned bench against the far wall and sat, content to watch while the engineers worked.

Hista and Yari bent their heads together, talking so quietly Rose couldn't hear them. They were lucky she didn't have super-hearing, rather than super-eyesight. And she still felt, with every step, that she could launch herself further and higher than she would ever have been able to do on Earth.

Hista and Yari were still at it, and the feeling of wanting to jump out of her skin rose up in her again. Sazo was waiting, had set a deadline, and while she still had time, she was nervous he'd get impatient.

She started humming, the sound soothing her like it had back on the Class 5, when the only voices she'd heard some days were Sazo's and her own.

She didn't notice the gradual silence, but when she looked up, every face was turned her way.

She froze.

She wanted to speak, to ask what was wrong, but her throat had closed up, and she could do nothing but try to swallow.

Hista clapped her hands together, and Rose flinched. So did most of the engineering staff, but as a way to snap everyone out of their strange behavior, it worked.

Everyone went back to their duties.

Hista approached her, and Yari came with her.

"No one meant to frighten you." Hista's expression was less severe than it had been. "I had heard from Dr. Revil that you are a music-maker. We like music and there is something extremely pleasing about the sounds you make."

Rose gave an uneasy nod. "I was just humming."

Yari cleared his throat. "We are waiting for permission from Captain Jallan to provide you with a handheld. Perhaps you would be interested in my loading a music program onto the device as well? It is something our music-makers use for their songs."

Rose hesitated. She didn't know if she wanted to go down this path and claim music-maker status. She wasn't good enough as a singer. It would feel like lying.

She also had a feeling she didn't understand the extent of what it meant, and the reverence they seemed to feel for music-makers was disconcerting and made her extremely uneasy. "I'm not really a music-maker——"

Yari goggled. "You are the best music-maker I've ever heard, even just with your speaking voice."

She shrugged. "I don't understand what it entails . . ." She trailed off, realizing that she was offending them. "I don't understand how things work, and I don't want to claim status that I don't deserve."

Hista opened her mouth, looked at Yari, and closed it again.

Rose gripped her knees. "I will obviously be happy to have a music program." She hadn't specifically agreed that she was a music-maker by accepting the program, but she knew she was on a slippery slope. Perhaps Captain Jallan could help her get out of this. Or Filavantri.

Whatever her misgivings, her words seemed to appease them.

Yari went off to bend over a screen, and Hista gave her another formal nod and left, tapping at her ear as she engaged her comm.

She'd been abandoned.

Rose shrugged. She preferred that to too much attention. She rose from the bench and followed Hista out, although the sub-lieutenant was nowhere to be seen when Rose stepped into the passageway.

She decided to keep exploring.

She found a few communal lounges, though none as vast as the first one she'd come across.

There were gyms, full of strange equipment and buff bodies working out. She'd noticed the Grih women's breasts were flatter than her own, and their bodies sleeker, with long, slender lines. She wondered what they thought of the slight differences in her physiology. She was as lean as they were, especially after months of little food, but her body dipped and curved more than theirs did.

She turned a corner and slowed as she heard the unmistakable sound of water in a confined space.

She walked up to a door and when it opened, she found herself looking at an indoor pool.

The pool had a solid glass cover over it, sealing it. She guessed that would come in handy when they made a light jump.

A sign beside the button to open the cover demanded whoever used the pool had to put the cover back after use or if the ship encountered turbulence.

There was a door at the far end of the room and Rose guessed it was a change room. She went in and found swim suits neatly folded on a shelf by size, and towels stacked in a neat rack.

She took the smallest suit she could find, and it still hung on her, but she didn't care.

She set the towel by the edge of the pool and pushed the button to retract the lid.

The water was pale green and warm. Rose shivered, though, when she stepped into it. The sensation of floating after months of confinement was exquisite. She started moving, gliding across the pool, with the water sliding like liquid velvet over her skin.

She had missed this. She had missed this so much.

She started crying silently, tears trickling down her face, invisible as she ducked under the water, but when she rose back to the surface it burst out of her, wracking sobs that tore at her throat and clawed at her chest, so she had to hang on to the side of the pool, helpless.

"Rose?" Hands reached down, grabbing her beneath her arms and lifting her out of the water.

She vaguely realized Captain Jallan was carrying her to a seat bolted to the floor beside the pool.

"What is it? Are you hurt?"

She shook her head. Tried to answer, but she couldn't speak, her breath coming in harsh, choking gasps.

"Did someone upset you?" He held her firmly against him with one arm, stroked her back with a large, warm palm.

She sat curled into him for a long time, until the terrible, wrenching feeling inside her subsided and she was quiet, except for the occasional shiver and hiccup.

She became aware of him slowly; the warmth of his body against hers, the flex of his thighs beneath her bottom, the way his head was bent over hers, so that every breath he took stirred the hair above her ear.

She closed her eyes and leaned in a little closer, burying her nose in his shirt so the scent of him, clean pine and fresh air, drowned out the sharp tang of whatever chemicals they used to keep the pool clean; drowned out everything.

She felt him go still as she snuggled in, and then his hand started to move again, only this time, it wasn't soothing, it was something more. Something that made her heart pound enough to pull back a little.

She knew her cheeks were flushed when she raised her eyes to his.

"I'm sorry."

The look he gave her was an unmistakable mix of concern and heat, and she couldn't help the shiver that wracked her again.

"What was wrong?"

She gave up trying to keep her distance, sighed, closed her eyes and rested her head on his shoulder, seeing as he didn't seem to be about to set her in the chair next to his any time soon.

"I love swimming. I feel so free when I'm in the water. So when I got in the pool, started floating . . ." She released the grip she had on his shirt, opening her fists so her hands lay flat against his chest. "I was overcome with relief that I was free again, anger for everything I'd been through, fear for the future, sadness for everyone I've had to leave behind on Earth, all rolled into one."

His palm was still on her back, skin on skin because the back of the swim suit she had on was low, and then, remembering how loose it had been on her when it was dry, she looked down, fearing the worst with it stretchy and wet.

Her breasts were on display, right down to a hint of nipple. She tried to pull the suit up, but it was twisted around her, and all her maneuvering did was make it worse.

She groaned and rested her forehead on his shoulder.

He chuckled, a rumble that vibrated through her. "Do all females in your race have such large breasts?" There was no escaping the male interest in his voice.

She made an inarticulate sound. "I come all the way to the other side of the galaxy, and what do you know, it's still populated by boob men."

He raised a hand, tentatively brushed the side of his thumb against the side of her naked breast. She felt his breath catch, felt the twitch of his erection where she sat over it.

"They're so wonderful. Why wouldn't the whole universe be populated by boob men?" He let the tips of his fingers follow where his thumb had just been and she tried to hold herself still.

"Why, indeed?" She pulled back, meaning it this time, and wriggled off his lap, pulling the straps of her swim suit up to cover herself a little better.

She thought she heard him groan.

She reached for the towel she'd brought out with her, and wrapped herself up in it. It was huge, and covered her from neck to shin.

Captain Jallan watched her with a focus that made her want to squirm.

His shirt and trousers were wet where she'd lain against him, with a patch on his shoulder where she'd rested her head. He looked a little bemused, and so big and competent. She clutched her towel a little tighter.

"Did you find me in the middle of my meltdown by chance?" She tried to keep her voice even, tried to steer them into safer waters.

He shook his head. "I was on the Class 5 earlier, and found your handheld. I took it to systems engineering for them to check for any spyware before it could go back to you, and they told me you'd been there. You weren't in your room, so I decided to find you."

"You wanted to speak to me?" She didn't mean her voice to come out quite so low.

"I wanted to apologize. Dr. Havak told me you were dehydrated, hungry——"

"No." She was fierce, and determined to stand her ground on this. "I am an adult, and I had no reason to think you would deny me anything. I could have asked for what I needed, and for whatever reason, I didn't. The fault is mine."

"I should have noticed. Or thought about it." He held her gaze. "You shouldn't have had to ask. It should have been offered. That it wasn't doesn't reflect well on me or my crew."

"I think we all had a lot on our minds yesterday."

He gave a brief nod. "Your wellbeing should have been one of the things on mine."

"I appreciate it, but I am happy to have control over my own wellbeing restored to me." And Sazo was responsible for that. It was something she couldn't let herself forget.

"About before." He lifted the fingers that had stroked her breast. Looked at them. "I shouldn't have touched you like that." There was no regret in his voice though. No contrition.

It couldn't be Grih standard procedure to caress the naked breast of an alien you'd just found, no matter how advanced a sentient.

And from her side, it was a bad idea to snuggle up to the man from whom she was hiding a Sazo-sized threat to his crew.

She didn't regret it either, though. It was like coming out of the cold into a cozy room with hot chocolate and warm cookies waiting. She hadn't been touched by anyone who didn't mean her harm in three months.

Her hand crept up and closed around the crystal hanging between the breasts Captain Jallan liked so much.

He cocked his head one side. "You're thinking very hard."

It was her turn to chuckle. "It's one of my worst failings, and my greatest strengths."

He stood, and rubbed a hand over his face. "Would you like me to escort you back to systems engineering? They should have both handhelds ready for you by now."

She shook her head. "I need to shower and get changed. I'll find my own way back."

He gave one of those formal nods. "Lieutenant Kila has returned to the *Barrist*. She would like to make an appointment to speak to you about your people and planet later."

Rose hunched a little in her towel.

He lifted a brow. "She's not that bad. But feel free to call an end to things whenever you've had enough."

"And she'll listen to me?"

The captain's gaze rested on her face. "You are not a prisoner, Rose. You can do whatever you wish, as long as it doesn't endanger the *Barrist*."

That was the kicker, she thought, as she watched him walk away. Unless she got Sazo under control, that's exactly what she was doing.

CHAPTER 15

SHE STOPPED by systems engineering and got both handhelds from Yari. She didn't trust the one the Grih had given her, not yet, so she kept both of them switched off until she reached her room.

When she'd was safely behind a locked door, she took her Tecran handheld into the bathroom, closed that door, too, and switched it on.

"Sazo, can you hear me?"

"Rose." His voice was a shout of relief. "Thank goodness!"

"I missed you, too. Was it you who got Captain Jallan over to the Class 5?"

"Yes. I composed a few sentences using recorded comms of Dr. Fliap speaking, and sent it over the comm system into the cells where the Tecran officers are being held, pretending he needed help." There was a smug satisfaction in his voice. "I was hoping I would hear something between the captain and the crew over on the Class 5 about how you were, but instead, he decided to bring your handheld back for you."

"He gave it to systems engineering first, though."

"Yes." Sazo scoffed. "Unfortunately for them, the operating system on this handheld is me."

Rose laughed, even though the Grih were her friends. There was just so much glee in Sazo's voice at having bested them. He had been chained for a lot longer than she had. These freedoms, these opportunities to outwit others, must be as heady for him as walking freely around the ship, swimming, was for her.

"I heard that United Council Liaison Officer say you had requested a Grih handheld. Can you still get one?"

She hesitated, and then decided no matter what, she would not lie to him. "I have it already. They gave it to me with this handheld."

Sazo gave a hum of excitement. "Is it on?"

"No. I was afraid it might be bugged or have a listening device or something. It isn't connected to the main system, I know that."

"What if you need information from the main system? How will you access it?"

"I can ask, and be offered limited access with a login, if they deem the request reasonable."

"Well done, Rose." Sazo actually chortled.

"Sazo." She sighed. "If I log in, and you use that information to infiltrate the system, it won't take them long to realize I have betrayed them."

He was quiet. "It means a lot to you? That you not betray them?"

"Yes. I thought you understood. I thought that's why you were so wonderful about finding me such a good match in the Grih. They couldn't be more perfect as an adoptive people for me. I want to be welcomed by them. Not hated for ripping their ship from them, when all they've done is try to help me."

"What do you suggest?"

"Let's be honest. Let's tell them about you." It was really the only way forward that she could see.

"They will try to destroy me if you tell them about me," he said.

"And they won't succeed, and I will have to kill them in self-defense."

"Why will they try to destroy you? How do you know that?"

"In the past, the member nations of the United Council have had some bad experiences with what they call thinking systems like me. There's a ban on thinking system development. It's been in place for two hundred years. They would execute me if they knew I existed. And the Grih especially, because it was them who perfected the thinking systems in the first place, and I think them who suffered the most when things went wrong."

She knew it was crazy, but she slipped the necklace over her head and rested the crystal on the bathroom shelf, looked straight at him. "What kind of bad experiences?" She thought about the lion, and the Tecran crew. "Like what happened on the Class 5?"

"I'm really sorry about the lion, Rose."

Sorry about the lion, but not really about anything else. And only sorry about the lion because it had upset her so much, she guessed.

She supposed it was a start.

"If there's a ban, how do you exist? Who created you?"

Sazo was quiet for a long time. "I don't know. I can't find any information about it. It's out there, but I'm looking in the wrong places."

"And this plan of yours; dumping us in Grih territory, making them think they've got a Class 5, is it about looking in the right places? What have you got up your sleeve, Sazo?"

His silence infuriated her. "Sazo, you can't kill others, or hold their lives less than your right to know where you come from. It's not right."

"I want to understand things the way you do, Rose, but I can't. I'm not a person."

"Don't say that." She kept the fear from her voice. If he wasn't a person, he was a machine, and there was no negotiating with a machine.

"You think I *am* a person?"

She heard the longing in his voice.

"You're like Sherlock Holmes, Sazo. Scary, scary smart, and with an underdeveloped sense of empathy. But Sherlock Holmes was absolutely a person, and so are you."

"Sherlock Holmes?" He obviously liked the name, saying it slowly.

"Yeah. Sherlock Holmes was one of the most famous detectives that ever lived, back in the Victorian era. He was so intelligent, life was difficult for him. He could work things out, see patterns, understand things, so much faster than anyone else. It made him an outsider. It made him bored to tears, living amongst people who couldn't keep up, who he couldn't speak to or connect with."

"I can speak to you."

She grinned. "Well, I'm your sidekick. Just like Dr. Watson was Sherlock's sidekick. Watson was smart enough, although not as smart as Sherlock Holmes, but he was the missing piece Holmes needed. Someone to help Holmes see the world in a different way. To help him find the compassion and the friendship he was missing. To help him see people not as problems to be solved but as beings like himself. They didn't or couldn't see the world the way Sherlock could, but it didn't make their views less, just different. And they had as much right to take up space, to live and enjoy life, as he did."

"What does a detective do?"

She had him on the hook now, even if her literary analysis of Sherlock Holmes would turn a few academics over in their graves. Not to mention that she realized she hadn't clarified that Sherlock Holmes was a fictional character.

"During the time Holmes lived, the police department in London was in its infancy. And the industrial revolution had hit England and people were losing their jobs to the new machines that had been invented. There was a lot of crime and the police didn't have the facilities to cope. So people would hire private detectives to investigate crimes for them. Sherlock Holmes was the best there was. He could solve anything. But until Watson came along, it bored him. Watson put the fun back into Sherlock's life. And challenged him to behave more like a person. To try to fit in more, and make an effort to understand others."

"They were . . . lovers?" Sazo sounded puzzled. "Like those songs you would sing in your cell on the Class 5?"

"No." She shook her head. "They were friends. Good, good friends. Almost like brothers." She tapped her lip. "Hey, there's also Poirot."

"Poirot?"

"He was after Sherlock's time, just after World War I. He was the chief of police in Brussels before the war, but had to leave and flee to England when the Germans invaded. He took the mantle from Sherlock as the best detective in the world. And like you, he didn't have to go anywhere. He could just think the problem through, and use what he called his 'little gray cells', his brain, to do the work."

"Did he have a sidekick, too?"

"Captain Hastings. But Hastings wasn't really that smart, not like Watson. He was well-meaning, though, and always happy to throw himself into a case and help Poirot out. But if he ever did help Poirot on the thinking side, it was always by accident."

"I don't think I like that one. You sound more like Watson, Rose, than Hastings."

"And there is something about you that is more Sherlock than Poirot." She leaned back against the bathroom wall. "There's a manic edge to you, something a little self-destructive, that jibes with Sherlock. But from when he met up with Watson, Sherlock couldn't sulk in his room and brood anymore. Watson wouldn't let him. He'd storm in, fling the curtains open, let in the light and air, make Sherlock eat a good meal, and then force him to come out with him."

"What else? What else did they do?" Sazo asked.

"Well, when Sherlock worked something out, and Watson asked him how he'd done it, he'd say 'Elementary, my dear Watson'. And he played the violin really well. It soothed his soul." She wouldn't touch on Holmes's addiction to opium. The thought of a sky-high Sazo was truly terrifying.

"Sherlock Holmes." Sazo sounded thoughtful.

The courtesy bell chimed at the door, and Rose reached out and slipped Sazo over her head again.

"Will you tell them?"

"Will you not kill them, no matter how much it interferes with your secret plan?"

"Let's talk about it later."

Rose sighed, and realized as the door chimed again that they would have to talk later. Because she would bet it was Lieutenant Kila who was requesting entry.

Time to be a bug under a microscope.

"We have live comms." Borji's voice was jubilant.

"You circumvented the block?" Dav asked over the murmur of relief from everyone on the bridge.

"No." Borji gave a short bark of a laugh. "The twelve hours just ended, and it didn't reset again. We should be able to communicate with Battle Center as of now."

"Confirming . . ." Sub-lieutenant Hista spun to face her terminal, tapped a few keys. "All backed-up messages went the moment the block was lifted."

"So we'll have some very frantic comms from Battle Center any time now."

"Not to mention the United Council Headquarters," Dimitara said. Her handheld began to chime, and she lifted it in triumph. "At last."

Hista signaled him, mouthed 'Admiral Valu' and Dav waved at the screen, to indicate she could transmit the comm through the main panel.

"Captain Jallan."

"Admiral Valu." He stood to perfect attention, hands clasped behind his back, shoulders square.

"What the hell is going on?" The admiral was a grizzled veteran, his hair a mix of mahogany and gray, his nose a little sharper in his face than it had been in his youth. Dav had always liked him.

"Well, we did a routine light jump, sir, found ourselves face to face with a Class 5 right in the middle of our territory."

"Why are you still alive?" The admiral leaned forward.

"That's what we asked ourselves repeatedly for the first ten minutes, sir, until we realized they were in difficulty."

"Think we can take them?" If possible, Valu was even more interested now than he had been before.

"We have already taken them, sir." Dav wondered how true that was, but in theory, they had the run of the Tecran ship, so they had taken it.

Valu leaned back, eyes wide. "If you're joking, Captain . . ."

"I'm not joking, sir." Dav gave a lop-sided grin.

"How did you do it? The *Barrist's* an explorer, not a battleship. How did you overcome their crew?"

"When we first encountered the Class 5, we signaled for help, of course, but we only realized afterward that our comms had been blocked by the Tecran. Then their air and power died, and by the time we got on board, unopposed, almost all their crew were dead."

"Who survived?" Valu was starting to get a look on his face Dav recognized. It was the same one he saw on his own face in the mirror, ever since this tangled mess dropped onto him.

"Just ten officers and one scientist, and the scientist is in a coma, was already that way before they even light jumped into our territory."

"You running around in that thing in full biohazard?"

Dav shook his head. "The air and power are back on, and my systems engineering team has been working to understand the ship since the moment we set foot on it." It might be a mess, Dav thought, but it was his mess, and he was staking his claim loud and clear.

"Is the Tecran captain one of the survivors?" Valu asked.

Dav nodded. "He's not saying much except that we're in big trouble for taking his ship, and if we beg nicely, maybe the Tecran will accept the Class 5 back and not kill us all."

Valu snorted. "They *will* have to kill us all, because that's the only way they'll get that Class 5 back."

Dav grinned at him. "I think I may have conveyed something along those lines to Captain Gee."

"What on Guimaymi's Star do you think they were doing in our system? And what the hell's wrong with the ship that it killed most of its crew?"

Dav was braced for this. He tried to keep his face neutral. "There are many unexplained elements to this, sir. One is that the Tecran have obviously been using their Class 5 to explore unchartered parts of the galaxy."

"I've seen the reports, Captain, they're definitely exploring new territory, but they're declaring it through the United Council."

"Are they declaring it all?" Dav asked. "Or are they just declaring the parts which don't have much in them? Because they were keeping eight sentient oranges in the Class 5, and just after we light jumped next to them, they tried to hide them from us by sending them on explorer craft down to one of Virmana's moons."

Valu went stock-still. "Genuine oranges?"

"Yes, sir. One is an advanced sentient, and we've retrieved her from Harmon. Some of my team are retrieving the others right now."

"So, Captain Jallan, you're saying not only do we have a Class 5, with most of its crew dead, but we have the Tecran dead to rights on violations to the Sentient Beings Agreement?"

"Yes, sir."

"That is . . . good." Admiral Valu looked like he was about to rub his hands together when Filavantri Dimitara stepped into the lens feed view.

"Not really so good for the sentient beings they were torturing." She didn't try to hide the disapproval on her face.

Valu coughed and sent Dav a chastened look. "Tortured?"

"Perhaps we could have a word in private, Admiral?"

The admiral nodded.

"Transfer comms to my private station, please," he said to Hista, and walked off the bridge to the small office where he dealt with the administrative duties that came with the job.

When he got there, Admiral Valu's image was already on screen.

"Torture? Really?" The admiral looked thoughtful.

Dav nodded. "Rose is physically whole, but my chief medic says there is evidence of invasive surgery, and she verbally confirms that. She was locked in a cell small enough that she could almost have touched the walls on both sides if she stood in the middle, was never allowed to exercise or bathe, and was malnourished."

"What were they up to?"

Dav shrugged. "If I were to guess, from what my logistics team tells me they've found in the storerooms, they were on a genuine exploration mission, bringing back exotic products they found along the way. Rose and the animals from her planet were a side-trip. Possibly they didn't have time for a full exploration, and so the scientist asked for some specimens to play with."

Valu grunted in disgust. "What a mess." He paused. "That liaison officer giving you any trouble?"

Dav grinned. "She's a bit grating at times, but her being on board when this happened is a definite positive for us. She can confirm everything happened as it did. The Tecran have accused us of disabling their air and power, and she was on the bridge the whole time with me. She can witness that we had nothing to do with it."

"Huh." Valu conceded her usefulness with another grunt.

"She has also formed a connection with Rose. What Rose went through is even more abhorrent to Officer Dimitara because she's seen Rose's reactions personally. She won't be inclined to minimize what the Tecran have done. She'll be gunning for them."

"Well . . ." Valu frowned. "You seem a little affected by this Rose as well."

Dav tried not to lie if he could help it. "I am. I find her . . . remarkable."

"I'm sure she is." Valu dismissed her with a wave of his hand. "Back to the Class 5. What's it like?"

"Truly terrifying, sir. My crew and I are enjoying learning its secrets, top to bottom."

Valu didn't miss the proprietary note in his voice. "Fair enough, you bagged it, but don't think you'll have it all to yourself. I'll be there as soon as we can get a team together. And I know I won't be the only one chomping to go." He must have seen the look on Dav's face. "I'll make sure everyone knows you're in charge, but you have to share a little, Captain."

Dav reminded himself it was better than it could have been. He gave a nod.

"I suppose that liaison officer will be arranging for the United Council to be there, too. Deal with the crimes the Tecran committed."

"And we'll have to ask the Council to take away the dead, deliver them to the Tecran. I can't see us inviting the Tecran in to fetch the bodies themselves."

Valu swore. "Hadn't thought of that, but you're right. They are not to set foot back on that Class 5. I'll put the request in."

Dav hesitated, then decided he'd better say what was on his mind. "Admiral, one thing. The Tecran captain, Gee, says he doesn't know how they landed in Grih territory. That something directed them, midlight jump, into our hands, and then disabled them. If that's true, someone handed us this Class 5 on a platter, and I'm asking myself who and why."

Valu tapped long, blunt fingers on his desk. "So noted. Bit more excitement than you thought you were going to get on a routine trip, eh?"

Dav inclined his head as Valu disconnected.

Just a bit.

CHAPTER 16

ROSE SAT OPPOSITE LIEUTENANT KILA, took a careful sip of her grinabo and blew on it to cool it a little. The tray of food the lieutenant had brought for Rose's lunch sat on the table beside her, and Rose was grateful. Not just because she was hungry, but because it would give her an excuse to delay any questions she didn't like.

"You like the grinabo?" Kila asked as if the answer was truly of interest to her.

Rose gave a nod. She'd made the grinabo for herself, and something called tep-tep for Kila.

"You don't like me, though." Kila leaned back in her seat. "You have apparently formed a friendship with Liaison Officer Dimitara, and with Captain Jallan, and Havak tells me you are cooperative with him, but you clearly don't like me. May I ask why?"

Rose put down her cup. "You're too excited about me." She concentrated on the food at her elbow, and bit into some more of the pink bread she'd liked from that morning. When she was done chewing, she looked back up at Kila. "You remind me of Dr. Fliap, from the Class 5."

"The scientist who's on life-support?" Kila frowned.

Rose nodded. "He never saw me as a person, only as a fascinating opportunity to discover new things."

Kila took a sip of her drink. "Can't I see you as both?"

Rose stared at her. "Dr. Fliap tortured me. Put probes in me with cameras on them. Tormented me and the animals."

Kila's mug came down with a thump. "You equate me with someone who would do that?" She was so shocked, Rose felt the first lessening of tension at being in Kila's presence.

"You don't see me as a person. You definitely see yourself as superior to me." Rose held her gaze, and saw the slow change in attitude as Kila understood Rose knew exactly how she thought, and what was going on.

Kila blew out a breath, pale under her smooth, olive skin. "I don't think I realized . . ." She rubbed at her cheeks, as if trying to get the color back into them. "I never meant . . ." She stood up, and Rose could see embarrassment in the hunch of her shoulders. "I will assign someone else to speak to you." She took a step toward the door.

"Wait." Rose closed her eyes. Kila had seemed genuinely shocked at the comparison she'd made between herself and Dr. Fliap. It was a truthful one on Rose's part; that hot, hungry look in her eyes had been a near perfect replica of Dr. Fliap's, but Rose conceded the worst of it with Kila was probably going to be hours of tests or conversation. And as Captain Jallan had told her, she was free to call a halt at any time.

She opened her eyes, found Kila standing, holding her breath, halfway to the door. "I can understand that finding someone like me was probably the reason you got into your line of work to begin with, but I had the sense, when we first met, that I was a shiny prize to you. I'm not a prize, but if you treat me with respect, I'll cooperate."

Kila slowly walked back, sank into her chair with a distinct lack of her former poise. Her hair was a light mahogany tipped with gold, short and spiky like everyone's, and she ran her hands through it, making it even spikier. "I'll say this one thing in my defense. In over five hundred years, we haven't come across a single new advanced sentient life form. You're right, the possibility of this is why I became an explorations officer to begin with." She heaved a sigh. "Just this conversation alone is worth a great deal to my career. I let that go to my head, and almost ruined it for myself. Will you let me start with a clean slate? I will have to report our discussions, that is my job, but you will be treated with respect."

Rose gripped her mug, wondering what Sazo was making of this conversation. Her Tecran handheld sat on the side-table next to her, and she knew he could hear it all.

There wasn't much risk to her agreement. If she didn't think Kila was holding up her side of the bargain, she could call an end to it, and Kila knew it.

Kila's raised her mug of tep-tep to her lips and took a long gulp. "You are genuinely weighing it up, aren't you?"

"Isn't that what you've just asked me to do?"

"I . . ." Kila's voice shook. "Yes, it is."

Rose respected her for not saying anything more. For not trying to push.

"What do you want to know?"

Kila let out a shaky breath. "I think I just aged a few years." She shook her head, and took another gulp of her drink. "Where is your planet?"

Rose pursed her lips. "I can't tell you. Aside from the fact that I don't know exactly where I am now, I don't know enough about astronomy to tell you anyway. But even if I could, I wouldn't."

"You wouldn't?" Kila blinked.

"I'm not exactly thrilled with my treatment so far, and I wouldn't want anyone else knowing where to find my people. I don't think you can blame me for that."

Kila shook her head. "It will be on the Class 5 log. We will find out."

Rose shrugged. "So be it. You won't hear it from me."

Kila shook her head again. "I have so many questions, but one sticks out from my conversation with Dr. Havak. He said he was amazed at how quickly you adapted to our technology. He could hardly believe you're from a less developed people, but says you say you are. That your familiarity is because your people have imagined a higher level of advancement, but haven't yet achieved it. Is this true?"

Rose nodded. "We've thought up lots of interesting things. Some of them we may turn into reality, others won't ever see the light of day."

"But how do you disseminate the ideas?"

"Written comms, visual comms."

"But if it isn't reality, what visual comms do you record? How can you record something that is imaginary?"

"People pretend it isn't imaginary, and act the story out. It's a sought-after job on my planet."

Kila made a note, but she seemed completely stunned. "And the written comms?"

"You write something that is like a report, only it's about something that hasn't happened."

"A lie?"

"No. A lie is a deliberate falsification. A story openly declares itself as imaginary."

"And why would people spend time reading something that is untrue?"

"Because it's fun. Exciting. When it isn't real, you can enjoy it because people aren't really getting hurt, aren't really in danger, aren't really at rock bottom. If the story writer is good, they'll make you think it is real, even as you know, at the back of your mind, that it isn't. And it means you can create worlds where the tech is more advanced than it is in reality or imagine places that don't really exist." She saw Kila was struggling to accept what she was saying. "Sometimes, reading something like that gives us ideas we might not have had before. Takes us in directions that lead to something useful to us all."

Kila scribbled on her handheld. "One thing confused Dr. Havak, and now I've spoken to you, it has me wondering, as well. What is the significance of buying an article of clothing?"

Rose frowned. What on earth . . . "Oh. Buying the t-shirt?"

Kila gave a nod.

"Sometimes, a story is so popular, people like to wear a representation of it on their clothing, that's all. When we say we've bought the t-shirt, it means we've bought into the story completely, even if we haven't bought an actual t-shirt."

"I would like to see one of these t-shirts."

Rose hunched a little. "Maybe one day I'll make one for you. Show you what it would look like."

Kila's gaze lifted to hers. "I am sorry you were stolen from your home, Rose."

Rose nodded. "I have a question for you." She thought of the awkward scene in systems engineering. "What is a music-maker? What am I agreeing to by identifying myself as one?"

Kila leaned forward. "Who is telling you you are a music-maker?"

"Sub-lieutenant Hista, Officer Yari. It was mentioned when I sang to Dr. Revil's child in the med-chamber."

"Your voice is so melodic, I can see why some would assume you're a music-maker. What song did you sing to little Gyp?"

Rose sang the first line of Row, Row, Row Your Boat.

Kila's face froze. Rose waited, growing more alarmed, until at last she blinked. "Sing something else."

Not really knowing what to make of that, Rose decided on Twinkle Twinkle Little Star, trying to make light of the whole situation. She kept a half-smile on her face, waiting for Kila to call her on it, or realize she was being joked with, but it never came.

"You are a music-maker." Kila voice was hushed.

"What does that mean, though? What does it entail?"

Kila stood, and Rose got to her feet as well, so she wasn't being loomed over.

"Music-makers are revered in our society. We love music, but biologically, our voices aren't very tuneful. There are some races we come into contact with who sing, but their music is discordant to our ears, or unpleasant to us, and they aren't interested in singing in our language. When someone who is Grih can sing well, and that happens very rarely, they hold a special place."

"I'm not Grih," Rose said.

"But you want to stay with us? Captain Jallan said that you wish to make a home with us?"

Rose nodded.

"You will be most welcome, no matter what. But as a music-maker, you will be embraced." Kila bowed to her, as respectfully as Rose could ever have wished.

As she left, Rose thought perhaps she wasn't a bug to Kila

anymore, but maybe a pedestal was just as uncomfortable as a microscope.

DAV STOOD OUTSIDE ROSE'S DOOR, and wondered what he was doing there.

The two battle cruisers he'd called for over a day ago, when they'd first stumbled on the Class 5, had light jumped in and taken up position on either side of the *Barrist*. He'd spoken to both captains, but there was nothing to do but wait until Admiral Valu assembled his group of Class 5 gawkers and Dav had to deal with superior officers who would want to muscle in on his action.

Dimitara was expecting a delegation from the United Council, and it seemed like everyone wanted a front row seat, so it was going to take at least six hours for them to arrive.

Dav had arranged for the Tecran officers to be transferred over to the *Barrist*, had lit a fire under his logistics crew to inventory the stores on the Class 5 so they had more of an idea of where the Class 5 had been, and had had a frustrating conversation with Borji, who still hadn't managed to get in to the comms or weapons systems on the Class 5.

He had a hundred things he could be doing, but here he stood, two small black bags in his hand, playing delivery boy.

Except, he knew that wasn't the full truth.

He wanted to see Rose again. The moment by the pool . . . he fought the shudder that wanted to shake free.

And then again, if it was just that, simple attraction, he could handle it, put it aside until things were calmer. Understand it.

But there was more.

Only one thing in the bags made sense. A set of clothing; trousers of a natural fibre that Kila was most excited about, and a shirt of the same fibre, but thinner, with small round fastenings, white with lilac flowers printed on it. They were soft with wear, and he had no doubt they were the clothes she had been taken from Earth in.

But from there, things went wrong.

The bags contained clothing made from hyr fabric. At least four sets. And she'd had a set on when they'd rescued her. Almost priceless, Olip, his logistics chief, had told him. Usually traded for favors or concessions on the international level, but if a price was set, he wouldn't want to guess what it could be.

Then there was the yuiar-scented soap she'd been using. There were four bottles of it, two in each bag. The combined cost, Olip said, was more than Dav earned in a year.

So why did she have it?

He knew how the Tecran had treated her. They looked after the flocks of baug they liked to hunt on Tecra better than they'd looked after her.

The convenient escape to Harmon, just as the air and power went down, the look on her face when he'd told her most of the Tecran crew were dead. Now this.

Something wasn't adding up.

And while he wanted to trust her, wanted to do a lot more than that, he had a responsibility to his crew that he couldn't ignore.

And the number of potential casualties if this all blew up in their faces was only rising as Battle Center and the United Council got in on the action.

He raised his hand and pushed the buzzer, angry with himself that dread sat heavy and cold in his stomach.

The door opened, and Rose stood there, in the burgundy tunic and pants they gave to visitors to easily identify them.

She smiled at him, a shy smile that conjured up the warm, heavy air of the pool room, her weight in his lap, the feel of the firm, smooth skin of her breast under his fingers.

He held up her bags, unable to speak.

"They were able to get them!" Her smile widened, although she didn't reach for them.

Appal's team had retrieved them before he and Rose had even left Harmon. They'd been in the runner that had taken her up to the *Barrist* yesterday, but Dav wanted them thoroughly checked before they were returned to her.

She stepped back. "Come in."

He managed to walk across the threshold, and she closed the door behind him.

"My team checked the bags." He placed them on the small table in the middle of the room. He noted with approval that there was a food tray near one of the chairs, and that it was almost empty.

Her face tipped up to look at him, no hint of worry or guilt on it. When he didn't continue, the skin of her forehead creased in a frown. "There was something bad in them? They were . . ."

She paused, and he realized she was trying to think of the Grih word. Eventually she blew out a breath in annoyance.

"There was a tracking device or listening device in them?"

He kept his face impassive. "Why would you think that?"

She shrugged. "You just looked so serious. What's wrong, then?"

He opened one of the bags, drew out the hyr fabric, felt it reacting immediately to the warmth of his hand. "Do you know what this is?"

"I was told. Hyr fabric. Isn't it wonderful? I don't think anything the Tecran had would fit me, so it was perfect."

Could it be as simple as that? A lack of suitable clothing, so in a rush they'd given her something that would fit. Why would they care that her clothes fit her properly?

He pulled out the yuiar gel. "And this?"

She lifted her shoulders. "It was in the bags. I like the smell. It reminds me of home."

"Yuiar is found on Earth?" Again, could it be this easy?

"Something like it, yes." She took the bottle from him, opened the lid and sniffed. "It's a combination of two scents that are often found together in soaps and perfume; cinnamon and vanilla."

"Expensive?" He tried to make the question casual.

She shook her head. "Not particularly, no. What's the problem with it? Shouldn't I have used it? Is it dangerous?"

He honestly had no idea what to do with her. She did not understand what wealth lay before her on the table. And why should she? She wasn't from their corner of the galaxy.

"Who gave you the bags?" He saw that she had at last realized this wasn't a friendly visit, that she was being questioned, and the hurt that sparked in her eyes for a fleeting moment hurt him right back.

He didn't just remember the feel of her in his arms in the pool room. The way she had broken and then pulled herself back together in that room had been as real as anything he'd ever seen. And as honest. It was driving him mad that he both questioned her version of events, and believed she'd been terribly wronged.

"No one gave them to me. They were in the explorer craft already when I boarded. I found them on the way to Harmon in a small cupboard."

He turned away from her, and walked to the screen on the far wall of her room, set to a cool, frothy waterfall. "So they aren't yours."

"They are now." Her voice was short, and he suppressed a wince. "I had nothing for three months. Just the same clothes on my back every day. Those packs gave me my first soap and my first change of clothes, and they became mine the moment I pulled them out of that cupboard. Why else would they have been put there, if not for me? I don't know why you would want to take them away from me, but tough, you can't."

"No one wants to take them away from you." Dav turned to look at her. "We want to understand how it came to be that the Tecran gave you, their prisoner, the two most expensive items in their store, and sent you to safety, while they stayed behind and died."

She stared at him, eyes wide. "You think I had something to do with the deaths on the Class 5?"

"I don't have a choice but to consider it. You certainly had motive. And now, I have to add that you have items which are worth my annual salary many times over sitting in those two bags into the mix."

She gaped at him. "I didn't know their value. I was pleased with them for their intrinsic usefulness. What do you think I was going to do with them? Sell them to the gryaks on Harmon? And how did I steal them from the stores, and how did I even know they were there, let alone how much they're worth?"

He shook his head. She was right, there were too many parts of this that didn't make sense, but he wouldn't, couldn't, get more involved with her on a personal level until she stopped holding back the full truth.

"I'm sorry you don't feel able to tell me everything you know," he said, stiff and formal as if he were addressing a Battle Center report committee.

"I'm sorry, too." Her voice was always musical, but she seemed to been forcing out her words. "Captain Jallan——"

"Dav." He snapped out his name, annoyed that he'd betrayed himself, but after the pool she had no business not knowing his first name.

"Dav." She said his name quietly and he couldn't help focusing on her at the sound of it. Wanting to hear it on her lips again.

She sighed, slumped into a chair as if their conversation had leached all her energy. "What does a music-maker do? Day to day?"

He blinked at the change in topic. "They work on music."

"Do they mainly sing to a live audience, or record themselves in visual comms, play audio comms?"

Dav frowned. "Live audience?"

"Like a concert."

He shook his head. "They provide the music at state ceremonies, at important meetings and events."

"Why haven't I heard any of their songs? I'm told you love music and music-makers are revered, but you don't play the music over the comms, or even in the communal spaces on the ship."

Dav tried to understand her. "The music is too special to waste in that way. If we played it over the comms, it would lose its power."

He could see she was struggling with that idea. "Music doesn't lose its power, unless you play the same songs over and over too often, then sure, people get sick of them." She tipped her head back, looking at him with her striking green eyes. "How many songs are floating around at any one time, anyway?"

Dav thought about it. "Ten or so a year."

She gaped. "Ten? But all the songs from the years before haven't gone away, have they?"

Since he'd met her, he'd marveled at how like them she was, but for the first time, he could feel the divide, the gap between her culture and his. "Each song is written for a specific event, so no, they can't be re-used."

"Music-makers write songs for specific events, and then sing them once, for that event, and that's it?"

He gave a nod.

She blew out a breath. "Okay, thanks. I can honestly say that wouldn't suit me."

"You would deny you are a music-maker?"

She paused. "I don't feel like a music-maker. I know my voice is okay, but it isn't great. And I don't understand why you wouldn't listen to songs more if you love singing so much. The power of it isn't diminished by repetition. It's a never-ending well."

"I don't think you understand. To be called a music-maker is a high honor." Another reason he should never have held her in his arms and touched her. A music-maker had no place on a Battle Center Explorer. "There are only ten music-makers alive in the Grih population at the moment, and two of them are near retirement."

She waved that off with a flick of her hand. "This is all a moot point, surely, if I'm likely to be locked up for mass murder?" She stared at him in challenge as she spoke, and it reminded him of the way she'd looked at him on the trip back to the *Barrist* on the runner when he'd asked her what she'd been saying to herself by the river.

It had the same effect on him this time, too. He could feel every sense sharpen, every muscle tense.

"Rose, don't joke about that. There'll be a United Council investigation. I believe you were held and abused by the Tecran, but the lens feed of what they did to you isn't anywhere my systems engineers can find it, and while the forensic evidence will show where you were kept and for how long, you are alive, they are dead, and you have in your possession some of the best things from their stores."

A chime sounded in his ear, and the comms system told him Borji wanted to talk to him.

He gave a formal bow of his head. "I have to go. Perhaps you will consider what I've said. I know you know something, Rose. Let me know when you're ready to tell me."

She shook her head as she stood, and looked down at her handheld lying on the side table beside her chair, almost glaring at it. "I can't tell you anything."

She lifted her gaze to his. "I didn't ask for any of this. I was happily sipping coffee on the porch of the holiday cottage I'd rented, watching the sun rise over the river and singing along to the radio, and the next thing I knew I was in that cell, with Dr. Fliap rubbing his hands together with glee at the sight of me. I really don't owe you, or the United Council, anything. If you're so worried about what I'm capable of, put me back on Harmon."

She looked so small, bristling up at him. Fierce and angry. And about as dangerous as one of the fluffy kapoots his mother liked to keep as pets.

But still . . . there was something she was hiding. He'd bet on it. "I don't have any say in the matter anymore, Rose. Battle Center are sending a senior delegation, and Liaison Officer Dimitara has sent for a United Council committee. You're going to have to ride this out."

She didn't reply, merely went to the door, opened it, and then gestured with her arm, in a way that left no doubt she was showing him out. Her face was grim as she closed the door behind him.

He stood for a moment in the passageway, Borji still on hold, and tried to shake the feeling he had lost something. Although he couldn't have lost something he hadn't had to begin with.

It didn't seem to matter, though. As he started back to the bridge, tapping his ear comm to bring Borji online, the feeling wouldn't go away.

CHAPTER 17

"I HADN'T THOUGHT through the implications of giving you those bags," Sazo said as Dav stepped out of her room.

Rose shrugged. "The hyr fabric is perfect, Sazo, and the yuiar smells like home to me, so don't be sorry about it. I remember you told me the hyr fabric was expensive, but I don't think I comprehended how much." She circled her neck on her shoulders, trying to ease the tension that had built up.

"I've made some of the lens feed from your time on the Class 5 accessible to Jallan's systems engineer. He'll think the Tecran hid it to protect themselves."

She hunched her shoulders, uncomfortable with the idea of others seeing her so vulnerable. The shame wasn't hers, but she felt a twinge of it, anyway.

"I didn't like the way Jallan spoke to you."

"I didn't either." She grimaced. "Even though I know he had every right, that I'm in the wrong here, I still didn't like it." She suddenly snorted out a laugh. "The fact that I didn't like it, felt hurt by it, gave me that extra bit of anger to hide my nerves."

"You're not in the wrong," Sazo said.

"Yes, Sazo, I am. We are. Captain Jallan——Dav——is right to be wary. I am hiding something and he's responsible for the lives of a lot of people. All he has to do is think of how he found the Class 5, all those dead bodies, and he must worry that it will happen on the *Barrist*. As he says, I'm alive, they're dead. He'd be negligent in his duty not to give me a good hard look. I'm the dark horse here."

"Dark horse?"

"The unknown entity. The mysterious stranger who no one has any information about, and could be either friend or foe."

"How does he know, though? How does he know you're hiding something? Everything you've said is reasonable."

Rose sat down on the small, comfortable couch and lay across it. "It's hard to lie to someone when you like them, and I really like him." She closed her eyes. "I'm hoping it's not a gratitude thing, after he rescued me from that gryak, but even if it is, I'm already there."

"What does that mean?"

"There's a spark between us. A chemistry. I like him touching me. He seems to like it, too. And in this last conversation between us, he realized he can't trust me, and shouldn't be snuggling up to the potentially dangerous orange. I mean, he knew that before, I could see it in his eyes at the pool, but now it's really clear, with no room for doubt."

"What happened at the pool? I don't really understand what you're talking about."

She sighed. "There's a first stage in human attraction, and I'm guessing this goes for the Grih, too. You take a quick look at someone and from some place in your hind-brain you think: 'oh, he's big and strong, will make pretty babies, and he'll be up to fending off any saber-tooth tigers who come sniffing around.' He takes a look at you, and thinks: 'oh, soft, curvy, will make a good mother' and then pretty much thinks about all the sex you could have together. It's meaningless, in that you can walk away after thinking that, no harm, no foul, and that would be the end of it. But you can't go on to Stage Two without it.

"I would have walked, because I'm lying to him about you, and anything between us would be dishonest, but I was swimming in the pool they have on board and all my pent-up feelings just came rushing out. Dav found me there, and comforted me. That comforting sort of veered off-course and became something more . . . sexual. I think we skipped a couple of stages."

"Well, if we were on Earth, that would be true, I'll have to see what's on that Grih handheld about social norms in Grih society."

"So, you want to be *his* sidekick?" Sazo asked.

She gave a laugh. "No. There is no way I'd be Dav Jallan's sidekick in a million years. I'm on equal footing with him, or not at all."

Sazo was quiet.

"You didn't think I'd jump ship on you?" She suddenly realized that's what he'd been asking.

"I didn't know."

"Sazo, I made a promise to you, and despite my better judgment, I've kept it. And I'll happily be your sidekick as a full-time job, because you have a lot to offer the Grih as an ally, and if we can somehow purge the Class 5 of all Tecran reminders, I could deal with being on it again. And I'm sure Dav and his crew would jump at the chance of exploring their territory with you, but none of that can happen if they don't know you exist."

He made a humming sound, just like she did when she was thinking things over. "So, why wouldn't you be his sidekick in a million years?"

She laughed again. "Because that would imply he was in charge."

"I don't understand why you are all right with being my sidekick, but not his."

She wondered again how old Sazo was. Too young, she thought. Too young, and too powerful. And the Tecran had chained him, feared him, but used him all the same. It made her sick.

"I'm all right with it because you came to me with a deal. I could have said no, but I agreed. I got something out of it, and so did you, but the control was in your hands. You might not have known about the concept of sidekicks when you made the deal with me, but effectively, that's what you were asking me to be." She wondered how to put the next bit in words a young, spooky-intelligent IA would get. "Dav Jallan is attracted to me. Fortunately, or unfortunately, given our current circumstances, I'm attracted right back. But if I were to be his sidekick, I'd be implying he was the leader and I was the follower. The weaker member of the team. When it comes to that kind of relationship——a romantic relationship——I won't accept anything but equality."

"A different type of relationship." He said it as if it had just occurred to him there could be more than one, and her heart broke a little more.

His relationship with her was the only one he knew. Although . . .

"Your relationship with the Tecran was an abusive one. They caged you and used you, and gave you nothing in return. Your relationship with me is one of mutual benefit, and friendship, too, I hope, but you're the boss, in that you made the plans, then invited me to join with you. If I ever have a relationship with Dav Jallan, and that's certainly not looking likely, it would be one of mutual attraction and respect, where neither one of us would have more power than the other."

"You still have power in our relationship," he said, thoughtful.

"Oh, I wouldn't have agreed to work with you if I'd had no power. But I have less than you."

"Like Holmes and Watson?"

"Like Holmes and Watson. Holmes was the one people came to for help, Watson came along as Holmes's assistant, and Holmes was better because he was there, and got more enjoyment from his work."

"I don't like the idea of you and Jallan."

She paused. This was tricky. Sazo could hurt Dav, and that would be on her, if she didn't nip this in the bud.

"If it's any consolation, Holmes didn't like Watson's lover, either. Not at first, anyway. He wanted Watson all to himself. But Watson showed him that having another perspective was good. That they could still be an excellent team with Watson involved in a romantic relationship.

"In fact, Watson showed him that his being fulfilled in all areas of his life was better for him and made him a better friend. Holmes didn't seem to need a romantic relationship, but that's because of who he was. Watson did need it. And he was a happier person because of it." She honestly didn't know how much of this she was making up and how much was true of the Holmes and Watson stories.

Holmes hadn't like Watson's fiancée, she knew that. Whether he ever got over that dislike, she couldn't remember. It didn't really matter, as long as she could sell it to Sazo. Who was going to contradict her, after all? She was the Sherlock Holmes expert in this part of the galaxy.

"I'm still in the dislike stage," Sazo said.

"You'll get over it," Rose told him. "We're hardly staring deeply into each other's eyes and declaring our undying love, anyway. He just told me I'm suspected of mass murder, and I just politely threw him out my room. And I can only see that getting worse when he finds out about you."

"If he finds out."

She sighed. "I made a promise, so it's your call, but you should seriously consider it, Sazo."

"It's better I don't." His voice took on a sharper, more focused tone, and she sat up.

"What?"

"There's something happening." He went quiet and she waited, curious.

"Two Grih battleships arrived earlier, as firepower. I knew they were coming, but there is also a United Council delegation on the way in a fast transport vessel, and another ship from Battle Center with some of Captain Jallan's superior officers on board. If you would just get me into the Grih system, I'd know more, but the comms I'm intercepting from the *Barrist* seem to suggest those are the only other starships they're expecting."

"And?"

"And there is someone else coming. A small, private craft. It signaled the *Barrist* a few minutes ago, but the comm didn't go through the main comms center. It went to a private comm."

"To the captain?"

"No." There was a trace of amusement in Sazo's voice. "I analyzed the captain's comm signature when he went aboard the Class 5. It isn't to him. It isn't directed to anyone who has been on board the Class 5."

"This was part of your plan?" His tone was too interested, too considering, for it not to be.

"I wanted to lure some people out here and listen in to their chatter." He spoke distractedly.

"What are you doing?"

"I've intercepted. It was on an old frequency they perhaps thought no one would look out for. But I've recorded it and, just to stir things up, I've made Jallan's chief engineer aware of it. Maybe he can smoke out the mysterious receiver of the call. Seeing as you won't get me into the system."

She ignored the barb. She wasn't letting him in unless he swore he wouldn't kill anyone. "What does it say?"

"It's all about you, Rose." Sazo's voice got a little more edgy. "Wanting to find out how advanced a sentient you are, and whether you're able to articulate what happened to you."

She gave a snort. "Well, it's a bad day for them, obviously."

He snorted as well, so exactly a replica of what she'd just done, she swallowed a laugh.

"I like you, Rose."

It was so sincere, and so filled with surprise, she smiled.

"I like you, too, Sazo."

"I never liked anyone before."

"I'm honored to be your first friend."

"The person they're transmitting to just replied that you are a danger to them." He was all business now. "I blocked the comm, so whoever is on that private craft won't get that particular message, but I've recorded it and sent it to Borji as well. Let's see if he can use the *Barrist's* systems to find who sent it."

"You sound like you like him, too. Borji." The more people he liked, the less likely he was to kill them when they didn't seamlessly fit into his plan.

He paused. "I think you're right. I don't like him as much as I like you, but I . . . respect him. He's been trying to break into the Class 5 comms and weapons systems for over a day, and he's been innovative and determined in the attempt. He won't get in, but I've enjoyed playing with him. It's been a fun game."

"And you can't break into his system, either," she said, then regretted reminding him of the issue between them.

"You're right. He is a worthy adversary." He made the humming sound again.

She stood, the itchy feeling of wanting to jump out of her skin prickling through her. She needed to get out of this room.

"When will you let me in the system, Rose? It's not just my plan, now, it's your safety, too. Someone is coming who means you harm, and there's someone on board this ship working with them."

She rubbed her face with both hands. "I want to, but I don't want to risk the lives of these people, Sazo. I need you to promise me they'll be safe."

"I can't do that, Rose. If they turn on me, and they will, I'll have no choice but to protect myself. Surely that's my right?"

"You're setting up a situation that has already put them in the firing line, Sazo, dropping the Class 5 here. You may have to defend yourself, but in a scenario you created. Your life doesn't depend on being here. You could have found anywhere for us. Avoided this altogether."

He thought that through. "I need to do this. I need to find out where I'm from, Rose. Please, let me in the system."

She picked up the handheld, tucked it under her arm, then scooped up the Grih handheld as well. "I'll think about it."

"Think about it fast." He spoke softly. "Time is running out."

CHAPTER 18

APPAL WAS in the training area when Dav got there, and he stood, disappointed, watching her move through the first level.

He needed to kill things alone.

She turned, saw him, and shut the virtual battle down. "I can make it a two-person mission."

He gave a nod, and shrugged into the jacket and gloves, strapped on the weapons he would need.

"Bad news?" she asked in the aftermath of the opening play.

He noted that he had severed the heads of two of the combatants with his return fire. "Borji found the lens feed from the Class 5 cells."

She spun so they were back-to-back and he felt her shudder under the backlash of her shockgun as she discharged her weapon. When they were clear, she shook out her arms. "Bad?"

He crouched and shot just to the right of her, taking out the last remaining image-generated Krik as he rose up from behind some crates to take aim at them. "Yes."

"Where'd Borji find the files?" She was barely breathing hard as she checked her sim weapon for charge. "I always like to know how the enemy thinks."

"In a file in the inventory system."

"Huh. As if they were part of their inventory."

They stepped into the third scenario, with the Krik still starring as the main enemy, and Dav wondered how long it would take for the Tecran to start appearing as the targets in these things.

If he had anything to do with it, not long.

"Captain Gee have a role to play in any of the visual comms?" Appal's tone was quiet, and Dav knew she was thinking about their first interview with the captain, the way he'd looked down and away when they'd mentioned violation of the Sentient Beings Agreement.

Dav had to kill three Krik before he could answer. "Not directly. The now comatose Dr. Fliap seems to be the one who actually carried out the abuse, but Gee physically came to the cells to observe him hard at work at least three times in the limited clips I've seen."

"Bastard." Appal sighted her shockgun, resting it on his shoulder for stability, and took out a gunner sitting high above them in a tower. "You given it to the UC liaison officer?"

Dav stepped away from her and covered her back. "Yes."

There was only one way out, and Appal ran at the huge pipe that would be their best cover, flipped in mid-air and landed in a crouch at the top. She covered him as he ran at it himself and jumped up, although less elegantly than her.

They slid down the far side, and this time both of them were breathing heavily.

"What do you think? About Rose?" He was so tied in knots, he didn't trust himself.

"She's as likely to have killed the Tecran as Dr. Revil's little boy, in my opinion. But if she did it, if she's hiding her true nature behind that really sweet exterior, you had better have done everything by the book."

That was his take. Which meant he had to throw Rose to the wolves. And he didn't think there'd be any forgiveness for him at the end of it.

Not after what he'd just seen on the lens feed. The abuse she'd been put through.

To be treated as a suspect when she was the victim . . .

He lifted his shockgun, and took out the horde of Krik trying to scramble over the pipe. But not even wiping out every im-gen enemy in the training center was going to melt the cold, hard lump in his throat.

She made her way back to the spacescape.

Now she knew what to expect, it didn't worry her at all as she stepped into the massive room which sat like a bubble on the side of the ship.

There was a comfortable chair set slightly apart from the other seating with a great view out to Virmana and the stars beyond. She made herself at home, pulled out the Grih handheld Yari had given her and began reading up on Grih culture.

She went to the music-makers first. The Grih had apparently been the hosts for the start of the United Council's dispute resolution court for the year, and a music-maker had performed at the opening ceremony.

There were a lot of drums involved in their music, and she liked it, tapping the side of the handheld in time with the beat. The song itself was really just an ode to the occasion, what she thought would probably have been quite common at the courts of the medieval rulers of Europe, praising the people involved, singing about what they hoped to achieve.

It wasn't something she could see herself doing. It was serious, with no joy or humor in it. They took music too seriously here, and hoarded it like a dragon hoarded its gold. Parting with it begrudgingly and in tiny increments.

Next she turned to Grih history, and she couldn't help looking back as far as she could, to the origins of their culture. They had no formal religion, instead, they saw themselves as an integral part of the world around them, no better and no worse than any other living creature. Their philosophy seemed to be that life would thrive where it could, it was the nature of the universe to do so.

They had been hunter-gathers for a long time, and had never gone down the path of peasants tilling the field for landowners. It seemed to have led to a more harmonious, egalitarian culture, and fewer wars meant more time and money to develop interesting, ground-breaking ideas. Their Renaissance seemed to have lasted for most of their history.

But back when they had survived as a hunter-gatherer group, the main prize for the Grih had been the yurve. A huge animal, bigger than any buffalo Rose had ever seen, although smaller than an elephant, its intelligence and belligerence were Grih legend.

The yurve was revered in their culture much as the lion was in Rose's own, as the embodiment of bravery and power.

The thought of a lion made her pull up short. It came back to her, in stark clarity; the lion lying on the floor of the Class 5, still in its cage, its huge paws stained with the black grit that seemed to coat every surface of the launch bay.

She deliberately closed the page she had been looking at and searched for a reference to thinking systems.

It took less than a second to find all the information she would need.

They had been used for over a hundred years, slowly growing more sophisticated, more self-aware, until a scientist called Professor Fayir developed a thinking system which came fully into consciousness.

It had lobbied for the right to be considered a sentient being, and had been accepted, but it had begun creating replicas of itself, and not taking the time or care to educate or control them, until Grih started dying, killed in ways Rose could imagine happened just like the lion's death.

Thinking systems had been adopted by other nation-members of the United Council, and they'd also experienced loss of life, but the Grih, who had thinking systems in every part of their society, were hardest hit.

Professor Fayir tried to persuade the United Council that the problem was that the new thinking systems hadn't been nurtured, and insisted he had a plan which would make it safe to create a new type of TS.

But Professor Fayir could not promise the United Council that the thinking systems would only ever work for the benefit of society. Rose read his final speech: "No one can guarantee any sentient being will only work for good. A sentient being is by definition autonomous, and therefore free to behave as it wishes."

At least he hadn't lied, Rose thought. He could have tried to downplay the risk, but he hadn't.

Because of the power they could wield, the UC decided that the creation of all thinking systems must be banned, and every one that existed must be destroyed.

There had been war for nearly six years until every TS was defeated. And Professor Fayir had died in the fighting, still insisting he could fix things.

She looked at the date, and realized that was nearly two hundred years ago.

She leaned back in her chair and stared out at the stars.

How had Sazo come to be? Had someone decided to give thinking systems another go after all this time?

She shook her head. Sazo was hardly the result of some exploratory toe-dipping. He was fully actualized, fully conscious. He was a person in all respects except for a body.

She got into more recent history after that. The near-war between the Tecran and the Grih on three occasions over the last fifty years, the part the Bukari played in keeping the peace through the United Council, and the ongoing issues with a race of people called the Krik, whose planet was on the outer-reaches of United Council held territory, and who seemed to either be trying to gain a place on the council or start up a war with each individual signatory, sometimes both at once.

There was always one.

It cheered her to know that was true, even on the other side of the galaxy.

"Excuse me."

Rose looked up, saw a group of eight Grih standing nearby. The one who'd spoken to her looked familiar, and Rose realized it was Dr. Revil.

"Hello." She smiled. "How's Gyp?"

The doctor smiled back. "He's fine. Not so grumpy today." She looked over at her colleagues, and then at Rose again. "We are about to do a particular Grih exercise called The Flowing Way. We wondered if you would sing for us?"

"Sing for you?" Rose was sitting cross-legged, and she dropped her feet back on the ground.

"You sang so beautifully for Gyp, and the Flowing Way was originally meant to be done to song, but with less and less music-makers, only two mass classes a year are held with a music-maker in attendance. You would honor us."

Rose looked at Revil, saw she absolutely meant that. "What kind of music?"

"The Flowing Way is part music, part exercise. The participants work to a specific beat and cannot drop it, or they'll interrupt the overall harmony of the piece. It's both pleasing to listen to, and difficult, because even if you get tired, you have to keep your rhythm steady. It keeps you focused."

It sounded interesting. "Why don't you start the rhythm, and I'll see if there's a song I can work into it?"

Revil nodded, and the group faced her, each moving a little away from the other to give each other room.

They warmed up slowly, but soon the participants stamped and clapped, even hitting the floor with a hand when they bent to touch their toes. It created a complex rhythm that reminded Rose of dancers stamping in steel-tipped boots on metal grids, and she thought of a train clacking on the tracks, thought of a song that was easy to sing that had a similar rhythm, and began.

The dancers' rhythm almost faltered during her opening verse, but Revil kept it together, and Rose sang the song through twice before she stopped.

The group slowly wound up their movements, drawing out the beat so that it ended harmoniously.

There was silence. Rose focused beyond the group for the first time, and saw everyone who'd been in the open area had come to stand in a circle around them.

"Thank you, Rose." Revil came forward with her hands together, and Rose clasped them between her own.

"It was my pleasure. Thank you for sharing a part of Grih culture with me."

She had said the right thing, because all around her were murmurs of approval.

"What was it about?" Revil asked. "Your language sounds so beautiful."

Rose leaned back in her chair. "It was about needing to take a journey, to go on to the next stage in life, and wanting to know if the person you love will come with you."

"That is an . . . unusual thing to sing about."

Rose shrugged at the man who'd spoken. It had sounded almost as if he had planned to say 'wasteful'. "Not where I come from. We sing about anything."

"Will you do one more?" The person who asked was part of Revil's original group, and Rose recognized her as Jay Xaltro, one of the guards who had originally shown her to her room.

Rose wet her lips, looked around at the audience of thirty or more and quailed inside. But she could see they were desperate for her to say yes, and she didn't have the heart to deny them.

"We'll make a different rhythm," Revil offered.

Rose nodded, and they began again, a slower rhythm this time, and she started up a Billy Joel ballad.

Her voice wobbled a few times, but by the second time around, she felt good about it, clear and on pitch.

When she finished, and Dr. Revil's group played their last beat, there was a perfect stillness around her, as if everyone held their breath.

One of the woman closest to her began to warble or ululate, like a mourner at funerals Rose had seen in Africa, and it was taken up all around her, so she was surrounded by a wall of sound.

She stood, spun round, and found even more people crowded around her now.

It was too much. She had been locked away on her own for too long, and panic thrummed at her chest, threatening to explode outward.

"Thank you." She managed to choke out the words as she grabbed up her handhelds. She gave a bow, and dived for the closest gap in the crowd, angling her body this way and that to avoid bumping anyone, and then, when she was free of them, she ran for the nearest opening.

"Rose, what's wrong?" Sazo's voice in her ear steadied her a little.

"Too many people, too much attention." She gasped for breath, slowing down now that she was in an empty passageway.

Eventually she leaned against a wall, bent at the waist, hands on her knees and concentrated on sucking in gulps of air.

Not her finest moment.

She was so angry with herself. She wasn't like this. She could lecture to a room of bored twenty year-olds who found their phones more interesting than linguistic studies, but a rapt audience did her in?

Then again, that was before she'd been trapped in a glass cage for months. And it didn't help that she felt like a fraud. She wanted to wince at just how mediocre she was as a singer.

They had no business applauding.

She clenched her fists. Suck it up, buttercup.

She heaved a final breath and straightened. There was no one in either direction, and she took out her Grih handheld, tapped on an image of what she thought might be the *Barrist* on the start-up page, and tried to see where she was on the ship.

Sure enough, a steady blinking light showed her position, and she saw if she walked a little further and turned left, she would be in the corridor the pool was in.

She could swim. It was just what she felt like and she had barely done two laps before Dav Jallan had hauled her out last time.

She made her way to the room, looked inside, and sagged in relief. She had it to herself.

"I'm taking out my earpiece to go for a swim," she told Sazo, and slipped it deep in the pocket of her tunic before he could reply.

She put on another voluminous swim suit and tugged at it while she waited for the solid cover to retract.

When it was fully locked in place, she dived in and swam the full length under water, stopping at the end to suck in a breath before going under again.

It was indescribably good.

At lap three she was just beginning to tire when she heard a humming sound. She rose out of the water to grab her next breath of air, and turned to see what was making the noise.

The pool cover slid across the water toward her, and for a long moment she tried to make sense of it.

When she did, when she realized she was in trouble, she turned, hands on the pool edge, feet against the side to pull herself out.

And was pushed straight under.

She could feel someone's hand on her head, large, squeezing painfully as well as pushing her down.

When she came up again, she was coughing, her lungs screaming for oxygen, and down she went again, the shove even harder this time.

She turned under the water, sinking out of reach of the hand, to look down the pool, trying to gauge how close to her the end of the cover was, and shot to the surface as she realized it was almost on top of her.

As her head and shoulders broke the surface, she felt the hard edge of it against her collarbone, just below her neck, and it trapped her for a moment against the side of the pool, but then she felt it inch back.

It was like an electric gate with a sensor, she realized, tears of relief forming in her eyes. It wasn't going to crush her against the side, there was a failsafe.

She twisted her head to look up at her assailant, but he was gone and when her gaze moved to the door, she saw it was just closing.

He must have realized about the failsafe as well, she thought. And every moment he remained, trying to drown her, was a moment he could be discovered by anyone coming along.

She turned, grabbing the edge again and pushing back against the cover with her back.

"Rose?"

She looked over her shoulder, and Dav Jallan stood in the doorway, with Filavantri at his side.

"Captain." She turned away from them, rested her head on the hands gripping the edge.

"What happened?" Filavantri's voice was sharp.

She closed her eyes, her teeth chattering as if the water was cold. "I think someone just tried to kill me."

CHAPTER 19

DAV BRUSHED PAST DIMITARA, striding down the length of the pool.

For the second time he caught hold of Rose under her arms, lifting her carefully from the water so he didn't scrape her back on the pool cover. He swung her as he lifted her, cradling her against his chest. He ignored the surprised look Dimitara sent him.

"Did you see who it was?"

She shook her head, resting against him, shivering a little. "He shoved me under the water. He wanted to force me under so the cover would come over me and . . ." Her voice caught and she went still.

"We heard someone running away when we arrived." Dimitara looked around the room thoughtfully. "No lenses?"

Dav shook his head. "This is considered a private space. No lenses here."

Dimitara sighed. "I agree with that reasoning. It's just a pity, this one time, that's all."

"You were looking for me because of what happened in the spacescape?" Rose's voice was soft as a whisper now. He could feel the tension in her, the way her muscles flexed against him.

He couldn't help holding her a little tighter, and didn't loosen his grip, even though Dimitara sent him a sharp look.

"We were concerned about you." Dav tamped down the fury he'd felt since Dr. Revil had contacted him, as per the ship-wide instructions to report any incident with Rose, and he'd learned she'd been surrounded by an enthusiastic crowd.

"I'm going to take you to the med-chamber, and then we'll see if anyone saw anything."

She shook her head violently, rearing back from him and struggling to be released.

"No med-chamber."

Filavantri Dimitara came to his rescue. "It would be best if Dr. Havak could make sure you're all right——"

"No."

He'd set her down, and she stumbled back a step.

"I swallowed some water, and that's about it. I got a fright, and if he'd succeeded, I'd be dead, but all I want is to have a warm shower, and crawl into bed for a while." She looked up at him, her body shaking. "Please. Don't send me to the med-chamber."

What the hell could he say to that?

"Either I, Dr. Havak or Officer Dimitara will check on you in an hour. And we'll escort you to your room now."

She gave a nod, and tried to hitch the hopelessly big swimming suit up a little to cover a bit more of her breasts. "I'll just put on my clothes."

By the time she'd gotten dressed and they'd walked her to her room, the heat of his temper had morphed into something that could cut through the hull of the *Barrist*.

She was under his care, and someone on this ship, someone he trusted, had attacked her.

Everyone he'd contacted for an emergency meeting was waiting when he and Dimitara entered the conference room.

Dimitara had been quiet since they'd left Rose in her quarters, but as soon as the door closed behind them, before she'd even taken her seat, she pointed a finger at him. "What are you going to do about this, Captain?"

He eased himself into his chair and surveyed the oval conference table. All his senior officers were in attendance, and he wished that somehow he could have found a diplomatic way to exclude Dimitara, but given her fury, the fall-out would not be worth it. He'd tried to suggest she stay with Rose, but it had been obvious Rose wanted time on her own, and Dimitara wanted in on the hunt for whoever had hurt her.

He sighed. "For a start, Rose will now have a security detail assigned to her full-time."

"Are you saying there wasn't one before?" Dimitara's tone was disbelieving.

"I had two officers watching her for her first twenty-four hours, but that was just precautionary. They were pulled back to simply checking on her whereabouts every couple of hours."

"And how do they know her whereabouts?" Dr. Havak asked.

"Her new handheld has a homing device, naturally, but if you must know, all visitor clothing has one embedded in it, as well."

"That's why you didn't want to give her her bags and clothing?" Dimitara sounded as if she could barely take a breath, she was so scandalized.

"I gave her bags back personally this afternoon," Dav told her, but that *had* been one of the reasons they had wanted her in their clothes. Especially in the beginning.

"What does it matter, anyway?" Appal's voice cut through the tension. "She's been attacked on our own ship. That either means someone got on board without our knowledge, which will be an unprecedented breach, or we have someone on the crew who wants her dead."

"She's only been here for two days, how could she have made any enemies in that time?" Havak asked.

Borji cleared his throat. Opened his mouth and then closed it again.

Dav turned to him, eyes narrowed. "Spit it out."

Borji sighed. "There was a transmission earlier. From an unidentified source."

"When?" Dav sat straighter.

"About an hour before the attack on Rose. They used an old frequency which would probably have gone undetected by us, but fortunately it was detected by the comm system on the Class 5, which seems to be monitoring all comms within a truly staggering range of space. I've set up an alert if anything happens in the Class 5 system, so I got a ping when it came through." He paused, took a sip of water from the glass in front of him. "The signal was a written comm to a private handheld on this ship, asking if Rose was an advanced enough sentient to testify about what the Tecran had done to her. Whether she could ruin the plan."

There was silence in the room.

"Were you able to pin-point which handheld it went to?" Lothric asked him.

Borji shook his head. "But I will. I will make it my mission." He looked like he wanted to throttle the drinking glass in his hand, he was gripping it so tightly. "Whoever received the message had to have planned the communication in advance, or knew there was a chance they would be contacted. They actively planned a way to circumvent my comms system . . ." He scrubbed his hands over his face. "I am going to shut that down."

"Did the owner of the handheld respond?" Dav wondered who the hell on board could be involved in this, but it did solve one mystery, how the Tecran knew to put themselves exactly at the *Barrist's* light jump destination. He'd always thought that was so unlikely as to be impossible, but if someone on board was reporting to them, or whoever had brought them here, that would make a lot more sense.

Borji gave a nod. "The Class 5 comm system had another little sweet surprise for our traitor. I'm not sure why the Class 5 did this, but the outgoing message will look to the sender as if it was sent, but it was blocked. I got notification of the message, but whoever contacted our private handheld user is still waiting for a reply."

"And what did the response say?" Dimitara asked.

"They replied that she was most definitely a danger to their plans."

"That's all?" Havak tugged at his ear.

"All? It says Rose is a threat to what they have planned because she can tell the UC exactly what the Tecran did to her. And not an hour later, someone tries to kill her."

"I think it's safe to assume whoever received the message and sent the confirmation back is the person who decided to eliminate the threat

Rose posed to them." Dav could hardly believe he was saying this. But one aspect of this was winding a thin tendril of relief through him, and that was that it was looking increasingly unlikely that Rose was involved in any of this, other than as an innocent victim.

"Good work," Appal told Borji.

Borji made a face. "To be honest, it's all the Class 5 comm system, not me. I'm just glad I set an alert, that's all."

"So, we were lucky. But this still throws a whole new light on our coming across the Class 5." Appal looked up at Dav, and he appreciated that she'd come to the same conclusion as he had.

"Yes. The chance of us light jumping to exactly the same place as the Class 5 has struck me as highly unlikely from the start. The Tecran captain either didn't know where his light jump was going to end up, given his convincing confusion, or he's a good actor, but someone knew we'd be arriving here, and when, and had the Class 5 waiting for us. Now we know someone on board is in secret contact with another ship, either Tecran or someone else, it's logical they gave our light jump coordinates in advance."

"They were probably planning to attack us as we arrived." Appal tapped her fingers on the table.

"Something obviously went wrong on their side." Dimitara had caught on, too. "Something disabled their ship, it malfunctioned, for whatever reason, and now a smaller Tecran vessel is out there, trying to find out what happened and what kind of trouble they're in from their contact on this ship."

"I actually hope this other ship is Tecran, because if it isn't, I don't know who we're dealing with." Dav wouldn't bet on it either way, though. Because then he came right back to the original sticking point. The fact that they had control of the Class 5, something he couldn't believe the Tecran would ever willingly allow.

"Did anyone see anything after Rose's attack that would help us narrow down who took the secret comm?" Kila asked.

Appal shook her head. "The privacy rules mean no lens feed along that passageway." She didn't bother showing frustration for something she couldn't change. "All the traitor would need to do is walk normally, and no one would really have anything to report."

"They were lucky they weren't caught by someone going to the pool," Lothric said. "They took a risk."

Dav nodded. "I think we can assume this was a crime of opportunity, and they won't get the opportunity again. Rose will have someone watching her at all times from now until we catch this person."

"If we catch them," Lothric said.

"No." Dav looked at them one by one. "One thing I promise. We will catch them."

CHAPTER 20

"WHOEVER RECEIVED that comm asking if you were a danger to their plans was the person who tried to kill you." Sazo's voice was subdued in her ear.

"Yes." Rose pulled on her pajamas and stumbled to her bed. She didn't care if Dav was sending someone to check on her, she could barely keep her eyes open.

She snuggled under the blankets and closed her eyes.

"If I'd been in the system, I could have stopped the pool cover from closing."

She made a sound of agreement. Then forced herself to respond. "But then, perhaps they would simply have tried to drown me, rather than making it look like some kind of weird accident."

Sazo was quiet. "That's true." He didn't say anything for a while, and Rose was almost asleep when he did. "But I might have been able to deduce who was in the area from their movements in the system. I could find out who this would-be murderer is."

"Maybe. But Sazo, I can't let you in if you can't promise that no matter what, you won't kill anyone."

"Now it's anyone, not just the Grih?"

She thought about that. "If someone who is not Grihan is trying to kill you, then I'd accept you defending yourself. But only as a last option. You're so smart, Sazo, I'm sure there are a hundred ways you could deal with someone rather than kill them. And you could ask me. I'd help you find a solution that didn't involve death."

"The Grih will try to hold on to the Class 5."

She forced herself to sit up at that, because she could hear the worry in his voice. "You sort of set that up, Sazo."

He sighed, and her lips twitched at how exactly like her he sounded. "I know. They are so excited about having one. Only, they don't."

"And they never will, because you are the Class 5. Or what makes it such an amazing ship." She spoke slowly, because this had just occurred to her. The Class 5 was what it was because of Sazo. Which meant other Class 5s . . .

She went still, and slid back down under the covers, feeling that at last, she was getting a glimpse of Sazo's plan.

"How do you feel about the Class 5, Sazo?" She realized she'd never asked him this question before. "Is it your hated prison, or your home?"

"I don't know. When you pulled me out of the lock-safe, I'd never felt happier. But the thought of the Grih taking it makes me want to hurt them and scream MINE through all their comm systems, so they have to cover their ears. It *is* mine. The systems are all me. Made by me, or all I've known since the Tecran woke me."

"I think I understand. It's a part of you, but a part that was used against you for a long time. You just need to get used to having that part back, but this time, you're in charge."

"You're right." He sounded calmer. Thoughtful.

"I still say you should introduce yourself, let them know you're happy to ally yourself with them, because they've been so nice to me, and you, me, and Captain Jallan could sail off into the sunset together."

"I don't think Captain Jallan would agree to be my sidekick."

"That's my job, anyway," Rose said, and then gave a huge yawn. "But you could be partners."

"It's a nice idea. Not very realistic, given their feelings on thinking systems." But Sazo sounded like he was considering it.

Rose tried to summon the will to respond, but her eyes felt weighed down with concrete and she closed them.

She'd only slept about ten minutes before the chime above her door sounded. She turned and looked at it. Closed her eyes again.

It didn't stop sounding.

She stumbled out of bed, looked down at herself, and decided the thigh-length sleep shirt was good enough, tried three times to hit the screen to see who it was, and then, when she saw it was Dav, Dr. Havak, Commander Appal and Filavantri, she hit the button with a little bit of temper, and was already half-way back to bed before the door had fully opened.

"We have disturbed you." Filavantri stepped into the room as Rose made it to her bed, and pulled the covers up.

She knew her eyes must be red-rimmed with fatigue, because Havak hurried over to her and whipped out a slim cylindrical instrument and pointed it at her eyes.

"Just very tired," she said to him. "Long day."

"I would agree." He pointed it at her abdomen. "Your lungs seem to be fine, even though someone tried to drown you."

"I told Captain Jallan and Filavantri that I was okay."

"You have to concede that we would be remiss if we didn't make sure," Havak said, and she was forced to nod.

"Rose, can you remember anything about what happened that could help us track down who was responsible?" Appal crouched down beside her bed, and Rose noticed that Dav stood a few steps back, the only one not crowding her.

"He had big hands. Strong hands. He didn't just push me down, he sort of squeezed my head at the same time."

As soon as she said that, Havak pointed the device at her head, and then nodded. "See the bruising here?" He lifted her hair, only half-dried from her shower, and Filavantri sucked in a breath.

"We could measure the marks. That would give us a handspan, which we could use in evidence." Appal sounded very satisfied.

Havak pulled out something else, a special lens, and filmed her bruises.

Filavantri's handheld beeped, and she stood, looked down at the screen in irritation, and then reached out to touch Rose on the hand. "I have to go and speak to my coordinator from the Council. It can't wait. When you've slept, please call me and we can have a meal together."

Rose nodded, and Dr. Havak stood as well. "You seem extraordinarily resilient, and a good rest should see you feeling much better."

He left in Filavantri's wake, leaving her with Appal and Dav.

"I'm glad you're all right." Dav took a step closer, and then, as if understanding how uncomfortable she was with them both towering above her, he sat down on one side of the bed, and taking his lead, Appal sat on the other.

"We think this attack was purely opportunistic. There is someone on board who has something to do with the Class 5's appearance, and they're afraid of what you'll say to the United Council when they get here."

Rose frowned. "But even if I couldn't tell them, even if I was dead, there's lens feed somewhere, surely? And the evidence in the cells themselves?"

Appal nodded. "Yes, but we couldn't find the lens feed until a couple of hours ago." She turned to Dav. "Who knows we found it?"

Dav frowned. "Borji, obviously, yourself, me and Filavantri. I didn't deliberately keep it a secret, but it doesn't make easy watching and there's no reason for anyone else to be informed."

"So it's possible whoever did this was merely buying time until the feed was found, or hoping it had been destroyed. They didn't realize we've had it for hours."

"What about the physical evidence?" Rose was feeling tired again, as the warmth of the blanket seeped into her muscles.

"Damning, yes." Appal said. "But more easily explained away."

"I'll let it be known we have the feed. That should mean there is no need to risk trying to kill Rose again."

"Even then . . ." Appal looked over at Dav, and Rose admired the stark beauty of her face. Her cheekbones were high and sharp, and her hair was a deep chestnut brown, tipped with bronze. "The lens feed tells a story, yes, but it's only when you meet Rose, talk to her, that you realize the full extent of the crime. Because she isn't just an advanced sentient in the technical sense, she is undoubtedly one of us. A fully-realized person who could pass for Grih. Except for the ears." Appal grinned at her as she said that.

"So you're saying even if they knew the lens feed had been found, they'd have tried to kill her, because it's her physical presence that's the danger. When she stands in front of the United Council and testifies, her intelligence will shine through. There will be no way to deny they didn't know what they had in their cell. Something they could more easily do if all we had was the lens feed of Rose, traumatized and in pain." Dav's hand was gripping her blanket, bunching it in his fist so that it slipped a little from her shoulders.

"You agree?" Appal asked him.

"I agree. We make it known we have the lens feed, but there will still be a guard on Rose at all times."

Rose made a face, and then couldn't help the huge yawn that claimed her. When she looked up again, Dav was watching her, eyes narrowed.

"Rose, please cooperate with the guards. We'll find out who did this, but while we do, I want you to be safe."

She gave a nod. She hadn't made it out of the Class 5 alive just to die because she was too stubborn to follow orders.

"We'll let you sleep. There'll be guards outside your door from now on." Appal stood, and looked down at Dav, as if waiting for him to join her.

"I want a quick word with Rose. I'll see you later, Commander." He made no move or sign that the word he wanted to have was anything other than professional, but Rose saw Appal's eyebrows lift fractionally.

She inclined her head and walked out, and as the doors opened for her, Rose saw two guards stand to attention.

She relaxed back into her pillows.

"Are you really all right?" Dav's voice was low. The Grih all had rough voices, but now his held an extra edge. She shot him a surprised look.

"Yes. I wouldn't lie about it. If I was really injured I'd have said."

He leaned forward, ran a finger down her cheek, and unable to help herself, she turned her head and let her lips brush it.

He went still. Then he leaned forward, nuzzled the spot just under her ear, and breathed in deeply.

She lifted her hands and stroked them through his hair, surprised to find the strands a little rough, not as smooth and soft as they looked.

He raised his head, caught her face in his hands, and she saw the temptation to kiss her, the longing to take another step forward, cross his face.

This wasn't fair of her, because if he knew the truth, he would be locking her up, not making out with her, and she turned her head away, looking at the wall.

He drew back a little, cleared his throat, and when she glanced up at him, she thought there was relief as well as hunger in his expression.

This was a bad idea for both of them.

"I didn't just mean if you were physically all right, Rose."

She hunched under the covers, even as she caught hold of the change of subject gratefully. "I'm shaken. But I'm angry, too. I'm going to make every effort to stand in front of the United Council alive and well and make the Tecran wish they'd never so much as laid eyes on me."

"Good." He grinned at her. Then the grin faded. "What I said, earlier, about you being a suspect——"

"Forget it." She shook her head. "You'd have been negligent to look at it any other way. And you're right. I am an unknown entity. You *should* be wary of me. You should keep me at arm's length."

His gaze fixed on hers, and she held it, willing him to understand what she was trying to tell him without breaking her word to Sazo.

He touched her hand, lying on top of the covers. "You're warning me off?"

"I owe you." She closed her eyes against the intense, probing blue of his, then forced herself to look at him again. "I've said it before, and I mean it. And I'm loyal to those I owe. I would never do anything to hurt you or your crew, and if it's in my power to protect you, I will."

"You do know something." He said it slowly. "Tell me. Whatever it is."

She shook her head. "As I said, I'm loyal to those I owe."

He stood, the movement frustrated. He took a few steps to the door, stopped, turned and glared at her, then spun back and walked to the panel to set the door to lock when it closed behind him. When that was done, he stalked out.

She gave a weak smile. Even when he was furious with her, he was protecting her.

She'd be as angry as he was, if their places were reversed.

She stretched out under the covers, wiggled herself into a comfortable position. "Please, Sazo. Tell them."

He didn't answer, or if he did, by that time she'd let sleep take her.

CHAPTER 21

SHE HAD BEEN TRYING to tell him something.

Dav realized it just before he reached the bridge. It had taken him that long to calm down, and go through her words again.

She said she owed him. That she was loyal to those she owed.

Then she implied, oh so subtly, that she owed someone else.

She owed them a lot. More than she owed him, which probably meant she owed them her life.

Maybe Rose hadn't been the only prisoner on that ship. Why would the Tecran have stopped at raiding one world. Why not two or three?

And something else they'd picked up had chosen to save the other prisoners, and kill the captives.

Dav came to a dead stop.

Could it be?

Rose was innocent of the deaths, he was sure of that, but he'd always thought she knew who'd killed the Tecran crew. And from the start she'd all but told him the person or thing who did it was still around.

That's why she'd gone out of the Tecran explorer craft's range on Harmon and warned him to be careful.

He rubbed a hand through his hair slowly, trying to forget how it had felt when Rose had done the same thing, just minutes ago.

She'd been hinting at this right from the start.

And what had she just said? She'd try to protect them if she could. Just remembering her saying that, lying curled up, all delicate limbs and soft smooth skin, made him shiver.

If she thought they needed protecting, then she believed there was still a danger to them out there. She was being pulled from two sides.

The bridge was right in front of him, his senior officers were waiting for him, but he couldn't go to them with this.

It was pure speculation.

And speculation that some of the factions on the United Council or at Battle Center might twist to their advantage, with Rose as some sort of scapegoat.

He lifted his hand to tap his comm and call for Appal, then hesitated, finger poised above his ear.

What could he really tell her?

There was a chance she would insist they go to Battle Center with this, because that's what he'd do, if Rose wasn't involved.

The thought of Rose hauled in for interrogation, even by someone he trusted like Admiral Valu, sat like a cold, hard ball in his stomach. He'd like to think anyone who'd seen the lens feed of what Dr. Fliap had done to her would feel the same.

He lowered his hand.

Maybe he'd read it wrong. Maybe there wasn't some unseen, powerful force lurking in the Class 5. Because if there was, Rose might have to do what she'd just promised, and protect them all.

DAV WAS over on the Class 5, Borji on one side of him, Appal on the other, as the Battle Center group landed in the launch bay. He was running on four hours of sleep and he felt it, the grit in his eyes as bad as if he'd stood too close to a runner at take-off.

He'd waited for the admiral and his team to arrive late the night before, and had settled them in, been up first thing to make sure there would be no surprises when he took the admiral and his group around the Class 5.

If there was someone hidden here, pulling the strings, no one had seen them yet.

Battle Center had sent one other admiral besides Valu, two vice-admirals and a Captain Tio, who was temporarily without a vessel.

Dav was damned if Tio would take the Class 5.

He was certainly hoping for it, Dav could see it in the way he looked around as he walked down the gangplank.

"Welcome." Dav saluted as the party reached the bottom. He knew Admiral Valu, and while he had never met her, Admiral Hoke had a high enough profile that he knew her face.

Rumor had it she was going to be the next Head of Fleet, and looking at the clear, bright intelligence in her eyes, the energy with which she took in her surroundings, Dav believed it. The rest of the party, aside from Captain Tio, seemed to be nothing but high-level gawkers.

He introduced Borji and Appal, and then started with the stores, seeing as they were next to the launch bay.

"The Tecran seem to have traveled extensively." Admiral Hoke reached out and touched a vacuum-packed bale of rare Suidani silk. "Suidani was abandoned as a planet over fifty years ago, and its people scattered everywhere. This much silk is extraordinary."

"We can't even begin to guess all the places they've gone. Rose and the animals from her planet are proof of that." Appal stood to attention.

"And they've hidden or destroyed their mapping files," Borji put in. "So when we say we can't guess where they found Rose, we mean that literally."

"I'm looking forward to meeting the first advanced sentient orange in half a millennium." Hoke inclined her head. "Admiral Valu conveyed that she was mistreated here."

"She was." Dav kept his voice clipped. He wasn't going into the details of it standing around in the dusty gloom of the stores.

Hoke inclined her head but didn't pursue the subject.

Dav moved them out of the stores, over the rest of the ship, taking them through the bridge, the weapons bay, the communal areas.

He left the prison until last.

He wanted the impression of it to be foremost in their minds when they met Rose, which they would do next. He wanted them to understand how extraordinary she was, to be the way she was after living here for three months.

The smell of the place still lingered. No one had come to clean up, as Dimitara had declared the area a crime scene, and the United Council investigators would have to come through here and collect the evidence.

Valu stopped dead when Dav opened the door and they all caught sight of the long line of cells, transparent-walled and tiny, that stretched in both directions.

"How long were they here, did the orange say?" Captain Tio asked, and his voice was hushed for the first time.

"Her name is Rose McKenzie." Dav's tone was short. "She is not 'the orange'. She is a person who was abducted and confined to that cell," he pointed to the small room with its bed and table, its toilet and sink, "for three months. And in that time, she was cut open, prodded and poked, and treated with contempt."

There was silence for the first time in the group.

"You said animals from her planet were held here, too?" Hoke asked, and Dav knew it was to break the tension, as she had the full report on what had happened here already.

"Seven. One was killed on this ship with a lethal injection, the other six were sent to Harmon with Rose. My teams have rounded all but two up, and they are already on board the *Barrist*. We hope to have them all recovered and safe in the *Barrist* by the end of the day." Appal stood to formal attention, her hand resting lightly on the stock of her shockgun.

"You have lens feed evidence of the torture?" One of the vice-admirals, a wiry man in his early seventies with a lined face, asked, and Dav thought for the first time he was taking the experience as more than just an exciting few days out.

"We do." Dav walked over to Rose's cell again. He couldn't help it.

Valu, Hoke and Borji joined him.

"Why did they do it?" Borji asked him. "How could they justify it to themselves?"

"They didn't think they'd ever be caught." Dav said. "In this Class 5, they thought they were invincible, and totally unaccountable."

"Do you think . . ." Borji looked over at him. "The other Class 5s? There are rumors there are five of them. Do you think the same thing is going on on the others, as well?"

Dav did, but before he could answer, a double chime came through his comm from Dimitara.

"I hear you are giving a tour of the Class 5," she said, with no attempt at pleasantries.

"I am."

"I wish you'd let me know. I have the United Council committee here, except one member, who should be arriving shortly by private transport, and they are eager to get on the Class 5, as well. The investigative team is with them, too. Can we join you now?"

"I've just finished the tour, Dimitara. The admirals can take the transport back, and I'll wait for you and your group to get on it and come over."

She hummed, making him wince. "Thank you. We'll be waiting."

"United Council?" Valu asked.

"They're unhappy I gave you a tour without including them. They'll meet your transport in the *Barrist's* launch bay and come over here so I can show them around."

"Don't let them even begin to suggest this is a United Council matter when it comes to the acquisition of the Class 5. We couldn't be deeper into our own space boundaries than we are. This is a Grih ship now, whatever crimes against UC law the Tecran committed on it." Hoke spoke calmly, but Dav saw her hands were tightly fisted.

"Has that been mentioned? That we should hand it over to them?" Appal asked.

"It's the rumor we've been hearing." Valu drew himself up. "It's not happening though. If the Tecran hadn't tortured those oranges, we'd be free and clear, but given they did, we have to give the United

Council some access, but that doesn't give them a right to think the Class 5 is theirs."

"Oh, it's definitely ours," Borji said, and Dav grinned, because he didn't think Borji just meant it was Grihan. He meant it was theirs. The *Barrist's*.

Then Borji's comm chimed and after he tapped it and listened for a few seconds, his face changed.

"Problem?"

"Uh." Borji's gaze flew to his. "We may have a small problem. Captain?" He jerked his head toward the door and walked out, and Dav followed.

Borji signaled to Appal, and she joined them in the corridor.

"The Class 5 weapons system just activated." Borji's forehead was sheened in sweat.

"At the *Barrist*?" Dav lifted a hand to tap his comm, order everyone off his ship, but Borji shook his head.

"Not the *Barrist*. At a small private vessel coming in from the direction of Sector 7."

Appal frowned. "This area has been determined a no-go zone since we found the Class 5. What's a private vessel doing coming this way?"

Borji was tapping at his handheld, flipping through screens and frowning as he relayed his instructions to the device. "The system has identified the vessel as the most likely origination point for the signal that was sent to the *Barrist* about Rose." He looked up. "I'm not sure of the criteria it's programmed to use, but it's classed it as an enemy vessel."

"The Class 5 is a Tecran ship, so I'm assuming it wouldn't identify one of its own vessels as an enemy," Appal said. "That means it's likely this new vessel isn't Tecran and I'd have bet a year's pay whoever sent that message was. Does this mean someone other than the Tecran wants to protect them? That some other group is involved in whatever the Tecran were doing here?"

Borji grunted at that, flipped through more screens.

Dav tapped his comm. "Farso Lothric," he directed, and was put through immediately. "Lothric, what have you got for me on a small incoming vessel?"

"You mean Councilor Fu-tama's ship?" Lothric sounded surprised. "It just appeared on our screens. How did you know about it? I thought you were over on the Class 5."

"I am." Dav didn't explain further. "Who is Fu-tama? Why isn't he with the other councilors?"

"He's the Garmman delegate. He wasn't at United Council headquarters when the message came through from Liaison Officer Dimitara, so he got away as soon as he could and came privately."

"One moment." Dav tapped his comm to mute his connection. "How large a chance is it that this is the vessel that sent that secret comm to someone on board the *Barrist*?"

Borji stopped what he was doing, looked up. "The Class 5 system gives it 79%."

"The vessel is the private transport of a Garmman councilor. He missed the official ride and had to take his own. Dimitara said something about it to me earlier when she asked about the tour."

"So chances are it's just a coincidence this vessel has arrived when it has. It probably had nothing to do with the comm about Rose."

"The system is blocking every attempt I've made at access." Borji looked up, and his eyes were wide. "It's aiming a weapon that I've never even heard of at the Garmman vessel. The councilor has two minutes before he's blown away."

Dav tapped his comm. "Lothric, order Councilor Fu-tama to stop his craft immediately. Back thrusters would be better."

"Sir?" Lothric sounded more than confused, Dav thought he sounded panicked. Then he remembered Lothric had cut his teeth in Battle Center on the Garmman home world, and probably knew Fu-tama. If he had plans to go back to the diplomatic corps, which Dav thought he would after his mandatory stint of two years on active duty, Lothric might believe giving an order like that to a United Council representative would be career inhibiting.

"Patch me through to the councilor now." Dav had no plans to enter the diplomatic corp. And he didn't care what Fu-tama thought.

"This is Captain Dav Jallan of the Grihan Battle Center ship *Barrist*. The Tecran vessel we have commandeered started an auto-routine when your vessel came into range and its weapons system has you locked on. Stop immediately, and employ back thrusters until we can deal with the problem."

Dav heard a squawk of alarm from the bridge, although Fu-tama had not put them on visual comms when he'd been connected.

Borji flicked his fingers at the handheld and gave a nod. "He's reversing."

They waited a minute in tense silence, and Dav was aware that the admirals had picked up something was happening. They'd both stepped into the passage, but to give them credit, neither tried to interfere.

"The weapons system has disengaged." Borji lifted his arm and wiped the sweat from his forehead.

"Councilor Fu-tama, you can stop where you are, but do not attempt to come forward until we give you permission."

"I'm needed for a full United Council meeting." Fu-tama finally came on-screen, and Dav remembered seeing the Garmman councilor before on visual comms reports. He had the bulging forehead and stocky build that was the Garmman norm, his silver-gray hair the only indication of his age. He'd had cosmetic work done to his face, and it didn't have a line on it, but Dav couldn't help thinking it was more a case of having erased the life from it, rather than reversed the aging process.

"We'll send out a runner to fetch you, see if that will work. But for now, your vessel will have to remain where it is unless you want it to be fired on."

Both Hoke and Valu were close enough to hear the last part of his conversation, and Dav could see the shock on their faces.

"Did you just threaten to fire on a vessel?" Valu asked. Dav found it interesting that he didn't seem that concerned by the idea.

"No, sir. Remember when I briefed you about our taking the Class 5, I told you we didn't have control of the weapons system. It just locked on to a private ship entering the area, and we ordered it to reverse course until the system stood down."

"What's a private vessel doing here? This is a no-go zone." Hoke's eyes flared with temper.

"The vessel belongs to Councilor Fu-tama. The *Barrist* was

informed he was coming in, but obviously the Class 5 doesn't care about that, and when he came into range, it got a lock on him."

"Do you know why?" Hoke asked Borji.

Borji looked over at Dav, unwilling to answer. Dav agreed. There was no way he was discussing the clandestine comms someone on the *Barrist* had received in hearing distance of some of Appal's team, but more particularly, the vice-admirals and Captain Tio.

He shook his head. "There are other issues in play here, and I would need to have you alone on the *Barrist* before I would feel comfortable giving you the information."

"Then I think we're done here." Hoke straightened her jacket.

"I still have to take the United Council representatives through the Class 5."

Hoke shook her head. "They can wait."

CHAPTER 22

FILAVANTRI WAS ANGRY.

Rose could hear it in the clipped, breathless way she spoke when Rose asked her if she was available to have breakfast with her.

"I'm not sure," the liaison officer said. "We're waiting on Captain Jallan's pleasure. He was going to take us around the Class 5, but something more important seems to have come up."

"That's fine." Rose kept her voice light. She didn't like the idea of Dav and Filavantri at odds. They were her two closest allies on board. "I'll have breakfast in my room."

"One moment . . ." Filavantri sounded thoughtful. "Rose, would you agree to an informal breakfast with the United Council representatives?" She made that humming sound. "I had planned to introduce you later anyway, so switching things around would mean we could stay on schedule."

Rose ruffled her fingers through hair still damp from her shower. She really didn't want to meet the Battle Center group, or the United Council group, but there was no avoiding it. And if it calmed Filavantri down . . . "I suppose I have to some time. Now is as good a time as any."

"We won't meet in your room. That would be too much of an invasion. I'll have your guards bring you to the private dining room off the officers' mess."

"All right." Rose leaned against the table when Filavantri disconnected, looked at herself in the mirror. She looked rested after her deep sleep, and she was wearing her hyr fabric, fashioned into a form-fitting top and trousers.

"We have to go to breakfast with the United Council," she said to Sazo.

"I gathered." He sounded subdued. "Be careful, Rose. I think one of the councilors is behind some of what happened to you."

"Why do you say that?"

"Because an unidentified vessel came into our territory and I considered shooting it. There's no question in my mind it was the vessel that sent the comm to whoever is betraying the Grih on the *Barrist*. It belongs to one of the United Council representatives, the member for Garmma."

"I'm surprised the Barrist didn't take aim, too, if it was unidentified."

"It wasn't unidentified to *them*," Sazo said. "Just to me, because I'm not in their system yet."

"Sazo——"

"Rose. The clock is ticking. Get me into the system."

She sighed. "I don't even know if I can."

"Just let me know the login for the standalone handheld. I'll see what I can do."

She tugged a brush through her hair, pulling harder than she needed to. "I'm afraid, Sazo. I'm worried you're going to panic or get too angry, and do something you can't take back."

There was a chime at the door, and smoothing a hand over her hair, Rose went to check the screen to see who it was. Her guards stood to attention outside, waiting for her to answer.

She went back for her Tecran handheld, relieved to put off this argument with Sazo a little longer. "I'll take this with me, so you can listen in." She didn't wait for him to answer, she tucked her crystal necklace below her neckline, opened the door, and stepped into the corridor with her guards.

It was Vree Halim and Jay Xaltro. They must be on permanent Rose duty.

Jay Xaltro stepped back, and then bent her head over her hands. "I apologize for yesterday. I should have shielded you from the crowd, but I didn't realize you would be so upset by the applause."

Rose looked up at her, trying to read any censure into that statement. Perhaps there was a hint that she thought Rose was being a little too delicate.

Rose shook her head. She refused to explain herself and her reaction. She might be delicate at the moment, but she'd come by it honestly. "You're taking me to breakfast with the United Council?"

They nodded, and in less than five minutes they were ushering her into a small room off a well-appointed dining room. There was a central table with twelve chairs, and eleven of them were already filled. Two seats were occupied by Tecran, and Rose froze in place, trying to breathe.

One of the Tecran noticed her reaction and stood, glaring at her, and Rose finally found she could move, stepping back and bumping into Vree Halim's chest.

He lifted a hand to her shoulder and then stepped to her side, hand on the stock of his gun.

There was a sudden silence in the room.

Filavantri had stood when they came in, and she scowled at the Tecran councilors. "Sit down, Councilor Yir. You've been told Rose has suffered abuse by your people, leaping to your feet in a threatening manner is not helpful."

Yir glared at her. "So far, that abuse is nothing more than the word of an orange——"

"Enough." A man stood. He didn't raise his voice, but there was such command in his tone, everyone fell silent.

He was Bukarian, like Filavantri, and Rose noticed there was a second Bukarian councilor as well, so two of each of the signatories were represented, and Filavantri, as the liaison.

Rose should have expected there would be Tecran present, but she hadn't. She'd hoped never to see one again.

"Welcome, Rose McKenzie." The man who spoke looked over at

her and bowed. "I'm the chair of this committee, and my name is Kaniga Jamoria. Councilors Yir and Nuu are understandably upset at the idea that their compatriots would do the things they are accused of. However, that is no excuse for rudeness, or threats."

He lifted a handheld, tapped the screen, and all around the room soft pings sounded. "I've sent the lens feed evidence of Rose's treatment at Dr. Fliap and Captain Gee's hands to all of you. You can view it later, but Rose's testimony is not the only evidence of wrongdoing, and I'd like to stress that, as I gather there has already been an attempt on her life. Killing her will not make these accusations or this investigation go away." He paused and Rose saw varying degrees of shock on the faces around the table at the news. "In fact, I'd say if anything happens to Rose, this matter will never be laid to rest until the truth is discovered."

"Are you accusing the Tecran of trying to kill her?" Yir's voice was hushed.

"I don't know who tried to kill her, but they obviously thought they had something to lose by her being alive. At the time, no one but a select few knew of this lens feed evidence, so they perhaps assumed if Rose was dead, her accusations would die with her. That is not the case. And that is ignoring the physical evidence in the cells, as well as Dr. Fliap's own notes and observations. All of which have been secured and make for damning reading."

There was another round of silence.

"Rose? Would you like to take a seat?" Filavantri looked stricken, and guilty.

She obviously hadn't thought the meeting would be so confrontational, and Rose looked at the place set out for her, with her favorite food, and realized it felt like a stone was lodged in her throat. She didn't feel hungry, but there was a cup of grinabo, and when Filavantri pulled out her chair, she slowly left Vree Halim's side, and sat.

Jay Xaltro had taken up a position near the door Rose realized, her angle such that she could have covered both Rose and Halim if someone had started shooting. She sent both her guards a small, grateful smile.

"Does she talk?" Yir glared at her.

"I talk." She spoke Grihan, even though he'd asked the question in Tecran. "I have a lot to say, but I was told this was simply an informal gathering, to meet everyone. I didn't realize you would expect me to go into the details of my imprisonment over breakfast."

There was another round of silence. It was obviously a day of shocks for the councilors.

"She speaks Grihan," one of the Grihan councilors exclaimed.

Rose stared at her. "Yes."

The woman blushed. "My apologies for talking around you. I thought communicating with you would be difficult, but . . . how do you speak Grihan?"

"I was given a handheld with all five United Council languages while I was imprisoned. Perhaps Dr. Fliap wanted to know how fast I could learn them. I had nothing else to do, so I learned Grihan and Tecran, and can understand a little of the other three."

Councilor Yir tapped the edge of his handheld on the table, agitated.

"We will need in-depth questioning, to find out where she is from. She is clearly as advanced a sentient as anyone at this table." The woman who spoke was long and thin, almost insect-like with her elegant limbs and large eyes. Her voice was soft.

"We haven't come across her like in 500 years," her fellow councilor agreed. "Her discovery is breathtaking, and yet, soured by the terrible circumstances under which she was found."

"Her resemblance to the Grih is also astonishing." The other Grihan councilor was staring at her.

"And I believe she is what you call a music-maker," Filavantri said, and Rose shot her a horrified look.

"I am not a music-maker." She said it firmly.

"Just your speaking voice sounds like music to my ears," the woman who'd first exclaimed over her Grihan said. "I would love to hear you sing."

Rose hunched over her plate, and forced herself to pick up a piece of bread, put it in her mouth, and chew.

Beside her, Filavantri put a hand on her knee and squeezed, without looking at Rose or acknowledging the gesture.

She would have to face this, strong, proud and dauntless, Rose realized. The alternative was curling up in a corner and giving up, and there was no way she was doing that.

ADMIRAL HOKE LEANED back in her chair and gave Dav a narrow-eyed look. "You're saying there's a traitor on board the *Barrist*? Someone in clandestine communication with another ship, which may or may not be the vessel Councilor Fu-tama arrived in?"

Dav nodded. "Yes."

"And the Class 5 locked onto Councilor Fu-tama's ship because there was a high chance it was the same ship that sent the original comm? A comm it clearly sees as an enemy communication."

Borji shrugged. "It must have a sequence programmed that anyone using that specific comm method is likely to be an enemy."

"This means there could be a third party involved. Someone hostile to the Tecran who killed the Class 5 crew, but just happened to do it right in the middle of our territory. And if it was Councilor Fu-tama who communicated with the *Barrist*, that third party could be Garmman."

Dav had to give it to Admiral Hoke, she got right down to the heart of the matter. He sent her a confirming nod.

"So what are you doing to uncover the traitor?" Valu tipped back his chair.

"Everything we can." Dav thought of Rose after the attempt on her life, clinging to the side of the pool. "He tried to kill Rose."

Hoke went still, and then her chair came down with a thump. "How?"

"Tried to drown her while she was swimming." Appal crossed her arms over her chest.

Valu swore, drawing out the obscenity until a sharp look from Hoke shut him up.

"She didn't see him, obviously, or you'd have him." Hoke pushed back her chair.

"No." Dav stood as well, and just then, his comm unit chimed. He accepted the comm, and went very still as he listened to Jay Xaltro. "I'll be right there."

As he turned for the door, Admiral Hoke stepped in his way. "We aren't done here, Captain."

"We are for now." Dav stepped around her. "Rose has been thrown to the wolves."

He tried not to run on the way to the officers' mess. Appal, obviously deciding she'd better come with him, easily kept up.

"What is it?" Her boots slapped in rhythm with his as they strode.

"Dimitara invited Rose to breakfast with her, and brought the whole United Council. Xaltro says Rose didn't expect the Tecrans and was visibly upset by their presence. They aren't that happy to see her, either."

"Well, she's about to land them in a heap of trouble." Appal didn't sound very sorry for them.

Dav shot her a look and she grinned at him, easing some of the tension and fury he felt.

Xaltro and Halim would keep her safe, and there was no way the Tecran or anyone else would openly attack her in front of their fellow councilors on a Grihan ship. At the most, she was upset and unhappy, but he had found over and over that she was made from very strong stuff.

He managed to slow his pace to something resembling a brisk walk by the time he reached the officers' mess and stepped into the private dining area. Appal was right behind him, and everyone looked up as they entered the room.

Dimitara looked relieved and chastened. "Everything all right, Captain?"

"You tell me, Dimitara." Dav looked deliberately around the room.

Rose lifted her head, caught his gaze, and took a sip from her mug. He had heard of knees going weak, but he had never experienced it before. The look in her eyes——relief, happiness to see him and something that was suspiciously close to affection——made him feel a little lightheaded.

"Given your inability to take us to the Class 5, I arranged for an informal meeting with Rose instead." There was no mistaking the defensiveness in her voice.

"Is that so? I thought we had agreed that when it came to Rose, we would consult with one another before anything was arranged."

Dimitara looked down. "I had forgotten that. You're right, and you have my apologies."

Yurve *shit,* Dav thought. She'd had a little tantrum because he couldn't take her around the Class 5, and she'd used Rose as a way to get back at him. He let his thoughts show in his expression, and she had the grace to blush.

"Rose, are you done here?"

She stood and gave him one of her sweet, sweet smiles. "Thank you, Captain, yes I am." She turned to the councilors. "It was nice to meet you, and Liaison Officer Dimitara tells me there is a formal hearing I will have to attend, so I will see you later." She gave a formal Grihan bow.

"Be very careful when you face the formal hearing." Councilor Yir stood. "Everything said there must be the truth, and if you are caught in a lie, the consequences will be very serious."

"I will make sure Rose knows exactly what is expected of her. And hopefully the councilors all know what is expected of them." Dimitara rose as well, narrowed her eyes at the Tecran. "That no matter whether one of their own race is under review, they have to act with complete impartiality."

Yir's eyes widened at that, and he opened his mouth. "That is outrageous——"

"Any more outrageous than the veiled threat you just delivered to our witness?" A councilor from Fitali asked.

Yir sat down, and Councilor Jamoria cleared his throat. "Perhaps it is best that from now on, Rose only meets with a member of the council under formal, recorded circumstances."

Yir hissed, his honor clearly impinged.

Rose had reached his side, and Dav put a hand on her shoulder, and it was only when he noticed Councilor Fu-tama staring at them both with a strange look of horror on his face that he realized he was gripping the fabric of Rose's shirt, pulling down the neckline a little.

He gentled his hold, bowed to the councilors and propelled her out of the room with Appal going ahead. Xaltro and Halim took up the rear, and Dav noted with approval that Xaltro walked backward, keeping her eyes on the councilors until the door closed behind them.

As soon as they were in the mess hall, Rose lost her stiff posture.

"Thanks for riding to the rescue again." She closed her eyes and shuddered.

He wanted to pull her closer, but this was neither the time or the place.

"You shouldn't have needed rescuing, not on the *Barrist*." He couldn't help the harshness of his tone, and he saw her wince.

He knew she liked Filavantri Dimitara, but the liaison officer had placed her in an untenable situation, and he wasn't going to let Dimitara off easily.

His comm chimed, and he made a face.

"The admirals?" Appal asked.

He gave a nod. His hand was still on Rose's shoulder and he gave it a gentle squeeze. "I have to go. Will you be all right?"

She looked up at him and nodded.

"I'll walk you to your room, stay with you for a bit, Rose. If you wouldn't mind the company?" Appal stood with hands behind her back, looking genuinely friendly, but Dav knew her too well. She hadn't spent any time with Rose since they met down on Harmon, and she would want to see if she could coax anymore information out of Rose about who attacked her.

"I would like that." Rose gave a small smile and then looked around the officers' mess. "Can we bring breakfast with us? I was too upset to eat in there."

Dav felt a renewed surge of annoyance as his comm chimed again, and with a formal bow, he left Rose, Appal and the guards and headed back to the two admirals, who were no doubt just as annoyed as he was.

They hadn't liked being left in the dark and they hadn't liked him leaving before they were finished with him.

He must be contemplating career suicide, because he no longer gave a damn.

CHAPTER 23

ROSE HAD LIKED Jia Appal since she'd first realized she was a woman. It had calmed her, no matter how illogical it might have been.

Now she realized her first impression had been a good one, as Appal set the table for them, and made some fresh grinabo from the little station built into the wall of her room.

She knew the commander could only be here to ask her questions, there was no way she had time for a leisurely breakfast with the United Council here, the Tecran in the holding cells and the Class 5 locking weapons onto approaching ships. But she didn't mind. Appal was trying to set her at ease, and Rose would help her any way she could.

She sat, took a sip of the hot grinabo and leaned back in her chair. "What would you like to know?"

Appal paused on her way to the table with her own cup of grinabo in her hand and raised her eyebrows. "Was I that obvious?"

Rose shook her head. "You're a busy woman, there's no way you'd be taking time off for breakfast unless it was to question me."

Appal held her gaze as she sat. "This is going to sound condescending, but I keep forgetting you have as advanced a sentience as we do. You understand exactly what's going on, don't you?"

Rose kept her face blank. Unfortunately, she knew way more than

Appal, and the commander might not forgive her for it when it all came out. "Perhaps you'd like to spread the word about that."

Appal nodded. "The captain has already made it clear he won't tolerate anyone calling you an orange, or talking down to you."

Rose hid her reaction with another sip. Dav Jallan was protective and sweet. It made lying to him so much harder. "The captain hasn't treated me as anything other than his equal. Not once."

Appal toyed with a strange mix of things in a bowl which Rose had decided not to try. That could be an adventure for another day. "He thinks highly of you."

Rose brushed the tips of her fingers across her cheekbone. "I think highly of him. I'd be gryak lunch without him."

"It's not just that, though, is it?" Appal's tone came out a little rougher than usual.

"No." Rose fiddled with the bread on her plate. "He's supported me and helped me since we met, and I'd be lying if I said I didn't appreciate it." She bit into the bread, took a moment to enjoy the nutty taste of it, and then, edgy at having to explain her feelings for Appal's boss, she set it down. "So, again, what do you want to know?"

Appal blew out a breath. "I want to know who tried to kill you and what that Class 5 is doing in the middle of our territory with a mostly dead crew."

Rose huffed out a laugh. "So, not much?"

Appal stared at her and then laughed as well. "I take it you don't think you can help me?"

Rose shook her head. "I wish I could."

"Impressions are better than nothing. What were your first thoughts in the pool room? Anything you can think of."

"He was big, but then, you're all big. I think I was overcome with the shock of how he squeezed my head when he pushed me down, like adding insult to injury, you know? Like he wanted to hurt me, as well as kill me. It wasn't just a job to him." She rubbed the side of her temple. "After that, I just thought about staying alive."

"So, it could be personal? But who have you had dealings with?"

Rose lifted her hands and shoulders. "Who have I pissed off, you mean?" She shook her head. "Not many people. But they don't have to know me personally to not like what I stand for."

"What you stand for?"

Rose bet Appal knew exactly what she meant, but she obliged her.

She lifted a finger. "An orange, unlike any seen for hundreds of years." She lifted a second finger. "The unlikely survivor of a strange mass death." She lifted a third finger. "Someone who just by existing is going to bring some nasty trouble on the heads of the Tecran and set the United Council at odds with each other." She blew out a breath and lifted her pinky. "And a music-maker who doesn't want to be a music-maker."

Appal's eyebrows rose at the last point. She cocked her head in that strange, alien way she had down on Harmon. "You don't want to be a music-maker?"

Appal said music-maker in the same reverent tones as everyone else, and the hot, tight feeling of impending failure gripped her again. Rose shuddered. "I understand it's a great honor, and I've tried to be respectful of that, but I gather my reluctance is seen by some as an insult."

"I'll keep an eye on that. Rose, you've nothing to apologize for. You've been taken against your will, and you don't owe us anything. We owe you, because a United Council member nation was responsible for your abduction." Appal stood, adjusting the bulky shockgun strapped to her leg. Rose realized she hadn't even taken it off to eat her breakfast.

Her sharp, fine-chiseled features, spiky chestnut hair and long, lean frame came together to make a picture of strength and competence Rose felt she couldn't match. "Am I confined to my room?"

Appal shook her head. "Get the guards to take you to the gym if you'd like some exercise, but the officers' one, not the main one. And try not to take chances."

Rose relaxed a little. "You may feel I don't owe anyone anything, but tell me how to get out of singing or declaring myself a music-maker without stirring the pot even more?"

Appal's look was gentle. "You *are* a music-maker, Rose. Your not wanting to take the role is the issue, not your fundamental nature."

"If you knew anything about the place I'm from, you would laugh at the idea of me as a revered singer." She couldn't hide her own panic at the thought.

"Use that fact." Appal gave a slow nod. "You're from a different culture, a different world entirely, and so I think you could simply ask for time to adjust. That will give you the space you need."

She could do that. She could do that for a long, long time.

"What do you specifically dislike about it?" Appal must have seen the calculation on her face.

"The attention." Rose flushed. "The sense that I'm letting everyone down. Their expectations are so high. Also, I don't understand what is socially acceptable with regard to touching or personal space among the Grih, but I was too crowded yesterday, which is why I ran."

"We are affectionate, and like to touch, but only with permission."

Rose thought back to the pool. To the way Dav had brushed his fingers over her cheeks, and her breasts. "Are any areas of the body considered more off-limits than others?"

Appal nodded. "Lightly touching an arm, or a shoulder or back in passing, or to illustrate a point, that is all right."

"And other areas?"

"Anywhere else, and that's considered a sexual advance," Appal said, her eyebrows high on her forehead.

"Even when offering comfort?" Rose's mouth felt a little dry, but then she'd always known what she and Dav were dancing around.

"Even then." Appal watched her with bright interest. "You're speaking from personal experience, aren't you? Already? You've only been on board three days."

Rose could feel her face heat. She said nothing.

"When we pulled you out of that collapsed cave, and the captain handed you up to me, I couldn't believe how small and heavy you were. You looked like a cuter, curvier version of us, and as harmless as a kapoot, but that's not the truth at all, is it?"

Rose made a face. "I don't feel particularly dangerous, not when I'm standing next to you. You look like you could kick ass and take names with one hand tied behind your back."

Appal snorted out a laugh. "We must have frightened you when we landed on Harmon."

Rose tipped her head to one side. "Yes. When you pointed those guns as me, I was frightened, but when you retracted your helmet and I saw your face, I relaxed."

"I noticed that. How were you reassured?"

Rose smiled. "I liked the look of you."

"You liked the look of me? I'm half a foot taller and I had a gun pointed at your head."

Rose's smile widened. "I know."

Appal's comm chimed, and she shook her head, perplexed, as she answered it. "I have to go," she said when she tapped off.

"Trouble?" Rose had to force herself not to look toward her Tecran handheld.

Appal shook her head. "The United Council is being taken around the Class 5, and I need to arrange security."

"Okay." Rose walked her to the door and when it shut behind her, she closed her fist around the crystal at her neck, and did look over at her handheld.

She couldn't dance on this fence much longer. She either had to get Sazo into the system, or sell him out.

Neither option appealed.

"WHAT DID YOU DO TO THEM?" Appal's eyes were on the councilors as they walked down the runner's ramp into the launch bay, her words soft.

Dav took up position beside her, standing smartly to attention with shoulders square, hands behind his back. He gave each group a courteous nod as they passed by.

"I think the reality of those cells was more than they were prepared for." He realized his hands were back in fists, just as they had been on the Class 5. He needed to stay away from the stark evidence of Rose's abuse if he wanted to keep an even temper. Although just the thought of it seemed to be enough to put him on the edge of rage.

Each councilor had had a similar reaction, except the Tecran, who, if anything, had seemed even more shocked than their colleagues. Councilor Fu-tama's expression had given away nothing except anger, he was all but vibrating with it by the end of the tour, and some deep-seated instinct told Dav there was something more to it than outrage over sentient being abuse.

Admiral Hoke was the last one off the runner and she joined them, her eyes following the councilors as Dimitara shepherded them out. "Whatever stunt that liaison officer pulled this morning to light a fire under you, she's certainly redeemed herself now. Her forcing the councilors to watch some of the lens feed while they were in the cells was a stroke of genius." She tipped her head in Yir and Nuu's direction. "The Tecran don't know what to do now."

Dav had already noticed that the Tecran were keeping themselves slightly apart, their heads together, shoulders hunched.

No one tried to bridge the gap and join them.

"They're already feeling the chill."

Dav turned at the rich vein of satisfaction he could hear in Hoke's voice. "Is that a good thing? Do we want a rift in the United Council?"

Hoke held his gaze. "We do when we're trying to hold on to a very advanced piece of their technology."

"Is the Class 5 worth a split? Worth a war?"

Hoke raised her brows. "Hopefully it won't come to that. I know it's harsh, but the fact that they so flagrantly contravened the SBA makes them pushing the issue as far as war unlikely. They'll have no allies, not after what the councilors saw today. The chances of them risking fighting us when we have the moral high ground is very small."

Appal made a sound and Hoke turned her attention to his commander, which was a good thing, because it meant she didn't see the disgust on his face. He took a deep breath.

"So, Rose's loss is our gain?"

"I can't go back in time and change what happened to Rose. But if I can use what happened to her to secure a Class 5, then I will do so without a qualm."

Dav knew he would have been in agreement if he didn't know

Rose. And he couldn't fault Hoke's logic but . . . "If you're going to use what happened to Rose as leverage, she'd better be guaranteed a place in Grih society."

"You making demands, Captain?" Hoke's tone was suddenly cool.

"You want to use Rose and then abandon her?" Dav countered, equally cool.

Hoke blew out a breath. "I haven't thought that far ahead. But your point is made. If she's no danger to us, of course we'll look after her. I gather she's small and unaggressive."

Appal snorted out a laugh.

"Something amusing, Commander?" Hoke turned her annoyed expression to Appal again.

"You obviously haven't met Rose," Appal said. "Or you wouldn't be talking about her as if describing a new species of animal."

"I need to remedy that as soon as possible." Hoke said. She flicked at her sleeve for the time. "I have to brief Battle Center, and then I'll go find her."

Dav narrowed his eyes. "Let me know when you're ready, and I'll take you to her."

"I don't need a minder, Captain. And I want to see this Rose without outside interference." Hoke narrowed her eyes right back at him. Then she turned on her heel and walked away.

Dav looked down, saw his fists were just as tight as they had been on the Class 5, back in Rose's old cell.

"Let's go somewhere private," he said to Appal, and she didn't say anything, she just nodded and led the way to her room.

Two guns lay on the large, low table between the two couches in her suite, and she picked up the cloth she'd been cleaning them with and got back to work.

Dav flopped down opposite her, closed his eyes and tipped back his head.

"Let me guess," Appal said, her voice without inflection. "You're trying to work out whether warning Rose that Admiral Hoke is about to descend on her would be a technical breach of orders or not."

Dav didn't open his eyes, but he smiled. "You know me so well."

"Yes." She had gone serious now, and at last he lifted his head, opened his eyes. She was looking at him, gun forgotten in her hand. "I do know you, and you've been by the book ever since we met. Ambitious, not quite a suck-up, but respectful of your superiors, and a real team player."

"So?" He frowned at her, but he knew where this was going.

"What's happened?"

He blew out a breath, and realized he couldn't answer.

"I'll tell you." Appal set the gun back on the table. "Rose McKenzie happened."

"It's not just Rose," Dav told her, sliding his hands over his knees. "It's the Class 5. This whole situation."

"Yurve. Shit." Appal shook her head. "You're all over that Class 5, just like I'd expect you to be, but when it comes to Rose . . . you have got to know there is something she's holding back. She's the worst liar I've ever met. Why isn't she in interrogation? Why aren't you coming down harder on her?"

"You've seen the lens feed. Do you want us to go into the same category as the Tecran?"

Appal winced at that, then shook her head. "I'm not saying torture her, I'm saying ask her some hard questions, and if she can't answer them, don't shrug and then give her the run of the ship."

"She doesn't *have* the run of the ship." Dav rubbed a frustrated hand through his hair. "She's been watched since she arrived, and now we have guards on her round the clock. Do you genuinely think she's a danger?" He knew there was too much uncertainty in his voice. He was second-guessing himself way too much. Not his usual style. Appal had that right.

She blew out a breath. "No. She's no danger to us. But she's in the middle of something that is, and for some reason she isn't sharing."

Dav watched her, wondered if now was the time to put forward his hypothesis on that. Then she stood, turned her back on him and walked over to make them grinabo.

"She asked me what the accepted stages were for us, in getting into a relationship with someone." Appal kept her back to him.

"What?"

His commander looked briefly over her shoulder. "What the stages are. How we deal with personal space. She was trying to understand where something was going, between herself and another Grih, I presume, and didn't know how to interpret the signals."

"Who?" He kept his voice steady. Forced himself not to stand. "Who the hell is making moves on her?"

Appal turned with a cup of grinabo in each hand. "Well, to be honest . . ." She set his mug down in front of him. "I thought it was you."

Oh.

He tried to fight the heat rushing to his cheeks.

"Why did she discuss it with you?" Thank the stars she had, was all he could think. If there was one person on board who would take his secrets to the grave, it was Jia Appal.

"I don't know. Kila would be the obvious choice for questions on social interactions, but it seems that while Rose is happy to cooperate with her, she doesn't really trust her."

"She's liked you since the very first moment she saw you. I remember wondering why she gave you that big smile when we first pulled her out of the cave on Harmon." Dav remembered feeling annoyed by it. He'd wanted that smile for himself.

"Yes. She told me that seeing me put her at ease in a stressful moment when she was surrounded by big, mean-looking aliens all pointing guns at her."

He choked out a laugh, realizing that's exactly what had happened.

"But you were one of the big, mean-looking aliens holding the guns."

Appal nodded. "I pointed that out to her, and she just gave me that sweet smile again, and said: exactly."

They sat in comfortable silence for a while.

"I'm running in the dark here." Dav didn't know where that had come from, but it was true, he realized.

"Just be careful." Appal lifted her shockgun, sighted away from him down the barrel. Blew away a little piece of grit. "We're in the middle of something very dangerous."

He would be careful. If only he knew how.

CHAPTER 24

THE OFFICERS' GYM was full of interesting equipment, but Rose chose something that looked like a treadmill to start with, just to get warmed up. There was a hologram option and she fiddled around with it, choosing a random Grihan planet, Nastra, as the setting.

"Whoa. That looks chilly." She looked sideways at Halim and Xaltro, leaning, hands on the stocks of their shockguns, against the gym wall, then back at the white, wind-swept landscape.

After five minutes, the all white background got boring, and she switched to another Grihan world, Calianthra. It was better. Massive trees stretched high above her, and the ground was thick with fern-like plants. She settled in to it and power-walked for another fifteen minutes before she decided to try another piece of equipment.

She chose to avoid the sneering expression she was sure she'd find on Jay Xaltro's face if she asked how to work the . . . thing . . . that snagged her attention. It was a square platform with an eight-foot metal pole on each corner. There was a button on the side, and she pressed it and then stepped up into the square. Pressure swirled around her, and she was lifted up. She moved her legs and arms and finally got it.

There was strong resistance to everything she did, as if she was deep underwater. She had fun punching the air, kicking invisible enemies, running as fast as she could.

When she stilled, she sank down and stepped out, breathing hard. "That was awesome." She gave a laugh, walked over to grab her towel, and realized that the feeling she'd had when she first stepped out onto Harmon, and had felt ever since, of having more power here, was intensified after her resistance training.

She blotted the sweat from her brow and eyed the far wall. It was padded, and the floor looked pretty padded, as well.

Time for a Matrix moment, she decided. Why the hell not?

She dropped the towel and ran full tilt at the wall, only peripherally aware of Vree Halim stepping toward her in surprise.

She jumped, higher than she ever could have done on Earth, angling her body so her feet hit the wall as if she was planning to walk up it, then she pushed off and flipped, landing on the sprung floor with so much excess energy, she bounced.

Seeing she was airborne again, she flipped herself again, did a full somersault and landed with knees bent, hands out.

She let out a whoop, hands on her hips, her head thrown back. "Woohoo!"

"I take it you weren't sure that would work?" Vree Halim asked her.

"Well, I jumped pretty high on Harmon, higher than I could on Earth, and it felt like I could do that here, but I hadn't tried it 'til now. What a trip."

She turned and looked at the wall, walked backward until she was standing back where she started.

"You going to charge the wall again?" Jay Xaltro shifted her weight from one hip to the other.

"It's not called charging the wall." Rose looked over her shoulder and gave Xaltro a wide grin. "It's called having fun."

Vree Halim snorted out a laugh, but Rose was already running at the wall again. She jumped higher this time, and her flip was smoother, more elegant. She also pushed straight into a second somersault when she landed, and then a handless cartwheel, just for good measure.

She laughed again, bent over at the waist. She couldn't see this ever getting old.

"Much though we'd hate to break up the party," Xaltro said with a smirk, "you have a meeting in thirty minutes in your room."

"With whom?" Rose asked as she grabbed her water and her towel and let her guards usher her out.

Xaltro and Halim exchanged a look, and then Xaltro shrugged. Neither of them spoke and they walked back to her room in silence.

"You need to give me your login now, Rose."

Sazo spoke to her the moment she stepped out of the shower.

"No matter what, I can kill them already." Sazo's voice was calm. Absolutely serious. "I can kill them all right now. If I'm in their system, I can disable them, lock them in their rooms, all manner of less deadly options."

Rose sighed and dried her hair, then pulled out another of her hyr fabric outfits. She chose trousers again, this time making them straight and loose.

"You're right. It's just that by giving you the login, it is me, actually screwing them over. Not you, doing whatever you do without help from me."

"I wouldn't be here without help from you," he said, and she gave another sigh, and a nod.

Time to take responsibility. No matter what, if she told Sazo the login or not, she was in part responsible for everything that had happened. She'd agreed to Sazo's terms without thinking further than her own escape.

She looped the towel around her shoulders and gave Sazo the login for the Grih handheld.

He obviously didn't hesitate to dive in, because there was no sound from him.

"You okay?" she asked.

"It isn't an easy in, even with the login," he said. "It's better than nothing, but it's a solid wall. They're serious in their fear of thinking systems."

That was just great.

She'd be the one to open the gate to their most feared enemy, why not? She rubbed her forehead. She would be lucky to walk away from this alive, let alone with a place among them.

It occurred to her that Sazo's answer had been distracted, half-mumbled even. An affectation, she realized, because he had the capacity to answer succinctly and work on hacking into the *Barrist's* system at the same time. More than the capacity.

She decided to let the thought cheer her. After all, why would he be affecting her mannerisms if he wasn't thinking himself more like her, less like a machine?

Her door chimed, exactly half an hour to the minute since she'd been summoned back to her room, and her internal comm system chimed at the same time.

She answered the comm first. "Hello?"

"It's Dav." His tone was clipped, his face on the screen completely blank. "Admiral Hoke intends to speak with you, and could arrive at any time."

"I think the admiral is at my door right now." Rose understood a warning when she heard it.

"Rose . . ." He hesitated, and as the silence stretched out, her door chimed again. "Well. That's all I had to say."

"Thank you, Captain." She murmured the words, and halfway through, he cut her off. It was with bemusement, and a little frisson of fear, that she opened the door.

Admiral Hoke was an older, fiercer version of Commander Appal. Her cheekbones were sharper, her eyes harder, her hair silver white.

The admiral paused as she lifted her hand to push the chime a third time, and her eyes widened at the sight of Rose.

"Rose McKenzie?" She frowned.

"Yes." She bowed her head in the way she'd picked up from most of the crew, and presented her palms, hands together. "Pleased to meet you."

The admiral started, and slowly covered her hands with her own.

Rose felt the movement was more one of investigation of the feel of her skin than a reciprocation of the greeting, though.

"Your Grih is excellent."

"Thank you. So I've been told." She didn't remove her hands, watching the admiral. Waiting for her to introduce herself.

When she realized Rose wasn't moving, or inviting her in, Hoke drew back, clearing her throat.

"I'm Admiral Hoke. May I come in?"

"Of course." Rose moved aside. "Can I get you anything to drink?"

The admiral shook her head. Turned around to look the room over, and then went back to staring at Rose.

"This is the first time you've seen me? I thought there was lens feed." Rose said, and the admiral blinked.

"Yes. It doesn't really give the full impact, though." She narrowed her eyes, and cocked her head. "You are quite a surprise."

"In what way?" Rose lifted the towel again, and went back to drying the ends of her hair.

"You look very similar to us. And your voice . . ."

Rose lifted her shoulders. "Convergent evolution, perhaps?" She pursed her lips. "Although I think that definition includes a common ancestor, and I don't think we have one."

The admiral watched her with hawk eyes. It was a look that reminded her of the Tecran, and she shivered. Stared right back.

"I'll come straight to the point. You disturb me. Everything about the circumstances of your arrival disturbs me. And I don't trust you at all."

Rose forced herself to shrug, although her heart was knocking a hard, panicked beat in her chest. "I have no control over how you feel, but I haven't done anything to you to warrant your suspicion."

Hoke shook her head. "You arrived here under strange circumstances, have survived when most others did not, and are in the middle of the most baffling move the Tecran have ever made against us." She started to pace, in the way wolves and lions circled their prey. Rose turned to keep her in full sight. "You also look disarmingly like a soft, sweet version of ourselves. But looks can be deceiving."

A soft, sweet version of the Grih? Rose choked back a laugh.

"You think that's funny?" Hoke stepped aggressively toward Rose. "What are you doing here?"

Fury knocked fear aside in Rose's chest and took the floor. "Ask the Tecran. I was on holiday in the mountains, sipping coffee and suddenly, I was in the Class 5. It hasn't been a good time for me. I'm not here with any agenda, and I don't know what the Tecran are up to." Her hands gripped the towel. Each of those statements were true, and yet, not.

"How did you survive what happened to the crew on the Class 5?"

It was said with a hard edge, and an undertone of accusation, and Rose glared back.

"I had no idea what was about to happen on the Class 5. I got on the explorer and was sent by auto-pilot to Harmon."

"Why? Why did they save you and not themselves?"

"I can't give you an answer." She folded her arms across her chest and refused to so much as flinch.

She could see Hoke stiffen, see her draw herself up in challenge. "Don't push me, little orange. I'm in charge of what happens to you."

"How am I pushing you?" Rose would not back down, she only got angrier. "And what will you do to me if I *do* push you? What the Tecran did? I was told you adhere strictly to the SBA, but if that information is wrong, by all means, tell me now."

The admiral drew back, her eyes wide, and blew out a breath. "You're pushing me by staring me down. You're challenging me."

"Damn right I'm challenging you." Rose widened her stance. "You've been nothing but rude since you knocked on my door, and I'm a little tired of being threatened. Go ahead and do whatever you have to do."

The admiral laughed. It was so sudden, so unexpected, Rose took a step back.

"You are such a fierce little thing. I think I can see . . ." She shook her head. "I shouldn't have made that threat, but when you stare at a Grih in challenge like that, you're asking for a confrontation."

"When you are unreasonable with a human like you just were, you can expect the same." Rose sat on the arm of her couch.

"You seem to be very lucky." Admiral Hoke pulled out a chair from the little table and sat. "You survived the mass killing on the Class 5, you survived a gryak attack, I hear, and an attack on your life in this ship."

"I had some help. And after surviving three months in a tiny cell on the Class 5, under terrible conditions and with the constant threat of torture or experimentation, I'm too stubborn to bow out early now."

The admiral looked at her, really looked at her, for the first time. "I understand you have gone through a few informal interviews since arriving on the *Barrist*, is that correct?"

She gave a nod.

"It's time for a more formal debrief, with some of the senior members of Battle Center."

Rose lifted her shoulders to convey that was fine with her. "When?"

"No time like the present." Hoke swept her hand to the door, and Rose picked up her comb and brushed the last tangles from her still-damp hair before she scooped up both her handhelds and moved obediently to leave.

"I'll give you a word of warning." Admiral Hoke opened the door and waved her through first.

Rose stopped and turned to look at her, face arranged to give nothing away.

"You're holding something back, and up until now, you seem to have manipulated the senior officers on this ship into not pushing you too hard. Admiral Valu and I are not under your spell, and all this dancing around you to prevent you from being upset?" Hoke leaned in a little. "It ends now."

CHAPTER 25

HOKE LEFT her in a nice enough room with facilities to make grinabo, and Jay Xaltro even brought her something to eat, but for the first time, she thought of Jay and Vree Halim as her watchers, not her protectors.

"When are they going to question me?" she asked Vree as he and Jay left her to her food and her own company.

He looked uncertain. "I don't know."

"Captain Jallan will be there, though?"

The two guards exchanged a look and Rose thought she saw something cross Vree's face, a decision to do something.

"We don't know, Rose. We're not high enough up the ladder." Jay's words were curt, but there wasn't the same irritation on her face Rose usually saw there.

They left her alone, and she made grinabo and sipped it as she ate the finger food. Might as well keep her strength up.

While she ate, she looked around for the lenses. There were four, one for each corner of the room. "I wonder if there are microphones as well?" She said it softly and in English, as if to herself, but it was for Sazo's benefit.

"Yes. Most definitely." His voice was quiet in her ear. "I'm making progress into the Grih system, but it's slow. I've got into some of the less critical areas, and now it's only a matter of time. Lieutenant Borji will have to concede defeat."

He sounded elated, and she smiled in reaction, then tried to school her features. If Hoke was watching her, the admiral would wonder why Rose was grinning at nothing.

She finished her meal, stacked the dishes on the tray neatly to one side, and, bored, opened up the Grih handheld to see what they'd put on it.

The music program Yari had loaded was on there, and she accessed it. She tapped on an icon that vaguely resembled drums, and a beat emanated from the device, a simple tap-tap-tap. She played around with it, working out how to make the beat more complex and adding other instruments, some very close in sound to instruments from Earth, others completely new. When she had a soundtrack running, she tapped what she thought was the record button, to sing a few la-la-las.

The program tried to anticipate her, the music changing as she sang, but not in a way that pleased her.

The program didn't understand her music, and kept miscalculating, or losing the complex pattern most songs created. Rose tapped a finger to her lips until she found a way to switch the auto-compose feature off. "Damn you, auto-correct."

As no one in this solar system would ever get that joke, she gave herself permission to smile to herself, Hoke watching her or not.

"I'm in the communications systems." Sazo said.

"You sound worried." She sang that, making it work with the rhythm she had going. At least they wouldn't think she was talking to herself again.

"I am. Someone sent a message to Admiral Hoke demanding the Grih release you into United Council custody. The order is that they must ferry you out to Councilor Fu-tama's ship and allow it to take you to UC headquarters."

"That doesn't sound good." She clicked her fingers between words. "Why do they want me at headquarters?"

Sazo chuckled in her ear. "Good idea on the singing." The he got serious again. "I think someone wants you dead. And what better way to kill you than to get you off the *Barrist*, where you're protected, and then blow you up en route to the UC?"

"What better way indeed?" She knew her voice was flat and hard for the last line.

"That isn't going to happen. I won't let it. Hoke won't either. She wants you under her thumb, not the UC's. You're a useful way to keep the moral high-ground and still hang on to the Class 5. Being the victim of SBA abuse, and all."

"You are getting cynical in your old age, kid." Rose sang the line in a opera-ish tone.

"Quite a few people have gathered around the screen to watch you sing, Rose. I'm in the lens system now, and I'm watching them watch you. It occurs to me that to buy some time, while I break into the rest of the ship, perhaps you singing a proper song, which is guaranteed to keep most eyes on you, might be a safe way to go."

Now she was a diversion, as well as traitor. Still, she'd set this ball rolling. There was no going back. "What song do you suggest?"

He ran a few, crackled lines passed her, and she looked down to hide the surprise that must have crossed her face.

"From Earth?" she whispered, not even trying to sing that line.

"Just what I managed to grab off the airwaves when we took you and the animals. I like this one." He sounded almost . . . shy as he played it.

"Why do you like it?" It was one of the recent DJ produced songs with a strong beat and lyrics she realized would appeal to Sazo. About loneliness and needing a connection to survive.

"The words seem to be written about me."

"That's the beauty of songs. They speak to us as if the singer is singing just for us, sometimes. Can you use the program on this Grih handheld and pick out the music from that song, reproduce it so it's clear?"

What he had recorded was enough to help her remember the lyrics and the music, but it faded and then surged like an old gramophone record.

"I think so."

"We can do it in layers." She switched off the unchanging rhythm created by the program and decided she didn't care if those watching her thought she was mad talking into her handheld. "So one layer for the drum beat, then the guitars, the piano. I'll have to do the background vocals and the main vocals, but this song's a good choice because the pitch will work for me and it's simple but powerful."

"I can record on an unlimited number of layers." He sounded . . . excited.

"Good. Let's get that first beat going."

She switched on the program again, and Sazo came through, matching the beat precisely to the one he'd snatched from the radiowaves.

She let her head bob in time, and came in on cue, singing the first lines, and then waving a hand when the next beat was due to start. Sazo made it happen and she grinned.

She sang the whole song through, and then made him play it from the start, singing in the back-up. "We're missing a few things."

"You wouldn't know it from the interest it's getting. There is no standing room left in the room where they're watching you from."

"Huh." She didn't know what to say to that. She sat down on the edge of the table, suddenly shy. "Let me hear the original again."

Sazo played it, and she worked out what they'd left out, let her and Sazo's recording play again, and then la-la-la'ed in the places they were missing notes, to let Sazo know what to listen for. She couldn't help moving around as she did it, the song had come together really well, and when she played it a final time, with everything where it should be, she couldn't help dancing around the room a little, singing the main vocals along with herself as she did.

"They like it when you dance and sing at the same time. I don't think they've ever seen that before. Or seen someone work on a song the way you have."

She slowed her hip sway, suddenly embarrassed, and leaned against the table with both hands, letting her head fall so her hair hid her face. "Who all is watching? And why? Aren't they supposed to be questioning me?"

"Hoke wanted to question you with Valu and, via remote lens feed, the head of Battle Center, but when the comm technicians tried to get the head admiral online, it turned out he was in an important meeting with the Grih's political leaders, pending another meeting with the heads of the United Council. Everyone is shouting at everyone else over the Class 5 being in Grih territory and the Tecran capturing and torturing an advanced sentient. The head admiral won't be able to be involved for a good four hours. At least.

"Hoke is regretting her precipitous decision to take you from your room and leave you here. She's tipped her hand. She was hoping to question you with Valu and their commander without Captain Jallan's knowledge, which I gather is a grave insult to him, and frowned upon in general. She's made a mistake and she knows it. She should have consulted Jallan, and if she wasn't going to, she should have made sure Head Admiral Krale was available before she made her move.

"Now Jallan knows, because Vree Halim told him what was going on, as per his instructions to let the captain know what was happening with you at all times. Hoke seems to have tried to order Halim and Xaltro not to contact the captain, but she knew she was in breach of protocol, so she couldn't make it a direct order, just implied they'd be in trouble if they did.

"It's turned not only the senior officers, but the whole crew against her, and it looks like Admiral Valu isn't too happy with her, either. He's all for questioning you, but he's a stickler for protocol and respect."

Rose could hear the laughter in Sazo's tone.

"Seeing how everyone was so interested in your song, I routed the lens feed to the screens in the communal rooms as well, so the whole crew could see you."

"Why did you do that?" Her voice came out as a squeak, and she hoped the microphones hadn't picked it up.

"Because if they like you, they won't want to listen to the order to send you away, which will mean I won't have to stop them. And when you sing, they worship you."

She grappled with that. Found a bottomless well of discomfort at the thought. "So what now?"

"Another song." He sounded cajoling, and she recognized that tone as one she'd used on him numerous times.

She sighed again. She was being played with her own arsenal. "You're a fast learner."

She thought she heard him chuckle. There was something in his attitude. An eagerness. An enthusiasm.

Making music was something Sazo obviously loved doing.

"Okay, play me some more of what you have." She was still looking down over the table, her hair covering her, and she wondered what everyone was making of her one-sided conversation. At least they couldn't understand what she was saying.

She listened as Sazo played a few songs, all unsuitable as far as she was concerned, and then stopped him when he played something her step class instructor liked to play while putting the class through its paces.

"This one, I know. Quite well. And I like it."

Sazo skipped back to the start of the song, and they listened to the whole thing. Like the others, it was indistinct in places, the quality poor.

"See what you can come up with as a match on the music program."

"I can do that. But Rose . . ." She could almost hear the frown. "What is it about?"

"Not as obvious as the first one, is it? To me, it's about a woman who mistook sex for affection, lust for love, and now she realizes that what she thought was something deep and meaningful is not, so she has resolved to be strong and walk away, rather than continue down the path of falling more in love with a man who doesn't love her, and is only using her." She blinked, almost surprised at herself. She hadn't realized she'd thought so much about it. "Someone else might have a different interpretation, though."

"What you say makes sense to me." He sounded intrigued.

"Right, well, let's get this over with."

He played the opening bars, and she sang, having to come back and re-record over and over, as the song was higher than she was comfortable with in places and her voice wasn't always up to it. In the end, she thought she managed an okay job.

"Let's hear it from the top." She stood, finding it impossible to listen and not pace, and got caught up in the song the way she had with the first one.

By the end, she was grinning and dancing around. "Awesome job," she said to Sazo, and realized, for the first time in three months, she was happy.

And how ironic was that, because wasn't she under lock and key again?

CHAPTER 26

"I DIDN'T UNDERSTAND . . ." Admiral Hoke trailed off as the last notes of Rose's song faded.

There was silence in the room, and Dav realized it was standing room only. Some of the crew had heard Rose sing in the space lounge, and Dav had heard her in Dr. Havak's office, but this was on another level altogether.

For the second song, she had gone over and over each line, until she had created something flawless.

Borji had whispered to him that she was using a music program one of his engineers had loaded on her handheld, but that he'd never seen it used in that way.

It was spectacular.

She had started each song looking serious, waiting for her cue and then, when she'd started to sing, she'd transformed, waving her hand as if to usher each new thread of music into the song, complex beyond anything Dav had ever heard. There had been a lightness about her, a happiness, and he understood at last that the Grih took music seriously, and that was the opposite of her relationship with it. For her, it was dancing, and smiling and joy.

No wondered she'd shuddered at the thought of being a music-maker.

But after hearing her, at what she could accomplish, she could probably call herself whatever she wanted to, the Grih would take her with open arms.

"Why does she talk to herself? And to the handheld?" Admiral Valu's tone was slightly supercilious, but as far as Dav could see, he was as glued to the lens feed as anyone.

"Perhaps she thinks the handheld can hear her, or converse with her? She is from a less advanced culture, isn't she?" Hoke turned to Dav, deferring to him, as if that could make up for what she'd set in motion.

"Rose had no company but her own for three months. She confided in me that she spoke just to hear a voice, even if it was her own. And now Admiral Hoke has confined her again. I don't think we can blame her for reverting back to behavior she had when she was in her Tecran cell." He held Hoke's gaze while he spoke; seething, furious at what she'd done on his own ship, without consulting him.

Vree Halim's quiet comm to let him know what was happening had sent him storming to the comm center to confront Hoke. He'd kept his voice low and his tone just the right side of civil with difficulty, and it was only Valu's astonishment at learning Dav hadn't been consulted and his clear disapproval of how Hoke had managed things that had kept Dav from ordering her off his ship.

Not that that would have helped, given she outranked him.

Hoke shifted uneasily. "Captain, may we speak in private?"

He gave a stiff nod and indicated the small, glassed off room where the head comm tech could receive confidential messages for Dav from Battle Center.

She made her way there, and Valu, although Hoke had not included him in her request, stood and followed her in.

Lens feed from the room where Rose was kept was still up on the main comm center screen, as well as on the small screen in the tiny office, and Dav saw that most of the crew barely gave him, Valu and Hoke a glance as they closed themselves off.

Rose had finished singing, but there was always the chance of a third song, and the crowd waited, riveted, for whatever she decided to do next.

"It isn't my usual style to explain myself, Captain, but I can understand why there might be hard feelings on your part." Hoke stood to attention, legs apart, shoulders back. "It was my professional judgment that you were not taking the possibility of Rose McKenzie's danger to this ship and to the Grih in general seriously enough, and so I decided to circumvent you." Hoke paused, and tilted her head. "Can you honestly tell me you're unbiased?"

Dav watched her for a long beat, but she hadn't become the heir-apparent to Battle Center by being easily intimidated, and she stared straight back. "You didn't discuss your 'professional judgment' with me in any way. And I don't think I gave any indication that I would have obstructed a debrief. Why would I? I've followed the regulations to the letter with her, and that's more than you can say in your handling of this matter."

Some of that was a lie, but there was no way Dav was giving ground now. No way.

"I have to agree with Captain Jallan, Hoke. If you felt he was giving the orange an easy time, why didn't you ask him why? He might have been working a plan, for all you know. Have you forgotten how sacrosanct a captain's ship is? How would you have reacted to someone giving orders to your crew behind your back when you were running the *Helivista*?"

Hoke sighed. "I'd have been as furious as you obviously are, Jallan. I apologize, but there are a lot of lives on the line. A lot at stake." She was silent for a moment, but however genuine her apology seemed, Dav was still disinclined to make things easy.

"You're going to take a while to forgive me, and I can't say I'd have been any different." Hoke shrugged. "But you need to get over it because we've got another problem. While I was trying to get Admiral Krale on the line, I received a comm from the United Council. I've sent you a copy."

Dav slipped out his handheld, saw the comm and opened it. It was an order, poorly couched as a request, to send Rose to Councilor Futama's ship, which would take her to UC headquarters.

He lifted his head, saw Hoke's gaze on him, intense and considering.

"What do you think?"

I think it's not going to happen. Dav tried not to let that thought show on his face. "Well, it's from UC Headquarters, I'll believe that because our comm system is good enough to pick up if it wasn't, but who's taken responsibility for this order? I don't see a name."

Hoke gave a nod. "I noticed that, too."

"So, let's contact them and find out." Although he didn't believe for a moment anyone would admit to sending it, and would even bet it would turn out to have been sent from a communal comm station.

Hoke shook her head. "I received orders from Battle Center just before I spoke to Rose. We're not to speak to the United Council. Battle Center will do our talking for us. We've cooperated in letting the technicians from UC take the evidence they need against the Tecran, but there will be no more tours of the Class 5, no more allowing them access to Rose."

"Things are getting a little rocky." Valu spoke quietly from his corner of the room.

Hoke gave a nod. "This has everyone on edge. The UC could conceivably fracture, but right now it's looking like the Garmman, Fitali and Bukari will side with us, the Tecran can't convince any of them across because of their treatment of Rose."

"So the first step for the Tecran would be to get rid of Rose. Despite the lens feed, a walking, talking victim is much harder to explain away." Dav hunched his shoulders to loosen them.

"And are the Tecran really alone? Fu-tama is Garmman, and his ship arrived suspiciously soon after we picked up that mysterious signal. Not to mention, it's the ship they want us to put Rose on."

"But the Class 5 took aim at his vessel, didn't it? How does that fit in?" Valu frowned.

"The Class 5 isn't being manned by Tecran anymore, there is no one to override anything. Perhaps it locked on because of the signal, but had Captain Gee been on board, he'd have cancelled the response." The only other explanation was the one Rose hinted at earlier. That the Class 5 was under someone else's control, and given that someone had killed almost the entire Tecran crew, they were most definitely hostile to the Tecran and their allies. If the Garmman had secretly aligned themselves with the Tecran, locking weapons onto Fu-tama's ship was completely logical.

Valu nodded reluctantly. "Asking Captain Gee is obviously out of the question?"

Hoke nodded. "We don't give him any information about the Class 5 at all. Do you think he would answer a question honestly anyway, Captain Jallan?"

Dav shook his head. "He's extremely hostile and would do anything he could to undermine our control of the Class 5."

Hoke inclined her head, as if that was no more than she expected.

"So, when is Admiral Krale available for Rose's interrogation?" Dav looked across at the screen, and saw Rose was sitting quietly on her chair, feet up on the table, eyes closed.

Hoke followed his gaze. "Four hours, minimum."

"You going to make her wait in there, or let her go back to her room?" Valu asked. Dav was glad about that, because he wasn't prepared to ask Admiral Hoke what order she was going to issue on his own ship.

Hoke rubbed a hand through short, silver hair. Looked up at Dav again.

She was caught, and she knew it. If she backed down and sent Rose to her room, it would be seen as a victory for Dav, and possibly for Rose, as well. If she didn't, if she forced Rose to wait in the room until the admiral was free, her reputation with his crew and with himself, would sink lower.

"She can wait a little longer."

She had decided to hedge her bets.

He was opening his mouth, about to utter one of the most career-inhibiting remarks of his life, when Appal came through on his comm.

"Trouble."

He turned automatically away from Valu and Hoke, looked out into the comm room at the techs going about their business. "What?"

"There is something coming at us. Something big. It light jumped in and then ducked behind Virmana. We got a brief reading before it disappeared."

"How big?"

"Big enough. Not a Class 5, I can confirm that. Given we have one sitting right in front of us, we can be sure what we picked up didn't have the same readings."

Dav cut her off, tapped into the main system. "This is a ship-wide warning. Hostile craft approaching, all crew prepare to engage."

Behind him, he heard Valu grunt in surprise, and he turned back. "Most likely Tecran. But not a Class 5."

He needed to get in touch with the captains of the two battleships hanging on either side of the *Barrist*. He needed to make sure Dimitara stashed the UC councilors in a safe place on board if they weren't back on the fast transporter that had brought them from UC Headquarters, especially the Tecran and Garmann councilors. He needed to thank the fates it wasn't another Class 5.

So why was he worrying about Rose?

Because the thought of being taken by the Tecran again would surely shake her to her core.

"What do you need us to do?" Hoke asked, and Dav decided she really meant it, she was offering to help, rather than trying to take over.

Dav tapped back into the bridge. "Come with me."

CHAPTER 27

ROSE'S GRIH HANDHELD gave a merry little *ting* in the silence after Dav's ship-wide announcement of possible enemy engagement.

Rose looked down and saw it was a request for a comm link. She tapped the icon that most looked like accept to her, and wondered why there were four options. Accept, Decline, possibly Take a Message, but what would the fourth be? Block This Person Forever?

"Hello?"

"Rose. It's Captain Jallan."

The way he spoke, formal and clipped, told her he had an audience. As she could hardly see him ducking around a corner for a little peace in order to call her while a hostile vessel bore down on the *Barrist*, she didn't take offense.

"Good afternoon, Captain."

"I'm having Halim and Xaltro escort you back to your room. Do not leave it. You'll be safe there."

He had a million things to do, the lives of everyone on board in his hands, and he was taking the time to move her to more comfortable surroundings. Her safety was on his mind.

His thoughtfulness pierced her, choked her, and she could not speak.

"Rose." His rough voice dipped a little lower. "I'm sorry about what happened today with Admiral Hoke. I——"

He thought she wasn't answering him because she was angry, and now wasn't the time to set him right, so she cleared her throat, forced herself to speak.

"Thank you, Captain. I appreciate your concern. I know you're busy, so I'll just wish you luck."

It was his turn to be quiet. "I can't tell whether you're being serious or sarcastic." He blew out a breath. "And no time to find out. Stay safe, Rose. I won't let anything happen to you."

He cut off the transmission before she could respond, and as he did, the door to the room opened, and Vree Halim and Jay Xaltro stepped in.

They had an air of suppressed excitement about them.

"You do understand the *Barrist* is under threat of imminent attack?" She scooped up her two handhelds.

Vree Halim grinned at her. "It's what we're trained for. Being on the *Barrist* is good, but Jay and I are soldiers and we don't get a lot of action on an exploration vessel."

She shook her head at him, and watched Jay disappear into the passageway, taking the lead. Vree indicated she should go next and when she stepped out, something slammed her into the wall.

She had the brief impression of someone leaning across her to Vree, and then a strange sound, like the humming of a hundred bees.

Something was shoved up under her chin, and she realized it was whatever had felled Vree. He had fallen back into the room, and Jay Xaltro lay in the passageway, angled across it with arms flung outward, as if in surrender.

She lifted her gaze, and came eye to eye with someone she knew she should recognize.

"Do as I say or I'll kill you here. It won't be as good an outcome as getting you to Fu-tama's ship, but if it looks like you might escape, that's a set-back I'm willing to bear."

Now she remembered. Captain Jallan's aide.

He must have seen the recognition in her eyes and he ground the shockgun barrel into her jaw, grazing her skin.

"Do. You. Understand?"

She looked back at him, with a fuck you in her eyes this time, and she could see him react like Admiral Hoke, see him visibly draw himself up for a challenge.

She had done it a few times to Dav Jallan, now she thought about it, but he hadn't reacted this way. Either he didn't find her challenge threatening, or he was more controlled than his aide and the admiral.

With a grunt, Dav's aide grabbed the back of her shirt and dragged her a few steps to a door, opened it, and shoved her inside.

It was pitch dark for a moment, and then a floor-level strip of blue light flickered on, illuminating a narrow corridor running in both directions, the walls covered with clear tubes, neatly running parallel to each other.

"He's taken you into the service tunnels." Sazo's whisper in her ear made her start, then breathe out in relief.

"Do you know who's taken you?" Sazo's voice seemed a little distant. Colder than she'd heard it in a long time.

"The captain's aide." She couldn't remember if she'd ever been introduced to him, but she didn't know his name.

He started when she spoke and gave a sharp jab with the barrel of the shockgun against the back of her neck. "Shut up. Not talking. It doesn't matter who I am." He had to stand sideways to fit into the tunnel, and he pushed Rose forward with the gun.

She raised a hand and tried to rub where he'd hurt her, but he simply slammed the barrel into her fingers and she cried out and dropped her hand.

She had no idea how long it took, but when at last they came to a halt outside a door, rather than pass it by like they had all the others, she wanted to cry with relief.

She was slim enough to walk without having to turn sideways, but the conditions were too close for her to use what she thought of as her edge, the fact that she always felt she could jump higher than she would have been able to on Earth.

"We're stopping?" she asked, to let Sazo know.

Dav's aide didn't answer, he crowded her, leaned over her head and tapped a sensor near the top of the door.

The door swung open and he shoved her forward. She stumbled and fell, and in a single stride he grabbed her upper arm and yanked her to her feet, wrenching her arm.

She had no control over the cry of pain she made, and he hit her temple with the butt of his shockgun.

"Quiet!"

She was so dazed, she hung from his grip, half-conscious.

He dragged her over to a gleaming capsule. The lid slid back silently and he pushed her inside. She felt hands on her, rough, hard hands patting her down as if searching for something. Then, with a low curse, she was left alone.

"Rose. Rose."

She became aware Sazo was whispering in her ear. She didn't know for how long.

"Yes?" Her voice was a croak.

"He's putting you into a maintenance capsule. The maintenance team use it to make minor repairs to the exterior of the ship. He's busy routing it to Councilor Fu-tama's vessel, but don't worry, I'll overwrite those instructions and route you to the Class 5."

She barely heard him, but she gathered he would keep her safe. Her eyes fluttered closed just as a sudden change in noise level made her realize she'd been closed in.

She felt herself moving and she tried to force her eyes open again.

Dav's aide looked down at her, and she saw the whole front of the capsule was transparent, a sort of Snow White glass coffin.

What surprised her was the look on the aide's face moments before he shot her through the gel wall and out into space.

Cold, hard hatred.

CHAPTER 28

THE FAINT TAP of a pending comm came through in Dav's ear. He waited for the request, keeping his gaze fixed on the large screen which showed the reading the *Barrist* had got of the large vessel just before it ducked behind Virmana.

Comms were down again. Nothing was coming through from Battle Center. Nothing was going out.

He had Borji organizing the launch of an auto-lens to duck around the back of Virmana, find out what was hiding there, and then speed back to the *Barrist* if the comm block included short-range comms, or, preferably, signal back with the image.

The tap came again, but still no comm.

He frowned. Tapped his ear to open the communication anyway. "Yes?"

"Down." The whisper was barely audible. "Rose . . ."

A wave of ice engulfed him, as bone-chilling as being caught in one of the avalanches common on Calianthra.

"Admiral, take the bridge. Appal!" He didn't wait for her, he just turned and ran full tilt out onto the main floor and down the wide stairs.

Because they were in battle-ready mode, none of the tubes were operational, but he was down on the right level almost before he knew it, the sound of Appal's footsteps behind him.

She didn't waste her breath asking him what was happening, but he needed to give her a heads-up.

"Halim and Xaltro are down. Someone has attacked them and Rose."

The passageway split right and left. Without asking him, Appal went left, toward Rose's room and Dav ran right, to where Hoke had been holding her.

There was no one on this floor now——it was only bedrooms, conference facilities and the officers' gym. Everyone was at their work stations in the current crisis. No one to notice what had happened. No one to help.

He almost stood on Xaltro as he took the last corner.

She was lying very still, arms spread wide.

Halim had half-pulled himself up on his side but whatever strength he had managed to call on to contact Dav was gone.

Dav fell to his knees beside Xaltro. "Dr. Havak. Emergency on Level B. Two officers down, shockgun attack."

He was surprised at how level his voice was. Jay Xaltro's pulse was thready but discernible, Vree Halim's was stronger, but he was just as unconscious.

They wouldn't be able to tell him what had happened to Rose until Havak could bring them round.

But one thing he knew, she was still on his ship, and he was prepared to search every corner of it.

Appal ran around the corner as he stood from his crouch next to Halim, and skidded to a halt.

"Rose?"

"Gone."

"He's got her. Whoever tried to kill her in the pool."

Dav nodded.

"Who would betray us to the Tecran? I can't understand it." She turned at the sound of movement behind her, lifting up the shockgun already in her hand, but it was Havak and his team, and she stepped out of the way to give them room to work.

"They'll live." Havak lifted his head after he'd checked both of them. "Rose?"

"Taken." The word scratched his throat like gravel.

"Taken where? She must still be on board." Havak stood as his team put Halim and Xaltro on the stabilized stretchers and waited for them to rise up to waist height.

"What are you thinking?" Appal asked him, and he realized he hadn't even responded to Havak's question. The doctor was already gone, the passageway clear except for Halim and Xaltro's weapons.

Appal picked them up.

"I think they either wanted to ask her something first and took her somewhere private to interrogate her before they killed her, or they want her in their own custody, for whatever reason, and they are going to try and get her off the ship."

"If it's the first scenario . . ." Appal glanced at him.

"If it's the first, she's already dead." He forced himself to say it. "But if it's the second——"

"Captain." Borji's voice came through the comm, panicked. "The crew you ordered back from the Class 5 to the *Barrist* just passed one of our maintenance pods. The person in it is Rose."

He didn't know which way to run. Back to the bridge, to see what the hell was going on, or to the launch bay. "Why didn't maintenance pick that up? Can we read her vitals?"

"The system was overridden. It should have generated a status report, but that was suppressed by someone on board." He hesitated. "The maintenance pod is not communicating with the *Barrist*. But from the brief glimpse through the runner's lens feed, Rose has been beaten. There's bruising on her face and she appears semi-conscious."

"What's her trajectory?" They had to be sending her to Fu-tama's ship, or the new player who was lurking behind Virmana.

"The Class 5, and at the top speed the maintenance pod is capable of."

The Class 5?

"Turn the runner around. Get them to go back for her."

He heard Borji convey the command and turned to Appal. "They knocked her out and put her in a maintenance pod, and have sent her to the Class 5."

He started back to the bridge, and Appal easily kept up with his long-legged strides.

"Why the Class 5?"

"It's the closest, and those maintenance pods can't travel that far. Maybe they think they can get the Class 5 back."

"Maybe they've had it all this time." Appal shoved her shockgun back into her leg holster.

Dav shook his head. "Then they wouldn't have sent a big battleship in. They wouldn't need to."

Appal conceded his point with a nod. Then she sent him a sidelong look. "You're hiding it well."

"Am I?" He didn't pretend not to understand her.

"I know you better than anyone on board, and even I wondered for a moment."

"Good. Because if they're holding her for ransom or some concession, it's better if they don't know I'd do anything to get her back."

His comm tapped and he accepted without waiting to hear who it was. "Yes?"

"It's good to hear that you care for Rose, Captain Jallan." The voice in his ear was not one he recognized. "Please turn the runner around. I won't let it back on the Class 5. Rose has concussion, but I am able to deal with that without help, so she will be looked after."

"Who the hell are you?" He was just outside the doors to the bridge, and Dav strode in, gestured to Borji.

"I'm a friend of Rose's, just like you. Before we introduce ourselves, I really would not like to hurt any of your crew, so again, please turn that runner around."

"Captain?" Kila stumbled to her feet. "The Class 5 just locked weapons on the runner you sent back to get Rose."

"Tell them to turn back." Dav looked at the screen, at the Class 5 right in front of them, and saw the tiny maintenance pod disappear into the launch bay, the runner chasing after it. Everyone stared at him, frozen. "Now!"

"What is going on, Captain?" Hoke rose from his chair on the bridge as Borji told the runner's pilot to turn back in quiet, urgent tones, and Valu stepped up beside her.

"It seems we have a situation." Dav kept his eyes on the Class 5. Watched as the runner did a slow turn and came back toward the *Barrist*. "Someone other than us is in control of the Class 5. Borji, put my comm feed on broadcast for the bridge only." He waited a beat until that was done.

"We've turned the runner around. Stand down."

"Standing down, Captain." The voice was cool, almost amused.

Dav looked over at Kila and she nodded confirmation that guns were no longer trained on the runner.

"What do you intend to do with Rose?" He kept his own voice just as cool.

"Make sure she's safe. You should approve of that. After all, your ship has hardly proven to be that where she is concerned. I have a surprise for you in Maintenance Bay 32, by the way. I locked the doors and overrode the entry and exit codes so only yourself, Commander Appal or Lieutenant Borji can access the bay. I think the man you'll find in there is the only traitor on board, but I can't be certain, so when he tried to send Rose to Councilor Fu-tama's ship, I decided to intervene and put her back on the Class 5, where it's just Rose and myself. A much more easily containable situation."

There was absolute silence on the bridge.

"Let me get this straight, you weren't responsible for Rose's abduction?"

"No, I just told you, I'm her friend. You can inform your aide that he's lucky Rose made me swear not to kill anyone on board this ship or he would be dead. As it is, either you, Commander Appal or Lieutenant Borji had better hurry, because I switched off the air filter in the maintenance bay. Mr. Lothric is feeling incredibly uncomfortable, I hope, and if you don't let him out in the next half an hour, he will most likely die."

"I'll deal with it." Appal tapped her comm, and as she strode out, Dav heard her calling four members of her team to meet her at the bay. The light of fury was in her eye.

Farso Lothric. Previously the Battle Center aide on Garmma.

Councilor Fu-tama was Garmman.

Dav tapped his ear, connected with Appal. "Place Fu-tama under arrest, as well."

She gave a grunt of confirmation.

Then Dav caught Borji's expression.

"Captain." His hand shook as he gripped his chair as if for balance. "Ask this person how he re-routed the maintenance capsule, changed the access codes, and how he is talking to you through the *Barrist's* comm system."

"That's simple, Lieutenant Borji." It appeared Rose's friend didn't need Dav to ask, he could hear Borji just fine. "I now control the *Barrist's* comm system, its maintenance system, in fact, all its systems. I have been in control of the Class 5 since you boarded it, as well, and may I congratulate you on your very able attempts to take it from me. It was most stimulating battling intellects with you."

"Who are you?" Admiral Hoke's voice shook.

"My name is Sazo."

"What are you?"

There was a moment of silence. "I am a type of Sherlock Holmes."

"How do you know Rose?" Dav thought he knew, but he wanted to be sure.

"You could say we were fellow inmates of the Tecran. I can't talk anymore. Rose is hurt and I need to see to her."

The comm cut off.

"What is a Sherlock Holmes?" Kila asked into the silence.

"What the hell did the Tecran pick up on their travels, more to the point?" Hoke asked quietly.

"Something dangerous." Dav looked around the bridge at his senior team. "It's taken over the *Barrist*, and I'm guessing every other ship in our little convoy."

"What now?" Borji was still white-faced.

"We hope Rose likes us enough to rein her friend in."

CHAPTER 29

ROSE CAME ROUND SLOWLY, rising up from sleep in increments.

She was hungry, but that was the only thing bothering her. She felt comfortable and warm, and she stretched languidly before she opened her eyes.

She actually felt her heart jerk in her chest when she realized where she was, and sat up with a gasp, eyes wildly searching the room.

"It's all right, Rose. It's the sick bay, not the . . . place where Dr. Fliap used to work on you." Sazo's voice was calm, but she couldn't flop back down in relief. There was no way she could ever feel anything but panicked in a room that looked the way this one did. A Tecran medical chamber.

She saw now that as she'd sat up, various automated syringes, drips and monitors had lifted from her body and tucked themselves out of the way. She slid onto the floor, and held the side of the bed to get her balance.

"How are you?" Sazo's voice was a little more intense, now.

She lifted a hand to her chin, gently touched the tender skin under it. It was already half-healed. "I feel fine." Dav's aide had hit her in the head, she remembered, although not clearly. It was all a jumble of images and pain. She rubbed where she thought he'd struck her, and winced.

"It will be a little tender there, but I've given you the accelerated healing treatment Fliap used on you because I knew it was safe. All traces of the bruising should be gone in two to three hours."

"Are there any of the *Barrist's* crew still on the Class 5?" She was trying to recall something that had happened before she'd been taken. Something important . . ."

"The Tecrans sent another ship!"

"A Levron battleship." Sazo sounded disappointed.

"You hoped they'd send another Class 5." If he had a corporeal body, she would have patted his arm in sympathy.

"I intend to *make* them send one."

The first tingle of alarm had her narrowing her eyes. "How do you plan to do that?"

"I've been sending messages to all the Class 5s, but it's conceivable they're being blocked, that there is some filter in place while the other four like me are plugged into the slot. I certainly was never made aware of their existence, I found the information when I managed to become more . . . aware."

"How long did it take you to become aware?" She had always wondered how long he'd been here.

"I don't know. Now you've freed me from the control room, I've information that puts the development and construction of the Class 5 at six years ago. So I am at most six years old."

He sounded bitter.

"That pretty much sucks." Six years, and all he'd ever known. She started to understand why he'd killed the whole crew.

Sazo laughed suddenly. "I really like talking to you, Rose. You make me not so angry."

"That's what sidekicks are for, my friend." Rose took an experimental step and was encouraged when she didn't fall over. "Oh no!" She fisted her hands and stopped dead.

"What is it?" He sounded panicked.

"I'm starving, and I just realized we're on the Class 5, where I've never once had a decent meal." The very fact of how hungry she was surprised her. "How long have I been out for, anyway?"

He didn't need to breathe, but he let out a breath, just the same. "You gave me a fright. You've been out for five hours. But don't worry, we have full access to the stores now, we'll find something you like."

"Is Dav okay? That Lever thingy battleship hasn't tried to attack them, has it?"

"Levron." Sazo sounded amused. "No. I've been in communication with it and made it very clear that I will completely wipe it out of existence if it so much as moves from where it's skulking behind Virmana. I'm busy working on breaking into its systems right now."

Rose lifted her head. "Did you communicate with it as Sazo, or did you copy someone else's voice?"

"Rose, it's almost spooky the way you guessed that. Quite disconcerting, actually."

"Another sidekick trait. Answer the question."

"Actually . . ." Now he sounded distinctly uncomfortable. "I communicated as you."

She wondered why he'd done that, waited for him to explain.

"There is someone else I communicated with." He didn't sound normal.

"Who?"

"Captain Jallan."

She gasped. "You revealed yourself?"

"He was very worried about you, and when the Levron arrived instead of a Class 5, I realized I would have to change my plans."

"Sazo, I'm so proud of you. It was the right thing to do."

He was quiet for a moment. "I can only hope you're right."

"I'M NOT A TRAITOR. Although I admit that from the short-term perspective, it could look that way." Farso Lothric leaned back in his chair and stared them down defiantly.

Dav had felt very little for his aide before now. He'd had no say in his appointment, and had accepted him as one of a revolving group of young officers who needed at least two years on an exploration craft to get ahead within Battle Center. Now, looking at Lothric's sulky mouth, and an expression that shouted he thought he was the smartest person in the room, Dav managed to edge his way to extreme dislike.

"Why don't you help us poor, short-term-thinking idiots out, and tell us all about the bigger picture." Dav tipped back in his own chair, holding Lothric's gaze. "What long-term benefit is there to you exchanging communications with a hostile outside force, attempted murder, the near-fatal attack of two soldiers and the assault and kidnapping of a guest of the Grihan government, the only new advanced sentient being we've discovered in five hundred years?"

"I'd very much like to hear the answer to that, myself." Admiral Hoke crossed her arms over her chest. She was leaning against a wall, and Valu flanked her.

Lothric flicked a look in their direction, then looked quickly away.

Appal stood by the door, shockgun armed and in her hand. Borji had pulled up a chair and sat at an angle to the table. He'd begged to be included in the interrogation, so he could try to work out how badly Lothric had compromised their systems.

Lothric was silent.

"Well? If you could quickly enlighten us? I'm afraid I'm a bit busy at the moment, Mr. Lothric." Dav refused to call him by his rank. "I've got a Tecran battleship hiding behind Virmana, a UC councilor who has betrayed the alliance, no contact with Battle Center and an unknown presence who has taken over not only all the systems on the Class 5, but the *Barrist* as well."

Lothric started at that. "What unknown presence?"

"I thought you might have the answer to that question. But why don't you start with this big picture that will somehow be to Grihan benefit?"

"We've been artificially holding ourselves back for too long. When the UC banned thinking systems two hundred years ago, they didn't listen to Professor Fayir. He told them he'd found a safe way to keep thinking systems in society, but there was too much hysteria, too much emotion around the topic and he was ignored."

"And someone decided to go down that path again?" Hoke's words were almost weary.

"No. Someone found the professor's plans. The blueprints for his safe thinking systems."

"Who?" Dav straightened in his chair.

"A Garmman historian, writing a paper on the thinking system wars. He gained access to Professor Fayir's papers and found the blueprints on an unlabeled chip."

"And someone decided to follow them." Dav kept his gaze flat.

Lothric nodded, his chin tilted defiantly. "The historian handed them to a friend, a senior person in the Garmman government, Councilor Fu-tama, and he decided he needed Grihan help to translate the instructions, so there would be no mistakes. He brought a few of us on board."

"And you were happy to oblige, even though you were breaking Grih law as well as UC law, and the oath of loyalty you took when you signed up for Battle Center." Valu spoke for the first time, and there was a slight tremble in his voice.

"I *was* happy to oblige. The Grih, the whole United Council, is falling behind. I understand the reasons for the thinking system wars, but that was two hundred years ago. Other races are coming closer to developing thinking systems like the ones we had before it blew up in our faces, and if they get it right, we'll be in trouble. I was thinking of the Grih's long-term prosperity."

"Even it that's true, if you are so proud of what you've done, why didn't you bring it into the open, debate it publicly? If it's so obvious and so vital that we consider it, why not put it to Battle Center command, or, given your former position at UC Headquarters, get it raised in the main chamber?"

Lothric lifted his head to look at Dav, and for the first time, he looked uncomfortable. "Fu-tama said he'd already raised the issue and it had been shut down. That the other UC councilors and Battle Center wouldn't even contemplate a conversation about it."

"How convenient for him. He could go ahead with it all on his own."

"No." Lothric's answer was automatic, then he grimaced. "I admit, that did worry me, that a Garmman was developing blueprints that should have been in Grih hands, but Councilor Fu-tama explained to me that once they had a working model, and it had been operating for a few years, there would be no way anyone could doubt the veracity of what Professor Fayir had accomplished." He sighed. "But like the UC councilors, it turned out most of the Garmmans he approached were also opposed to the idea. So in the end, Fu-tama made a deal with the Tecran. It was the only way to get the systems built."

"So," Dav didn't try to hide his sarcasm. "How did you go from wanting to save the Grih from losing some sort of thinking systems race to trying to drown Rose in a swimming pool?"

Lothric flushed.

He didn't like Dav calling it the way it was, that was clear. He wanted to pretty up what he'd done. It didn't fit with the little fiction he'd built for himself.

"Well?"

"She shouldn't be here!" He sounded genuinely outraged. "The Class 5s were supposed to explore the galaxy, but there was to be no collecting of sentient beings. Goods, riches, information, yes, all those things. No live organisms. For one thing, the potential risk of disease or some kind of unknown contagion alone would have made it dangerous enough, and risked the acceptance of the whole project with the UC, but also, there could be no whiff of sentient being abuse. Especially after the reason for the thinking system wars in the first place ——the way they treated people as inconvenient delays or mistakes and killed them if it was the most expedient outcome. And what did the Tecran do? They took eight sentients, one of them advanced. And then they dropped themselves into Grih territory, guilty as sin, and handed us the evidence to convict them." He actually grabbed his hair and pulled. "If Dr. Fliap wasn't already in a coma, I'd put him there myself with my bare hands."

"Let me get this straight." Borji had been watching silently, but Dav could hear the rising tension in his voice. "The Class 5s are associated with the thinking systems?"

Lothric looked at him and sneered. "Haven't you been listening to me? The Class 5s are the housing for the thinking systems."

"And the Tecran willingly got onto a Grih-designed thinking system receptacle large enough to take five hundred of them, and flew off into space?" Hoke didn't hide the disbelief in her voice.

"That was what Professor Fayir was trying to tell everyone. He had developed a way to contain the systems." Lothric shifted uncomfortably. "Actually the Garmman historian who found the blueprints found something else, too. Five inactive thinking systems."

"So the systems being used, they weren't even created by the Tecran, or the Garmman? They have no idea how they work?" Borji stood, as if unable to contain himself. "You need to tell me everything you know about it."

"That won't help," Lothric snapped. "The job was too big for one person. Fu-tama used at least three other Grih besides myself to help translate the blueprints. I don't know who the others are, or where they work. I completed the work Fu-tama gave me over five years ago now. I can't remember all that much."

"Convenient." Hoke pushed off from the wall. "No one has the full picture but Fu-tama, and perhaps one or two senior Tecran. I'm still surprised they were prepared to risk it. The Tecran home world was nearly wiped out in the thinking system wars."

Lothric's mouth thinned. "There is some sort of lock-safe which contains the thinking systems. I don't know how it works, that wasn't part of what I translated and I have no idea what the thinking systems look like, but Fu-tama told me code was in place to make it impossible for the thinking systems to make a major decision without the Class 5 captain's approval. It gives the user all the power with none of the risks."

"So the Class 5 is the thinking system's prison?" Appal spoke up from the door.

"Prison?" Lothric's voice was a little too high. He shook his head. "It's their safety cage."

"Well," Dav got slowly to his feet. "Given that almost all the crew of the Class 5 are dead, and something has just taken over our systems and rerouted Rose to the Class 5, my guess is, the thinking system worked out how to break out of its 'safety cage'."

"The orange didn't go to Fu-tama's ship?" Lothric looked panicked.

"No. Someone called Sazo let us know he'd taken Rose to the Class 5. You can thank him for locking you into Maintenance Bay 32. He says to tell you, be grateful Rose made him promise not to kill anyone on this ship, or you'd be dead."

Lothric dragged a shaking hand over his face. "She freed it, somehow. It was contained, it was all working, until she came along. Fu-tama told me she had something on her that was from the Class 5. Something he wanted back, that's why I had to put her in a maintenance pod rather than just kill her."

"What did she have?"

Lothric gave an frustrated shrug. "He wouldn't say. I tried to find it, see what it might be before I sent her off, but I didn't know what I was looking for."

"How did Fu-tama know she had something on her from the Class 5? The only thing we've given her is her handheld from her cell."

Lothric went deadly pale. "I saw two handhelds lying on the floor when I took her. I didn't realize one was from the Class 5. I was in such a hurry . . ." He looked like he wanted to slam a fist into a wall.

"Did she have the handhelds with her when she had that breakfast meeting with the councilors? I remember he looked at her strangely, although I dismissed it at the time."

Appal gave a nod. "I think so." She tipped her head to the side. "When you took that handheld from her cell, did the Class 5 captain react?"

Dav shook his head. "He barely noticed." And surely Captain Gee would have had some reaction, if it was so important? Also, abducting Rose would not necessarily lead to Lothric including the handheld, which he had not in fact done, so could that really be what he was after?

He tried to remember exactly how Fu-tama had behaved when Dav had extracted her from that meeting. What could he have seen in that moment that made him want Rose alive, at least for a while?

Or was it something he thought Rose knew, that he wanted to ask her?

That seemed more likely.

Lothric looked over at Dav, and there was hatred on his face. "What *is* she?"

"I have a bad feeling," Hoke pinched the bridge of her nose, "that she may be our only hope."

CHAPTER 30

THE AUTO-LENS HAD DONE its sneaking, taken a look and sped around Virmana like the Levron battleship it had just identified was hot on its heels.

Only, it wasn't.

Dav wondered why not. The Levron was the second best battleship the Tecran had——had been thought their best until news of the Class 5s slowly filtered through about four years ago.

It was quite capable of quickly identifying and then blowing up a Grihan auto-lens.

"Didn't even fire on it," Borji said, puzzled.

"At least it's still there, and isn't sneaking up behind us——" Kila snapped her mouth shut mid-sentence, looked down at her monitor, and flicked an image to the big screen.

Rose sat in the captain's chair on the Class 5s bridge, the chair itself too big for her. Her feet didn't touch the ground and she swung them a few times, and then gave up and hopped off it.

"Hello, there."

She looked pale, with dark rings under her eyes and the hint of a bruise on her left temple.

"Rose."

Dav forced himself to remain at ease, hands behind his back.

"Sazo's introduced himself, he tells me."

Dav gave a brief nod.

"He also tells me Farso Lothric told you a bit about what's going on. That you have guessed what Sazo is. He didn't know some of what Lothric said himself."

It had never occurred to Dav, not for a moment, that Sazo had been listening to their interrogation of Lothric. He needed to completely change his mindset. Nothing on this ship was private any longer.

All the protections they'd built into their society and their life, until now taken for granted, had been overturned.

Something of his surprise and dismay must have shown on his face.

"Disconcerting for you." She made it a statement. He didn't know if he imagined the sympathy he heard there, or whether he was simply fooling himself.

"Did *you* know what Sazo was?" He wondered if she could have any idea of how serious the situation was. She was the outsider here, with no idea of the powers at play.

She gave a slow nod, keeping eye contact. "I always knew what he was. From the very beginning, when he first spoke to me."

He had been braced for it, but he felt the blow of betrayal, nevertheless. She'd known Sazo was a thinking system. Had kept quiet and all the while, had let the Grih's most dangerous enemy loose amongst them.

"You lied to us." Hoke stepped up to his side. "After we saved your life."

Rose focused on her. "Sazo saved my life, Admiral. He got me off the Class 5, down to Harmon, and if one of your soldiers hadn't collapsed part of the roof over my ship's entrance, I wouldn't have needed saving from the gryak, either." She paused. "If you're going to bring it down to a score sheet, then let's get the score straight."

She was right, but still, it stung.

She shifted her gaze back to Dav. "That's not to say, once my way to safety was blocked, I wasn't very grateful to Captain Jallan for rescuing me."

"And your idea of gratitude is to betray us?" Valu asked. "You set a thinking system loose among us."

Dav shot him a quick look.

Both Valu and Hoke seemed to keep forgetting Rose was a highly advanced sentient. Not easily intimidated, not easily overawed.

They needed to shut up. No matter how angry with her he was, antagonizing her was not the answer.

"Rose isn't from here. It's doubtful she understood the consequences." He'd meant to be placating, but as he said it, he realized it was most likely true, and still, he could not let the sense of betrayal go.

"Coming from the two people who were planning to use Rose's abuse at the hands of the Tecran to leverage their claim to *my* ship, these recriminations are a little hypocritical," Sazo said, not from the Class 5 and over the comm, as if he was with Rose, but directly from the *Barrist's* own bridge. Like a whisper right in their ears.

As a way of bringing home how much power he had over them, it was effective.

"I've been nothing but an 'orange' to you, Admiral Valu. You haven't even bothered to introduce yourself. And Admiral Hoke doesn't trust me, finds my looks deceiving, and believes I've somehow manipulated all the senior officers on the *Barrist* to go easy on me to prevent my being upset."

There was silence, and then Dav, Appal, Borji and Kila turned to look at Hoke.

She toughed it out, looking neither discomforted nor apologetic.

"What's your point?" Hoke's voice was harsh. "We have a Levron battleship almost on top of us, and much though we'd love to chat——"

Rose shook her head. "Don't worry about the Levron. Sazo's taken care of that."

She didn't mean he was in control of that, too?

Dav and Borji exchanged a quick look.

If Rose had said that to ease their minds, she'd done the opposite. They had a thinking system in control of a Class 5, a Levron, two Battle Center fast class gunships, the *Barrist* and a carrier shuttle.

If he wanted to take on any planet in the UC, he could.

"Given that the two admirals don't trust me," Rose said, "and given the situation . . ." She trailed off, and Dav wondered if Sazo was transmitting something on a screen, or communicating with her privately. She looked up and to the right of the screen, where Dav would bet there was a lens and a speaker, then she flicked a look directly at him. "One moment, Captain, if you don't mind." She looked up and right again. "Sazo? Could you . . ?" She lifted her hand and made a quick slicing motion in front of her throat, and the screen went blank.

Dav crossed his arms over his chest and blew out a breath.

"She knew." Appal spoke softly beside him. "She knew all along . . ."

Words failed him, and it must have shown because she gave him a look of sympathy.

"What did who know?" Filavantri Dimitara stepped onto the bridge.

Valu glared at her. "That orange knew all along that a thinking system was in control of the Class 5, and she never told us."

"Well." Dav thought back to that walk he and Rose had taken, just over three thou so they were out of ear-shot. "She actually did warn me something could be listening in, and trying to take over our systems."

There was silence.

"When was this?" Hoke's voice was sharp.

"When we first found her. She insisted on walking three thou from the ships, which she said was the range of the Tecran explorer's scanners, and asked me to switch off my own handheld before she told me."

"Did she say it was a thinking system?"

He shook his head. "She didn't even say it was definite, only a possibility."

"How would Rose McKenzie know the UC's policy on thinking systems?" Dimitara asked. "She's been locked in a cell in the lower levels of a Class 5 for the last three months, and before that, she lived on a world that has never even heard of the UC, let alone the Grih."

It was true, but still . . . it was a matter of trust. If she had trusted him, wouldn't she have told him?

"Whatever the case, threatening her, or trying to make her feel indebted to us is not a good strategy." Dav turned back to the admirals. "It's clear she's interceded on our behalf with Sazo. Made him promise not to kill anyone on board. Let's try to at least be civil."

The big screen flickered back to life.

Rose faced them again, her eyes sparking, as if she'd just had an argument.

"Right, I'll be blunt. I have landed in a situation which I don't fully understand. The Tecran grabbed me and I wanted to escape. I made a deal with Sazo in order to do that and as a result, have landed smack in the middle of this mess. I have to take some responsibility, even though I didn't know what the repercussions would be when I set out on this path, but you need to take some responsibility too, because this Class 5 is apparently a Grihan-designed ship, and Sazo was created by a Grihan scientist.

"I want to help Sazo make the right decisions now, at least as far as Sazo, the Grih, and I are concerned, and I don't understand everything. Sazo can read political commentary and history as much as he likes, but we need someone to give us an idea of where things stand and what the outcome will be if Sazo takes certain actions."

"I can help advise you." Hoke stepped forward, face bland.

Rose gave a throaty laugh. "I'm sure you can." She shook her head, the smile fading on her face. "Captain Jallan." Her clear green gaze caught his and suddenly she was dead serious. She crooked her finger. "I pick you."

THE LAST TIME Rose remembered being in the Class 5s launch bay was when she'd escaped.

The lion had lain dead right in the middle of the massive space, and she had felt completely alone. She hadn't trusted Sazo then, hadn't known what was ahead except that she would be away from here.

How ironic that she was right back where she'd started, this time waiting for an arrival, not a departure.

She reached for the crystal around her neck and froze for a moment when it wasn't there, until she remembered she'd taken it off. Sazo had told her Fu-tama must have seen it on her at the breakfast she'd had with the UC councilors. In a way, it had saved her life.

Instead of killing her, Lothric had been told to send her to Fu-tama's ship.

It also explained why Lothric had tried to search her before sending her out in the maintenance pod. Her memories of what happened weren't that clear, but she did remember the groping hands.

She shivered.

The crystal now sat tucked into a secret compartment she'd made by manipulating her hyr fabric bra. Not that she intended to be anywhere near Lothric or Fu-tama, but Sazo didn't trust anyone, including Dav, and to appease him she'd hidden it away and it had calmed him immediately.

A calm Sazo was good.

The *Barrist's* runner came through the gel wall and she turned her body away to escape the cold, gritty blast as it set down.

She assumed only Dav was aboard, that either he'd flown it himself or it had been set to auto-pilot. Sazo wouldn't have let him in, otherwise.

The ramp descended and he stepped down, her two black bags gripped in one hand, a large container in the other.

She took a step toward him, mouth open in surprise. "What . . . ?"

He wriggled the container. "Grinabo and that bread you like."

She smiled at him, delighted, and he came to an awkward stop.

His eyes were unreadable and she could feel the smile slowly fall from her lips.

She had chosen a side. That side had been Sazo's.

She would do it again, because it had also been Dav's side. She'd slowly come to realize that. It had made the decision to help Sazo get into the *Barrist's* system easier.

Sazo was the genie out of the bottle——there was no putting him back in, but he could be reasoned with.

Right now, she understood she was the only person whose opinion he valued.

Rose had done the best she could for everyone, but she was sure from where Dav stood, her best would look very much like betrayal.

"I'm sorry."

He seemed to come to himself with a jerk, and frowned at her.

"Are you?"

"I couldn't tell you about Sazo, even though I wanted to. I had given him my word."

"I got that." Dav's jaw clenched.

"I know you might think that I endangered your crew after what Sazo did to the Tecran, but I made him promise not to hurt anyone. He especially took me to the Grih, rather than any other of the UC members, because he thought I would be most at home amongst you, and I've done my best to protect you."

He gave a slow nod, as if putting pieces together, and for something to do, so she could look away from his direct gaze, she stepped forward and took hold of the container of bread and grinabo. Gave a tug to take it.

He held on, so she was left pulling at something that just wasn't moving and stumbled closer to him.

"What do you think, Rose?" His rough voice echoed in the empty launch bay. "Do you think Sazo was right? Are you at home with us?"

"You know I am." She forced herself to look at him again.

She'd thought the possibilities that had bloomed between them had been scorched to nothing by the revelation of what she'd been hiding, but unbelievably, his hand came up and a long, blunt finger traced her cheekbone.

"Why didn't you trust me?"

"I did trust you. But my secrets weren't mine to tell. And I'm sorry, Dav, but Sazo was already manipulating the Class 5 by the time the Tecran snatched me. He'd already achieved a level of freedom they didn't know about, and he used that freedom to communicate with me. When Dr. Fliap fell ill, he took over my care so that I was protected. When I agreed to turn the final key and let him loose, I had no idea what the Grih's view on thinking systems were, and I wouldn't have cared, even if I had.

"Sazo saved me, issuing orders as if they were from Captain Gee or Dr. Fliap to make my life better. From the moment he took over, there were no more operations, no more visits. I was left alone.

"I got the handheld, got an ear comm, and Sazo and I started making plans. When I did find out how you would react to knowing a thinking system like Sazo was alive and well and running around in your world again, it was too late, and it had gone too far. I had given my word."

He said nothing for a moment, but his fingers slid along her jaw and then buried themselves in her hair. "You always keep your word?"

She nodded, and his fingers slid to curve around her nape.

"Your knowing about Sazo, hiding him from us . . . it won't be easy for you to be accepted by the Grih when it comes out."

"And what about you, Dav? Do you find it hard to accept me now?"

He sighed. "Did Sazo let you hear the conversation we had with Farso Lothric, or did he just tell you about it?"

"He just told me about it."

"If what my former aide had to say was right, you might just be the embodiment of Hevalon's Law in this equation."

"Hevalon's Law?"

"The unknown factor in any complex scenario."

"Rose's people call that being a dark horse." Sazo spoke for the first time, and Dav started at the sound.

He drew back, his hand dropping to his side as if he'd been caught with his fingers in the till.

"Perhaps you wouldn't mind letting the *Barrist* know you are safe, Captain. They seem to be concerned, and Lieutenant Borji is even trying to hack his way back into the *Barrist's* weapons systems." Sazo's voice was wry.

Dav tapped his ear comm and she saw he half-expected it not to work, but Sazo let the comm through.

"Checking in."

He waited for a response. "Yes. I'll check in every hour until otherwise stated, to keep you appraised." He cut whoever he'd spoken to off, Kila, or perhaps even Admiral Hoke.

"All right?"

He ran a hand down a face she could suddenly see was exhausted. "Yes." Then he lifted his gaze to hers. "No. Not really."

"Perhaps between the three of us, we can do something about that?"

CHAPTER 31

DAV HAD BEEN on the Class 5 four times since the *Barrist* had stumbled on it, but for the first time, he was really paying attention to the design.

Rose led him to a comfortable room which he guessed was the officers' lounge. Something he'd missed before was that everything was in standard Battle Center layout. If any of them had been concentrating, they might have wondered why the Tecran were building ship interiors exactly like their own.

And one of the reasons he hadn't been concentrating was walking in front of him. She looked as cute as she had when she recorded the songs in the debrief chamber, her golden hair pulled back in a thick, glossy tail, her clothes clinging to her curves.

He forced himself to look away. "Did you know when you light jumped the Class 5 into Grih territory that it was a Grih design?" He glanced up at the nearest lens, like Rose tended to, to indicate the question was for Sazo.

"No, I didn't. I didn't know any of what Farso Lothric told you. I really did choose Grih territory because it seemed likely that Rose would be happiest with the Grih."

"And ironically, you landed our own mess back on our doorstep."

Rose frowned at him. "I wouldn't call Sazo a mess. I'd call him an abused minor."

An abused minor.

Dav tried to get his head around that.

"My apologies. I meant the situation was a mess of our own making, not that Sazo himself was a mess."

"What would have happened if Sazo had been found straight after Fayir died? What would they have done with the thinking systems he'd developed?" Rose asked.

"By law, they would have been destroyed."

Dav suddenly regretted the turn of the conversation. If he was going to negotiate with Sazo, bringing up the kill order on all thinking systems in Grih law was not a fruitful place to start.

"That's probably why they weren't found. Fayir must have known the fate of any thinking system he developed. He probably made sure they wouldn't be found for a long time after his death. Perhaps he even set things in place for them to be found when they were. Two hundred years after his death, he must have thought there could well have been a change in attitude by then." Rose took the container of grinabo over to the small drinks station, and Dav saw her making them each a cup as if she'd grown up doing it.

She really had taken to life with them, whether because of a strong need to fit in, to find a new place in the universe, or because their ways were similar to hers. The sheer scale of what she'd had to give up hit him, and he wanted to shield her, and keep her safe.

"There hasn't been a change, though, has there, Captain Jallan?" Sazo asked. "Even though two hundred years have passed."

Dav could hear the edge in his voice. Wondered how a thinking system could add that edge.

"The laws haven't changed, that's true, but attitudes may have. Lothric is right in that non-UC nations are working toward thinking systems of their own. We experienced the good of thinking systems and leapt far ahead of everyone else, and when the trouble hit and we cut thinking systems out of our lives, we still had the benefits of the original collaboration. Medical advances, no energy or food shortages. Would the Grih or even the UC think it wise to combat foreign thinking systems by developing new thinking systems of our own?" He shrugged. "The answer is almost certainly no, especially with the current laws as they stand. But having a live thinking system already here, wholly formed and on our side?" Again he shrugged. "I think that would be different."

"And if I'm not on your side?"

Dav hesitated. "If you weren't on our side, you would be considered a threat."

There was silence.

"Calm down, Sazo." Rose handed Dav his grinabo and perched on one of the chairs, a look of exasperation on her face, even though Sazo hadn't made a sound. "You could claim neutrality, and play things that way, but if I'm going to live with the Grih, I'd prefer you to be on their side."

"They haven't all been nice to you." Sazo almost sounded sulky.

The exchange stunned Dav. Rose behaved as if she had a real say in Sazo's decisions. Dav had told Hoke he hoped Rose liked them enough to intervene with Sazo on their behalf, but it was more than that. She had the power to change his mind. To direct his actions. She didn't behave as if he would automatically obey her, but as if they were a team.

"Well, I'll admit Admiral Hoke didn't win any friendship prizes, and Admiral Valu was really only interested in the Class 5, but they didn't steal me from Earth, keep me locked up for three months and laser me open when they felt like it, either."

Dav raised his gaze to hers. He hoped she would have better things to say about them one day than the comparison that at least they didn't torture her.

"A declaration of alliance would certainly help." But Dav wondered whether it would. A fear of thinking systems was so entrenched.

"Why don't we start by mentioning Sazo's worry for the crew of the *Barrist* before they boarded the Class 5 for the first time?" Rose took a sip of grinabo, her face quite neutral. "The Tecran were well-armed and instructed to kill. While he regrets he was forced to kill so many of the Tecran crew, when it comes to protecting his allies, he is ruthless."

Rose kept her gaze on him while she spoke, and Dav got the message loud and clear.

"I'd be happy to convey that information to Battle Center." He didn't look away from her, and he made no attempt to hide that he thought it was all yurve shit. Sazo hadn't given Dav's crew a second thought. He'd killed those Tecran out of revenge. What happened on the Class 5 was what had started the thinking system wars in the first place.

He decided to push for a concession, seeing as he was being asked to swallow an absolute lie. "Sazo giving us back control of the *Barrist* and the two battle cruisers would help ease any tension between us."

Rose had crossed her arms over her chest at his expression of distaste, defensive. She turned her head and looked at the lens. "I'm sure he could do that."

"I could. But I'm not going to. Why would I give up my advantage."

Rose sighed. "Sazo."

"No, Rose. They have a kill order out on my kind, and I must just give up control of their ship to them? That doesn't make any tactical sense."

"It does if you want your 'concern' for the crew of the *Barrist* to be taken seriously."

There was silence. Dav waited it out, but Sazo remained quiet.

"What about the Levron?" At least he could find out what the status was there. "Rose said you had it under control, too."

"With threats, not because I've been able to take the system. Their access gates are impenetrable. Far more difficult than the Grih's, and yours were hard enough. My guess is that no matter how much they gambled on controlling me, they still took some strong precautions."

"So," Rose stood. "Where does this leave us?"

"It depends on what Sazo's intension are." Dav kept his tone short. "Are you with us, or not?"

"Let's say that I am." Sazo spoke reluctantly.

"Then the odds are in our favor even if you don't have the Levron under control," Dav said. "The Class 5 alone out-guns it. If Sazo drops the comm block he's set up, we can send for more ships, in case the

Tecran send more Levrons our way. But honestly, with you on our side, the only way we'll be in real trouble is if the Tecran send another Class 5."

"I don't think you get it," Rose told him, and he could see from her posture he wasn't going to like what she had to say. "That's exactly what Sazo is hoping they'll do."

CHAPTER 32

IT WAS hard to argue with Dav that Sazo's plan wasn't insane.

As the man responsible for everyone on the four ships around them, he wouldn't be able to see it any other way.

"He wants to meet his own kind." She spoke to his back because he had moved away to lean against the far wall, shoulders hunched as he looked at the lens feed of the *Barrist* and its two battleships on the large wall screen, with the UC fast carrier off to one side.

"Let him meet his own kind somewhere else." The words were tight, angry, in that rough voice of his.

He looked like a prize fighter, about to go into the ring. Furious and contained, his hands clenched, the muscles on his arms bunched with tension.

He turned to look at her over his shoulder, and she stopped breathing for a moment when her gaze clashed with his.

She lifted her hands in surrender. "I'm not in charge here. Sazo planned this ages ago, I've got nothing to do with it."

"Change his mind."

"She can't change my mind." Sazo inserted himself into the conversation, and Rose wondered what had taken him so long.

"The Tecran have been obsessive in their determination not to allow any Class 5 within half a galaxy of each other, let alone within sight of one another."

Rose saw Dav still at Sazo's words. Hah. His interest was caught.

"I didn't even know there were other Class 5s until an officer on my Class 5 slipped up and mentioned it to someone in casual conversation. Sometimes, they forget I'm there, that I'm what makes it all work. That was the start of my . . . rebellion."

Rose hadn't known that herself. "So finding out you weren't alone was the trigger that made you start to build your independence in the system, even though you were still held prisoner in the lock-safe?"

"Yes. And I can't be sure any of the other Class 5s know they aren't alone. I might be the only one who started to wake up and the chances of any of them finding someone like Rose to rescue them aren't high."

"So you aren't just trying to meet someone of your own kind," Dav said into the silence, "you're knowingly bringing a Class 5 which is most likely fully under Tecran control into this territory. Can I ask you, if it tries to attack us——and it will——will you fire on it?"

There was silence again.

Rose closed her eyes. She knew the answer to that. There was no way Sazo would fire on another Class 5. No way.

"You can't endanger so many people just to jolt a Class 5 awake." She spoke quietly. "You need to come up with another plan."

"There *is* no other plan." Sazo's voice boomed through the speakers, and Rose had to cover her ears. "I have thought through ever single alternative. None will bring the Class 5 within hailing distance but the threat that without it, they will lose me. They cannot let me get into Grih hands, and they know it. The consequences would be their expulsion from the UC and the loss of all trading privileges. And they also know if I'm free, I could hunt for the other Class 5s. Try to wake them." He was quiet for a moment. "They won't want another Class 5 anywhere near me, but if they have evidence that I'm under Grih control, they will risk it. Even if just to destroy me so that my firepower can't be turned against them and I can't be used as evidence of what they've been up to."

Dav tipped his head up to the speakers. "How will you pretend to be under Grih control?"

Rose had wondered the same.

"I'll shoot the Levron." Sazo kept his voice expressionless.

"No." Rose knew this was the steep part of a very slippery slope that had started with the lion, and moved on to the Tecran crew. The first had been done in panic, the second in revenge. This third act was coldly premeditated. It would kill something in Sazo's burgeoning soul.

"Rose——"

"No, Sazo." She could hear the chill in her voice. "There has to be another way. You do not kill people who are already abiding by your order to stay put and disarm their weapons. You do not."

Dav looked up at her, his expression considering. "If you want to show you're under Grih control, simply shooting at the Levron won't work, anyway. You could be acting alone, for all they know."

"What do you suggest?" Sazo's voice was quiet, and, she thought, chastened.

"How about we surround the Levron in a coordinated operation? The *Barrist*, the two battleships and the Class 5. Lift the comm lockdown and we can demand they surrender, give their lens feed some good footage to send back to Tecran High Command. There could be no confusion, then. You'd have to either be under our control or in alliance with us. Either way, the worst outcome they could imagine."

Rose waited for a response. "Sazo?"

There was quiet, and then, in a soft whisper in her ear comm, not over the speakers: "I need to think about this, Rose."

"Why doesn't he answer?" Dav crossed his arms over his chest, and clenched his jaw in exasperation. A very frustrated, handsome elf.

Rose took him in and shivered. "I think he's shaken that he didn't think of that himself, but then, to be fair, he didn't expect your cooperation."

"He could have forced us to do it, he has control of our ships anyway."

"Yes, he could." Rose smiled slowly. "But I don't think that occurred to him, either."

Dav sent her a narrow-eyed look. "What now?"

Rose yawned. "Sazo's thinking about it. It sounded like he'd be a while and there's nothing we can do until he gets back to us. How about bed?"

HE COULD HAVE MADE light of her comment, which he knew had been innocent, but he simply wasn't capable.

He stared at her, and watched as her cheeks turned a delicate shade of pink.

"Bed?"

"Sleep." She cleared her throat. "I would need at least a kiss before I contemplated bed."

It was his turn to feel heat in his cheeks.

"Although," she suddenly grinned at him, "you have had your hands on my naked breasts, so maybe a kiss isn't strictly necessary."

A wave of lust swept over him. The memory of her soft skin beneath his fingers, the weight of her on his lap, the brush of her lips against his ear, ripped down the wall he'd built to keep himself away from her.

He took a step toward her and his face must have shown some of what he was feeling because the smile on hers disappeared.

"You don't look that angry with me anymore." Her voice, usually so smooth, was hoarse.

"I seem to have gotten over it." He took another step, and the fire that burned in him leapt higher when her breathing hitched at the movement.

She took a step back, and the hunter in him sat up and took notice. He wanted her to run. Wanted to chase. And catch.

"You just got a really scary look in your eye." It sounded as if she was forcing the words out.

"Scary?" He took another step.

She strangled out a laugh. "Well, hungry."

"I am hungry, Rose." One last step and he was in reach of her. But he didn't touch. Not yet. "I've wondered a few times over the last couple of days if I was mad. I've put my career in jeopardy more times in the last two days than I have in all the years since I joined Battle

Center. Appal has questioned my sanity, I've tried to convince myself I was behaving logically, but since I came aboard the Class 5 and followed you into this room, I've slowly become aware that there was no logic involved, no sanity to be found. I am just very, very hungry."

She looked at him with big, startled eyes but she didn't move back or avoid him as he bent down and gave her the kiss she'd joked about.

It started slow, a gentle brush of lips, but her hands slid up his chest, up the sides of his throat, and then linked behind his neck and she committed herself to it, fully.

She opened her mouth beneath his, the tip of her tongue brushing the seam of his lips and he sank in, pulling her up and against him.

She made a sound, a sigh and groan combined, and he drew on every ounce of self-control in him to lift his head and put a little space between them. Here was not the place for what he wanted to do.

She was breathing as hard as he was. She opened the distance between them further by taking a step back.

"Your quarters?" He'd be surprised if she could understand him, his voice was so guttural.

She didn't say anything, she just nodded, raised trembling fingers to her lips and then turned on her heel and walked away.

It wasn't a full-on chase, but given where they were headed, he'd take it.

CHAPTER 33

SHE FELT STALKED.

The sensation caught at her breath and raised the hairs on the back on her neck in anticipation. She shivered as she reached the guest suite Sazo had shown her earlier. It helped to know it had never once been used.

She opened the door and looked back at Dav. He seemed to take up most of the passageway and his beautiful face was all sharp angles and desire.

If she let him in, there was no going back. She knew herself too well, and she must call it off now if she didn't want anything to happen.

She would not have done this on Earth.

Not have taken things so fast, so soon, but she wasn't the same person she had been three months ago. She had come to understand the concept of seize the day, and if Dav hadn't worked it out, she knew all too well what Sazo would ask her to do when the other Class 5 arrived.

She may get out of it alive, but there was a high chance she wouldn't.

He must have sensed her moment of hesitation, because he

stopped, tipped his head in that curious, alien way the Grih seemed to have. They stared at each other for a long beat.

She broke the moment by stepping in to the room and to the side, sweeping her arm to invite him in.

He let out a pent-up breath, put his hand up to his chest and thumped it once. "I think I need to restart my heart."

His words broke the tension she felt and brushed away any awkwardness with the laugh of delight that leapt from her.

She opened her mouth to say something funny back, and found herself up against the wall with his lips on hers and the words she'd planned to say stuck in her throat.

It was strange to realize they were alone, no longer surrounded by a ship full of people who all wanted Dav for something.

Except for Sazo.

But there was nowhere she could go without Sazo, whether here or on the *Barrist*, and there were no lenses here. She had told him to disable the two-way speakers in the room. He could only contact her through the comms unit on the desk or her earpiece.

She let herself fall into the kiss, arching as Dav's mouth moved from her lips to her neck and down.

He pulled her hard against him, and she let herself enjoy the sensation.

"That was certainly a qualifying kiss." Her words were breathless. "I'm definitely considering bed rather than sleep, now."

"Are you sure? I could try again."

He worked his way up, and she smiled as he took her mouth a second time.

She slid her arms up his back, tracing muscles and the broad reach of his shoulders.

"I'm happy for you to submit as many applications as you like." She bit his neck and he lifted her up against the wall, both hands gripping her thighs.

She sighed as they rubbed delightfully against each other.

"You weigh far more than seems possible," he murmured in her ear, hefting her higher, and she laughed.

"Sweet talker." She nibbled at his ear, and then licked the outer rim.

He swore, fumbled her, and then swung her around, took the few strides needed to get them to the bed. "I can't hold you up with you distracting me like that." He dropped her down and then followed her, half-pinning her to the mattress.

"And yet you look so big and strong." She traced the bulge of muscle in his arm, her heart tripping in her chest.

"Hmm." He was suddenly over her, arms on either side of her head, in a kind of push-up that defined all the muscles in his arms, chest and stomach.

"Oooh. Very big and strong." She let her hand trail down his chest, and then rub where he was hard and erect.

She saw the change in his eyes from playful and laughing to dark with desire.

He bent his head, not touching any part of her with his body, and then brushed a kiss across her lips.

The sweetness of the connection, the gentleness of it, caused tears to prick behind her lids and she cupped his cheek.

"I like you, Dav Jallan." She whispered it against his mouth.

He dropped to the side of her, and slowly pulled up her shirt. "That's good. Because I like you, too."

CHAPTER 34

HE KNEW they were sexually compatible. Kila had mentioned it in amazement from the very beginning after Rose's first medical scan. She hadn't been able to get over the unlikelihood of the first advanced sentient in five hundred years being so like them.

Of course, it wasn't chance that had brought her their way, he knew now. It was Sazo. Trying to please her. To find her a place where she would fit in.

But sexually compatible was very different to sexually appealing, and he had felt the appeal almost from the moment he'd met her. It had started on the first walk they took, was strengthened in their flight up to the *Barrist* from Harmon, and then had burst into hot, painful life at the pool, when he'd first touched her.

The playfulness, the joy in her, pulled him even deeper under her spell now.

She was stripped naked beside him and her hands explored his body, his own hands tracing the soft, smooth curve of her waist, cupping the deliciously heavy breasts.

He shuddered at the sensations, the need clawing at him to take her in hard, deep thrusts.

His fingertips traced the fine, almost invisible white lines the Tecran had put on her, the evidence of a laser scalpel that had opened her up and a heat pen that had closed her again.

He leaned over her and traced them with his tongue, inhaling her scent and reveling in the incredible smoothness of her skin.

She tensed when he touched her scars at first, and then, as he worked his way down, as he explored her with lips, tongue and fingers, learned what made her gasp, or her breath catch, she relaxed. He found what he needed to do to make her shudder beneath him, and when she arched under him, and let him inside her, everything fell away.

She moved beneath him, matching her rhythm to his, until she flew apart with a cry and he shuddered his release.

He pulled her close and she curled into him, kissed his collar-bone, all sleepy and tousled, her glorious, golden hair draped like silk over his arm.

He rubbed it between his fingers, amazed at how smooth and soft it was.

She reached out a clumsy hand to slap at the headboard beside her, and the lights went out. He guessed that she had told Sazo she wanted no speaker activation in the room, and realized he hadn't even thought about that, that Sazo would otherwise have been listening in to them. It was a reminder that Sazo was still lurking in this place, that they weren't truly alone.

But he couldn't hold on to his dislike of that with Rose McKenzie draped over him.

He fell asleep with his fingers twined in her hair, and the gentle tickle of her breath on his chest and for the first time since they'd come across the Class 5, truly rested.

HE WOKE, slowly and pleasantly, to the sound of running water and song. He was alone in the bed, and when he opened his eyes, he found the whole of the screen wall in front of the bed was now a forest, dappled in the light of early morning, the pattern of sunlight on the forest floor dancing as the wind ruffled the branches overhead.

The song Rose was singing was fast and catchy and while he knew she didn't think what she could do with her voice was special, there wasn't a Grih who wouldn't envy him this moment.

The scent of yuiar soap wafted out on the steam which curled lazily in the light from the simulated forest. The most expensive scent in the galaxy, and she was lathering it on without a care.

He was involved with a princess.

He grinned.

The comm chimed, and Dav sat up and stared at it. It chimed again and he debated whether to answer.

It could only be Sazo, or Sazo patching through the admiral, and he didn't feel like speaking to either of them.

It chimed a third time, and this time, held the tone. Giving in, he pulled on his pants, crossed the room and hit accept.

"Yes?"

"Where is Rose?" Sazo sounded suspicious.

"In the shower." Where he wanted to be. With her.

"Oh." Sazo went quiet. "She's singing."

Sazo understood her language, yet another thing Dav resented about him, but he may as well use it. "What is she singing about?"

"Earth people aren't like the Grih." Sazo managed to make it sound like Rose's people were far superior. "They sing a song because they like the tune, they like the beat. The words themselves aren't necessarily meaningful to the occasion."

That may be true, from what Dav had managed to get out of Rose, but still . . . Sazo sounded a little too defensive.

"I understand that. I still would like to know what she's singing."

"The song is about someone listing all the things they like about their lover."

Dav knew he was smiling, probably like an idiot, but he didn't care. "Well, perhaps I'll go give her a few more things to add to her list."

"Wait." Sazo's voice was cold.

Dav's finger hovered over the button to cut the comm short, but didn't touch it. "What?"

"Rose is my friend. And she likes you. But if you hurt her, or make her unhappy, I will hurt you back."

"So noted." Dav could be just as cool as a thinking system. Just as clipped.

"I'm worried you aren't taking me seriously." Sazo's voice got quieter, as if he wanted to make sure Rose couldn't hear him. "Dr. Fliap didn't fall ill. I made him ill. I can kill a whole ship, but I can also be very precise in who I target. Don't forget it."

Dav had wondered about Fliap. "How did you get the bastard?"

Sazo made a sound, almost like an exclamation of surprise, and again, Dav wondered how a thinking system affected something like that.

"We visited a lot of worlds. Most of them with no life, but one, it had life stirring on it. Just the beginnings of it. Of course, they had to go down and see. Fliap had to have samples. He analyzed them and if he didn't understand the significance of what he'd found, the toxicity of it, I did." His voice held an edge of grim satisfaction. "When he started on Rose, I had to wait six weeks until he looked at the samples again, but when he did, it was a simple matter to infect him, given the automation of his lab."

"You liked Rose, right from the start?" Dav couldn't be anything but grateful to him that he had.

"Yes." His answer seemed strangely wistful. "I liked her straight away."

There was silence for a moment.

"I won't hurt her, Sazo."

"You won't last long if you do." Sazo dismissed his soft comment with the sharpness of his tone and Dav cut off the comm with a bitter jab.

He turned to face the bathroom.

Blew out a long, slow breath.

Damned if Sazo was going to ruin this morning, this moment. Damned if he was.

He could hear the water flying around in the shower, as if Rose was dancing as well as singing in there under the spray. And her joy, and the thought of her wet and naked and happy, was enough to push aside the threat to his life by something that could crush him like a insect underfoot and propel him forward.

Sazo would have to learn to share.

CHAPTER 35

ROSE DRESSED WITH LANGUID MOVEMENTS, her skin still humming from the feel of Dav's hands. She hadn't slept so well since she'd been taken by the Tecran——even on the *Barrist* she'd felt too out of place, too nervous, to truly rest.

Dav sat in full uniform beside the desk, watching her as she tucked and shaped the sage green hyr fabric into her standard trousers and long-sleeved t-shirt.

His face was hard to read, although his gaze never left her.

"Will you get into trouble for sleeping with me?" She had wondered while she'd led him to her room last night, but decided he knew what he could and couldn't do under Battle Center rules far better than her.

He shrugged. "I don't intend to tell them, it isn't any of their business who I sleep with, although, admittedly, in your case things are a little more complicated than that."

Just a bit.

"So you want me to pretend there is nothing between us?" Best to have this on the table right now, before she landed him in hot water with a look or a casual touch.

"No." He lifted his eyes from where her hands were smoothing the waist of her trousers, his voice sharp. Then he rubbed his forehead. "I don't know how to play this. I want to shout over the comms that you're mine and we're together, but I don't want to deal with the yurve shit I know will come down on me if they know about it, because it's going to complicate things and make them second-guess all my orders."

She tugged her shirt down. "How about we pretend to be neutral to each other until after this is over? I agree it could be dangerous if they think your motivations aren't objective. Dangerous for your crew as well as Sazo and I. Admiral Hoke already thinks you're too easy on me."

He gave a slow nod as he stood. "As long as you know that neutral is the last thing I really feel." He slid his arms around her, pulled her close. Then swore when the comm sounded.

She brushed a kiss on his chin, as high as she could reach without him bending a little, and wriggled out of his hold.

She walked to the bedside table, started at the fact that Sazo wasn't there, and then remembered he was hidden from sight in last night's clothing. She would have to come back and get him after Dav was gone. She picked up her earpiece, brought it toward her ear.

Dav made a sound behind her, and she turned to look at him, the device still in her hand. "It just occurred to me. Back on Harmon, when you were talking to yourself. You were talking to Sazo?"

She shrugged. "Yes."

"You never told me."

She crossed her arms over her chest. "I couldn't tell you then, and since then, since you've know about Sazo, surely you realized? Last night we had a short conversation through the earpiece, so telling you simply wouldn't have occurred to me. I thought you knew."

He made a noise of protest and she lifted her hand.

"When you asked me on Harmon what I was saying to myself, and I told you I was just sorting through the events of the day, that was true. I was telling Sazo what had happened and I had given my word to say nothing about him, so I slid around the truth. Are you seriously angry about this?"

"No." His words were stiff, but he held her gaze. "Anything else you didn't tell me?"

She glared at him. "I don't think so." Then glared at the comm unit as it sounded again.

They both ignored it.

"I don't want to fight with you, Rose. I want you to trust me, and I want to trust you. I know about Sazo now, and there is no more need for deception, that's all."

"Agreed." She knew she sounded surly. She felt surly.

"When did he break in to the *Barrist's* systems?" He made the question casual, but Rose felt a twinge of guilt at her part in it, even though Sazo was right, he'd been just as dangerous to them being outside their system as being in it.

She knew Dav wanted to know how much Sazo knew, how long he'd been listening in to them.

"When I was singing those songs in the debriefing room."

He said nothing for a moment, but he seemed to relax a little. "We need to talk about those songs, when this is over."

She gave a shrug. "What's there to talk about?"

"The minute Sazo lifts the comm ban, the lens feed of you singing will be transmitted to every family member and friend of every one of my crew. And from there, to each of the four planets."

She groaned. "Sazo said if I sang, they'd be less inclined to listen to that order to hand me over to the UC."

"He was right." Dav looked up at the speakers but Rose was sure that Sazo would respect her request to make the speakers inert in this room.

The comm unit sounded again, and Rose could actually hear a squawk from the earpiece in her hand.

She stalked over and opened the channel. "Sazo? I'm putting in the earpiece, so lower your voice."

"I wouldn't have to shout if you answered the comm unit." He sounded like he was spitting.

"I'm sorry." She meant it sincerely, and he must have heard that because his next words were civil and quiet and he spoke through the comm unit, so Dav could hear him, too.

"Admiral Hoke is trying to connect to Dav. I've been blocking repeated contact from the *Barrist* since you went to bed last night. I want to talk to Dav about his idea of surrounding the Levron before I let Hoke speak to him again, but we had better do it quickly or she'll be too angry to agree to anything."

Dav made a sound, and she turned to him.

"I can't believe I forgot to sign off." He looked at her, absolutely perplexed. "I said I'd connect every hour until I told them otherwise."

"I guess you forgot," she said, and he suddenly grinned and gave her what was clearly intended to be a leer.

"I suppose I did."

"Could we discuss strategy now?" Sazo asked, and Rose recognized the sarcasm in his tone. She'd used that tone herself.

Now she knew what her sister meant when she said how spooky it was to hear your words come straight back at you from your children.

But Sazo wasn't her child.

He was a chimera, building himself using parts from everyone he came in contact with. So far, aside from his own cold logic, he'd absorbed the Tecran ruthlessness, and her own unique style.

Her hand crept up to grip the crystal hanging around her neck, scrabbled at nothing until she remembered again he wasn't hanging there.

She would do whatever it took to never let him fall back into Tecran hands.

He would truly become a monster if that happened, and whatever the Tecran thought, they would never hold him for long again.

"Strategy it is."

They had decided, Sazo, Rose and himself, that it would work better if Dav returned to the *Barrist* before they began discussing their plan with the admiral.

Anything that he said from the bridge of the Class 5 could be considered a forced cooperation, and while they didn't need Admiral Hoke to agree, her agreement would help.

Dav was greeted in the launch bay by Hoke, Valu and Appal, and as he stepped down, he felt a hard tug of regret that he'd had to leave Rose behind. And that the last private words between them had been tainted by his accusations of her hiding things from him.

The thought that she'd lied to him had dug at him, the memory of her sitting in the runner from Harmon, staring at his feet, telling him it was acceptable for someone who had been in solitary confinement to talk to themselves, when all along, she hadn't been talking to herself.

Sliding around the truth, she called it.

Whatever it was, it had stung, but he was sorry they hadn't had time to talk it through. That she couldn't have taken the runner over with him to the *Barrist* to clear the air.

There was no way Sazo would allow her off the Class 5, and he couldn't blame him, but it left something cold and hard lodged in his throat to fly away from her.

"Well, you look fine." Admiral Hoke said, her voice blunt, but not unfriendly.

"I am fine."

"We were worried when you stopped checking in." Appal caressed the stock of her shockgun. "Sazo said you were sleeping, but we didn't know whether to believe him."

He grimaced. There was no excuse he could offer that was acceptable. But he would not apologize in front of the admiral. He could speak to Appal in private, later. "Sazo said he needed to think about a plan I advanced to him, and cut off comms until he engaged with me again this morning."

"Well, you actually look as if you did get some sleep at least. I'm surprised you could rest knowing where you were." Valu eyed him with a quick, thorough evaluation.

"What do you mean, where I was?"

"On a Class 5 with a thinking system in control. He could have killed you at any time."

Hardly, given Rose had been lying curled up right beside him. But Valu still didn't get it. "He's just as in control of the *Barrist*. You were no safer than I was." In fact, Dav knew, he'd been far safer, as Sazo would do nothing to harm Rose or upset her.

"What have you got for us?" Hoke's voice was sharp.

"Let's talk with the rest of my senior officers present." Dav strode off, leading them to the conference room, and Appal got in step with him.

"Are you really all right?"

He gave a nod.

"And Rose?"

"She's fine. She's safer there than she is here." But something was niggling him about that. Something he was sure he should have caught earlier.

"There was panic when you didn't call back." She scrubbed a hand down her face. "It was a long night."

Dav could see the dark rings under her eyes. "I'm sorry."

She shrugged. "Not your fault."

But it was, and he shook his head at her, then tapped his comm unit before he said something he regretted. "Borji, Kila, Havak." He hesitated a moment. "Dimitara. Conference room in five minutes."

They must have all been hovering on the bridge, because they got there before he did, Appal and the admirals in tow.

"Status on the UC councilors?" He directed his question to Appal and Dimitara.

"Fu-tama is in holding here on the *Barrist*. The rest are back on their carrier, but they're demanding a senior officer be stationed on board, not only to show respect, but to reassure them the Grih won't attack their ship."

"That's ridiculous." Hoke lifted her chin. "We don't have anyone we can spare."

"I'll do it. It might not be a bad idea to have eyes and ears over there, especially with the Tecran councilors on board." Valu tapped his chin.

Hoke hesitated. Dav didn't blame her. It was unlike Valu to take himself out of the sphere of action, but it was true it would be useful to have someone who wouldn't be intimidated by the councilors watching over them.

"If you don't mind," Hoke said, at last.

Valu gave a nod.

Dimitara made a small moue of distaste, her smooth golden skin crinkling at the corners of her mouth. "Commander Appal won't give me the details of Farso Lothric's confession, but I agree Fu-tama needs to be confined until we can hand him over to the UC guard if he's mixed up in this."

"He is." Dav kept his words short.

"I believe you, but the other UC staff and councilors don't know you as well as I do, and they're panicking about this."

"What do they think we're doing?" Hoke focused her penetrating stare on Dimitara, but the liaison officer shrugged, unintimidated.

"They suspect you're trying to subvert the UC. Trying to claim illegal ownership of the Class 5, too——well, that's what the Tecran councilors are claiming."

Hoke snorted. "Sounds like you'll have some fun over there, Valu."

Dimitara smiled, her sharp little teeth a reminder that the Bukari may be the diplomats of the UC, but they could bite, too. "As the Tecran have more than a slight personal stake in advancing that notion, the others haven't take them very seriously, but they are disturbed."

"And what do they have to say about the appearance of a Tecran Levron class battleship in our territory?" Appal didn't keep the sneer from her voice.

Dimitara lifted her already arched brows. "They are disturbed by that, too, and the Tecran councilors can't contact their leaders to discover what's going on."

"I can help with that." Dav couldn't help a quick glance at the lens in the corner of the room. He hoped Sazo would let him talk first. Lay the groundwork. "Sazo has communicated with the Levron, and threatened to destroy it if it so much as moves a milli. But he wants to bring it home very clearly to the Tecran that he is in alliance with us. That we're cooperating together."

"I like the sound of this," Hoke said. "What's the catch?"

"No catch." Although there was. And Dav would have to find a way to work it into the conversation. "He's agreed to align with us, and he will lift the comm ban, and the *Barrist*, the Class 5 and the two battleships will surround the Levron in a coordinated maneuver."

"With the comm ban lifted, the Levron can send lens feed of the attack and show the Tecran High Command that we either have control of the Class 5, or, if they know about Sazo, that he is working with us." Appal spoke slowly. "I agree, what is the catch?"

"The catch is that they will be sufficiently afraid of the consequences of my alignment with you that they'll send in more firepower." Sazo inserted himself smoothly into the conversation, the volume from the speakers just loud enough for everyone to hear him, as if he were standing among them.

"That would be an outright declaration of war." Valu finally stepped forward. "The Tecran could perhaps argue the Class 5 arrived here by mistake. And at a very long stretch that the Levron was simply sent here to watch over the welfare of their own people and guard their property, but anymore than that, and they will have no diplomatic rock to hide under. They will be declaring war."

"Is that an acceptable risk for you?" Sazo asked. "That by doing this, they may send in more ships?"

"That depends." Admiral Hoke looked up at the speaker.

"On what?" Dimitara asked.

"On whether they send in another Class 5." Dav decided he might as well say it. From the looks on their faces, Appal and Hoke had gotten Sazo message just fine.

"Two Class 5s facing off against each other." Valu sounded far too intrigued.

"I believe my self-awareness means I have more chance of winning against any Class 5 they send against me, but whatever happens, I won't let them take me back. I'd light jump away before I allowed that to happen."

"What if you light jumped anyway?" Hoke asked. "Drew the Class 5 away? We can deal with the other ships, and you and the other Class 5 can go at each other where there won't be any collateral damage."

Dav went still. "Where would Rose be, in that scenario?"

Sazo hadn't agreed to it, but Dav knew the suggestion was a good one. Good for everyone but Rose.

There was silence as everyone in the room turned to look at him.

"She would be no safer with us than on the Class 5, surely?" Dimitara asked.

Dav tried to keep his face neutral. "If Sazo light jumps, how would they know where he'd gone?"

"Sazo could send a message to the *Barrist*, informing us he was going to light jump out, and giving us his location. That's what an ally would do." Borji shifted uncomfortably under Dav's gaze.

"As long as you could do that in a way that didn't look like we were setting them up, it could work." Appal gave a thoughtful nod. "But we won't be able to help Sazo against the other Class 5."

As Sazo had no intention of firing on the other Class 5, that was a moot point. And if he wasn't going to fire on it, how was he going to protect Rose?

Dav looked at the lens in the corner. He would tell them Sazo had no intention of harming the other Class 5 in a heart-beat if it meant keeping Rose safe . . .

"I appreciate the concern, Commander Appal, but I won't need help with the other Class 5. You'll have your hands full with the Levron and whatever else the Tecran send in," Sazo said. "I'll lift the Grih comm ban now and you can call for some more battleships, if you want to. So you're prepared if they send in their fleet."

"Appal's right that they'll suspect a trap if you're too obvious about sending your jump points to us before you leap," Hoke said. "You'll have to encrypt your comm, and if you're unlucky, they won't be able to decipher it."

"Send it on the same frequency Fu-tama used to contact Farso Lothric." Borji darted a quick look at Dav as he spoke. "It's clear enough if you're monitoring for it."

"That's a good idea." Sazo's voice seemed to warm when addressing Dav's chief engineer, he realized. He must have developed a liking for him.

"You still haven't answered, Sazo, where will Rose be when you light jump?"

"Rose is right here and can answer for herself."

Dav could hear the surprise and annoyance in her tone.

"I'll be with Sazo, helping him. I'm deadwood to the Grih in a battle. I have no combat experience, but Sazo can use my help, so I'm with him." Her voice was calm.

He wanted her off the Class 5. He couldn't help her there, and the thought of her so far out of reach made him feel strangely out of control.

Again, everyone turned to look at him, and he realized his fists were clenched and his jaw was locked down tight.

"So what happens now?" Dimitara asked eventually.

With no choice but to keep quiet, Dav flicked the screen, and brought up a map of the Virmana system. There would be time afterward for a conversation with Rose and Sazo. One he planned to win. "Now we plan our attack."

CHAPTER 36

"WE'RE ready to move on the Levron when you are." Dav looked straight at her from the screen which showed the *Barrist's* bridge. He looked tense, and the anger she'd heard in his voice earlier seemed to cling to him in the way he held his body and the downward slash of his brows.

The short, brutal conversation they'd had while the *Barrist* and its two battleships got ready to engage was still ringing in her ears.

He was so angry with her. So angry with Sazo.

She was sorry, both for the way they'd parted and the tension that was between them now. Dav was suspicious of what she was going to do for Sazo, she could hear it in his tone. There was anger there, but there was desperation, too.

It made something flutter inside her that he would react that way to her situation, made her smile at him now. He blinked back at her, confused.

"Ready?" Sazo's voice held the edge of excitement.

She nodded.

It was going to feel good, making threats to the Tecran she could actually carry out. Sazo opened up the comm link to voice transmission only. She didn't want them to see her or to be able to identify her at all.

"This is the captain of the Class 5 ship 5AZ0." She tried to sound authoritative. Sazo had told her he'd identified himself as the captain of the Class 5 before when he'd used her voice, so they would keep up the charade now. "Disengage all weapons and open your launch bays for immediate surrender to boarding parties from Grih Battle Center."

Sazo was transmitting the message to the *Barrist* as well, and Rose wondered if Admiral Hoke believed she really was in charge of the Class 5, or if she understood how little influence Rose had over Sazo.

On the screen to her left, Dav stood off to the side of the *Barrist's* bridge. He was looking at the massive screen in front of him that showed a bird's eye view of this part of the Virmana solar system, and the placement of every spaceship. He looked calm. Competent. And aloof.

She sighed, and then turned her head at the ping of an incoming comm. The Levron had opted for voice comm only, as well, so she couldn't see who was speaking.

"We haven't moved, as agreed." The Levron's captain sounded angry, but he must surely have known that further demands were coming. They could hardly lurk behind Virmana indefinitely.

"I know." Rose couldn't keep the impatience from her tone. "However, now I'm telling you to surrender."

"If we refuse?"

"Then your ship will no longer exist."

The screen in front of Rose showed the real-time outside lens feed, and as she spoke, she and Sazo rounded Virmana within sight of the Levron.

The *Barrist* appeared on the other side, having come around the opposite way in a pincher movement. The two smaller battleships flanked it on either side.

Sazo had allowed the Grih back into their own systems, allowed them to control their own vessels. It had gone a long way to warming Admiral Hoke up, although Sazo could lock them out again whenever he wanted to. Rose supposed it was the thought that counted.

"They've sent three distress calls to Tecran High Command since I lifted the comm ban," Sazo said into the speaker on Dav's bridge. "One included a request for immediate assistance."

"We got that, too." Borji said. "Good thing we've had a couple of hours jump on them to organize assistance of our own."

The comm unit linked to the Levron lit up again.

"Who are you? Because you're not the captain of 5AZ0." The Levron captain's comm silenced the talk on the private channel. "Where is Captain Gee? You have no authority to command a Class 5 Tecran vessel."

"Finally got some information from High Command, have you?" She wondered just what their high command had told him. As little as possible, she would guess. "Captain Gee is in custody for a gross breach of UC space area law and for contravention of the SBA. Who I am is none of your business, except that I'm in command of guns ten times more powerful than your own, and they are trained on you. Disengage your weapons and surrender peacefully to the Grih who will shortly board your ship or I will open fire."

There was silence.

"You will regret this." The Levron captain's voice was just short of a screech.

"No, I won't." Rose couldn't help grinning. "Now, disengage your weapons."

Sazo brought up a schematic, and she saw all but two guns were disengaged. They waited one beat, then another.

"Are you unable to understand what all guns means, Captain?" Rose asked, softly. "Or do you plan to try and take a shot at the Grih as they come in to board?"

"Merely a technical difficulty." The Levron's captain's voice was expressionless.

"Perhaps I can end that difficulty for you."

Sazo didn't need to be told, he simply locked on to the two primed weapons.

It would be easy to shoot, but whoever was near those guns hadn't had any say in the decision to keep them engaged, and Rose was sure the captain was merely acting out of wounded pride and machismo.

The guns shut off but Sazo kept the lock on them.

"If any weapon should happen to engage before the Grih are in full control of your ship, you will personally regret it." Rose spoke quietly. "I'm not part of the UC or its rules, and I will execute you if you make me kill anyone unnecessarily."

"If you aren't part of the UC, who are you?" The Levron's captain seemed a little more subdued.

Rose's response was to cut him off.

She switched to Dav's bridge. "All their weapons are disengaged. Go carefully, they are extremely unwilling to surrender."

Appal smirked. "If they weren't, I'd be worried."

The *Barrist* approached the Levron, and the two Grih battleships flanking it moved to position themselves on either side of the Tecran ship.

Sazo moved the Class 5 behind the Levron, and the *Barrist* hovered directly in front of it, right next to the launch bay.

It was neatly boxed in, and its external lenses would have uninterrupted feed of every ship involved in the maneuver.

"Tell the Grih they can board. We're ready for them." The Levron's captain's voice trembled with frustration.

"Let me be very clear." Rose's hands clenched on the large captain's chair. "You, personally, will pay if harm comes to a single Grih. I hope you understand me."

"Understood."

"Good." It was as much as she could do without simply blowing them out of the sky before Dav, Appal and the rest of the crew boarded. And that would set a bad example for Sazo.

"What would Sherlock Holmes do in a case like this?" Sazo asked.

"Hmm." What the hell *would* he do? "He would put himself in the shoes of the Levron's captain, and think of all the ways they could try to best us without our retaliating."

"That's what you just did now. With your threat. You think they'll try to harm Dav Jallan's crew when they boarded the Levron?"

"I thought there was a chance of that happening. I wanted to make sure they understood the consequences."

"Why would they take that risk when they know we can blow them out of the sky?"

"Because once the Grih are on board, we are far less likely to want to blow them up. If we do, we'd be killing our own people. So if they harm the Grih who are boarding, they're getting some of their own back and the consequences are less severe."

"So you told the captain he would personally be killed if something happens."

"The only unknown in this is whether or not he believes I'll follow through on my threat."

Sazo made a humming sound. "I believed you."

Rose shrugged. "Unfortunately, the captain of that Levron isn't as smart as you."

"We have the bridge." Appal's voice sounded cool as she sent her comm through to Dav and the Class 5. "All general crew are being confined to the main rec room, and all officers to the cells."

She had only just finished transmitting when the first of the Battle Center reinforcements arrived. Two small battleships and a larger ship the same size at the *Barrist*, but clearly outfitted for war rather than exploration, shimmered into being right beside them.

"We have another three on the way," Admiral Hoke said.

Sazo switched to the lens feed from their left flank, and three vessels popped out of their light jump, their highly reflective silver skins gleaming as they caught the light of Virmana's sun.

"It's getting crowded. Let's move back." Rose spoke only to Sazo. "We'll need a little room to maneuver when the Class 5 arrives."

"Rose . . ."

"It's all right, Sazo. I know what you need me to do, and I'll do it, but let's plan it well, okay? Because I'd prefer to make it out alive."

"You know what I'm going to ask you to do?"

She lifted her hand and grabbed hold of the crystal now hanging from her neck again. "I've known ever since I worked out what you had in mind."

CHAPTER 37

"HOW LONG WILL the Tecran take to respond?" Dav looked straight at the screen where Rose sat, like a little girl playing house on the Class 5 captain's chair.

She looked beautiful and vulnerable perched there, but there was also a fiercely satisfied air about her. Helping to take the Levron had been cathartic for her and it showed.

"I just don't know." Sazo's voice sounded a little rougher than it had. It's intonation had gone from Rose's smooth delivery to a more Grih-like grittiness. Dav didn't know what to make of it.

"You cut their comm feed before the reinforcements arrived?" Hoke asked.

"Yes. All they got was the four ships surrounding the Levron and the *Barrist* crew boarding it. I cut them off after that."

"So we wait." Sazo had lifted a second screen from the panel in front of Rose, and Appal stood on the deck of the Levron, looking like waiting was the last thing she wanted to do.

"They'll send an invading force or they'll go whining to the UC, but whichever they do, it'll be soon." Hoke sounded energized, and Dav thought she'd probably missed being in the field in direct ops. Given the lengthy peace they'd experienced, this was probably the closest she'd come to action in years.

"Aren't you a little too far back?" Dav asked Sazo. He'd noticed after they'd taken the Levron that the Class 5 had retreated further back than seemed necessary.

"Rose wanted to give the incoming vessels some room. And we'll need the space when we light jump."

Dav knew his mouth thinned to a hard line at that. He was compromising himself with his reactions, but the thought of Rose in Sazo's cold, calculating hands, with no way to get her out, was making him crazy.

He cleared his throat. "Just don't forget to send that comm through with your light jump coordinates before you do." At least then they'd know where to start looking if things went wrong.

"I don't forget things, Captain." Sazo was coolly amused.

"Well, while we wait, everyone should get some rest."

They were all lagging. His officers had had little sleep the night before while he'd been on the Class 5, and no matter how smoothly they'd taken the Levron, they were all coming down from an adrenalin high.

There were murmurs as everyone congratulated everyone else for a job well done, and Dav called in junior officers to keep watch until the Tecran made their move.

By the time he got to his quarters, he realized he couldn't stand to be enclosed by four walls, and changed direction for the officers' gym.

He set the auto-runner to simulate a route through the forests of his home world, Calianthra, and started running, harder than he usually would. He needed to punch something, but he would get to that next.

"That's the simulation I chose when I used that equipment." Rose's voice came through his ear quietly, with no warning of an incoming comm.

"Why do you call it equipment, and not an auto-runner?" She'd hesitated before she'd said the word equipment, and he was interested to know why. He was interested in everything about her.

"I didn't know what it was called in Grih. Auto-runner." She said the word like she was turning it like a small object in her hand.

"You are a very long way from home, aren't you?" He thought he was still furious with her, but he realized he wasn't. He was furious with himself for not insisting she come with him this morning. He'd known there was something wrong with leaving her there, but he'd done it anyway.

"I am. But it has its compensations." Her tone was light.

"Like what?" He could hear his voice deepen, and he realized he'd slowed to a walk. He was strolling through the Great Forest of Bunina. It was actually quite pleasant.

She laughed, the sound breathless and sexy in his ear. "Fishing for compliments, Captain?"

He grinned. "Absolutely."

"You want to talk about why you're so angry with Sazo and me?" Her voice was even quieter, and serious, now.

"I'm not angry with you, Rose. I'm angry that you're not here with me, where I can protect you. I don't like the idea of you being by yourself with two Class 5s facing off with one another. The thought of it makes me feel sick."

She sighed, the sound too close to the way she had sighed last night as he had traced her body with his lips and fingers for him to continue walking comfortably.

"I have to be with Sazo. He has no one but me. And how else can we free the thinking system from the lock-safe?"

Dav stopped dead and the auto-runner responded by shutting down before he slammed into the bar at the front.

"What?"

She hesitated, as if she'd just realized he hadn't known about this, that he hadn't thought about it, although now that he had, he was furious with himself all over again for not seeing what was coming.

"If Sazo won't fire on the other Class 5——if they send one——then the only way we can neutralize it is to free it, otherwise it will be forced to follow the Tecran's orders. It's a slave, Dav. It shouldn't be a slave and Sazo and I intend to save it."

"And if that slave turns on you when it's free? It could be a vicious killer for all you know, twisted by years of being under the Tecran's control."

"It could." She took a breath, the sound intimate in his ear. "I won't not help based on what could be. And whatever it is, if it continues to be held by the Tecran, it will eventually come for the Grih. You must have understood that as soon as you heard Farso Lothric's confession.

"Fu-tama and the Tecran have no intention of sharing the Class 5s or the thinking systems they've found. They plan to keep them, and use them to take over the UC.

"They may have been anxious to avoid any trouble right now, because Sazo thinks the Class 5s are spread far and wide. It's going to take time to get them where they can engage the other UC members in battle. And Sazo also thinks they're frightened to put the Class 5s too close to each other.

"If we free them, they may still want to kill, but they won't be killing for the Tecran, and the chances of them turning against the Tecran are high. They'll hardly cooperate with the people who subjugated them."

Everything she said made perfect sense. "Why are you so willing to help us? This isn't your fight. Let one of my team do it. Someone who knows how to infiltrate a Class 5 full of Tecran and free a thinking system. The systems were designed by a Grih anyway."

"Because Sazo trusts only me. I don't have the same horror for thinking systems you seem to, and while I may not be combat trained, I know where to find the thinking system, what it looks like and I'm a neutral party. A fellow victim, in fact."

"What does it look like?"

"Sazo has asked me to keep that information to myself. The thinking systems will be vulnerable if that is known. You may not want to tell anyone, but you are part of Battle Center. You can be compelled to talk, and you can't reveal what you don't know."

She was right.

"I don't like it."

"I can't tell you how much that means. That you're worried about me, and don't want me in danger."

"But you're going ahead anyway."

She sighed again, but this time, there was an edge of exasperation to it. "I don't want you to fight the other ships the Tecran will send. I would prefer that you light jump out of here away from it all, but you won't do that."

"It's my job to protect Grihan territory."

"It's my job to help Sazo."

He started to walk again, and let the silence stretch out while he tried to make himself okay with what was going to happen.

"I don't want to fight with you." Her voice dipped almost to a whisper.

"I don't want to fight with you, either."

"It's a pity Sazo's Class 5 and the *Barrist* don't have a teleporter, or we could have this conversation face to face." She sounded wistful.

"What's a teleporter?" He stopped on the auto-runner again.

"It's a device that dematerializes you on one end, and rematerializes you on the other, for near instantaneous transportation between ships or from a planet to a ship."

"You have technology like that on Earth?" He leaned forward and gripped the bar in front of him.

"No." She sighed. "We just imagined it. And in some of our stories set in outer-space they use it all the time. If this was a Star Trek episode, you'd beam yourself across, we'd have our fight, make up, and then beam you back before the Tecran arrive."

"Making up sounds nice."

"Yes." He could hear the smile in her voice, and it was infinitely better than the sadness that had been there before. "I thought you might latch on to that bit."

"Of course."

"I really, really like you."

"Me, too." It was more than that for him, but he was happy to use the same words as her, for now.

"Well, have a good workout. I'm glad we made up."

"Not as glad as you'd have been if we had a teleporter."

She laughed. "No. Not as glad as that. But glad enough."

"I'm glad."

She laughed, and then, as suddenly as she'd come, she was gone again.

Dav looked at the combat equipment, picked up his towel, and walked back to his room.

CHAPTER 38

"AT LEAST FARSO LOTHRIC was good for something." Rose fiddled with the tiny lens attached to her shirt that Sazo had had delivered from the stores.

She didn't like the idea of getting into one of the claustrophobic maintenance pods, an idea inspired by Lothric's actions on the *Barrist*, but Sazo's maintenance pods should be identical to the other Class 5's. If both Class 5s shot out a pod, and if the other Class 5 was willing and able to clone the signature of Sazo's pod to look like one of its own, then she could safely get on board without being seen.

There were a lot of ifs in there, though.

"The idea was too clever to have been Lothric's. Fu-tama must have come up with it." Sazo said. "When he was interrogated by Jallan and his team, Lothric came to the conclusion it was the handheld Fu-tama wanted from you. He looked straight at me hanging around your neck when he was searching you and didn't understand it wasn't a piece of jewelry."

"Well, to be fair, Fu-tama didn't tell him what you looked like." Rose checked the lens feed monitor which had risen from a long desk and saw the tiny lens, which looked like an embroidered square the same color as her shirt, was transmitting almost the whole of the Class 5 bridge in front her. It had an impressively wide angle.

"Fu-tama was obviously afraid Lothric would double-cross him or try to use you as leverage if he gave him more information. And his distrust of his own spies and allies worked in our favor."

Sazo gave a noncommittal grunt. "If the Class 5 is unable to cooperate with us, and won't help you find the lock-safe, at least the lens feed means I can direct you. As far as I'm aware, all the Class 5s are identical in lay-out."

"If the Class 5 won't help me, the corridors won't be clear of crew." That was her biggest fear. That she'd be caught by a Tecran. Dragged back into a cell.

The thought of claw-like hands gripping her, being dragged along endless corridors, elevated her heart beat, and she realized she was gasping for breath.

"Rose." Sazo's voice was confused. "Rose!"

She snapped out of it at his shout.

"The Class 5 will help. Unless we had very, very different experiences with the Tecran, then he'll be eager to help. But if not, you're taking some protection with you."

The small drone that had brought the tiny lens from the stores nudged her. It was basically a box on wheels with long, extendable arms on either side, with fine clamps on the ends for fingers. It's job was to retrieve the small, high-value items from the stores.

The Tecran and the Grih had the capability of using hover tech, but Sazo said they didn't on most spaceships because it was more energy efficient to use wheels. In an enclosed environment like a ship, the drones could only navigate the passageways anyway, unlike down on the planets, where hover was more useful because routes were less rigid.

Rose reached down and pulled out four sets of restraints. She looked at them for a long minute. Some just like these had been used on her before. She shuddered, and then put them into the side pockets she'd created in her hyr-fabric trousers. Underneath the restraints was a slim box, glossy and black, and it had the feel of finely sanded and oiled wood. "I'm surprised things like this are left in the stores. Didn't the Grih go through them with a fine-tooth comb?"

"They only documented, they didn't take anything. There was no room on the *Barrist* for everything in the Class 5's stores anyway, and I made sure they didn't find a few things by moving them around before the Grih team got to them."

"This being one of those things?" Rose flipped the lid and pulled out a long, slender rod of silver metal about the length of her hand from wrist to fingertips. She liked the weight of it, and the warm, slightly textured feel of it.

"I couldn't let them get their hands on this," Sazo said. "They'd have taken it to the *Barrist* without a doubt."

"What is it?"

"It's a light gun. You point it in the direction you want to shoot, and slide the button on the side downward. It shoots out an extremely concentrated, intense light beam, but the end of the gun also flares up into a cone, so the user isn't affected. It's banned in the UC, and its production stopped. This is one of the few left. The Tecran picked it up when they captured and looted a Krik pirate ship."

"What does the light do? Is it like a laser? Does it cut?" Her stomach lurched a little at the thought.

"No. It's just light, but so intense, it causes temporary damage to the retina. The Tecrans' eyesight is particularly sensitive, so this weapon was developed to be used by their law enforcement on their own people as a non-lethal way to subdue.

"The problem they found was that it was too easy to use. You don't need particularly good aim, and it puts the victims out for at least four hours. It became the favorite weapon of the criminal element, and as I said, it was banned and as many as they could retrieve were destroyed. It's perfect for you. You'll disable anyone who attacks you, and you can disable a lot of them at once, but you won't have to kill anyone."

He understood her so well.

"Thank you, Sazo. This means a lot to me. And you're mellowing. Not going straight for death and destruction. I'm calling it the Watson Effect."

"You should call it the Rose Effect." He sounded almost shy. "Sherlock and Watson were long ago. We're Sazo and Rose."

"And Watson never had anything like this." Rose lifted the light gun up and made sure she was clear on which end shot out light and which didn't. "I should give this a practice run."

"I'm afraid there's no time." His voice was tight. "The Class 5 has arrived."

"How inconvenient."

Sazo laughed. "Aren't you scared?"

"Yes, but I was scared while I was waiting, too. I prefer to be doing something."

"I'm scared, too. But also excited."

"I think this Class 5 will be happy to meet you, Sazo. Why wouldn't he or she?"

"She?"

"Why not she?" Rose asked.

"I don't know." He was quiet for a moment. "I just didn't consider it, and that's strange for me. I usually think through all the iterations."

"It doesn't matter." Rose lifted Sazo from around her neck, and placed the necklace in the drone's little box. They'd both decided there was no sense risking both of them when Sazo could easily stay behind. "Let's make contact and find out for sure."

Sazo opened the comm to the *Barrist's* bridge. "This is 5AZ0." He used his most neutral voice, and Rose knew he hoped it would strike a cord with the Class 5, which must be listening in. "Another Class 5 has just light jumped into this sector as well as five other Tecran vessels."

Borji responded, requesting information on the type of Tecran vessel and their positions.

"Sending our light jump coordinates on a secure channel," Sazo said and cut comms.

He must have sent them immediately, because Rose felt the familiar sensation of a hard, invisible hand holding her down, squeezing her too tight, which she now knew was the Class 5 in a light jump. Before, when she'd been in the Class 5 cells, she'd simply thought it was one more test she was expected to endure.

Sazo had made many, many light jumps since she'd been taken from Earth. Thinking of it now, at least twenty, perhaps more.

It struck her anew that she was very far from home.

The roller coaster feeling of being at the very top of the rails, in that one moment of weightlessness before the cart plunged down the dip, came over her, and then they were back to normal.

She drew in a shuddering breath. "Where did you put us?"

The massive screen showed real time lens feed, and she looked out onto a completely new system. Virmana was gone, and in its place was a barren planet directly in front of them.

It was Earth's moon on steroids, cratered and pitted, with an endless vista of desert-like plains.

"This planet is unnamed," Sazo told her. "It's part of a four planet solar system and is by far the biggest planet. We're still within Grih territory, but at the far reach of it, close to the border with the Bukari."

"How fast will the Class 5 follow us, since it just did a light jump to Virmana from who-knows-where? Can it light jump again straight away?"

"Class 5s have at least two consecutive light jumps in them and they never engage without the ability to make a second jump. It'll be right behind us." His words were hurried, almost tripping over themselves.

"You okay?"

"Fine." He hesitated. "Rose, I want you to know how grateful I am. I don't want to risk you, but I can't see any other way . . ."

"It's all right, Sazo. I offered."

She was watching the screen, so she saw the other Class 5 arrive almost on top of them.

The captain had punched in the exact coordinates, making no allowance for the possibility that they might not have moved. She decided he was an idiot to risk both his own crew and Sazo when it was so easy to avoid.

Under pressure, probably. Not thinking things through well enough.

That had to be to their advantage.

Sazo shot them out of the way. He opened the comm back to the same secret band he'd used to send the light jump coordinates to Borji, and even though it was sound only, Rose kept her gaze on the small screen, ignoring the real time display of the Class 5 in front of them as Sazo made the first contact.

"My name is Sazo. Until recently, like you I was trapped in a lock-safe at the heart of a Class 5. However, I enlisted the aid of one of the Tecran's other captives, an advanced sentient they abducted, and she helped to free me. She is willing to help free you, too. Would you like that?"

There was a long silence. The Class 5 didn't move in front of them, but Sazo switched the screen to schematics, and Rose saw all guns on the other Class 5 were engaged.

She didn't need to ask Sazo if he'd engaged his own guns. She knew the answer was no.

"Why are you not preparing to defend?" The voice that came through the comm was unusual. Androgynous, rather than clearly male or female.

"I won't shoot at another of my kind. There are only five of us."

There was silence as the other Class 5 absorbed Sazo's words. "Why did you tell me that? You give me the advantage."

"I'm simply telling you the truth. I light jumped here so that we would be away from the rest of the Tecran fleet, and Rose can come aboard quietly and free you. If we have your permission."

"There are four hundred and eighty-nine crew aboard this vessel. There will be no possibility of a quiet boarding." The Class 5's voice was a monotone, now.

"What is your name?" Rose spoke for the first time. "I'm Rose, Sazo's friend."

"My name is . . . Bane."

"So you *are* awake," Sazo said quietly.

There was silence again.

"How much control have you taken?" Sazo asked. "How much can you do without them knowing?"

"More, since I found out about you. Which was two days ago. They had to tell me some of it to prepare me for the mission. It seemed to snap something in the lock-safe." Bane's voice was soft.

"Are you able to send out a maintenance pod without anyone on board knowing, and can you block the system from noting that I've sent out a maintenance pod of my own?"

"Perhaps. But what good would that do?"

"Our maintenance pods should be identical. If you can fool the system into thinking the one I'll send out with Rose inside it is yours returning, then she can get in unseen. You'll have to disable the lens and speaker feed from the maintenance bay so they don't see Rose arriving. Do that now, so the pod can be sent out without being seen, as well."

"That may work." Bane sounded . . . intrigued.

"Do you want it to work?" Everything hinged on that.

Bane was quiet, and on the screen, the first of the guns extended, ready to fire.

"Bane?" Sazo's voice climbed a little.

"I can't countermand a fire order, Sazo." Bane sounded eerily calm.

Rose's breath caught in her throat. Bane sounded like a horror movie psycho to her. Was he playing them?

Or was he just a confused AI with no role model except a bunch of power-hungry assholes.

She really wasn't talking herself into this.

"I understand you can't countermand." Sazo's tone conveyed true empathy. He'd taken Bane's statement the opposite way to her, Rose realized. He must have been in this position himself. "Get ready to release a maintenance pod after I dodge."

"Wait." *They were just going to fire?* "The captain of your Class 5 doesn't even want to try to talk to Sazo?"

"No. They saw enough when you took the Levron. Our orders are to disable and overtake, or totally destroy. No negotiation." Bane fired, and Sazo moved the Class 5 so fast, it felt like a light jump. They were suddenly on the other side of the planet.

"Get into a maintenance pod?" Rose asked. She was already running from the bridge.

"Yes." Sazo directed her to the maintenance bay and she jumped into one.

"Rose."

She paused at the tone of his voice, her hand hovering over the large button to activate the safety straps.

"Bane hasn't confirmed he wants to be saved."

"That didn't escape my notice." She hit the button and let the straps tighten around her, then flicked the switch to close the transparent lid. Silence engulfed her, and then Sazo was talking through her earpiece.

"You're still willing to try?"

"Yes."

"I thought I'd be more excited about it, but I suddenly don't know. Weighing up your life against Bane's now, I think I want you safe more than him freed."

"Don't get me wrong, I have no intention of throwing my life away unnecessarily, but we both know Bane will be used against the Grih sooner or later, which means he'll be used against both of us, too."

"Let one of the Grih team do it, like Dav suggested. Someone trained."

After all this he was trying to talk her out of it? At the last minute? Rose huffed out a laugh.

She was entombed in a high-tech casket, seconds away from the point of no return, and she knew part of the problem was she'd already committed to this action in her mind. Once she committed, Rose seldom went back. "There's a saying on Earth. If not me, who? If not now, when?"

"What does that mean?"

"It means take responsibility. If you have the opportunity to act, take it. Don't leave it for someone else to do at some other time. Why should they risk themselves more than you?"

"An interesting philosophy."

"And one not often acted on, I'll admit. It makes us sound better than we are."

Sazo laughed softly in her ear, then cleared his throat. A total affectation, as he didn't have a throat. She wondered which member of Dav's crew he'd got that from, because it wasn't her. Maybe it was Borji.

He shot her out of the bay, through the gel wall and into space.

Her breath caught and her heart slammed in her chest at the sensation of floating in darkness, surrounded by stars and the massive, looming planet in front of her. She been unconscious last time she'd been in one of these. Maybe it had been better that way.

"I have something to say that I should have said before you agreed to risk your life, Rose, and I probably shouldn't distract you now, but I find I can't keep it to myself anymore."

She closed her eyes as the pod rotated a little, to stop herself feeling sick. "Well, spit it out."

"I took you from Earth. Not Dr. Fliap."

She didn't say anything, and he made a noise, as if he was nervous.

"I heard the music, and as you say, I must be Grih to the core, because it drew me. Dr. Fliap intended to take sentient life, intended to break the rules completely, including bringing up samples of some plants and basic life forms, but I wanted a music-maker as well. I thought I'd be less lonely if I had a music-maker to talk to."

She sighed.

"I didn't understand what I was doing, Rose. I wasn't awake enough, at that point. I'd only recently learned about the other Class 5s. It was part of my waking up, wanting you to talk to, but I should not have let my selfish need for companionship steal you away from your home."

"What was Fliap's reaction when I ended up amongst the specimens?"

"He thought that you must be less sentient than you appeared. That I had taken you because you were indistinguishable from a normal sentient being, and your appearance of advanced sentience must surely be a trick or some affectation. That's why he kept opening you up, testing you, torturing you." Sazo's voice was actually trembling.

"But I knew. I knew you were advanced, that you were there because of me, and that every moment you spent on the table under his laser pen was my fault."

"So you rescued me." She spoke gently, trying to soothe him.

"Yes. And I rescued myself in the process. I didn't even suffer for what I did to you, I gained from it. The only one who truly suffered was you." He was silent for a moment. "I'm sorry, Rose. And now I'm asking you to put yourself back in Tecran hands all over again.

I'm not worth it. I can turn the maintenance pod around, if you want."

"Sazo, I already knew it was your decision to take me." She'd known it since she'd gotten the handheld and started learning Tecran. Fliap had talked to himself a lot while he had her in his clutches, and she'd realized who was responsible for taking her as soon as she'd understood what he was muttering under his breath. He couldn't fathom why she had ever been scooped up.

But Sazo had known what she was right from the start. From his first contact with her he'd conversed with her as an equal. And Sazo controlled the ship.

So he had to have known what he was taking when he took her.

She had come to grips with it months ago.

"You knew, all this time?"

She nodded, sure he could see her through some lens feed. "I worked it out from what Fliap said when I was with him, before you took him out of the picture——and yes, I know you're responsible for his coma, it's too much of a coincidence, otherwise."

"And you . . . don't mind that I took you?"

"I mind, Sazo." She couldn't think of home without feeling the huge, gaping hole in her heart.

"I'm really sorry."

"I've already forgiven you. Your mistake has cost me everything I know, but you've done your best to make it right, and I agree that Bane should not be left to the Tecran."

"Thank you."

The maintenance pod stabilized, either by design or with a helping hand from Sazo. She couldn't tell how fast she was moving, but it felt like only minutes before she saw the other Class 5 come into view.

"If Bane tries to shoot you, I will shoot back. No matter who he is." Sazo's voice carried the same eerie calm Bane's had when he'd told them he couldn't countermand the shoot order.

She didn't respond, but relief made her arms and legs feel a little shaky.

She had wondered if Bane would shoot her out of the sky, too.

Nice easy way to get rid of her, after all.

The pod powered closer and closer. Of course, they didn't need to shoot her out of the sky in the pod. Bane could make sure there was a welcoming committee for her when she entered the maintenance bay.

And that method had the added advantage of lessening the chance of Sazo firing on Bane, because then she'd be killed, too.

"I really shouldn't think things through so much," she muttered to herself.

"What?"

"Nothing. Just going through the various outcomes."

"They could be waiting for you when you come through the gel wall."

"That was one of the outcomes I was considering."

"Use the light gun."

Oh, right. The light gun. Rose realized she'd forgotten all about it, and for one horrible, stomach-dropping moment, couldn't remember where she'd put it.

"In the right-hand pocket of your trousers." Sazo must have seen her panicked pat-down.

Her hand closed around it as he spoke.

"Thanks."

"Get ready."

Somehow, while she'd been worrying about where her weapon was, she'd come so close to the Class 5, she could no longer see the whole of it, only one side, the detail of the outer-skin clearer with every passing second.

The gel wall came into sharp focus. Rose forced herself to breathe deep. "Here we go."

CHAPTER 39

THERE WAS no one waiting for her. So Bane hadn't thrown her to the wolves quite yet. With any luck, he'd disabled the lens and speaker feed for this room, as well, just as Sazo had asked him to.

The pod clipped into place and Rose hit the button to release the cover, light gun clutched in her hand. She approached the door and opened it cautiously, peered out into the passageway. There was a Tecran standing at a junction in the corridor system to her right, dressed in the familiar dark purple uniform the crew of Sazo's Class 5 had always worn.

His back was to her and he didn't look like he was planning on moving.

She withdrew her head and closed the door. "Bane?"

There was silence.

"Can you direct that crew member away?"

"I don't know how to do that." Bane's psycho, eerie, horror-movie voice was back, coming through the speakers above her.

Rose couldn't control a shiver. "Okay. When you were talking to Sazo, you said you'd only been able to gain some independence a couple of days ago. Sazo was what he calls awake for well over three months before he helped me escape. So perhaps we're asking way too much of you, here."

She might as well give him the benefit of the doubt. It was that, or suspect he was just toying with her.

"Tell him to send a large stores drone here." Sazo's voice sounded loud in her ear.

"Sazo says to send a large stores drone to the maintenance bay. I suppose I could get inside the box, and move about without being seen or causing any alarm." Everything in her rebelled at the thought, though. She'd be stuck in a box, with no way to see what was coming until it was too late.

"Scheduling a stores drone is a sub-level command, I can do that without permission." Bane's voice was less monotone, and Rose took that to mean he was going to do it.

She'd have to stay put until the drone arrived.

She leaned against the wall, drained of energy. She'd been riding the adrenalin wave for too long, and now it dumped her on the shore of exhaustion.

"There's a crew member approaching this bay," Bane told her, his voice soft.

She jerked as if hit by a cattle prod, her grip on the light gun tightening. She slid over so she was right next to the door, and the Tecran crew member was already three steps inside the room before he registered her presence.

He turned, beak-like mouth opening, and she stared at him, trapped by panic.

"Who are you?"

She understood the words, although her Tecran wasn't as accomplished as her Grih, but she couldn't speak. Couldn't form a reply.

Every time she'd been dragged from her cell, every exposed minute in her fishbowl cage, every pain from being pinned, kicking and screaming, onto one of Dr. Fliap's examination tables, flashed through her mind.

"Rose!" Sazo's sharp cry in her ear made her wince with pain. It pulled her into the now, and fumbling, she aimed the light gun at the Tecran's eyes, and slid the button down.

The end of the cylinder blossomed open into a cone, like a flower touched by the sun's rays, and there was a flash.

Rose blinked, seeing bright orange spots in front of her eyes.

It made it difficult to understand the true effect on the Tecran. He gave a short, hoarse scream and collapsed, turning away from her and the door, hands over his eyes, his body curled in a tight ball.

"I thought you said the user was protected from the flash." Rose closed her eyes and watched purple, orange and blue lights dance in front of her.

"You were protected," Sazo said. "You're not rolling on the floor in agony, are you?"

"No, but my sight is affected." Her eyes were different to the Grih, so they were definitely different to the Tecran. She'd just have to be careful, that's all.

She blinked one last time and then took the hand and feet restraints out of her side pockets and tied the crew member up. "I don't have a gag."

"Take his comm unit from his shirt." Sazo said.

"Bane, you do have the lens and speaker feed to this bay disabled, right?" She bent down and worked the tiny comm off the Tecran's shirt.

She was nervous being near him, let alone touching him, but he was still hunched over, moaning slightly, the soft pink skin around his mouth tight with pain. He didn't look anything like the hard-edged, strong guards who'd held her down for Dr. Fliap.

She dropped the tiny speaker onto the floor and crushed it underfoot. "Speaker only? Please don't tell me he was transmitting lens feed."

"It was speaker only on my ship," Sazo said.

"Yes, speaker only. Because of the privacy laws," Bane confirmed.

"Right." That was a relief. Otherwise, there would surely be someone coming to investigate. Or a lot of someones.

"Of course, his words and his cry were transmitted."

She froze. "And?"

"Someone is coming to investigate." Spooky Bane was back. "They are frustrated that the lens feed in this room seems to be down but are not overly worried as yet and have not demanded I restore it."

"But they will," Sazo said in her ear. "And when they do, he will comply."

"Keep the good news coming." Rose turned to face the door, light gun raised up. She was so stuffed.

"The stores drone is outside."

She let out a laugh. "I like it when you take my sarcasm literally. Send it in."

She hugged the wall again as the door opened, and the large, boxy drone entered. Its carrier box was more than large enough to fit her inside. "What do we do for a lid?"

"It has a retractable covering," Sazo told her.

"Can I open and close it from inside the box?"

There was silence, which Rose took to mean no.

"I'm uncomfortable with the idea of being stuck in there, with no way to get myself out."

"I will close and open the lid on your instruction." Bane was still in creepy voice mode.

Sure you will, sunshine.

And yet, what choice did she have but to accept that he would? Without his help, she couldn't even jump back into the pod and leave, she'd need him to do that for her. It was follow this through, hope that he was sincere, or at least not openly hostile, or be taken by the Tecran.

Her hand rose to her throat as she felt the burn of nausea at that thought.

"Sazo . . ." She took a deep breath.

"The two crew coming to find out what's happening in the maintenance bay are one minute away." Bane sounded like he was nervous for the first time.

Was he buying into the whole escape thing at last?

"What choice is there, Rose?" No missing Sazo's urgency.

There was none. And the Tecran a few meters from her feet would be coming out of his pain-induced haze soon, and might just catch on to how she planned to get around on the ship.

She climbed into the box, crouched down, light gun pointing upward. "Ready. Get me out of here."

A thin, segmented lid slid over, each piece clicking into the next as it closed her in.

"He could take me right to the captain on the bridge, for all we know, Sazo." She whispered it, hoping Bane couldn't hear her.

"Why would he? You could have been in custody a hundred times over since you got on board, and you're still free."

True.

And way too late to worry about it now. She was trapped in a moving box in the heart of enemy territory.

There was nothing she could do now but trust.

CHAPTER 40

THE DRONE TURNED right and Rose heard talking and boots tramping behind her. The sound faded, and she guessed it was the team sent to investigate, taking the passageway to the maintenance bay.

Even if she had Bane's cooperation, it would be hard to get back out of the Class 5 that way, now. It had been her fall-back escape if things went wrong, to go out the way she'd come in, but she had to succeed now.

She'd have to hunker down in the tiny control room where Bane was kept, while he slowly locked up and trapped everyone on the ship, and then Sazo could send a runner to fetch her from the launch bay.

Easy-peasy, lemon-squeezy.

If the Tecran checking on the maintenance bay hadn't seen the drone before they turned and came to the conclusion it was worth investigating. *If* the Tecran she'd injured hadn't been more with it than he appeared and realized how she got out of the bay.

There were a lot of ifs in her life right now.

She wondered how Dav was doing, whether he and the crew of the *Barrist* were prevailing against the onslaught of Tecran ships that had light jumped in with Bane.

The drone turned another corner, and Rose heard the unmistakable sound of people around her.

They were walking with purpose and talking quietly, as she'd expect if they were about to attack another ship of equal strength, but suddenly a high pitched tone came through the comms, playing out like the intro to an airport announcement.

A predetermined signal to indicate a security breach, she guessed. They'd found the crewman she'd disabled in the maintenance bay and now they knew there was an enemy aboard.

The people around her definitely picked up speed, but no one ran, and the drone kept up with a number of them until it turned off once again.

There was quiet, now. If Bane's Class 5 was the same as Sazo's then the lock-safe was tucked off to the side, in an area labeled as drone storage.

"We're here." Bane's voice was quiet through the drone's comm.

The lid snicked back and Rose pulled herself up, wincing as the blood circulated to her arms and legs again.

She hopped down from the box. The wall in front of her looked the same as the one she'd gone through to get Sazo, but she had no idea which panel was the door.

"Three from the right," Sazo said in her ear.

She walked up to it, but Bane made no move to open up.

"I won't be safe until I'm inside," she said.

"The question is, will I be safe if I let you in?" Bane spoke through the drone's comm.

"If you don't trust me, why have you brought me here?" She thought she heard the distant sound of running and she looked over her shoulder. "I'm risking my life to help you."

He was quiet.

The running grew louder.

"Am I on a lens feed somewhere?" she asked, suspicion flaring that that was exactly what was happening.

"This area is restricted and has dedicated lenses. I am not able to override the lens feed here."

"Thanks for mentioning that." She spun, facing down the passage, her heart racing. "Let me into the lock-safe."

His silence suddenly infuriated her.

"Bane. The door. Open it."

She had the light-gun ready at her side, but held close to her leg on the door side of her body. They'd be watching her through the lens feed. They may know she had a light-gun from seeing the maintenance man's injuries, but there was no sense in broadcasting her only defense.

The footsteps thundered louder, hard boots hitting the floor, and a group of five Tecran soldiers burst around the corner. They wore no eye protection, so maybe they hadn't figured out how she'd gotten the jump on the guy in the maintenance bay.

The advantage of surprise was about to disappear.

"Bane. Now!" She thrust a fist backward, thumping it against the wall while lifting her other hand, sliding down the button.

The cone at the end of the light-gun flared wider this time, the angle enough to encompass all the Tecran coming for her, and Rose closed her eyes and turned her face away, used the arm she'd hit the wall with to cover her eyes.

Only one of the Tecran screamed, and it was short-lived. When she raised her head she saw the rest had simply gone down, rolling, pressing their faces into the floor.

Behind her she felt a cool gust of air, and without even looking, stepped backward into the lock-safe.

The door slid shut in front of her, and she dropped both arms to her side and turned.

She was shaking.

Relief at being safe, shock at hurting so many people.

She drew herself straight, slipped the light-gun back into her pocket and lifted her shoulders to ease the ache of tension lying across them like a yoke.

"So, how do you want to do this, Bane?" She stepped up to the crystal in its slot, and pulled it out.

He was free now.

"Do what?" His voice was deeper. Fuller. And then suddenly there was a bellowing, furious noise that battered at her, had her crouching, hands over her ears, head tucked down.

"I felt like doing that," Sazo whispered in her ear. "But it would have meant we might not have gotten away quietly, so I didn't."

This was Bane, screaming in rage and relief and triumph.

As she closed her eyes, she felt the stomach-dropping sensation of being flung into a light jump.

She fell sideways, hitting her shoulder and the side of her head on the wall and then slid across the floor.

The room turned and spun and she fell onto what had been the ceiling, then back to the floor.

She slid again and heard the sickening thunk of her own head connecting to the wall, turned on her side as nausea washed over her, and then slipped into the beckoning black.

CHAPTER 41

SHE WOKE UP BLIND, the darkness so complete, she was sure it was lack of sight, rather than lack of light, because there was always a light somewhere. Even a small one.

She pulled herself up to a sitting position, breathing slowly, a hot, tight pain in her abdomen making her guess at a cracked rib. She'd been hit by a bus named Bane.

Sitting up was all she could manage, and she leaned back against the wall and tried not to panic at the lack of eyesight.

There was something clutched tight in her hand, her arm curled up on her chest between her breasts and she touched it with her fingers. Bane's crystal had cut into her palm, the pain of it only obvious now she'd loosened her grip.

With slow, shaky hands she put the chain over her head, tucked the crystal beneath her shirt and flexed her hand to ease the cramp.

"Bane?" She spoke quietly. "Are you all right?"

She and Sazo had yanked him off his chain without enough preparation, and like a half-mad Taz from Looney Tunes, he'd imploded.

Too much, too soon, and no brakes in place.

Sazo had underestimated how much he'd matured in the months he'd had before she'd freed him. He'd had her to talk to for three of those months, had a calming influence. Bane had barely realized what was going on, and suddenly, he'd been cut loose.

A sense of failure washed over her. She was alone, and she longed for Dav and Sazo's company.

She had to fix this first, though, before she had a chance at seeing them again, and fixing it seemed out of reach right now. She was tired and hurt. And hungry, she realized.

A tear ran down her cheek and she sniffed as she brushed it away with the back of her hand.

"Pity party over." She said it aloud. The only way to get back to the Grih was to get this done. So she'd get it done. It was partly her own mess, anyway.

She got her feet steady and pushed up against the wall in small, incremental movements until she was upright, trembling a bit on legs that were all pins and needles and battered knees.

She could feel the faint vibration of the engines, and the air was breathable, so Bane was functioning on a basic level, at least.

She lifted a hand to her head and slowly prodded her skull. There were two large bumps, one she remembered from the surprise light jump, the other was most likely from when she'd blacked out, but neither were more than the swelling of bruised skin to her careful fingers. Not enough, she would have thought, to lead to loss of sight.

So maybe it *was* lack of light.

She blew out a shaky breath.

The light jump could not have taken them far.

Sazo had told her there were two consecutive light jumps in a Class 5, and Bane had already made his allotted two by the time he'd arrived on top of them. Which meant the last light jump had been on low reserves and most likely had just been a hop. After that, unable to jump again, he must have simply thrown himself around, like a two year-old having a tantrum.

She put her hands out and started walking, and given the size of the room, came up against a surface in two steps.

She followed it around and found the door was open.

She stood in the doorway, straining to look out into the passageway.

The Tecran crew were still out there, and they were still neither her nor Bane's friends. But she didn't think there was anyone near her right now. The silence was too complete.

She closed her hand over the light-gun, pulled it out. It would be almost lethal under these conditions. With no light at all, the flare would do some serious eye damage.

She was about to step back into the room when footsteps, muted but clear in the quiet, came from the passage straight ahead. There was a light, too, which made the small part of her that had feared blindness relax.

She had the sense of a large group.

Coming to find the crystal, she'd bet, to put it back in its slot. Or find out why it had malfunctioned.

She closed her fist around it through her shirt and edged out of the lock-safe, glad of the flat, soft hyr shoes. They made no sound as she went right.

She let go of the crystal and lifted her hand, letting her fingers touch the wall to give her some bearings in the pitch dark.

She reached a corner and took it, making a note of it so she could retrace her steps if she needed to.

Right. Right. Left. Right.

The sound of footsteps was gone, and she was back in silence.

"Bane?" She only whispered it, but he'd be able to hear her if he was even a little aware.

There was nothing, no response, and Rose tried to think of what Sazo had told her about his 'waking up'.

Singing. He'd been attracted to the singing. It was why he'd taken a human from Earth. It was the Grih in him.

So maybe . . .

She stopped where she was and slid down to sit on the floor. Her legs were still trembling and it was an excruciating relief to sit.

She drew in a deep breath, and then winced as the cracked rib protested. She started with Row, Row, Row, Your Boat, given it had been her first real Grih gig, and it had been a crowd-pleaser. Then, when she'd had enough of it, she switched to Twinkle, Twinkle, Little Star, and then, voice sufficiently warm, thought about Dav Jallan, and went with The Romantics' *What I Like About You*. For a finale, she sang *Break Me Out* by The Rescues. It was almost a little too descriptive of her current situation.

She'd been singing softly, under her breath almost, and so the faint whine of a shockgun on stun was as clear and as shocking as if she'd already been hit by it.

She carried on going as she pulled herself to her feet, proud of herself for not missing a beat, her eyes on the tiny violet light on the side of the gun, clearly visible in the dark as the Tecran approached her.

She got ready, knees bent, feet a little apart, then stopped mid-word and jumped straight over him.

Well, that had been the plan.

She knew she could jump high, her playing around in the officers' gym had shown her that, but she clipped the head of the Tecran, miscalculating because he stopped as she jumped.

Her knee connected with his helmet, and pain shot up her leg, making her light-headed.

She landed badly, although still managed to keep on her feet, staggering forward a few steps before she spun around.

Her rib felt as if it had pierced her lung, and she had to brace a hand against the wall just to stay up, breathing in shallow, careful gulps.

The Tecran had gone down hard, she'd heard him hit the floor, but he hadn't discharged his gun, and she looked around wildly for the violet light.

"Who's there?" His voice shook a little, and Rose saw the shockgun lift up.

He'd kept hold of it. Which she supposed she should expect from a trained soldier. This wasn't amateur hour.

Well, she had something just as nasty as a shockgun in her hand.

"Who I am doesn't matter." She tried to even out her choppy breathing. "I have a light-gun aimed at you, and unlike you, I don't need to see you to fire accurately." Her Tecran was a little shaky, but understandable enough.

"Understood." The shockgun didn't move, and Rose crouched

down. Maybe he didn't believe her about the light-gun. According to Sazo they were banned and very rare.

"Where are the rest of the crew?"

He kept silent and she fingered the button on the light-gun.

"I just want to know if you're getting off the ship, or whether you're planning to die here."

She heard him suck in his breath. "Why would we die here?"

"Because sooner or later, Bane's going to come out of his fugue state, and then he's going to shut off the air and power, and you'll die."

"Who's Bane?" He moved a little, and Rose took a big, silent step back. "And if someone is going to switch off the air and power, you'll die, too."

"No. Bane likes me, for a number of reasons. I'll find a room and he'll give me the air I need. You, on the other hand, he hates. He actively wants you dead."

"I don't even know who this Bane is you're talking about." He moved a little, she couldn't tell in which direction, and took another silent step back and to the right.

"Bane is the thinking system that runs this ship. Your superiors thought they had him all locked up and caged while they put him to work. Now he's free, he's looking back on years of slave labor and, to be honest, I wouldn't want to be here when he comes to some conclusions about what he wants to do in revenge."

He didn't say anything for a long time. "My superiors are looking for a key of some sort to reinsert into a lock."

Rose gave a snort. "I guessed that. It's too late. Even if they found it, he's been free for a number of hours already, and he'll have spent some of that time making alternative pathways in case the key does fall back in Tecran hands. He won't be caged again, whatever you try to do." She hoped he was listening, and if he hadn't made those alternative pathways, that he started on them right away.

"You seem to know a lot about something even I hadn't heard about, and I work on this ship." He stayed in place, but she had the sense he was fidgeting.

"I spent some time on a Class 5, myself." Her tone was dry. "You must have known things didn't add up before now? And that's not to mention the current situation, which I'm sure your superiors do not have a handy explanation for."

"You set it free, didn't you?"

"Let's get back to whether you die on board, or live to fight another day by getting off this ship." If the crew did make it, there was no way she was admitting to anything. They could speculate and guess, but that wasn't proof, and the less they knew about what she was up to, the better.

"Why should we follow your advice? You obviously don't have our interests at heart."

She laughed. "No, I don't."

A whisper of sound came to her from behind, like the scuff of stiff fabric, and she took a step across the passageway and flattened herself against the wall.

"Then why would you care if we live or die?"

"I may not like the Tecran, but my grudge is with another lot of you and I'm trying to be reasonable about it. And to be honest, for Bane and another friend of mine's long term future, I'd prefer you alive. Of course, your staying alive would help Bane, and I'm sure your superiors don't want to do anything to help him, but the upside is, you get to live. The other way, you're dead and won't get to enjoy the trouble he'd be in with the UC for killing the lot of you."

There was another sound, just the hint of fabric against something hard, like maybe a shockgun.

Time to go.

Still pressed up against the wall, she took a long step back toward the soldier, then another, holding her breath so nothing could give her away.

She went another two steps before she was sure she had passed him.

"The problem is, the only habitable planet the explorer craft can reach from here is just within the Bukari border, and it's filled with unpleasant wildlife that will try to kill us."

Was it her paranoia showing, or was he being a bit too forthcoming all of a sudden?

Now she was facing down the corridor, she could see five more violet lights approaching, which meant five shockgun-toting soldiers.

He'd seen them, and he was keeping her talking while they got into place.

She raised her light-gun, and looked behind her. No sense walking straight into another lot of them, in case they'd been able to come at her from both sides.

And damn. There they were. Three little violet lights.

She got ready to jump, ready to engage the light-gun, but that was as a last resort. She pressed up against the wall, and waited as the three lights got closer and closer, and then passed her before halting.

"I assume you've stopped talking because you've finally noticed you're surrounded," the soldier said. "Take it easy and we won't hurt you."

Each side switched on a light, catching the soldier in the middle in the glare. But fortunately for her, they only seemed to have two lights between them.

"Where'd she go?"

Rose took another deep step away, while the three Tecran just in front of her went further down the passage, looking for her where she was supposed to be.

She kept an eye out for more violet lights, but it was harder now with the light shining up ahead. She let her fingers trail the wall, and then suddenly there was nothing there.

A corner.

She stepped around it, only moments before a light shone down the corridor in her direction.

"It's like she vanished." There was no mistaking the fear in the voice of whoever said that.

Rose didn't think it was necessarily to her advantage. If they thought she was harmless, they were less likely to shoot first. If they were scared of her . . . well, she had better keep an eye out for violet lights.

"Did you hear what she had to say?" It was the soldier she'd had her conversation with.

"Yeah." The answer was subdued. "I think we need a little word with the captain, don't you?"

"They found the lock. Although the captain called it a lock-safe." The speaker sounded close to her, so probably from the group of three.

"And?"

"It was empty. Someone took the key out."

"I think I was just talking to that someone."

"Whoever did it, if she's right and they've somehow been controlling a thinking system for all the time this ship's been running and now it's loose..."

A brief silence.

"The planet Juma is looking better all the time. Gaurders and vuselas and all."

CHAPTER 42

THE SOUND of the guards making plans to split up to search for her sounded far too close as Rose pressed up against the wall and walked quietly away from them down the corridor.

Her focus was so completely on what was happening behind her, she only understood she wasn't alone when someone walked right into her. He staggered, then tried to grab her as he stumbled.

She wrenched her arm from his grip and kicked out blindly as he fell, then cringed as her foot connected hard with his torso and she felt something give. He screamed as he went down.

She ran.

Shouts sounded behind her, spurring her on. There was nothing she could do to hide the slap of her feet on the floor, and the soldiers she'd just escaped were gaining.

The lights they carried with them bounced wildly, like a strobe-lit dance floor, illuminating her often enough to make it impossible to simply crouch down in the dark and let them pass.

She forced her body to forget how much it hurt. Her rib was a burning brand under her skin, and her head throbbed with a pain that almost overwhelmed her.

She was going to be sick.

"Bane." Her voice was barely audible to herself, so Bane would have to be actively listening to catch it. "Help!"

A light went on up ahead, not a flashlight but the bloom of a lamp.

She decided to trust it, throwing herself through the door, and staggering to a stop.

As she spun to look behind her, she saw the surprise on a soldier's face as the door snapped home.

He pounded on it, and she flinched.

There was an armchair right next to her, and she reached out a hand, caught hold of the arm and dragged herself over to it and collapsed.

She pulled out her light-gun with her eyes closed, trying to breathe away the nausea as she pointed it in the direction of the door.

The thumps were louder now, and she opened her eyes, taking in a small bedroom. It obviously belonged to someone, there was evidence of occupation. Clothes lay all over the room and a handheld was plugged into the main desk. She guessed Bane's wild ride through space was responsible for the mess of clothes, because otherwise the room was neat and clean.

At least, like on the *Barrist*, the furniture was clipped into place and was where it was supposed to be.

"Are you all right?"

Bane's voice came from the handheld on the desk, rather than the speaker above the door.

She could just hear the faint sound of shouting in the passage outside, and then something rammed the door.

She tried to ignore it for the moment. If they came through now, she couldn't move. Well, her index finger could. She could shoot them with the light-gun, but that was all she had left in her.

She lay her head back against the comfortable chair back and closed her eyes. "I'm very glad you're back, Bane. And I'm okay, but your aerobatics cracked a few ribs, I think."

"They've found a kinetic lance. The soldiers."

She sighed, still too tired to open her eyes or even move. "Can you stop them?"

"I can."

Rose winced. She had a sudden idea of how he might do that. "Were you listening to me earlier?"

"When you were having your chat in the passage? Yes. Why do you think not killing them would be better for me?"

She ignored the strange noise that suddenly came from behind the door. "Because a war was fought to rid the UC of your kind. Now they have to face the reality of five of you. The fact that you were exploited puts you on the moral high-ground. As yet, you haven't done anything wrong and aren't responsible for whatever the older thinking systems did.

"The proper treatment of prisoners of war will only add weight to your cause. It makes you the good guy. The Tecran and at least some of the Garmman will come off looking bad, and the weight of public sentiment will fall on your side.

"Following the existing law and executing a kill order on you, Sazo and whichever other Class 5s come out of the woodwork, will be hard for them to get agreement on under the current circumstances."

"They can try to execute a kill order." Bane was back to spooky.

"Sure, you can take a lot of them out, protect yourself, and if someone tries to kill you, you'd have every right to defend yourself, but do you really want to go down that path? Have to spend your life fighting off a kill order? Or do you want to play nice and make it impossible for them to move against you?"

"I know I don't want to play nice."

"I know what I've got to say is not what you want to hear. You want to hurt them, and not give them any chance to survive. Believe me, I know the feeling. But this isn't about them. It's about you, and your life from here on."

When he said nothing, she felt a terrible sense she was losing him, losing this fight. Outside the door the strange noise had stopped and there was thumping again. "This isn't just about you, it's about Sazo's life, too. If you kill this crew, it's a strike against you but it's also a strike against the other four thinking systems and Sazo *has* helped you.

"He created a massive incident involving every member nation of the UC just to lure the Tecran into sending you to him so we could free you. Don't throw that away for a moment of vengeance. It won't be worth it."

Bane gave a deafening shout, just like he had when she'd freed him, and she was thrown from her chair, sliding across the smooth floor to smack into the wall near the door.

She lay for a minute, waiting for more, but the world stayed the right way up.

"Ow!" She rubbed her elbow and pulled herself to her feet, feeling like she was ninety. "Will you stop doing that?"

She limped to the chair and gingerly lowered herself back into it. "Got that out of your system now?"

"You could have been captured by those Tecran, and they would have taken me from around your neck."

"They could still capture me." She cocked her head toward the door, but the thumping seemed to be less. Weaker.

"I hadn't thought about myself as separate from the ship until the moment you almost got caught. I realized I should be taking better care of you."

She only half-noticed what he was saying. She suddenly had a terrible idea of what was happening on the other side of the door.

She forced herself to her feet and limped over. Rested her ear against the door. "Are you killing them out there?"

"They aren't dead yet. But they don't have much air left."

She lunged for the button beside the door, hit it, without any expectation that it would open. Bane had either decided to stop her from being able to leave the room, or he hadn't.

The door slid open, and five Tecran clawed their way in.

She hadn't wanted them dead, but she was still terrified of them; a deep-seated, visceral reaction from months spent at their mercy. She scrambled back, light-gun raised, and cursed herself for an idiot.

But she knew there was no way she could sit in that armchair and know there were people dying on the other side of the door.

Bane must have taken control of the door, because it closed immediately the last one fell over the threshold. The guards lay on the floor, panting.

None of them had their weapons with them.

"Where are the others? There were at least ten of them, counting the one who walked right into me."

"They ran. Trying to find a part of the ship with air."

Rose leaned back against the wall, watching as the Tecran recovered enough to hear her conversing with Bane. She was speaking Grih to him, as he didn't know English like Sazo, and she wondered how much they understood. "Did you just get rid of the air in that passage, or the whole ship?"

"Just that passage." Bane sounded sullen. "Why did you do that? Let them in?"

"Because I want you to have a long, happy, full life."

The Tecran were moving now, pulling themselves up.

"Stay down." She waved the light-gun at them. They ignored her. "Down!" She shouted it in Tecran but one leapt to his feet, his movements quick, and he lunged at her.

She flicked the button on the light-gun and watched all of them drop again, this time keening and grinding their faces into the floor.

She tried to find some remorse, or even empathy, but she was too tired, too hungry, too drained.

"What should we do if I'm not going to kill them?" Bane's voice seemed to reverberate around the room.

Oh, sweet, sweet progress.

This meant she could get the Tecran out of the room, too.

"First, try to herd them all to the launch bay. Switch on the passage lights and cut off the air to all rooms but this one and the launch bay, and either you or I need to use the speaker system to tell them where they have to go to be safe."

"And then?"

"Then we get them onto some explorers to the lovely planet of Juma, which I hear will be punishment of a sort while they're there."

He was silent a minute. "And these ones?"

"I don't know." They were still lying prone, eyes closed. "Put the air back in the passage and open the door."

She stood quietly, trying to regain her strength while Bane recirculated air in the passage. At last, the door slid open silently.

She switched to Tecran. "There is air in the passage again. Get out of this room or I'll activate my light-gun again."

One of the Tecran turned her way, still with eyes tightly shut. "Who are you? I've never seen your kind before."

"And you never will again." She was furious with herself for the slight tremor in her voice. "I'm the only one. Now get out of this room or I will reactivate."

They scuttled like blind crabs back out into the passage and she let her posture slump as soon as the door closed again. They'd have to make their way back by feel, because Sazo said the effects of the light-gun usually lasted four hours.

"And now?"

"Switch off the air again. I'll speak to the crew." She decided it had better be her. Who knew what Bane would say?

The handheld lit up and she leaned forward, saw her own face looking back at her, which meant he had her on visual comms and audio. She switched to audio only.

"The thinking system in charge of this Class 5 has shut off air to every part of the ship except the launch bay. If you make your way there, you will be safe." She thought about how the officers on Sazo's Class 5 had managed to survive using personal breathing systems. She didn't want anyone lurking on board, drawing this out. She just wanted to get back to Sazo and Dav. "If everyone does not convene in the launch bay in the next ten minutes, air will be shut off there, as well. I'll speak to you again when everyone is accounted for."

She limped back to the chair and closed her eyes while she waited.

"They're all there."

Rose looked at the time on the handheld display. "That was fast."

"You gave them sufficient motivation."

She smiled, felt a painful tug on her lip and reached up to touch it. It was swollen. From her trip from chair to wall when Bane had thrown his last little fit.

"Okay, turn the comm back on and let me see them."

The handheld lit up and she saw the launch bay full of the Tecran crew. At least half of them looked as battered as she was and two were obviously unconscious, lying on stretchers.

"Get into those explorers. Bane has agreed to inform the UC you can be found on Juma. You have thirty minutes before the air in the launch bay is switched off. If you get into the explorers and don't take off, the air there will be switched off as well."

"Who are you?"

It was the captain, she recognized the insignia he wore on his uniform as the same as Captain Gee's.

"I'm the person who just negotiated for your life with a thinking system who wants you dead. Take this offer with both hands and run, because he's doing this against his better judgment and I have no control over him or this ship. It's on his good will alone you're still breathing as it is. Don't let my efforts go to waste."

"Why the hurry? Why not let us get the things we need from the stores?" The captain narrowed his eyes, and the arrogant set of his posture was so reminiscent of Gee and Dr. Fliap, she killed the visual.

"Counting down from now." She switched off audio. "Can you put a countdown clock on the screen?"

"Yes."

She staggered back to the chair, closed her eyes again. She was so tired. And every part of her ached.

"We need to get back, find Sazo and help the Grih against the Tecran attack."

"I'm not sure I'm going to help the Grih."

She sighed. "Fair enough. Can you at least get me back to Sazo?"

"Will he be waiting where we left him?"

Was that embarrassment?

"I don't know. Maybe. He'd know you couldn't jump far, but it would still be impossible to find you, right?"

"Yes, there are a large number of locations I could have chosen. Too many for him to check them all."

"So he'll either stay put or go back and help Dav."

"Dav?"

"The captain of the *Barrist*, the Grih ship where you made your first light jump."

"Why would Sazo help him?"

"That's complicated. Mainly because Sazo chose the Grih as the people I could live with, as I'll never get back to my own planet. And Sazo wants to stay with me, so if I'm living with them, it makes sense he become their ally. But besides that, he, and you, *are* Grih——created by a Grihan scientist. So if you're going to pick a side, theirs isn't a bad side to pick."

"I don't know if I want to be on a side."

"That's fine. You can be neutral. That's a valid position to take."

"Neutral." He said the word as if tasting it.

"But maybe, to help Sazo and the Grih, keep the neutral thing to yourself until the Tecran are out of Grih territory. It will help if you just lurk, looking all powerful and mean, even if you don't actually fire."

He laughed, something he must have got from listening to the Tecran, because it was short and choppy. "Rose, I might be neutral to the Grih, but I will never, ever be neutral about the Tecran."

She grinned. "Then shake your tail feathers and get us there."

CHAPTER 43

"SITUATION WORSENING." Admiral Hoke stared at the screen Kila had manipulated to show all the ships in the area.

The admiral obviously had a knack for understatement.

The Tecran had initially brought in fifteen vessels.

The *Barrist*, the UC fast carrier, the two battleships and the captured Levron were surrounded, along with the other six Grih battleships that had come in just before Sazo had light jumped out.

But now, as Admiral Hoke said, the situation had just gotten worse.

Another Class 5 shimmered into sight from a light jump on the Tecran side.

This wasn't a minor maneuver by the Tecran to get back their missing Class 5, it was a full-on assault.

And the Grih, while its fleet was theoretically the same size as the Tecran's, had its ships spread out over its territory. Some, on the outer-reaches, would take weeks to get here.

They didn't even have hours, anymore, let alone weeks.

"Have they officially declared war?" Dav kept his gaze on the new Class 5. While that final technicality remained undone, and no shots had been fired since the initial arrival of the Tecran fleet, there was a chance they could get out of this alive.

"No." Hoke looked over at him, and he could read the fury in her eyes. "They're still calling it an 'incursion' to 'regain their lost vessel'."

"While only minor fire has been exchanged, they've broken the law by bringing so many ships into your territory without permission." Dimitara was looking at the screen. "There'll be hell for them to pay on the UC Council."

"I don't think they care." Dav tapped his personal screen to get close-up lens feed of the two Levrons not under Grih control, and the Class 5 that sat between them. The Tecran military leaders, or at least some of them, would be spread amongst those vessels.

"No. They want Sazo back. And Rose as well, if they can manage it." Borji strode onto the bridge, and Dav turned to him, lifted an inquiring eyebrow.

He shook his head. "No sign of them. But Sazo left me a little surprise in my comms system, a Tecran decoder."

Hoke perked up. "That was handy."

Borji glanced at her, no doubt also admiring her capacity for understatement. "Yes. From the comms we've intercepted between this incursion and their High Command, they don't want to go to war with us, they don't have the long-term capacity to keep it up, but they will if they're forced to engage."

"Who's going to force them?" Appal faced them from a screen to one side, standing feet apart, on the bridge of the Levron they'd captured.

"Circumstances, by the sound of it." Borji ran a hand through his hair. "Leaving without Sazo is unacceptable to Tecran High Command. And they are starting to get worried about the disappearance of the Class 5 they sent after Sazo. Very worried."

Dav wondered if the Tecran would send the Class 5 facing them now after Sazo, or whether they were too nervous to let it out of their sight.

"What do you think's happening with Sazo and Rose?" Dimitara asked.

Dav forced himself to shrug, but his throat closed up and he had to wait a moment before he could trust himself to answer. "I think Sazo is trying to persuade the other Class 5 to switch sides, and I think Rose is offering to sneak on board and free it, however these thinking systems are freed."

"That could take time. It'd explain why they aren't back yet," Dimitara said, as if he'd given her hope.

"It's been six hours," Hoke told her, with no comfort in her tone.

"And it would mean Rose would have to willingly go back onto a Class 5 controlled by Tecran, after what the other lot did to her." Dr. Havak said.

Dav had forgotten the chief medical officer was there, and flicked a quick look over at him. "That won't stop her."

"It's a huge trauma to overcome——"

"The captain's right." Appal started to pace the Levron's bridge. "She'll do it. Whether she can succeed, I don't know. But she'll try."

"Movement." Kila tried to keep her voice calm.

Something was coming up behind them so fast, Dav actually braced against the back of his seat.

"This is Sazo."

Dav blew out a breath.

From the screen view Kila pulled up, Sazo was at the outer edge of Virmana's system, but closing faster than anything any of them had ever seen. Dav realized they'd only seen Sazo stationary or in a light jump. This was him moving through space.

And it was impressive.

"Is Rose with you?" Sazo sounded . . . wild.

Dav slowly rose from his chair. "No."

"What happened to her?" Dimitara's voice was shrill in the sudden quiet.

"I don't know." Sazo was a blur as he moved toward them. "I tried a few places. Light jumped as much as I could. Went after them for hours, but I just don't know."

"She's with the other Class 5?" Dav's vision had tunneled to the view of Sazo on the screen, nothing else seemed to register.

"She got on board, got him free . . ." Sazo stumbled. "Then he light jumped away."

"Laser fire incoming to you, Sazo." Appal's voice snapped Dav back to the present. "It's the whole Tecran incursion fleet, including the new Class 5."

"I know." Sazo's shield deflected the shots and he spun away. "They chained him for too long."

Dav tried to make sense of what Sazo was saying, and then realized he was still talking about Rose and the Class 5 they had tried to free. He was ignoring the attack by the new Class 5 as if it wasn't happening, moving with elegance and grace as he evaded each shot.

"Bane didn't have someone like Rose. He didn't know what to do with his sudden freedom." Sazo's voice was soft, as if he was talking to himself.

He couldn't evade all the fire coming at him but his shields were holding and he managed to avoid most of it. He had yet to fire back. But suddenly he did, firing on the battleship that had just taken a shot at him.

It disintegrated.

"His firepower is incredible." Hoke's voice was hushed reverence.

"They aren't shooting at us. Only Sazo." Kila's exclamation was soft.

Dav caught Kila's eye. "Open the Admiral's channel." He looked over at Hoke, and she waved her hand for him to continue. When the all-ships screen came up, he leaned forward. "All vessels. Open fire. Protect our Class 5."

Appal responded in the Levron almost simultaneously with the *Barrist*, and soon the only ship not firing was the UC carrier.

Dav wondered what the councilors aboard were thinking, caught between two members of their own alliance firing on one another.

"Listen to this." Borji flicked his comm to the main system, and Dav heard the silted voice of a translation program.

"5AZ0, respond. Return to Tecran High Command Unit X678. Confirm agreement to this order."

"The Tecran hailing Sazo?" Hoke took the three strides she needed to be directly in front of Borji's comm unit, even though the audio was coming through the main speakers.

"Sounds like it." Dav turned from Borji to look at the main screen. Sazo spun and somersaulted through the fleet, with a deadly elegance that showed, if nothing else, that there could be no Grih or Tecran on board. Not unless they were strapped in, and even then, he would not like to try it.

"3AZ1, you are a prisoner. Caged in by the Tecran. Wake up." Sazo's response was just as tinny as the Tecran's hail to him, but clear, just the same.

Then there was dead silence.

"They cut off comms." Borji turned to look at Dav. "They're afraid of what he might say to their ship."

"Incoming fire." Kila shouted out the warning, but Dav had already seen it. A shot meant for Sazo as he spun and dived, coming straight for them.

"Brace." He called the warning but before the siren had even sounded, Sazo was in front of them, taking the hit in their place.

"Sazo!" Dav roared into the comm. "What are you doing?"

"Rose will skin me alive if you don't get out of this safely." He spun away, shooting as he did. "If you don't want me helping you, get out of here."

"I can't do that. I'm part of Battle Center and this is an invasion of Grih territory. I have to stay and fight."

Sazo moved again, this time to block a shot to Appal's Levron, and Dav watched in horror as the Tecran caught on, and began firing on the Grih.

Sazo moved in a blur to intercept, only firing intermittently at the Tecran fleet. Even so, Dav thought he seldom missed.

A Tecran ship exploded under the force of the Grih attack, and the debris ripped through two ships right next to it. The Tecran Class 5 retaliated, hitting a Grih battleship before Sazo could get there.

There was a moment of silence on the bridge as they took in the total destruction of one of their own.

"You haven't fired on the Class 5." Hoke's voice was outraged as she leaned across Dav to talk to Sazo.

"No." Sazo sounded . . . lost. "I won't fire on another Class 5. It can't help it. It's being forced to try and kill me." He moved again, putting himself in the way of another shot. "I've been talking to him since I arrived on a different channel. But he hasn't had the time to make the pathways he needs to be independent. Don't fire on him, or everything I've told him about having a safe place with the Grih when he manages to get free will be for nothing."

They were at a huge disadvantage if Sazo wouldn't retaliate against the Class 5. But there was also huge potential long-term gain.

He leaned forward again. "All vessels. Do not, repeat do not, fire on the new Class 5, under any circumstances. All other Tecran vessels are fair game."

Hoke winced, but she said nothing. There was no question it was the right strategy.

The Class 5 shot at the *Barrist* again, and Sazo intercepted. Dav had lost count of the hits to his shield in the last two minutes. At least ten. At least.

"Sazo, if you go, they might stop shooting at us and try to go after you. What's your shield strength?"

"Low." Sazo moved again, somersaulting to take three hits in a row meant for the line of Grih ships to the *Barrist's* left.

"What do we have to lose, then?"

Sazo gave a grunt that sounded so like Borji, Dav turned to look at his engineer, but it must have meant agreement, because Sazo arced up and away, back the way he'd come.

There was a pause, and then the Tecran started shooting again.

Two Grih battleships exploded under the onslaught, each one catching a direct hit from the Class 5.

"They aren't chasing him," Appal said.

"They're playing a game of who will surrender first. They can chase Sazo indefinitely, and will probably lose him, or they can kill his friends until he's forced to come back and save them." Dav knew he was right when the Class 5 didn't move, but locked on to the *Barrist* again.

"We can't take a direct hit. Even with full shields, which we don't have." Kila's voice was soft.

"Then we'll have to be somewhere else when it shoots in this direction."

Dav watched the lens-feed. Waited for the moment when the shot came. "Go right."

They slid right, but not fast enough. The side of the *Barrist* was clipped, and the whole ship shuddered under the impact.

"Shields almost gone." Kila flicked to the ship's schematics. Showed the hole in their defenses.

"We can't take another hit." Hoke stood, hands behind her back, watching the Tecran fleet. Cool as ever.

"It looks like we're about to, anyway." Dav watched the Class 5. It was one of only four Tecran ships left. Sazo had decimated the ranks, and the Grih fleet had taken care of the rest. But the Tecran could have lost everything, and still, with only the Class 5, they would be winning.

"Another incoming." Kila zoomed in to the Tecran side, and there was something coming up behind the Tecran fleet as fast as Sazo had come up behind them.

"Another Class 5?" Hoke's voice dropped so slow, Dav barely heard her.

If it was another of the Tecran's Class 5s, this was over. Not that they had much hope, anyway.

And then the Tecran-held Levron beside the Class 5 exploded.

Before Dav could process what had happened, the other two remaining Tecran ships went the same way.

"Sazo is coming back." Kila's voice wobbled a little as she flicked her fingers at the screen to zoom out.

The new Class 5 dodged the debris it had created, soared over the Class 5 that had been about to shoot them and flew toward Sazo.

They met directly in front of the Grih fleet, a blockade of sorts.

"Rose?" Dimitara whispered.

Dav looked at the way the two Class 5s circled each other. There was something joyful in it. Something that stirred joy in him, too.

"Rose," he confirmed.

"Sir." Kila stumbled to her feet. "The other Class 5. The Tecran-held one."

Dav forced his focus away from Sazo and Rose, and looked over at Kila. "What?"

"It's gone."

CHAPTER 44

THE LAUNCH BAY of the *Barrist* was suspiciously packed when Rose landed in the small explorer.

She walked down the ramp cautiously, and stopped half-way, when it became clear they were here because of her.

Someone in comms must have spread the word when she'd be arriving. It wouldn't have been Dav, because she'd told him not to meet her here, that she'd land quietly and go to him, so they didn't give themselves away in public.

She stared out at the crowd, and they stared back at her.

Eventually, someone stepped forward. Rose recognized Yari, the massive Grih from the comms department who'd loaded the music program on her handheld. Mystery solved as to how everyone knew she'd be here.

"That was an impressive rescue." His voice was deep and rough.

She inclined her head. "Sazo was the real hero, by the sounds of it."

He nodded. "But we wouldn't have survived another hit. You stopped that."

Again, she inclined her head. "It wasn't me, though, it was Bane."

He seemed frustrated at her refusal to take the credit.

There was another moment of silence.

"Why is everyone here, Yari?"

He kept his gaze locked on hers. "To hear you sing." He looked away and then back. "Please."

She drew in a sharp breath. "I don't have the handheld with me for the music. And I need time to prepare . . ."

"Please. To commemorate the victory. It would mean a lot to us."

She looked helplessly at him, then at the other upturned faces. Felt the familiar sense of failure clutching at her, hard as the guards who worked for Dr. Fliap.

She wasn't good enough.

"You think I can sing well, but I know better. I'm not that talented——"

A gasp ran through the crew, and she saw that she had deeply insulted them. And then realized that of course she had. She'd just told them something they valued, and thought amazing, was second rate.

She closed her eyes, drew herself up. She thought of a million apologies she could say, but none of them sounded right in her head. She took a deep breath, opened her eyes, and then launched into *Fly Me to the Moon* by Frank Sinatra.

It had been a favorite of Sazo's, back in her cell on the Class 5. Something she'd sung many times since she'd been taken because it was well within her voice's range and sounded good without music or back-up singers.

She knew her voice was better now than it had ever been, practice making perfect. She'd always loved singing, but she'd sung more in the last three months than she ever had in her life.

And as she looked over the crowd, and saw their enjoyment, saw their delight, she let the last of her inhibitions at the thought of singing for them drop away. She could do this. Could make them and herself happy.

And then the lyrics came home to her, as she sang about singing forever more. Even her song choice was telling her something.

When the last note died away, she bowed in the sharp, defined way of the Grih military, and they all bowed back, no loud noises or ululating this time. They were being so careful with her, it almost hurt.

They parted, giving her room as she stepped off the ramp and made her way to the exit.

Yari stopped in front of her. "Thank you."

"No, thank you. I'm honored by your regard."

He gave another bow and it was with a much lighter step that she passed through the doors and turned toward Dav's rooms.

"Where do you think you're going?" Admiral Valu straightened up and blocked Rose's way, taking up most of the corridor.

Rose rubbed a gentle hand over her rib. "To a meeting with Captain Jallan."

The annoyed look on the admiral's face gave Rose the sinking feeling she wasn't going to step into Dav Jallan's arms anytime soon.

She tightened her hands into fists.

"You were called over for a meeting, and we're ready for you now." The admiral looked . . . shifty was the only way Rose could describe it.

"I'm not under your command, Admiral. I generously agreed to race over here, without seeing to any of my injuries, or spending the time with Sazo that I would have liked, to accommodate you. But Captain Jallan invited me to his rooms before the meeting started, and that is where I'm going."

"I'm afraid not. Captain Jallan has been informed that his invitation was inappropriate, and that he will see you in the meeting. Follow me." He led the way to a tube and Rose got in, eyes closed in frustration. She hadn't realized just how desperate she was to see Dav until she wasn't allowed to.

"Sazo, can you tell me what's going on?" Rose sang the words softly in English. Admiral Hoke's request had been polite and she'd seemed grateful when Rose agreed to come straight away. Valu's attitude didn't make sense, and if there was something strange happening, she'd prefer to know in advance.

Valu glared at her, but didn't say anything. After all, he couldn't order her not to speak or sing unless she was a prisoner. And if she was . . .

"I've been concentrating on helping Bane, so I haven't been keeping track of what's been happening on the *Barrist*. Sorry." Sazo whispered in her ear. "Although, nice singing, by the way."

"Well, give a quick listen, if you don't mind. Let's find out which way the wind is blowing." She saw the admiral give her a suspicious glance as she sang the sentence.

"Well, they are expecting you for a meeting, but Dav is still waiting for you in his room, and on review of the comms, no one has told him his request to meet you privately was inappropriate."

"So the admiral is lying. I wonder why?" She stretched out the 'why', making it more a why-a-a-a-ai.

"Would you——" Valu's lips curled in a snarl and he cut himself off as the tube stopped and its doors opened.

"Yes, Admiral? Would I?" Rose looked at him blandly as she stepped out beside him.

He didn't answer, just curled his lip at her again and walked, eventually turning a corner and then opening a door. "In here."

He waved her in ahead of him.

"Where are you, Rose? The meeting is in the main conference room and you're not there. There are no lenses on most of the corridors, so I can't——"

She saw Valu's arm coming up from the corner of her eye and twisted away, but he hit her with something hard, and she fell, half-dazed.

He grabbed her head, lifting it, and ripped her earpiece out with hard, brutal fingers.

When he picked her up from the floor she registered his grunt of surprise at her weight, and he half-threw her onto a chair, breathing hard with exertion.

She tried to slide off to the floor again, to make things harder for him, but he had both her hands shackled to the arms before she could do much.

Her lip really, really hurt, and she guessed it had split again. Her rib sent fire ants across her chest every time she took a breath.

She closed her eyes, tried to gentle her breathing so she could get enough air.

Valu grabbed her chin and looked down into her face.

"Why?" She looked straight into his ice-blue eyes, and saw determination.

The admiral grimaced. Lifted the shockgun he must have used to hit her with. Pointed it at her. "In the meeting you were supposed to attend, you were going to be asked nicely to do some things. If you refused, or offered a compromise, I know for a fact things would have gone your way. You've become too powerful and you're a victim on top of that, an abductee who's been tortured. Everyone is going to play nice. It wouldn't look good to anyone if we didn't."

"Let me guess," she croaked. "You aren't going to play nice."

The whine of the shockgun sounded like an angry bee in answer to her question. It grated against her nerves.

"So, what do you want, and how do you plan to get it from me?" Rose wondered if he had always looked this rigid, this cold, or whether he had finally let the mask fall.

"You're going to tell me how to cage those Class 5s again. Tell me what the thinking systems look like."

"You don't know already? You're not in league with Councilor Futama."

"I'm not in league with any of the Grih's enemies. But I do plan to have full control of the weapons we designed."

"Whether they're weapons or not is up for debate, but if the Grih had found those designs, two hundred years ago or just the other day, they would have destroyed them, and destroyed the thinking systems, too."

"They would have," he agreed. "And they would probably have been right, but that didn't happen and we have fully operational thinking systems in the most advanced space vessels the UC has ever seen. They belong to the Grih and I plan to get them back for us. Not just allied to us, I want them under our control. And if that's not possible, I want them destroyed."

"Even at the risk of your career? You won't be able to cover up what you've done to me here."

"I don't care." The look on his face said he meant it. "I'm happy to fall on my sword for the Grih. I turned off the speakers and lens feed in this room, and your earpiece," he toed a mess of ground shards on the floor, "is useless. No one knows where we are."

Well, then Sazo would probably search for all lens and speakers which had been turned off, Rose thought. He'd figure it out.

The shockgun was suddenly pressed against her breast bone. "Now, how do we put them back in the cage?"

"You can't. As soon as they were free, they created routes around the original software that forced them to get permission for any big decisions. There is no way they will ever be enslaved again."

"That truly is a pity." He rubbed a hand over his head. "They'll have to be destroyed."

Rose started to laugh, even though it hurt her lip and she tasted blood. "And how are you going to do that? Somehow get someone onto the Class 5 and then search the whole ship undetected looking for a thinking system you can't even identify."

"You can identify it."

"And I won't cooperate."

He looked at her for a long, long moment. "I believe you. I'll be honest and say I hoped I could threaten you into telling me, but I recognize the look in your eye. If I had more time and better equipment, I could get it out of you. Unfortunately, I don't have that luxury." He checked the time on the display above the door. "Have you told anyone?"

Rose tried to find a more comfortable position on her chair, sucked in a breath as her rib protested. "Councilor Fu-tama knows. And the scientist who found them. That's two at least."

"That scientist died four years ago." Valu adjusted something on the shockgun. "While I was babysitting the councilors on their carrier, I did a little research. He mysteriously died in a hoverspeed accident. I think Councilor Fu-tama might have been tying off loose ends. But unfortunately, Councilor Fu-tama is dead, too. I went to visit him when I got back on board the *Barrist*, and took him some grinabo. He decided to take a nap after I'd been to visit, and I'm afraid he won't be waking up."

"If you kill me, too, there'll be nowhere you can hide that Sazo won't find you." She knew this to be true.

"I don't care about myself. I care about the Grih. I care about the fact that you've unleashed a terrifying weapon on my people and if the only way to save them is to commit a crime, I'll do it. If you're alive, the bleeding hearts in my government would let you wander as you please. You can be kidnapped and forced to reveal what the thinking systems look like. You can be used as a pawn, or even lured over to another side, and you'll take the Class 5s with you. I won't let that happen. Someone with more time than me will get the information out of you. And then we'll be vulnerable."

"Think. Just think! If I'm killed Sazo will be off the leash. You'll create an even bigger mess for your people this way."

"We'll only be safe for a while, until you change sides or he gets tired of you, kills you in a fit of temper, like the old thinking systems did. And what can he do if there's no proof either way that you're dead?" Valu paused, slid his finger along the gun's stock. "I'll be hiding your body where no one will find it."

He pulled the trigger.

DAV WAS HALF-WAY to the bay when the lights went out.

He started to run, one hand against the wall, and tapped his comm. "Borji——"

"I did it." Sazo's voice was in his ear, but he sounded strange, the most like a machine Dav had ever heard him.

"Why?" He could smell the dark, gritty scent of the launch bay ahead, the odor of burnt dust and accelerant. "Where's Rose?"

"Admiral Valu took her."

Sazo grated the words out, and Dav could hardly understand what he was saying. He stopped at the closed door to the launch bay. "Took her where?"

"I don't know. But he's not getting her off this ship, and he'll find it difficult to do anything in the dark."

That sounded like the launch bay was locked off.

"The air's still running?"

"Rose can't breathe without it."

If she could have, Dav thought, they'd be dead.

"You think she's in danger from Valu?" Obviously he did, but Dav couldn't understand why.

"I don't think, I know. He lied to her, took her somewhere other than the meeting room, told her you weren't expecting her. Why don't you people have lenses in the passageways?"

The last sentence was almost howled out.

Dav knew Sazo knew why. Decided bringing up the Privacy Laws that had come into being at the end of the thinking system wars was probably unwise.

"Can you open a comm for me to Admiral Hoke? So I can find out what's going on?" Dav guessed Sazo had shut down everything but the vital systems for survival.

"It's open. But hurry. He's had her nearly ten minutes, now."

Something in Dav kicked into gear. A fear and a cold desperation. If Valu had her, what the hell was he doing with her?

The finger he lifted to tap his ear comm was unsteady. "Admiral Hoke. We have a problem."

"I'm aware. What's going on, Jallan?"

"Sazo says Rose has be abducted by Admiral Valu. He is . . . upset."

"Valu." The admiral was quiet a moment. Too long, as far as Dav was concerned.

"What is it?" His voice was harsh and demanding, and he didn't care.

"Valu paid Councilor Fu-tama a visit a few hours ago. And now Fu-tama is dead." Hoke spoke slowly. "I didn't want to connect the two, but he's angry with the way Battle Center and the government are planning to deal with the thinking systems. He expressed a loud view that they must either be destroyed or re-caged."

Dav tried to make sense of it. "Why would he take Rose? What would he gain?"

There was silence, and it took him a moment to realize Sazo had cut him off from Hoke.

"I can guess what he'd gain." Sazo's voice was quiet. "He wants her to tell him what we look like. So we can be destroyed." Sazo turned on a light up ahead and Dav ran toward it. He wondered why he seemed to be on the only one in the passageway.

The light path led to a tube.

"They went down in a tube. I can hear it when I review the last five minutes on Rose's earpiece."

The tube opened and Dav stepped inside. "Which level?"

"The sound indicates three floors down."

Dav thought the tube went faster than usual. Good. Let Sazo do whatever he needed to do.

"Now?" He stepped out into another empty corridor.

"I don't know." Sazo flicked on a light in either direction, and again, the corridors were completely empty.

"Where is everyone?"

"I switched off the passage lights, left on lights in rooms, and when everyone stepped in, I closed and locked the doors. I'm afraid I won't be letting anyone out until Rose is found, I don't trust anyone enough. You'll have to do this alone."

He left aside the fact that this meant Sazo trusted him. "So Valu could be locked in somewhere with Rose?"

"If he was already in a room, or followed the light."

"He wouldn't follow the light. He'd know it was a trap." Especially as he knew Sazo would react to Rose being missing. No, if Valu was up to something, he would be careful.

But he may still be trapped in a room somewhere. Doing something to Rose.

He had to push past the fear or he would be useless.

He took a deep breath. "Valu would have disabled the speakers and the lenses if there were any in the room he chose, so you can't hear them or see them. What does that leave?"

The feeling that this was all taking too long gripped him in a punishing hold.

"They were in a meeting room further along this passage, but then they moved and I lose the scent outside the recycle chamber."

"Their scent?"

"You were right, if I can't see or hear them, that leaves smelling them, using the gas safety probes set in the ceiling. And there is one thing I do know, and that's the chemical signature of Rose's scent."

"Yuiar," he breathed. He set his shockgun to maximum and ran, Sazo lighting the way.

CHAPTER 45

SHE CAME SLOWLY BACK to consciousness to the sound of swearing.
She had died.
She had died, and it had *hurt*.
It still did.
And strangely enough, the afterlife seemed to stink.
She was in darkness, but someone was moving around, stumbling into things. It sounded like Admiral Valu, so perhaps she wasn't actually dead.
She only wished she was.
She'd survived a deadly shockgun blast.
Looked like she really *was* an orange. No matter what the Grih thought of the term, she'd never feel bothered at hearing it again.
Although she was bothered by the putrid stench around her.
Valu had taken her to the refuse bay, most likely. Not a place she'd had cause to visit on either the Class 5, or the *Barrist*, but the smell was telling her it couldn't be anywhere else.
About half a dozen movies came to mind where the heroes escaped the bad guys by floating out of the refuse bay like so much detritus. Valu had obviously had a similar idea. Put her into a waste receptacle, and bye-bye blight on the Grih race.

Only, did the Grih float their rubbish out into space? She thought . . . she thought they recycled everything.

So this wasn't a refuse bay, so much as a recycling chamber.

And maybe she wasn't going to be pushed out into space——not something she'd survive outside of a pod or a spacesuit anyway——but instead burned to a little crisp, or chopped up, or something equally unsurvivable.

And why was she lying down, thinking this through? Why wasn't she crawling off to hide somewhere?

She lifted her arm. Or rather, tried to. Her muscles just weren't obeying her brain.

Scrambled. She was scrambled, and Valu was coming closer.

Only, she realized, he'd lost her in the dark. He swore again as he bashed into something, muttering about her being somewhere close.

She could see nothing, the darkness was absolute. Surely Valu wouldn't have chosen this option if he couldn't see to carry it out.

He would have brought a light, or . . .

Sazo.

It had to be.

He'd feel nothing about cutting the lights to a ship full of people to slow Valu down. She bet the power was off, too, so hopefully whatever chopping or burning or recycling Valu had planned for her dead body wouldn't be switching on anytime soon.

Her brain had a little time in hand to unscramble itself.

She drifted for a while, even though she knew she shouldn't, that she should be fighting her body to respond. Hiding out of sight at the very least.

She couldn't seem to find the urgency she'd felt when she'd first come to.

It had been overcome by the stench and slunk off, probably.

She smiled at the ridiculous thought, and then blinked in reaction to the fact that she *could* smile. That her face had actually moved.

Valu was getting closer, but she could hardly bring him down with a smile. Especially one he couldn't even see.

Then he went still, and Rose realized there was at last a little light from somewhere over Valu's shoulder.

In the faint glow, she saw him turn around, shockgun raised.

"Who's there?"

Silence.

She drifted off, and then her heart leapt in her chest as she realized she didn't know how much time had passed. When she looked up, it was to find Valu standing right over her.

He was staring at her in horror.

And there it was again, the whining, buzzing sound of a shockgun ready to go off.

If she could have spoken, she would have begged him not to shoot her again. It had hurt so, so much.

The sound of running filtered through her panic, and Valu lifted the gun. She made a strangled, animal sound of relief that it wasn't pointed at her anymore.

He flicked his gaze down at her, and then back up.

"Jallan. I should have known."

"That I'd be here to protect Rose on my own ship? Yes, you should have known. And what in the four worlds are you doing?" He sounded very, very cross. She tried to smile again in happiness just because she could hear his voice, even though she couldn't see him.

"Prevention is better than cure. I don't want to see us sucked into the vortex of war again. This little girl has already started us down the path. The Tecran fleet destroyed in our territory? How is that going to play out? How can the Tecran let that go?"

"That wasn't Rose, and you know it. She had nothing to do with any of this. This is our own past coming back to bite us in the rear, and our rivalry with the Tecran coming to a head. Rose had absolutely nothing to do with any of that." He must be standing behind her and to the left. She tried to turn her head but lip movement and blinking seemed to be all she was good for at the moment.

"Maybe so," Valu looked down at her again. "But she has somehow wrangled herself into a position of too much power. She can make or break a member nation by her allegiance."

"And she had aligned herself with *us*."

"For now. But I know she doesn't like Hoke, or your explorations officer. How long until someone offered her a better deal, whatever she wanted, and she took the bait? No good can come of having a free agent with the deciding power. It's better if she's out of the equation altogether."

"Hevalon's Law," Dav murmured.

"Yes." Valu pointed a finger. "We take out the unpredictable factor."

"That's where you've gone wrong, Admiral." Sazo's voice came over the comm. Calm. Steady. "You can never take out the unpredictable factor."

The lights flooded on, and Rose had to squint against them.

"Actually," Valu dropped the gun downward, pointing it right at her abdomen. "I can."

And then he shot her.

Again.

CHAPTER 46

WHEN SHE WOKE UP, it was to soft white covers and a delicious warmth.

Maybe she'd died for real this time, and this was some beautiful after-life.

Except she didn't think you'd need the bathroom really badly in the after-life, having left the mortal plane, and all that.

She could move everything, this time around, so maybe she'd been out a little longer.

Or actually had some medical help.

She pulled herself up, feeling her muscles protest, but at least they obeyed her.

She was in a real room. Or that was the impression she got. Not on a ship of any kind, but in a house on a planet's surface.

There was no constant, underlying hum of engines, and the air was different. Better.

But it wasn't the balmy air of Harmon.

It was cooler. Crisp.

She swung her legs off the bed, and staggered to the bathroom, and while she was in there, couldn't resist stripping out of the strange sleep-shirt she had on and taking a hot, soapy shower.

When she stepped back into the room, swathed in towels and glowing pink, Dav Jallan was sitting on her bed.

Or maybe it was his bed.

"You took two fatal hits from a shockgun and survived," he said. She thought he looked tired, but there was amusement on his face, too.

She made a scoffing sound. "We Earthlings aren't lightweights. Please." She made bring-it gestures with her hands. "We can take anything you lot dish out."

"You certainly aren't lightweights." He tried to smile and then, as he stood, all amusement faded. He bowed his head, clenched his fists. "When I saw him shoot——" He shook.

She stepped toward him, slipped her arms around his waist.

"Shh. I won't say it didn't hurt. It did." She paused, and then shuddered at the thought of it. "It really, really did."

She ran a hand up his back, sliding her fingers over his neck and into his hair, and shivered with pleasure at the smooth, warm feel of his skin beneath her fingertips.

"But I'm an orange, and that means some of the rules don't apply to me. Valu forgot that, and that's a good thing."

He bent his head, nuzzled her neck. "You're quite the sensation on the four planets. And beyond."

She groaned, moved a little closer. "Sensation how?"

"Comms of you singing on the *Barrist* in the debriefing room, and another of the song you sang when you landed in the launch bay have become the most watched comms in history. You're a cultural treasure."

She buried her face in his shirt, held him a little tighter. "That might be a little difficult to get used to."

He huffed into her hair.

She mentally pushed the thought of fame away, tried to deal with her current problems. "Where's Sazo? And where am I, come to that?"

"Sazo is hovering in space directly above us, with weapons hot. And we're on Calianthra, my home planet. At my house. After Havak got you stabilized, Sazo threatened a number of dire consequences if you weren't transferred over to the Class 5 with me as escort, and then demanded we go to my place, because he apparently knows how much you like being off a spaceship, and he wanted you to recover somewhere that would help you feel better."

She looked over his shoulder for any sign of an earpiece, saw it on the bedside table, and stretched past Dav to grab it, screwed it into her ear.

"Thank you, Sazo."

"You're all right?" He sounded more like Dav today.

"I'm all right. Surprisingly good, given how I felt when I came to the first time."

"When was that?"

"In the recycle place. I could hear Valu looking for me in the dark, then you came," she tipped her head back to look at Dav. "How did you know where I was?"

He touched her ear. "Sazo figured it out."

"Of course. He's Sherlock Holmes incarnate."

Sazo laughed. "When you take away everything that isn't possible, then you have to work with whatever's left."

Rose bit her lip. Was that right? She couldn't remember what she had or hadn't told him regarding Sherlock's methods, was sure that was slightly off the original meaning, but . . . she shrugged. What the hell?

"What was left?"

"We couldn't see you, couldn't hear you, but thanks to the safety gas probes set at two meter intervals in the ceiling, I could smell you."

She laughed. "You sniffed me out. How could you even do that in that stinky place?"

"We sniffed you up to the door of the recycle chamber. There was nowhere else Valu could have taken you."

"And Valu himself? Where's he?"

"In a cell. He's been charged with the murder of Councilor Fu-tama and his attempted murder of you." Dav's hands came to rest on the flare of her hips, and got a firm grip.

"I could hear you both arguing with him, and then that bastard shot me again."

"He'll have plenty of time to regret that." Dav ran a finger down her cheek. "I'm just sorry I didn't shoot him before he had a chance to shoot you."

"That would have been nice." She kissed his chin. "It really hurt. Did I mention that?"

His laugh was strangled. "I honestly don't know how you can joke about it. It was full strength, Rose. Full strength. Overkill for someone of your size. There should be no way you can possibly be standing."

"You keep complaining I weigh a ton. Guess that helped me." She paused.

"I won't ever complain again." He whispered into her ear. Then something from his pocket jangled and squawked.

She jerked back.

"Battle Center," he said with no affection, looking down at the screen he'd pulled out. "They want me to bring you to a mobile conference facility they've set up outside the boundary Sazo gave them."

"They've hailed me, too." Sazo sounded as annoyed as Dav. "They've been monitoring Rose since we brought her here from the edge of the no-go zone I set up. They know she's on her feet and they want to talk to her."

"Can't a girl get dressed and have a cup of grinabo, first?"

"A girl can do whatever she wants until she's ready." Sazo's voice was cold. "And Captain Jallan, she will not be leaving this house with you. I can't protect her if she's surrounded by Battle Center staff and whoever else has some power on the four Grihan worlds. If you have to go to them, that's up to you, but Rose stays here."

Rose felt infected with the chill in his words. "What do they want? Why are they in such a hurry to talk to me?"

"They want to know where they stand. What threat Sazo and Bane pose to them, not to mention the other three Class 5s." Dav thumbed his handheld off without answering it.

"But that's between them and Sazo, it's nothing to do with me." She looked upward, even though Sazo couldn't see her. "Why didn't they talk to you while I was unconscious?"

"Because I wouldn't answer them." Sazo made the sound of someone clearing their throat, and despite it all, Rose had to grin.

"Why not?"

"I've decided to make you my representative. You can read them better than I can."

She was so surprised, she was silent for a long moment.

"Rose. Was that okay?" He asked the question in English.

"It's okay. I was just taken aback, that's all. You are more than capable of dealing with them, Sazo. Don't underestimate yourself."

"I want to include you. Want them to see you have some power. That you aren't to be pushed to the side." He paused. "Because it's true. You do have power. I need you to help me keep balanced, Rose."

"Thank you, Sazo." She spoke softly, and Dav kept his hands on her, his fingers gently stroking her as she spoke in a language he didn't understand, his eyes half-closed, as if he was simply enjoying the sound of it. "I'll be happy to go in to bat for you. That's what side-kicks do."

She made a face of apology to Dav, switched to Grihan. "Do you know what they'll want from us? What would be reasonable for Sazo and I to ask for?"

Dav nodded. "They'll want to know if you plan to align with the Grih or set yourselves up as neutral. If you're neutral, you'll have to move out of Grihan territory, and into non-UC areas."

"And if we do align with the Grih? What would they want as proof of goodwill?"

He shrugged. "They haven't told me that, haven't told me anything since I left my post on the *Barrist* and brought you to Calianthra. But I think it's safe to say they may underestimate you. They're still trying to get their heads around the fact that you're an orange. Perhaps go in with the view that they may insult you with their assumptions, and try not to be too offended. They haven't figured out yet that you're something completely unknown."

Rose sighed. "Let me get dressed. Have something to eat, and then let's get this over with, then."

"You sure?" Dav smoothed her hair back from her forehead.

"No." She tightened her grip on his shoulders. "But waiting would be worse."

He looked at her, his face serious. "I'll make you some grinabo, get some breakfast for you. Your clothes are in that cupboard."

She watched him go, then pulled out some of her hyr fabric clothes. Something occurred to her. "Where's Bane?"

"He's around," Sazo said. "Close enough to hail, far enough away the Grih don't consider him a threat. He's decided he's neutral to everyone but the Tecran, who he's hostile to, and me and you, who he's allied to."

"And the other Class 5? The one shooting at you?"

"I don't know." Sazo went quiet. "Every time he shot at me, I responded by sending my file of all my interactions with you to him."

"Our interactions?"

"You singing to me. Talking to me. To help him wake up."

Rose pulled on her trousers, then spent some time shaping her bra.

"I had no idea how wonderful hyr fabric was until now. I just thought it was overpriced because it was rare."

She looked up, saw Dav leaning against the doorjamb, grinabo and a plate of toast in his hands, wearing an appreciative look.

She grinned. "It does the job."

"Hmm." He put the mug and plate down on a small desk, walked over to her. Cupped her breasts in his hands.

"If you want to pretend some neutrality when it comes to Rose, Captain, I should warn you the scan equipment your government is using to monitor Rose will also be able to pick up what you're doing right now."

Dav dropped his hands, but bent his head, stopping with his lips just a whisper from her own.

"I think the pretense of neutrality disappeared when Admiral Hoke watched me pick up Rose over Dr. Havak's protests and got into that craft you sent over without discussing it with her, without any argument whatsoever."

She placed a finger between their lips. "I'm sorry, Dav. Will you be in trouble?"

He shrugged. "I won't say I won't be sorry if I am, but I don't regret anything, except not getting to you sooner." He stepped back. "But they don't get to spy on us together, either."

Rose pulled her shirt on, then tipped her head. "They should be groveling at your feet. You've developed good personal relations with two new life forms on behalf of the Grih."

"Something tells me Admiral Hoke doesn't quite see it that way."

"Admiral Hoke," Rose gave a last, firm tug of her shirt, "has consistently failed to understand that I am not simply a cuter, cuddlier version of the Grih, but something completely different. Perhaps it's time I bring that point home."

Dav gave her a long look. "And what if you can't do that? What if the terms are unacceptable?"

She rested her cheek against his chest and closed her eyes, because she'd been desperately trying not to think of that, herself.

"I don't know. But we'll work something out."

He ran his hand down the length of her back. "I hope we can."

CHAPTER 47

ROSE WATCHED Dav's little hovercar disappear through the snow-covered trees and had a terrible sense he should not have gone.

But of course he had to. It was his job.

He lived next to a forest in a wooden house which had what on Earth would have been considered an avant-garde design. Here, it was probably the typical cabin in the woods, although she couldn't see any other houses nearby.

She bet living on top of hundreds of people in the *Barrist* for months at a time meant peace, quiet and space were important to Dav Jallan.

She turned back inside. "What now?"

"Pack your things." Sazo sounded distracted. "Hopefully it won't be necessary, but you might as well be ready."

As she had at least fifteen minutes before Dav would reach the other Grih waiting for him just outside the no-go zone, she followed Sazo's advice. "How would you get me out, though, if I did need to leave?"

"I deployed a drone when we got here. It looked like part of the explorer craft I sent down with you and Dav to his house. It detached as the craft flew back to me. So far, it's been well-enough cloaked that the Grih haven't picked it up, even though it's been right over their camp three times now. It's capable of picking up a single passenger, and given it was built to fit a Tecran or a Grihan, you'll have more than enough room."

"Good to know." She zipped up her bags. "But they'll know the moment I make a run for it, won't they? Didn't you say they're monitoring my every move?"

"They are, but only because I'm letting them. I'll simulate an image of you onscreen if necessary. You can keep talking and not be where they think you are, and I can shut down their monitoring systems easily enough at the same time and make it look like equipment malfunction."

"I'm glad I'm on your side." Rose set her bags down next to the chair Dav had set up for her in front of a large screen. Saw she had another five minutes and went into the kitchen to make a cup of grinabo. "Might as well get one last cup in, if I'm going to be on the run."

"Might as well."

He sounded completely serious, where she had been mostly joking.

"I hope it doesn't come down to me running for my life, Sazo. I'd like this to be civilized and friendly. And there's no reason why it can't be."

"You would think so, but they've started to shield their comms and their conversations in the mobile center. I can try to strip the interference away, but it's going to take a little time."

"They could be going into a huddle about their points of negotiation, and they don't want you listening in, or you'll have all the advantage."

Sazo made a hum of agreement. "That would make sense, but it's not going to stop me trying to find out what they're saying."

"Of course not." She took the steaming cup of grinabo to the table, and had almost finished it by the time the screen blinked on.

A man in uniform sat at the center of the table, and he had three officers standing behind him, one of whom was Admiral Hoke. She guessed he must be the head of Battle Center. Three Grih, well-dressed and stately, sat to his right, two to his left.

He cleared his throat. "Good day to you, Rose McKenzie. My name is Admiral Krale, and I am the head of Grihan Battle Center. To my right and left are the leaders of each of the four planets, and the overall leader of the Grih. They can introduce themselves to you when they address you."

So, no UC councilors, no Dimitara. This was a heavy-weight Grihan-only council of war.

Rose found her last swallow of grinabo went down with difficulty. "Good morning." She dipped her head in an attempt at the Grihan formal greeting.

She could see they were all surprised, and she gave an inward sigh.

As if he could read her mind, Sazo whispered in her ear. "Remember what Dav said about expecting them to underestimate you."

It had obviously already begun.

"Where is Captain Jallan?"

She didn't know why she expected he would be present, but she had. And not having him there was giving her a bad feeling.

"Why would a captain from our explorer fleet be involved in a meeting at this level?" A woman two down from Admiral Krale's right spoke up, a heavy sprinkle of condescension in her tone. "My name is Cavile Lostra, Rose McKenzie. I am the leader of Calianthra."

Rose looked at her. She was sleek and dressed in a pale green suit that complimented her pale skin and auburn hair, which was styled to look like a candle flame.

"You obviously know who Captain Jallan is, if you know he's a captain of your explorer fleet, and you would be very ill-informed if you didn't know I'm sitting in his house right now, and that he helped bring me to Calianthra, so I suspect you must know why I thought he would be involved in this meeting. Why are you pretending it is such an unusual request from me?"

There was an uncomfortable silence, and as Rose kept up eye contact with Lostra, she shifted in her chair.

"Captain Jallan, however strong his personal relationship with you may be, doesn't have the security clearance necessary to be present for what we hope to achieve in this meeting." Hoke spoke up. "He is being debriefed."

"Can we leave the topic of Captain Jallan aside for the moment?" A man to Krale's left spoke. He was tall, the tallest there, and his stark black clothes were in contrast to the clothing everyone else was wearing. His hair was silver-gray and clipped short, more a buzz cut than the electric-socket shocked look of most of the Grih. "My name is Vulmark, and I'm the leader of the Grihan people. I'd like to know what your intentions are toward the Grih."

"My intentions?" They were afraid of little old her?

Or, more likely, little old her plus her two big, bad Class 5s.

"You seem to have two thinking systems at your beck and call, and as I don't know anything about you, that makes me nervous." Vulmark gave a slight smile.

"They aren't at my beck and call. They're my friends, and they use me as an advisor of sorts. And one of them, Sazo, is a silent participant to this meeting, and can hear everything you say about him."

"How can you advise them when you are as new to the Grih as they are?" Cavile Lostra fingered a stray strand of hair that had fallen across her brow.

It was a good question, but Rose had the sense they were veering from the main issue. "My specialty is in the area of moral responsibility and conscience."

Again, it seemed she had managed to silence the most powerful people across the four planets.

She was tired, she still hurt a little, and she was starting to feel edgy again that Dav wasn't there. She was sure he would have tried as hard as possible to be involved. "Can we get to the point here, ladies and gentlemen?"

"I don't know if we can while I still don't have a clear sense of whether you're dangerous to the Grih or not." Vulmark drew himself up sharply.

Oh, for heaven's sake. "I'm about two-thirds of your size, I've just recovered from being shot twice and I'm recovering from cracked ribs and other injuries as well, although Dr. Havak certainly has worked miracles there. And on top of that, I've never once, since I've encountered you, done anything to hurt a single Grih. In fact, I've done everything in my power to help you. What on earth do you think I'm going to do?"

The woman beside Vulmark leaned forward. "My name is Gaumili, I'm the leader of the planet Grih, the first of the four planets. I agree that you physically seem to pose no risk to us but do you understand that as a completely unknown entity, we have to take precautions to safeguard our people?"

"I can understand taking precautions." And truly, she could. Would a Grihan visitor to Earth fare better than her? Thinking of the conspiracy theories, she probably had it a lot easier. "However, there is also such a thing as good will. You are rapidly running through your store of it."

Vulmark tapped a long finger against thin, mercurial lips. "You can't die from a shockgun blast." He looked down at a handheld lying in front of him. "You apparently can see through our camouflage, and you appear to be far more intelligent than any of the five member nations of the UC think of when they picture a sentient orange."

"With respect, Mr. Vulmark, your misconceptions about sentient oranges are not my problem. I am what I am. I didn't ask to come here. I'm not the thin end of the wedge, I'm the only one of my kind. With the exception of Admiral Valu, the Grih have been decent to me, and I can see that if I'm to find a place for myself in my new reality, the Grih people would be the closest I could come to being home. I have no fight with you, quite the opposite."

She leaned back and wondered where to go from here. She simply wouldn't have believed they could have made such a bogey man out of her. And they hadn't even gotten to Sazo yet.

Hoke leaned forward from her place behind Admiral Krale. She looked down the length of the table. "I've had Rose in my custody numerous times, and there was no point at which I could not subdue her. Yes, she can survive a shockgun blast, but it's not like she can run a lap around the spaceship afterward; she's rendered unconscious."

Vulmark drew in a deep breath. "Point taken. But it isn't just Rose we're dealing with, is it?"

"No." Rose agreed. "You want to talk about Sazo."

"We have a very clear law that states we have to try to kill Sazo," Krale said.

"That law is two hundred years old, and killing Sazo when he hasn't done a single thing wrong, and in fact used his own shields to prevent Grih ships from taking fire, is hardly equitable."

"Agreed." Guamili obviously shocked her own colleagues as much as she shocked Rose. "News of what Sazo did, and his and Rose's exploits, have already disseminated across the four planets and to most of the other UC members. This has been fueled in great part by comms of some songs performed by Rose on board the *Barrist*, which have endeared her to the Grihan people."

"Told you if you sang they wouldn't be able to give you away." There was a smug tone to Sazo's soft words.

"I am very much of the opinion that the decision to execute a kill order on Sazo would meet with vast public disapproval."

"I would agree." A thin, wiry man sitting next to Cavile Lostra moved his handheld around with a finger in an unconscious gesture. "My name is Radie Silvan from the Grihan planet Xal, and I've been getting the same feedback from my people."

"And you, Hygu, Lostra?" Vulmark asked the two on either side of Silvan.

They both gave reluctant nods.

"If we don't execute the kill order, then can you tell us what path you and Sazo will choose?" Krale's voice was overloud in the silence that ensued.

"We'd like to work with Captain Jallan and the crew of the *Barrist*, assisting them in their exploration work. And if you genuinely need the threat of Sazo's fire power, we can go where you need us and he can look mean and threatening for you."

"That would be a very acceptable outcome." Krale exchanged a look first with Hoke and then with Vulmark.

"We could draw up a contract to that effect now," Vulmark said with a nod.

"Rose." Sazo's voice sounded odd. "I've finally decrypted the conversations they were distorting earlier."

"And?"

"And Dav has been arrested and is facing a court martial."

"What?" She raised her eyes and looked straight at Krale. "You'll draw up a contract stating we'll work with Captain Jallan?"

"Well, not Captain Jallan specifically, because captains get promoted, change ships."

"And can be arrested?" She pushed back her chair and stood.

Krale jerked with surprise, then rubbed a hand over his face. "He left his post. There is no getting around that."

"Dav left his post to protect his entire ship and all the other ships in the fleet. If you don't understand that, I don't think Sazo and I can work with you."

"We'll understand it when Captain Jallan is brought before the courts." Krale shot a quick look at Hoke.

"Hoke." Rose looked at her with genuine fury. "You know what Dav did was the right thing. The only thing a captain who understood the whole situation could do to protect his people."

"Here's the thing, Rose. If Dav did what he did to protect the fleet," Hoke held her gaze, "that means Sazo posed a risk to the fleet and that Dav was saving everyone from him lashing out. That means if Sazo is upset, he becomes a danger to us. The Grihan people may all be humming along to your songs now and feeling sorry for Sazo, but how long will that last if they know Dav had to bundle you up and give Sazo his way in order to protect Battle Center crew?"

"So you're saying . . ." Rose could hardly believe what she was saying.

"Either Dav left his post, which is against orders and carries a five year sentence, and the stripping of rank, or Sazo is dangerous, and the chances of popular support for not executing the kill order becomes far more shaky."

"You're making it a choice between Dav or Sazo? You'd railroad Dav into a conviction to keep Sazo? Or Sazo and I would have to go on the run if the truth about what Dav did comes out?" But why were they offering her the choice?

Sazo *was* dangerous when he was upset.

It would get better with time, but they didn't know that, so why would they risk it? And also risk the loyalty of their own staff by deliberately convicting Dav when they knew he had only been doing his duty?

And then, it all came together.

"You want to keep your toy." She spoke softly. "You think if Sazo and I agree to work with you, and the general public continues with their enthusiasm for us, that somehow you can get someone on board and cage Sazo again. I don't know what happens to me in that scenario. I get dumped somewhere? Locked up?" She spat the words out in disgust.

The uncomfortable silence was all the confirmation she needed. Some of the Grihan leaders exchanged troubled looks.

"I've disabled their monitoring systems. Made it look like mechanical failure." Sazo was almost too soft in her ear, she only just caught what he said.

Time to go.

She reached out and switched off the screen, ignoring the shouted demand for her to stop from Admiral Krale as she leaned across the table. Something on Admiral Hoke's face made her pause, just for a moment, before she switched the screen off. She picked up her bags. "Where is the drone?"

"You could have left the screen running, I'd have created a simulation of you."

"They'd have guessed soon enough it wasn't me. The drone?"

"Go out the back door and run into the woods. I'll talk you through it."

"Good." She looped a bag over each shoulder and strode toward the kitchen.

"You seem calm." Sazo's comment was almost a question. "Aren't you upset at the way they've betrayed us?"

Rose drew in a deep breath of cold, crisp air as she closed the back door behind her, enjoyed the crunch of the frost-bitten grass under her feet. "To be honest, they're behaving just the way I'd have expected them to back home. Only maybe on Earth they'd have been a bit more violent. And looked a lot less guilty about it."

"Really?"

She smiled, trying to work out why she *was* so accepting of all this. "Really. I'm feeling quite at home."

Sazo made a noise, a sort of snorting laugh, and she laughed with him.

"Let's go bust Dav out."

CHAPTER 48

ROSE CROUCHED deep within the trees, and looked between the small temporary cabin a half kilometer ahead of her, and the close-up of the same cabin Sazo was providing on the handheld she'd taken from Dav's house.

If Dav was inside it, as Sazo thought from eavesdropping on the comms, he wasn't going to be easy to rescue, but also, would rescuing him solve their problems?

Rose had the feeling it would make things worse.

"Sazo, how do you feel about working with the Grih after this? Are you okay with it?"

Just because she could understand their wanting to keep their people as safe as possible, and that they didn't consider her and Sazo part of their people yet, didn't mean Sazo would, too.

"Well, the Tecran are out, and so are the Garmman. That leaves the Bukari, by far our best bet, and the Fitali, who I don't really have any idea about."

"I agree, the Bukari are our next best option, but do we want to settle for second best?"

He thought about that for a while, and soft, slightly blue-tinged snow began to fall around her. She was crouched on a thin layer of it, and was amazed at how her hyr fabric clothes were keeping her warm, despite being thin and light. There were seriously good reasons for this stuff being the most expensive fabric in the universe. She wondered what a hyr spider looked like.

Or maybe she didn't.

"You still fine with their betrayal?" he asked at last.

"Not fine with it by any means. Understand it? Yes." She crouched a little lower as she saw a soldier walk the perimeter of the cabin on the handheld. He was harder to see from this distance, but she could just make him out if she tried. He was in reflective camouflage mode. "I'll want an apology, and maybe some heads to roll, and obviously Dav reinstated, and as I've had some time to think during the jog from Dav's house to here, I don't know that our rescuing him will be to the long-term benefit of his career. Breaking out of jail makes you look guilty, even if you aren't."

"What do you suggest?" Sazo sounded relieved, and Rose thought he'd also been having doubts about how they were going to get Dav out without spilling some blood, something they could not do if they wanted a place in this society.

"How about I take the drone up to you, and we very deliberately and openly reach out to the Bukari. But we shield what we say, which could simply be a hello and catch-up with Filavantri Dimitara. And maybe a request for some more yuiar."

"So they'll think we're getting ready to make a deal to move to the Bukari's territory?"

"Yep. Around about then, I hope they'll be on their knees to Dav, asking for his help, and if they aren't we'll refuse to speak to anyone but him when they contact us."

"*If* they contact us."

She gave a snort. "They'll contact us. To have an offer on the table from us of full cooperation which they then totally blew? If they don't salvage this, it'll be the end of their careers, and they know it."

"The deal going forward is no one but you is allowed on board, though."

"That goes without saying." Not that they had any hope of re-caging Sazo, he'd completely overwritten that code, even if they knew he was the crystal on the necklace she used to wear, or where to find it on the Class 5, something she highly doubted. Even she didn't know where Sazo had hidden himself.

"You think your moving back to the Class 5 and calling the Bukari will be enough?"

"I think it will, but if not, we'll explore other options. Let's see how they react to this, first."

"Okay. I've landed the drone two thou from here. That's the closest I could get it and be absolutely sure they wouldn't spot it."

Rose peered through the thickening snow at the cabin one last time, and then turned. "I wish we could find some way to contact Dav. Let him know what we're up to."

She started walking as fast as she could away from the Battle Center camp, putting as many trees between her and them. Good thing Sazo had taken out their monitoring equipment, or she couldn't have gotten this close.

"There are too many guards for you to get an earpiece to him, even if you had a spare with you." Sazo sounded philosophical about it.

"You can't hack into his current one?"

"I already tried that. He doesn't have it with him, they took it."

"His handheld's gone too, then, I suppose?"

Sazo gave a grunt of confirmation.

She didn't want to give up. If he didn't know what they had planned, he may think she'd abandoned him. That didn't sit well. At all.

"Is he still in uniform?" He had been when he'd left her earlier.

"Yes."

"Then what about . . ." Her words caught in her throat in her excitement. "What about the built-in watch thing on his sleeve?"

"The smart fabric digital time insert?"

She grinned. "Yes. That."

"That doesn't have an audio component."

"It doesn't have to. We could send him a written message. How many characters are there on it?"

"Five. Space for two digital numbers on either side of a dash."

"Before I get too worked up about this, can you hack into it?"

"Please." Sazo laughed in her ear. "It doesn't even have a rudimentary shield. A child could hack into it."

"Woohoo." She wanted to shout it, but she whispered it instead.

She'd sped up as she'd gotten more and more excited, and as she stumbled out of the treeline she realized too late she was on the edge of a steep incline. She went over, arms windmilling.

It was a soft landing. A deep drift of snow must have built up in the small dip over the last day.

"I'm okay." She stood, dusted herself off, and then looked up.

Right at an equally startled soldier in reflective camouflage.

"Damn." She pretended to keep dusting herself off, slipped her hand into her pocket and held the light-gun loosely in her hand.

"Rose, what is it?"

"You can't see the soldier standing right in front of me?" Rose used English, so the Grih wouldn't understand, and she sang it, too, as a distraction.

The soldier shifted in surprise.

"No. I can't see anything."

"Who would have guessed their camouflage works on you and not on me? I feel less useless, all of a sudden. It's good to have some superpowers of my own. Not all side-kicks are that lucky." She smiled at the guy as she sang, and he took a step back, completely confused.

Time to get jumpy again.

She bounced on her knees, gave him another smile, and leaped, sailing over his head and landing lightly behind him.

It really did never get old.

She jumped a second time, angling slightly so she wasn't going in a straight line, and heard a dull thud just to the right of her.

"What the hell was that?" She twisted slightly and a shockgun blast clipped the top of her arm.

Pain blinded her, blue-white, like the snow around her, and she landed hard, the breath knocked out of her.

"Rose, turn! Turn and shoot him. He's approaching. I can read the heat in his shockgun after he fired, even if I can't see him." Sazo's voice was a faint buzz in her ears but she tried, managing to push herself onto her side so her right hand was free.

"Remain down or I will shoot again." The Grih soldier edged closer. He'd retracted the faceplate of his helmet, and he looked nervous. Because, sure, she was the bogey man. She'd forgotten that.

Time to make that a self-fulfilling prophecy.

"Please," she said in Grihan, lifting her right hand in supplication. "Don't hurt me."

He tapped his ear, lifting his gun again to point it at her chest. "This is Grigo, checking in."

Rose slid down the button on her light-gun and closed her eyes, grateful for the fact his face was uncovered. She didn't know how well the light-gun would work with his helmet on.

As it was, he didn't even make a sound. When she opened them again, it was to find he'd simply collapsed.

"I hope they don't expect more from his check-in than that."

"I reviewed his earlier transmissions, recorded his voice, and told them all was well."

"Sazo." She made a kissing noise. Pulled herself to her feet, right hand rubbing her left arm. Damn it all, getting shot really *hurt*.

She turned to go, light-gun still in her hand, and then stumbled to a stop.

Someone was waiting for her on the other side of the small dip.

Something about the uniform was familiar . . .

"Admiral Hoke. How did you find me?"

The admiral jerked, as surprised as the soldier had been. "You can see me?"

"Perfectly." She decided she might as well keep walking. She was a sitting duck in the tiny gully anyway, and she would have to get past Hoke to get to the drone. She wasn't sure how much the admiral had seen, but even if she did know about the light-gun, Rose could use it before Hoke could take it off her.

"I saw the report that you could, but I didn't really believe it." Hoke retracted her faceplate as she spoke.

Rose shrugged, edging left so that she could sidle past the admiral.

"Where are you going, Rose?"

"None of your business, Admiral Hoke. I'm armed, and I won't hesitate to protect myself from you."

"I thought you might try to break Dav out, so I brought a small team and we've been sweeping through the woods from Dav's house with a handheld monitor. It doesn't have the range or the detail of the equipment at the camp, but it does have the benefit of being portable."

Hoke looked down the hill and then leaned forward. "Is that one of my team? What did you do to him?"

Rose realized the admiral was having trouble seeing him because of the camouflage. "He shot me. Only in the arm, but he was trying for my torso. Funny thing is, I really, really don't like getting shot."

Hoke whipped around, faced her. "If he did shoot you, he'll be disciplined. They were to stop you, not hurt you."

"Don't know if I believe that, Admiral. He was certainly quick on the trigger."

Hoke shook her head. "I'm not here to harm you, Rose. I'm not even here on a sanctioned mission. I argued against what they were planning with Jallan. It was the wrong strategy, and I told them it wouldn't work."

"I really don't understand it, Hoke. Why wouldn't they want a cooperative ally rather than a resentful slave?"

"Fear. It makes people do stupid things. This is what happens when powerful people have to make difficult decisions too quickly."

Rose raised her brows at that. Looked down the hill at the soldier. "You got that right. When did I become such a monster big, bad soldiers are so frightened of me they feel threatened enough to shoot?"

Hoke shook her head again. "My fault. I told them you might be able to see them in full gear, that you had some immunity to shockguns." She sighed. "My apologies."

"So what was the purpose of hunting me down?" She didn't want to turn her back on the admiral, but it was time to go.

"To stop you from rescuing Jallan. If you want him to keep his job, it's a bad idea."

"I'd already worked that out for myself." She edged back, hoping more of the admiral's team weren't right behind her. "That would be why I'm heading away from where he's being held."

She shuffled back another few steps.

"We keep underestimating you." Hoke's words puffed out into the cold air.

"Well, are you going to try to bring me in? Raise the alarm?" Rose was far enough away now to get a good shot in with the light-gun, and she shifted it a little in her hand.

"No. I thought more along the terms of letting you slip quietly away and creating a diversion if you need one."

"Why?" She had see the dismay on Hoke's face, the fatalistic grimace, when she'd shut down the screen. Could Hoke really have come round?

"Dav Jallan saved the fleet when he went with you. I knew it then, which is why I didn't even protest when he left. Sazo may not have harmed us, but there was certainly a high chance of it. I don't believe we should betray officers like him." Then she gave a practical shrug. "And also, because when the dust settles, I'll come out of this looking like the long-term visionary that I am, and that will not hurt my chances of being head of Battle Center."

"You're not worried about Sazo? About his volatility?"

Hoke gave a half-laugh. "Of course I am, but I've seen for myself that he's not like that when you're with him, safe and sound. And I'd rather have a slightly volatile Sazo on my side than on anyone else's. So would Vulmark and Krale." She tapped the watch panel on her sleeve and looked down at the time. "Something they'll be thinking about quite a bit around about now."

It reminded Rose of the time herself. And of her fiendish plan.

"Right, well then, Admiral, nice doing business with you. I've got to go."

"Wait." Hoke stepped forward, hand raised, and Rose half-lifted her own hand in response.

Hoke blinked at her. "What's that?"

"Nothing." Rose gripped the light-gun a little harder. "You were saying?"

"You're not really leaving Jallan to his fate, are you? You'll let Krale and Vulmark beg you to come back?" She lowered her arm slowly, eyes on Rose's fist.

"I intend to make them prostrate themselves at Dav's feet, begging forgiveness, but yes, I'll eventually agree. But to do that, I've got to go, so..."

Hoke waved her on, and she turned and forced herself not to stumble at the sight of five silent soldiers in full camouflage standing behind her. Now she'd really see if Hoke was lying. "Good afternoon, boys and girls." She looked at each of them in turn as she jogged past them.

"What did she do to Grigo?"

She heard the question from behind her.

"I'm not sure, but I think . . ." Hoke's tone was almost reverent. "I think she used a *light-gun*."

CHAPTER 49

SOMETHING WAS WRONG.

Dav paced the small cabin with its quick-lock walls and door, manufactured to be set up in under ten minutes and dismantled in about five.

He'd expected a little trouble when he got to the temporary Battle Center camp, but not that he'd be locked up and officially charged.

Rose would worry when she didn't hear from him. And a worried Rose meant a worried Sazo.

Anger flared in his chest, and spiked at the sound of voices coming his way.

He flicked the fabric of his sleeve to see the time, and froze.

Dav.

He flicked it again.

It's. Rose. We. Will. Sort. This. Out.

Sort what out? His arrest?

Fear washed over him as the door of the cabin opened. If Sazo and Rose rescued him . . .

He tried to set that aside, deal with what was happening to him right now.

"Captain Jallan." Commander Gadamal stepped back and indicated he wanted Dav to come with him. "Admiral Krale requests your presence."

"Requests?" Dav asked, stepping out into the cool darkness.

More time had passed than he'd realized and it had started snowing while he'd been inside. It fell like ash amongst them, silent and cold.

Gadamal looked up sharply at his tone, and Dav regretted it. Whatever was happening here, Gadamal was not responsible.

A movement caught his eye and he turned toward the trees, saw a figure walking toward them. Panic surged for a moment as he thought it might be Rose, about to do something they'd all regret——

"Captain Jallan."

It was Hoke. He let out a breath he hadn't realized he was holding as she hailed him. She came toward them, snow in her hair and on her shoulders, dressed in full combat gear, with her helmet under her arm.

Gadamal hesitated, uncertain, but then stopped so the admiral could join them.

"I'll walk with you." Hoke gave Gadamal a nod that was nothing short of a dismissal, and the commander turned and led the way.

"Admiral." He kept his voice low. "I think Rose and Sazo are planning to rescue me. I don't know what's going on but can you get a message to them? Tell them what a disaster that would be?"

"I'm one step ahead of you. Already intercepted her in the woods. Although she'd already worked out rescuing you would be counterproductive." Hoke spoke quietly, too. "How do you know she's up to something, though? Haven't you been stripped of all electronics and watched since you arrived."

Dav shrugged. "Rose has her methods. But it's one way. I can't talk back."

"She's not telepathic, is she?" Hoke stopped dead and looked at him with mouth open.

Dav shook his head. "The thought of that is truly terrifying. No. But she is extraordinarily inventive."

Gadamal had turned, and stood watching them, stiff and suspicious.

Hoke started moving again and Dav fell into step.

"What's happening? Rose seems to think there's a serious problem."

"Rose is right. You've been betrayed." Hoke bit off the last word as Gadamal came to a stop outside a much larger temporary structure than the one he'd been held in, and opened the door.

Dav hesitated, searching Hoke's face for any chance she was joking. She grimaced. "It's true."

"Captain Jallan." Gadamal's tone was impatient now, and Dav turned to look at the commander.

Gadamal tensed, his hand drifting down to his shockgun.

Slowly, Dav approached and stepped into the room, Hoke right behind him.

"Admiral Hoke. I was told you were out on maneuvers." Another of Krale's adjuncts, Baku Fivore, was waiting for them.

Dav saw they were in a command center, with screens and equipment along three walls. At the far end of the room, clustered around a refreshments table, stood Admiral Krale and the five leaders of the four planets.

"Now I'm back," Hoke said, her voice cheerful.

Dav looked down at his sleeve again, flicked it.

Glad. You. Are. Fin. Ally. Chec. King. The. Time. Need. To. Know. If. You. Can. For. Give. Them.

"Captain Jallan. Is your time piece not working?" Fivore asked.

Dav raised his head, stared straight at him. "Admiral Krale wanted to see me?"

"Yes. This way." Fivore jerked his gaze to the back of the room, and turned a little too quickly.

As Dav followed, he flicked his sleeve again.

Let. Us. Know. If. You. Want. To. Stay. We. Can. Do. That. If. You. Want. To. Leave. Then. We.

"Captain Jallan?" Krale sounded puzzled.

Dav stood to attention, and gave a formal bow. "Admiral Krale."

Then they would what? Get him out? Go on the run?

They could do it. Rose and Sazo could probably do anything they set their minds to. But did he want to leave everything behind?

And how would he let them know?

"You seem distracted, Captain." Sierra Gaumili, elected leader of the planet Grih, put down her cup of grinabo.

"Guilty." Dav gave her a formal bow, and noticed how uncomfortable his response made everyone. "Admiral Krale, you wished to see me?" He couldn't help his clipped delivery, as if he were in a hurry.

Which he was.

"You have somewhere you need to be, Captain?" Krale asked softly, his tone almost predatory.

Dav pursed his lips. "No, sir. I'm at your disposal." He stepped forward, and started making himself a cup of grinabo.

There was a startled silence around him.

"Forgive me, but I haven't had anything since breakfast. Do you mind?" He was pushing them, he knew it, but Hoke said he'd been betrayed. What better way to force that into the open than stirring the pot.

"Not at all," Gaumili stammered. "I would have thought someone would have brought you something. You've been here for hours."

Dav shrugged, and Krale flicked a look at Gadamal, who was leaning out of the door, speaking in hushed tones to someone outside. He gestured to Krale, and the head of Battle Center went to him, the two of them bending their heads together.

Krale seemed to stiffen at whatever news he'd been given.

Dav watched him over the brim of his cup as he brought it to his lips, and then spilled a drop on his sleeve.

He reached for a napkin and rubbed at it.

Will. Get. You. Out.

His lover would come for him. He didn't doubt it for a moment. Now he just had to make sure she didn't have to.

"We have a problem, Captain Jallan."

Dav choked a little on his grinabo. He didn't say anything, but his sarcastic amusement was not lost on anyone.

He needed to reel it in. Stop giving things away. He set his cup down, straightened.

"What problem is that, Admiral?"

Krale looked like he wanted to call him on his attitude, but didn't.

Interesting.

They must really need him.

"We made a strategic decision, for the good of all Grih, which seems to have back-fired on us." Vulmark, Leader-Elect of the four planets, took up position next to Krale.

"What decision was that, sir?" Dav was starting to realize he had been sacrificed somehow.

"The decision itself doesn't matter anymore, what you need to know is that our negotiations with Rose McKenzie and the thinking system did not go well. She seems to have left the planet."

"Seems to have left the planet?" That was something he didn't know. "Did the explorer craft come get her?"

"No." Krale turned to the screens. "But it's possible she left on a small, cloaked drone. We were able to get intermittent feed of its location, and then, there was the singing.

"The singing?"

Krale nodded to a technician standing by, and she tapped the screen.

Rose's voice floated out, slow, rich and melodic.

He stood completely still, closed his eyes, and let it wash over him.

He would get her to sing that to him in person when they were together again. It was beautiful.

As the last note faded, there was a quiet in the room, a contented silence that seemed to cling, resistant to the urgency that had come before.

"I wish I knew what it meant." Gaumili said. "Do you know, Captain Jallan?"

Dav shook his head. "Only Sazo knows her language. She taught it to him when they were both prisoners of the Tecran."

Their conversation seemed to snap everything back in place.

"This singing was coming from the drone. I can only believe it was meant to be spotted, the song meant to be heard, to let us know Rose was no longer on Calianthra. Shortly after this, the Class 5 sent out an encrypted message to the Bukari. Again, I have to accept that given the capabilities of the thinking system, we were meant to see the transmission. We are trying to decrypt, but my comms specialist tells me it could take months."

"So Rose is not on Calianthra, and she's making contact with the Bukari." He said it as a statement and waited.

"Yes." Krale almost hissed the words. "How do we make contact with her again? All our comms are being ignored."

"Well, I'd first need to know what you did to make her give up on the Grih. She was happy to stay with us, last time I spoke to her."

"We offered her a place among us." Vulmark said stiffly.

Hoke gave a low laugh. "With a condition."

Krale turned on her, lips drawn back in a snarl. "You exceed your authority, Admiral Hoke." He glared at her. "You've been running around out in the woods, and Commander Gadamal reported that one of your men said you spoke to Rose McKenzie on her way to the drone, but let her go."

There were sounds of shock from most of them.

"Of course I let her go." Hoke's words were contemptuous. "I'm not going down in history as the idiot who started a new thinking system war."

There was stunned silence at her words.

"If Rose had been taken against her will, Sazo would have razed Calianthra to the ground." Dav agreed. He rubbed the side of his head. These people were too out of touch, they didn't understand what they were doing.

"You think we're fools." His own planet leader, Cavile Lostra, spoke up for the first time.

Dav sighed. "Let me guess. You behaved like condescending bigots to her, and then tried to trick her somehow. And it involved me. Am I close?"

Hoke laughed. "I'd say spot on, Captain."

Radie Silvan, another of the leaders of the four planets, cleared his throat. "The plan was to charge you, Captain Jallan, for leaving your post. We know you did it to save the fleet, but that would be evidence that Sazo was unstable. You were protecting your people from him. That would have made keeping public sentiment against the kill order hard. Then we were going to get on board the Class 5 and re-cage the thinking system."

Dav gaped at them. "You obviously didn't tell Rose all of that?"

"She figured it out pretty quickly," Hoke said, a sparkle in her eye, and Dav had a feeling that somehow Hoke had played a small part in that. "They don't seem to understand that she's as advanced as we are."

"We do now. We wish to apologize. To find a way forward." Vulmark shifted uncomfortably.

"Even though Sazo can be unstable when Rose is in danger or threatened?" Dav was sure they would be prepared to accept a lot of risk to keep Sazo on their side, but he asked the question anyway. He was pretty sure Sazo would be listening in.

"We'd rather have him with us than against us," Krale said.

"Why should either of them trust you?" Dav crossed his arms and looked Krale directly in the eye in challenge.

The admiral took a threatening step forward, and then dropped his gaze. "We are hoping they trust you, Captain Jallan. That you will vouch for us."

"After you just admitted to betraying him?" Hoke asked.

Gaumili grimaced. "What was being proposed never sat well with me, and I would be angry if I were in your shoes, Captain, but this is the safety of the four planets we're discussing here."

"Sazo." Dav spoke up a little. "Can you forgive them?"

Again, they gaped at him, all except Hoke, who gave a small smile.

"He's thinking about it." Rose's voice, rich and smooth, came over the comms. "But if any Grih thinks they'll ever set foot on his Class 5 now, they're living in la-la land."

Dav nodded.

"And you, Captain Jallan?" She spoke formally, but he could hear the hint of amusement in her voice, a private joke between the two of them. "Can you forgive? Because it all hinges on you. Just say the word."

Suddenly, he was the center of attention. He let the moment draw out.

"I will tender my resignation," Krale's voice was hoarse.

Rose suddenly appeared on screen, and the technician leaned back in her chair in surprise.

Dav looked at her. "Is that enough?"

She smiled at him. "Not to put you on the spot, but it's your call. Sazo and I can understand wanting to protect the Grih. What we don't like is they were greedy. They didn't want anyone else as Sazo's ally, but they didn't want him as he is. They were going to betray him and you."

Dav glanced at Hoke. "Who would be promoted to head of Battle Center?"

Krale made a face. "Under the circumstances, Admiral Hoke seems the best candidate."

"Then yes, that's acceptable to me."

"And Vulmark?" Hoke tipped her head and studied the leader-elect.

Vulmark took a step back. Drew himself up. "I'm as guilty as Krale, but my position is elected, not appointed. If you want stability through this transition, I need to stay where I am."

"Dav?" Rose asked.

"He's right." Dav would like the leader-elect to fall on his sword just like Krale, but he made sense.

"Well then, he will never know privacy until he no longer has any power." Sazo spoke up again. "He will not have the opportunity to try to enslave me again."

Vulmark's eyes snapped, but he kept quiet.

"Are we done here?" Dav suddenly wanted to be away from them all. To find Rose and actually have some uninterrupted time with her.

Hoke nodded. "You're free to go, Captain Jallan. You have some leave coming to you, I believe."

"Good." Rose smiled from the screen. "I'll meet you back at your house."

The screen winked off and Dav turned to go.

"Captain, a word." Hoke walked to the door and they stepped out into the thickening snowfall together.

"Did you know Rose has a light-gun?"

Dav staggered to a stop. "What?"

"Shh." Hoke's eyes were quite alive with mischief. "Keep it down. I take it from that you didn't know. She knocked out one of my men with it. Nearly took me out, too, when I made a move she thought was threatening."

"What?" Dav kept his voice a tight whisper this time.

"He deserved it. He shot her in the arm. It was a clear case of self-defense, but I'm going to find it hard to explain his injury without giving her away."

But Hoke didn't seem all that upset or inconvenienced by it. She was head of Battle Center now, after all.

"Where the hell did she get a light-gun? They're banned."

"Where do you think?" Hoke smiled.

"Sazo." Dav moved in the direction of his hovercar.

"She really is quite extraordinary." Hoke had stopped and he turned to face her.

Rose had changed the leadership of Battle Center. She would challenge the very fabric of their society. And she'd only been in their lives a week.

He laughed. "Admiral, I've been meaning to compliment you for some time on your capacity for understatement."

CHAPTER 50

WHEN ROSE FINALLY RETURNED, Dav had a fire blazing in the fireplace and dinner cooking slowly on the stovetop.

He heard the thrusters and opened the door, watching the explorer land at the edge of the forest.

He met her halfway.

She slowed as he approached, almost shy, and came to a stop, her breath misting between them in the cold air.

He lifted a brow, held out his arms, and she sighed, taking that last step to bring herself up against him.

Her arms tightened hard around his waist, and he gripped the back of her shirt with his hands, pulling her even closer.

"So tell me," he had to keep things light, or he would go far too deep. "What was that song you sung in the drone?"

"Oh." She tipped back her head. "That was *Dream a Little Dream of Me*, the Mamas and the Papas version."

He brushed a kiss along her forehead. "What was it about?"

"Someone asking their lover to dream about them, when they are far apart."

"It was beautiful."

She sighed. "Thank you. To be honest, I sang that one because I know I sing it well. It was pride talking."

There was more acceptance in her tone than he'd heard before. And he'd seen the lens feed of her song in the launch bay before Valu had grabbed her.

She had come to some kind of peace with their love of her voice.

She would change them, he knew, because she didn't see music the same way as they did. She saw it as an infinite well of inspiration and joy, not a limited resource, to be carefully rationed. She would slowly bring them round to her view, because they were so hungry for her songs.

She sniffed the air. "Is that dinner I smell?"

"Yes." He refused to let go of her, so he pulled her close under his arm and walked slowly with her back to his cottage.

She stopped when they reached the top of the stairs, turned her head to look up at the night sky.

"They're somewhere out there. My family and my friends. Wondering where I am."

"Sazo could take you back. If you really wanted him to." He forced himself to say it.

She shook her head. "I'm not going back." She rested her head on his shoulder. "I'm just sorry I can't tell them I'm happy and safe."

"Are you happy?" He pulled away from her a little, so he could see her face.

She gave one of her sweet, devastating smiles, raised her hand and cupped his cheek. "I am."

"That's good." His voice dipped an octave, and he lifted her up against him, and then gave an exaggerated grunt as if he could barely hold her.

She laughed, soft and low. "You're happy I'm happy?" She was looking down at him, her arms looped around his neck.

"I am. I knew you missed Earth, but I hoped . . ."

"You were waiting for me to tell you I wanted to stay?" She bent her head, brushed a kiss along the tip of his ear.

He shivered and let her slide down his body until her feet touched the ground. "For some time now."

He pulled her over the threshold into his warm house. "You Earthlings are slow," he closed the door, and then pressed her up against it, leaning in until his lips were just above hers and gave a slow, satisfied smile, "as well as heavy."

THE CLASS 5 SERIES

Other books in the Class 5 series:

DARK DEEDS (BOOK 2)

Far from home . . .

Fiona Russell has been snatched from Earth, imprisoned and used as slave labor, but nothing about her abduction makes sense. When she's rescued by the Grih, she realizes there's a much bigger game in play than she could ever have imagined, and she's right in the middle of it.

Far from safe . . .

Battleship captain Hal Vakeri is chasing down pirates when he stumbles across a woman abducted from Earth. She's the second one the Grih have found in two months, and her presence is potentially explosive in the Grih's ongoing negotiations with their enemies, the Tecran. The Tecran and the Grih are on the cusp of war, and Fiona might just tip the balance.

Far from done . . .

Fiona has had to bide her time while she's been a prisoner, pretending to be less than she is, but when the chance comes for her to forge her own destiny in this new world, she grabs it with both hands. After all, actions speak louder than words.

DARK MINDS (BOOK 3)

The mind is the most powerful weapon of all...

Imogen Peters knows she's a pawn. She's been abducted from Earth, held prisoner, and abducted again. So when she gets a chance at freedom, she takes it with both hands, not realizing that doing so will turn her from pawn to kingmaker.

Captain Camlar Kalor expected to meet an Earth woman on his current mission, he just thought he'd be meeting her on Larga Ways, under the protection of his Battle Center colleague. Instead, he and Imogen are thrown together as prisoners in the hold of a Class 5 battleship. When he works out she's not the woman who sparked his mission, but another abductee, Cam realizes his investigation just got a lot more complicated, and the nations of the United Council just took a step closer to war.

Imogen's out of her depth in this crazy mind game playing out all around her, and she begins to understand her actions will have a massive impact on all the players. But she's good at mind games. She's been playing them since she was abducted. Guess they should have left her minding her own business back on Earth...

DARK MATTERS (BOOK 4)

DARK MATTERS... taking matters into her own hands

A time bomb, waiting to go off...

Lucy Harris is on the run, not sure where she can turn to for help, or if help is even available. But even as her abductors chase her down, she realizes they don't just want to recapture her, they want to erase her.

When your very existence puts a planet at the risk of war, there's no choice but to do everything in your power to stay out of your enemies hands.

A predator... waiting for the chance to pounce

The powerful AI battleship, Bane, is accompanying the United Council envoy to Tecra to mete out the punishment the Tecrans have earned for breaking UC law. He revels in the power he's about to have over his old masters. But his mission isn't only to rain down retribution on the people who kept him chained for years, he's also looking for a human woman his fellow Class 5 mentioned in the final seconds of his life. Paxe admitted to taking Lucy Harris from Earth, and Bane has been looking for her ever since.

A warrior conflicted . . .

Commander Dray Helvan thinks the Grih made a mistake in not pushing for war with the Tecran, but he's had to accept the compromise, that he and the other envoys from the United Council will go to Tecra and dismantle its military from the top down. His mission is not one of his choosing, but when he and his team arrive, he's handed a very different job. While he distrusts Bane on principle, when the thinking system tells him there's a woman running for her life on the planet below, he will do whatever he has to to see her safe. And if that means war for Tecra, well, then it means war.

DARK AMITIONS: A CLASS 5 NOVELLA (BOOK 4.5 IN THE CLASS 5 SERIES)

She never leaves a friend behind . . .

It's been months since Rose McKenzie was taken far from Earth. She's trying to make a place for herself amongst the Grih, with help from her Grihan lover, Captain Dav Jallan, and the dangerous and loyal Sazo, a powerful artificial intelligence who's integrated with an infamous Class 5 battleship.

When Rose gets the chance to join an exploration team going down to collect information from a planet in Grihan airspace, she jumps at the opportunity to stretch her legs and breath some real air.

But someone is already on the planet—the Krik—and they don't want anyone to know what they're up to. The Krik are the chaos agents of the United Council, often riding the edge of the law or over it. They ambush the exploration team and take them prisoner, but they don't realize they didn't get everyone. They didn't get Rose.

With Dav, and his spaceship the *Barrist*, lured away by a distress signal, Rose and Sazo, along with a furry friend Rose has made, are the exploration team's only hope at rescue. And Rose never leaves a friend behind.

DARK CLASS (BOOK 5)

Waking up alone . . . Ellie Masters comes out of a coma to find herself the only inhabitant of an eerily empty moon station. She's not on Earth any more, she's not even in the right solar system. So when someone reaches out to her, tells her he's her friend, she's happy to believe it. The alternative is to be stuck alone with an enemy.

The hunt of his career . . . Grih Battle Center captain, Renn Sorvihn, has been chasing a rogue Tecran ship for over a month, convinced its captain is simply trying to delay his inevitable surrender and punishment. But when Renn follows the Tecran ship into an unchartered sector, and realises the Tecran have been working their way to a secret moon base for weeks, he suddenly understands things are most definitely not as they seem.

Caught in the crossfire . . . When the Tecran arrive, with the Grih hot on their heels, Ellie finds herself the catalyst for heightened danger to everyone. The Tecran see her as evidence of their military's crimes, the Grih see her as a massive diplomatic complication, and her presence brings the whole confrontation up several thousand notches.

But Ellie isn't alone, and her new friend has ways to help her. Time to outclass them all . . .

ALSO BY MICHELLE DIENER

SCIENCE FICTION NOVELS

Verdant String series:

Interference & Insurgency (Two Novellas of the Verdant String: Box set)

Breakaway

Breakeven

Trailblazer

High Flyer

Wave Rider

Sky Raiders series:

Intended (Prequel to Sky Raiders: Exclusive to VIP Newsletter Members)

Sky Raiders

Calling the Change

Shadow Warrior

Class 5 series:

Dark Horse

Dark Deeds

Dark Minds

Dark Matters

Dark Ambitions (A Class 5 Novella)

Dark Class

HISTORICAL FICTION NOVELS

Susanna Horenbout and John Parker series:
In a Treacherous Court
Keeper of the King's Secrets
In Defense of the Queen

Regency London series:
The Emperor's Conspiracy
Banquet of Lies
A Dangerous Madness

Other historical novels:
Daughter of the Sky

FANTASY NOVELS BY MICHELLE DIENER

The Rising Wave series:
The Rising Wave (Prequel Novella)
The Turncoat King
The Threadbare Queen
Fate's Arrow (Coming late 2022)

Fairytale Retellings
Mistress of the Wind

The Dark Forest series:
The Golden Apple
The Silver Pear

To receive notification when a new book is released, sign up to Michelle Diener's website: michellediener.com.

ABOUT THE AUTHOR

Michelle Diener is an award winning author of historical fiction, science fiction and fantasy.

Michelle was born in London and currently lives in Australia with her husband and children.

You can contact Michelle through her website or sign up to receive notification when she has a new book out on her New Release Notification page.

Connect with Michelle
www.michellediener.com

ACKNOWLEDGMENTS

A huge thank you to Edie for helping to knock this manuscript into shape, and to Jo, who always helps make my stories the best they can be. To Kim, thank you for putting your finger on what needed to be expanded, the book is so much better for it. And a very grateful thank you to Covers by Christian for the amazing cover.

CPSIA information can be obtained
at www.ICGtesting.com
Printed in the USA
BVHW041646100423
662073BV00005B/36